About the Author

Doug Stumpf is a deputy editor at *Vanity Fair* and lives in New York City. *Confessions of a Wall Street Shoeshine Boy* is his first novel.

CONFESSIONS OF A
WALL STREET **SHOESHINE BOY**

CONFESSIONS

OF A

WALL STREET
SHOESHINE BOY

DOUG STUMPF

HARPER

NEW YORK · LONDON · TORONTO · SYDNEY

To Jeff

HARPER

A hardcover edition of this book was published in 2007 by HarperCollins Publishers.

CONFESSIONS OF A WALL STREET SHOESHINE BOY. Copyright © 2007 by Doug Stumpf. All rights reserved. Printed in the United States of America. No part of this book may be used or reproduced in any manner whatsoever without written permission except in the case of brief quotations embodied in critical articles and reviews. For information address HarperCollins Publishers, 10 East 53rd Street, New York, NY 10022.

HarperCollins books may be purchased for educational, business, or sales promotional use. For information please write: Special Markets Department, HarperCollins Publishers, 10 East 53rd Street, New York, NY 10022.

FIRST HARPER PAPERBACK PUBLISHED 2008.

Designed by Joy O'Meara

The Library of Congress has catalogued the hardcover edition as follows:
Stumpf, Doug.
    Confessions of a Wall Street shoeshine boy / Doug Stumpf, 1st ed.
    p. cm.
    ISBN 978-0-06-088953-1
 1. Securities industry—United States—Fiction. 2. Stockbrokers—Fiction. 3. Corruption—Fiction. 4. Wall Street (New York, N.Y.)—Fiction. I. Title.

PS3619.T854 C66   2007
813'.6—dc22

ISBN 978-0-06-088954-8 (pbk.)

08 09 10 11 12   ID/RRD   10 9 8 7 6 5 4 3 2 1

MONEY, here you got to HAVE IT, man.
If you DON'T have it, you're just NOBODY.

—Aguilar

INTRODUCTION
Aguilar Benicio

THIS IS MY STORY that was written by Greg Waggoner, and most times he told the truth, though there was some things that he had exaggerate. I don't know if anybody in America care about the life of a shoeshine boy, but I have the hope that some bigs will read it to see that I had a hard life but I'm an honest person, very hardworking, and that I never had done anything wrong. I'm a little person with no power, but I still be an American. My daddy did the citizenship thing back in the day.

Seriously, why Mr. Greg want to do this book is a question that is hard to answer. I don't know until today. It's cool, though. It gives me props. You know that word—props? To me, it is a word that you use when you have a lot more confidence on yourself. It's kind of ghetto: giving you props, son.

If this book hit big, maybe I will go on TV to show what's like the real shoeshine boy. You know which show that I usually used to watch it in the morning, but it's just for really famous people. That guy, Reggie, I think, on channel seven, him and this other blond lady. That's a good show. If I went on that, I think I would wear jeans and a shirt on and tie. I want the shirt to be different, like green and white stripes. Like that. I think a blue tie would go good. Or either a blue shirt, or white and blue, with a pink tie. Some pink, that would be good. And then a blazer. A blue blazer.

I love dark glasses. Versace. But I wouldn't wear them, because

I think they wanted to see right into the eyes. And I'll wear a Von Dutch hat, a really different style that's fashion. Like if I wear blue and white and pink tie, I'll get a hat that is stripes—blue, white, and pink, matching with the other colors. And a brown pair of Gucci shoes, those that kind of pointed but not pointed. It's really a nice style. I haven't seen them in a while. With no laces, only a buckle.

I come onstage, kind of nervous, until Reggie start asking me questions. I would tell him that the message of the book is that not everybody is the same in life. A lot of peoples is born in a gold crib, but it is not everybody that has that great opportunities.

Maybe, if Bill Clinton sees it, I will be able to call him up. Not that many peoples is capable to have a friendship with Bill Clinton. That would be the biggest thing. Imagine! Him and me in the TV, just walking and talking.

If the book hit big, the thing that I think I would do: travel the whole Europe. I really wanted to do that. Travel the whole Europe. I think I would like to take no less than five month just to do that. If you go different countries, you get to know the peoples. You explore every little country. Let's say you would go to Italy. You don't think the peoples in Italy is very interesting? You stay there for two weeks, three weeks. Then you go to another country: France. Then you go to Turkey. Just to see. Greece. Trying to be nice, trying to be cool. You learn a lot doing that.

I don't think I would ever want to be born rich, though. Because peoples don't usually know what is it to come from the bottom. Like my mom say it; If you got nothing and you go up to the top, if you lose, you'll be fine, because you on the same life you lived before. But when you come from the top and you lose everything, it's really hard. Peoples that have it never thought that thing going to happen. They do anything not to lose. They just go crazy.

INTRODUCTION
Greg Waggoner

THIS IS THE STORY of how I got the biggest story of my career. Regrettably, I can publish it only as a novel, with the events and characters disguised.

My main source was Aguilar, nicknamed Gil (not his real name, but he chose it—Aguilar means "eagle" in Portuguese, he tells me). I met him while I was working at the newspaper, and my route to the office took me by a shoe-repair store named Yuri's, after its Russian owner. Three shoeshine guys, all Brazilians, worked there. One looked fifty, but was around thirty-five. With a scowl and bad posture from bending over other people's feet all day, he cursed in Portuguese at customers who didn't tip enough, two dollars being the generally recognized minimum tip for a shoeshine in New York City. (Most customers don't realize that a shoeshine man's tip is his salary—he is paid little or nothing by the shoe-repair-shop owner. Yuri, who had nearly starved to death as a child in the siege of Stalingrad, gave his men $80 a week for shining the mountains of shoes left at the shop for repair. For Christmas, he gave each man a chocolate bar.) The grouchy guy had a good excuse for being that way, Gil later told me, in that he sent $1,200 a month home to his wife and four kids in Brazil, which left him enough only to live on rice and beans and share one room with a roommate, far out in Queens. Still, you'd think he would have realized a bad attitude was bad for business. Gil says he tried several times to point that out, but with no success.

In his late twenties and gay, the second guy was the opposite—friendly and eager to please—but he would try to engage you in conversation even when you didn't feel like talking, so I tended to avoid him.

Number three was Gil, only seventeen when he started. Good-looking, with curly, light brown hair and blue eyes, he was friendly in just the right way. If you weren't interested, he kept his head down and did the job; if you responded, a grin would bloom on his face, and he would start to talk sports or about some item in the morning's tabloids. When business was slow, he followed me out onto the sidewalk to chat for a few minutes about himself: he lived with his mother in the large Brazilian and Portuguese community that clustered around Ferry Street in Newark, New Jersey; he already regretted dropping out of high school; soccer was his passion, but he also loved the Knicks and the Yankees.

Gil was so green and sweet that he developed a fan club among the customers. My two-dollar tip increased to five, and I saw customers give him tens and twenties, not to mention the basketball and baseball tickets they couldn't use, from their fabulous corporate season tickets. You'd think Gil's colleagues would have resented him for soaking up so many tips and so much attention, but they didn't. On the contrary! He was the only one who could make the bad-attitude guy smile, and the two entertained themselves by ogling women on the street through the plate-glass window and bantering in Portuguese. The gay guy was always trying to enlist the customers in his campaign to get Gil to finish high school.

When I turned thirty-three, I quit the newspaper grind and signed a lucrative contract to write for *Glossy* magazine. Since I worked from home for the new job, I didn't wear leather shoes as much and wasn't as often in the neighborhood of Yuri's, so I lost touch with Gil. One day, though, I was passing by the store and thought to drop in for old times' sake. Gil was gone. He had a new job, the gay guy told me, not at another stand but at a Wall Street firm. I was surprised that Wall Street firms had their own shoeshine men, but a banker friend assured me that most of them do.

Gil and I met again, however, under circumstances soon to be described.

Like most journalists, I try not to become a character in my own stories. That was obviously not possible here, because a major part of this story involves its scaffolding, i.e., my working method in getting it. My wife, Annie, asked how I thought the reader would perceive me. I told her, truthfully, that I had no idea.

PART ONE

STREET SMART

ONE

GIL

I WAS BORN in this place named Santo Andre that is part of São Paulo, Brazil. It's not a bad area, not rich, not poor, but middle class. It's the same thing if you go in Astoria, Queens, or Newark, New Jersey. That's where a lot of Brazilians lives. You never going to see people getting robbed in the street, but then you never going to see people driving real nice cars. Santo Andre's a normal, quiet area.

In Brazil my daddy used to legalize papers. His dad came from a really poor place of Brazil. Really poor. When my grandpa came to São Paulo he didn't have anything. He probably didn't even have a pair of jeans. I don't know how he made his way up, but he became a guy who regularized houses. You know, if you want to build a house in Brazil, you got to have all this paperwork, so that's what my grandpa usually used to deal with. He taught my daddy how to do it, and then my daddy used to legalize the houses that his daddy used to send him to. It was an easy job because in Brazil everything is so corrupt. You got to know peoples. If you want your papers to work, you got to pay the peoples that deals with the papers. You already know them, so you go there, and you pay them. And then they pay somebody, and then they hurry up with the papers, because otherwise the papers would sit there for two years.

My grandpa used to deal with big stuffs, like supermarkets, but my daddy was never the greedy type. If a guy would tell him, Oh, we still building up the house, and we got to spend money on this and that, then my daddy would be like, You know what? Just give me some money so I can go and buy some groceries, and he was not like, You got to pay me this percentage. He's like that until today.

My mom was adopted. My mom's mom used to clean the house for this family. And one day she went to the family and said she was going to give away my mom for adopt because she didn't have enough money to support her. So the lady said, Why don't you bring her here because we don't have any kids, so she brought my mom to the lady when my mom was about two and a half.

The couple used to love my mom. But my mom's mom used to come to them every month for money, so they used to get into some fights with her. And the lady was really religious, so that's why they sent my mom to Catholic school. You go to live there with the nuns. My mom said it was really, really bad. She hates church even today. She never goes to church. She hates the nuns. She never explain to me how it really was, but she said her life was miserable in that convent.

After a while, she got out and went home to live. Her adoption parents were really nice, but they were really strict. She couldn't go out, she couldn't do anything. Until today, my mom doesn't go out, she doesn't do anything. I tell her, Look, you're fifty-some now. How many years do you have left in your life? That's why I want her to go on vacation and stuffs, but she don't do it.

Then my mom met my daddy. Back then the only way for you to get out of your house was getting married. This is the way I see it: my mom just wanted to get out of that house, so she got married to my daddy. She was eighteen, but my daddy was twenty-eight. My mom was really into work. She used to work in a big Brazilian company. It went out of business a long time ago, but back in the day she was the one, after the manager, that used to hold the keys where they put the money, and she used to know the codes and everything. She used to make a lot of money doing that. My mom was a really smart woman. She still is until today, but the job that she does here, clean houses, it's not the same. Because if you don't speak the language in this country, it's hard. Really, really hard. And my daddy, he shines shoes.

If I came from a real rich family, I don't think I'd ever be able to do it. You know when you're rich, you don't want to do that, you don't want to shine shoes. Sometimes when I used to walk into that place, I was like, Damn, how they look at me, the traders? Not now. Now, I'm more comfortable. Because I don't go there to shine their shoes. I go there more to socialize. To talk, see how they doing.

I'm more like an entertainer. I like that. It makes me feel good.

The trading floor has this HUGE desk, and everyone will be sitting next to each other like if you go to a high-school computer class, they have the kids. There's rows of those. There's peoples that will be having three flat-screen computers in front of them. There's peoples that will be having four, five. There's numbers on the computers. I don't know what they stand for.

That's the thing: I got to get to know the difference. Sometimes they tell me what they do, but I don't keep that in mind. It's kind of hard, though, because there's a whole bunch of little things. It's not just traders that is there. It's like one thing led to the other. One sells this, another one sells just that. One got to sell to this other guy that sits two rows away. It's so confusing. I never know.

Today I was shining Mr. Turner's shoes, and I was looking at his screen, and I was like, Damn, there's so many fucking numbers. How the fuck you know which ones good, which ones not good? You got to study that for years, I think. You got to know the business. It's hard though, because you dealing with numbers.

It's always packed, loud, because everyone be talking and answering the phones and just walking around, having a conversation without stopping. It's like you going to Times Square, you see so many peoples, but a lot more is sitting down than just walking around. They talk back and forth. Meanwhile, they on the phone, but then they go, Hey! Wait! They put their hands on the phone where you talk, and they just ask questions to each other. Or they will be on the phone, and the line rings. Someone has to answer, and the person who answers, if it's not for him, which it wouldn't be—it's always for someone else—they would be like, Hey, this guy, he wants to talk to you.

And the person just go with the finger around, and it means Later. Or Tell him I'm not here. I think that depends if the transaction good or not, they will answer your phone. But they usually go, Oh, I'll call him later. They do that a lot.

They have this little microphones, so they beep each other. They will go on those, and they know the extension. The person be sitting three rows ahead. They be like, Hey, I got some buhbuhbuh share. Are you interesting on it? The other person will respond yes or no. I think some persons just do that as a favor because the day before they bought something to them. Most peoples do it just for favors, I think.

It's a whole bunch of TV screens that stay up by the windows. It's always this lady—I don't know her name—on the afternoon. Peoples usually talk about her hair all the time because she change her hair all the time. Beautiful girl. Black hair.

In my job I'm trying to be kind of professional and kind of funny, so peoples can like me, and they can give me the job even if they don't want to. I go over there in the morning, the first thing that I do, I don't go over there and grab my box and go like, desperate, Yo, you want to shine your shoes? No. I leave my box in a little corner, and I say good morning to everybody. Hey, how you doing guys? Hey, what's up? Hey, Mr. Pearson! Hey, what's up, Tim? What's up, Jim? Everybody doing okay? How's your son, Mrs. Alice, that little genius kid? Hey, the Knicks clobbered the Spurs last night, Jared, you see that?

I always like to make peoples laugh. I'll talk about anything to anyone. I'll just go to one guy, and we only talk about soccer. And there's a guy behind him that I'll talk about clothes. And there's a guy that sit on the other row that I'll talk about NBA. And a guy I'll talk about baseball. And there's a guy that I'll ask about his family, how they doing. And a guy that will like to talk about Brazil. I know who is who and who likes what, everyone's name, if they have kids. And it's not one person, it's more than a hundred persons at my job that I know pretty well what to say and how I approach them. There is guys that will be very serious, and I will be very serious. I'm like, Hey, hi, sir. I'm the guy that cleans shoes here. You need my service? But with some certain ones, I'm like, Hey, how's it going. How you doing, dude? Like there's a guy, Tim, he will come and scare me, pushes me. So when I go by his row I kick his chair. I kind of grab on the back and shake him. I tap on his head. It's pretty cool, though. There's some certain guys that they don't like to talk about womens. I try a couple of times. They married, very serious. Damn, there's tons of different individuals there. You got to know how to approach peoples. You got to make them laugh.

It's not like I'm desperate to shine their shoes. Because they might not want my service today, but they might want tomorrow. Because sometimes they doesn't even want to shine their shoes, but if you treat them nicily, they going to be like, Well, you know, Gil's here today. Good, let's shine the shoes.

Maybe 68 percent have the shoes off their feets to shine, the other ones are on the feets. There was one guy that got it shined off, and I asked him, Why? Why don't you shine your shoes on your feets? And he said to me, it's mean. Very mean. That's what he said it.

With the ones that want it shined off, I get the shoes from the rows, and I sit on the end, shining. To buff them off the feets you got to put the heel between your legs, a little bit up from your knees, and hold with your legs, with the point a little bit out, so you got space to buff them up. You put a towel to cover up your whole pants, so you don't dirt it.

Or I can get my box and I can go right in the middle of the row and shine one person's shoes on the feets and then come back out of the row. Or shine right in the hallway. Or I can stay in the row and shine everybody's shoes. I can take any spot in the whole building and shine the shoes. But there's one little corner I take for myself.

Some certain peoples just want it on, some certain peoples just want it off. The ones that get it shined on, they usually pay attention to the time you spend. Or some peoples just don't like to walk around without their shoes. Or sometimes they just like to hear my stories.

There's always someone who sits on the end, and I'm talking to that guy. And sometimes it's like, Hey, they busy, and he goes back to work. So, I know when to talk to him and when not to talk to him. I respect a lot of that. This guys, they have little times that they just bullshitting, watching the TV on the screens, ordering food. And sometimes they busy. So you got to know how to approach them. It's funny, because when the interns come, they don't know. They want to ask some question, and the guys are like, Get! Out! They treat the interns worse than they treat me. Because they never treat me with no respect. When I go over there, if they really busy, they just roll the fingers, saying they busy.

When I first start working there, they didn't know me. When I first walk in, they thought that I was an immigrant, that I didn't know how to speak a word of English, because I used to go like, Hey, shine shoes? You want to shine shoes? That's the only thing I used to say. I didn't communicate with peoples.

I went through times at my job. I used to dress really ghetto when I first started. Imagine the kid with the do-rag, Jordan sneakers, Rocawear jeans. I used to wear army pants. There's this army pants that used to go white, black, purple, and gray. It's crazy colors. With the blue Jordan sneakers. Baby-blue. Yankee hat, turned back. That's right in the beginning. Peoples used to look at me. I used to talk to peoples like, Yo, what up? I used to be me, me, me. And I don't know who you are. And I don't care who you are, mostly. Because that didn't used to do me any good. I'm just there for the money. Most times.

After that I started to treat peoples better. I went from ghetto to more cool—Armani Exchange, really cool guy. I'm talking to peoples more civilized, niclyier, sophisticated. Trying to pick up what peoples have to say it. They talk about clothes, I get into a conversation about clothes because I read the magazines, and I have a lot to talk about. Even though I don't know, I get my way through it. The person's talking about selling the house that they live. They live in Westchester, I know Westchester. I know Rye. I know Larchmont. You name it. All the areas that the peoples in my job lives, all the place that the rich peoples lives. Even though you went there once.

TWO

Gil

YOU KNOW HOW I really got noticed, though? After I went to Miami for spring break. Me and my cousin Fabio drove the whole way. I took pictures there, a lot of pictures of the kids I hung out with in that place. Before I went to Miami, the traders were cool with me, but after, they started giving me, not respect, but they started seeing me in a totally different way: Oh, this guy's pretty cool. You know, because if you see the pictures, most of the kids I was hanging with are American. So the traders probably thought it, Oh, Gil don't hang with Mexicans.

Yo, peoples just loved this pictures, man. That's when they turned. They turned really big. Everybody was like, Whoa, Gil! They just went crazy, you know? Because they saw crazy stuffs on the pictures. This girls that I got with down there, I took naked pictures. Yeah, I have that in my house! I'm serious! I showed it to this guys at my job. First I didn't think I was going to show it, because, you know, this guys can get me fired. But I showed it to Mr. Tim, this guy I'm cool with. I woke up really early that morning, because I wanted to show it to them. It was around eight something. I was like, Mr. Tim, *come here, come here, come here, come here, get out of the row!* Just take a look how my vacation was.

Tim got up, but when he saw it, he was like, Oh, dude! Oh, my God! You are my hero. Gil, what have you done? Let me see this pictures again. He look again. He's like, Gil, you made my day! I wish I was you. He make me kind of big. It's funny. I liked that.

Mr. Tim went around and start showing everybody. Mr. Pete, when he saw it, this is what he did: he give them back to me. He was so shame. You know you can see the person's shame, they get red, and they put the head down.

There's another guy, Mr. John Pearson. Mr. Pearson saw it, and he was like, Gil, next time you go, tell me, I will pay the hotel, the plane tickets. You going down with me. You just got to call her up and bring her back to the hotel. He said just like that. I'm serious. I was like, Okay, Mr. John. I don't know if he was fucking around, but he cool. He plays around once in a while, but with this guys sometimes it's like you fishing. You throw the line and if the fish catches—Hey! I bet you if I tell him I'm bringing you, maybe he will go. You never know. Humankind could be so crazy. I would be like, Look, Mr. John, between me and you, you going to pay for everything, we go down, and you do you, and I'll bring the girl. But you got to pay for us. Down there. Come on. You don't think he will go? He will. He's married. To a supermodel. Russian. But he loves womens. A guy that probably worth about a couple of millions. He's old, forty-something.

A lot of peoples there only start treating me good because they see the other ones that is really on the top treating me so nicily, stop and talking. So they like, Fuck, if this guys talking to Gil, I better do. Just a few miserable motherfuckers that don't treat me good. They look down at me because I'm there to shine shoes. They like, This kid is probably not worth a penny. They don't say hi to me. They walk by me for three years, they don't say a word. It's like I'm not there. I shine their shoes once in a while. They like, Hey, can you shine my shoes? They don't want to know my name. It's business. They don't care, they don't want to know anything.

But some of them, they really care. They want to know about my life. The way they treat me, it's like they care. Who's going to give you that?

This is the way I deal with peoples at my job. The shoes to me doesn't really matter. It's the way the persons going to treat me. Some of them, they can be looking like a millions dollars, they can be a dick to you. They going to treat you like you nothing. The way I treat peoples is the personality. In the whole firm that I work there's two, maybe three guys that if they ask me for a favor, like take their shoes into the shop for new soles, I'm not going to do it right away. It's not for the money, it's for the attitude. They don't treat me right.

The fee for a shine is three dollars. But most of them, they give five. There's just a few, I can't even count on one hand, that give me three. Now, when they come and try to give me three, I tell them, Sorry, sir, I raise to four dollars. One guy that is British has a lot of pairs of shoes. He has a pair of shoes that cost $2,000. He usually dress all British and European style. Now I don't go there all the time, because he give me three dollars. The British man is cheap. I used to like that guy, but I waste my time.

One guy give me ten dollars, Mr. Fred Turner. He's about six foot three, blue eyes, thirty. Comes from a wealthy family. A very wealthy family. He's there, but he's already rich. He really knows how to use the money, but he's not a snob. I think he's Catholic. Jewish or Catholic. He makes a lot of money. He used to just say, Hey, how you doing? But then he'd stop and look at me and ask, How you doing, Gil? That was from him to me. I was surprised. Then he start talking to me, ask me how my life was, so I tell him about that. He was like, Oh, your mom cleans houses? I think he looks at me, and he kind of feels bad for me. Because the way he looks at me, maybe he wants to help me out, but he doesn't know how.

It was just the way he treat everybody else and he treat me, I used to see it, that it wasn't different at all. He was kind of paying attention to me. He wasn't like, Oh, whatever you saying. Sometimes when I used to say things that he wasn't interesting, he used to stick to his own little world, watching his computer. He wasn't a man of a lot of words, but he always amaze me.

First he didn't used to tip me good, but then he ended up tipping really good. He's kind of a simple man, because the way he dresses is nice but not too expensive—nice shirt from Pink, nice pants, nice shoes, Johnston & Murphy. He doesn't walk around like he's the hottest shit, but if you see him, you might think that he's the hottest shit. Just the way he is.

He has a fiancée that the secretaries say doesn't look that good for him. The secretaries there, most of them, they old. They gossip about the guys. Who look the best, who dressing the best, who making the most. They know about the traders' lives more than their own lifes. Because they listen to everything, when the traders on the phone, when they talking to each other. A lot of womens who have that imagination of the job that they can get near the traders and marry them. Because the traders don't spend that much time with their wifes. So from there the secretaries could start an affair, and then they could become the future wifes. Then they could stay home all day and spend the cash. But that usually happen right in the beginning, when they young, or that will never happen. A lot of them still there and still dream about it, but if it doesn't happen, it doesn't happen. Like Rona.

Rona's the secretary that book all the financials for the traders, like when they go to dinner and stuffs. She's like, Oh, Fred's girl was here. I was like, So, how she look? Like a supermodel? Nah, Rona says, she's not all that. Not for him. She look like just a regular girl.

I'm cool with Rona. Rona know everything, like how much this guy make and how much that one. She make good—probably about $70,000 and she own a nice car. A Z3. Live by herself in Astoria. Three cats. She *loves* those cats. She look good. Blond. Nice ass. Thick body, but the guys on the trading floor, the white guys, they like skinny womens with big titties. They don't like womens with big ass, you know, with nice body the way she has.

She's Greek. Thirty-six years old. She goes to the tan machine. A lot. Sometimes she almost black. Sometimes I go up to her, and we have a conversation. Sometimes I go up to her, and she doesn't even say hi to me. She's like good mood, bad mood. And it's not anything with me. It's with her. Some people funny like that.

She knows everybody's gossip. Like if some guy cheat on his girl or his wife. She knows everything about that. Because she sees all the paperwork for the big guys, the guys that make money. She knows if they go to a hotel when they not supposed. There's this guy, right? To me he was the boss. Like, fucking, this guy spend a lot of money on suits and shoes. The way he dressing, he must be the boss. One day Rona saw me talking to him, and she was like, You know that guy? And I was like, Yeah, is he the boss? She's like, No, this guy probably make the half the amount of money that I make. I was like, Are you serious, Rona?

Rona's type is really old and rich or a guy with muscles—like a strong kid. If the rich guys would date her, she would. But they don't want her, so she had gone out with Fabio, my cousin. He's Brazilian, but he has the Italian look. The type of guy, really built up. He only lives for that—the gym.

Fabio, he's the copy guy. Whenever the fax is broken, he goes and replace it, or when there's no papers in the copy machine, he helps to put, or if there's no tint inside, he will go there and replace it. Little stuffs like that. If peoples leave papers to get copied, he got to do the folders. He got a car, a Subaru.

He went out with Rona, but he didn't get with her. She said he's too much on himself. He was about his muscles and his car. Then I talked to him, because I know boths of them, and he says she probably have cellulite in her ass, her ass wasn't that hard, this and that. And he was saying, You see all that tittie? That's all flat. It'll probably be hitting her belly soon. I was cracking up.

I went to see Rona today. She put her feet on the box: Nine West shoes. They okay, affordable, sixty, seventy dollars. Okay leather. Stylish. Would last you a year and change. But today, she kind of mad. She wanted to tell me who does she likes and who does she doesn't like in the firm, and why it's the reason. Sometimes it was more how the person ask her to do things. Some peoples demand and never say thank you and never be nice, and she put it that whatever they doing not cool. But they can't never fire her, she say.

She's like, Gil, I know stuffs about this guys, what they do. She's like, I could get some certain of these guys into a lot of trouble. I was like, Are you serious, Rona? She's like, I'm dead serious. That's what she say. *Dead* serious. But I think she must be exaggerate because she was mad at them just that day. She's like that. Some certain times she get really, really mad, but the next day she erase it from her mind, and she's like, Hey, how you doing? Beautiful day. Everything cool?

THREE

Gil

WHEN THE PERSON'S not busy, they just love to listen to my stories. Like Miss Lindsay Minter, she loves it. Yeah, she does. She's thirty-one years old. To me she look super good, five foot ten, blue, blue eyes. Modeling type. Body's like, Whoa! She told me she's from a strict Catholic family. She spend money for shoes like no other: Manolos, Guccis, Ferragamos. Every day I see her she's in a different outfit. Different shoes. Different this. She treat me really nice, always talking to me, ask me how was my day. She's a great tipper, six, seven dollars.

She loves to hear how I live my life. But she always trying to put it like, Oh, me and my boyfriend, we went to this place and this hip-hop star was there, the guy that sang that song, and she trying to play it up that she knows about the guy. But she doesn't know. She doesn't even know what the guy, if you read about hip-hop in magazines, then you know. Like how gangsta the guy was and how bad the guy was.

I know she would never like to live in my world. When I tell her about Newark, she thinks I live in the ghetto, in the really bad part. Everybody thinks that. Because they never going to think that, Oh, Gil is able to live in an okay place, you know, that is not going to have no crime. They think I come from the subway stations, like the rats. That's the way they see me. They don't think I am capable to work a computer or that I make enough money to go to clubs. They like, Oh, Gil you really went to that place? Or, You are really capable to do that thing? I get that all the time.

They don't know Newark. They don't know Queens. They only know Manhattan, part of Jersey, Hamptons, Connecticut. That's it. They don't go to any other place. They don't even know where I live.

Mr. Tim and Mr. Jim, young guys, twenty-some, they sit by Lindsay. They like brothers. Twins. I swear. Same blond hair, real short. Same shoes, Tods. You know what they be doing usually every day? They be tackling each other. You know tackle? I'm serious. They come and they try to put each other down on the floor. Like kids. They drag each other down to the floor. Or sometime Tim is sitting, so Jim comes and tackles him. They talk back to each other, like "I'm going to get you." Just fucking around with each other. I think they want attention. Like two kids. Everybody's working and them showing off over there, grabbing each other, using the force. Tim is like, Yeah, you got me this time, but the next time I will get you harder. Then Jim is like, I'm going to slap your head. This and that.

They boths like Miss Lindsay, but she doesn't care. Her boyfriend's wealthy. Jim put it that he's a really rich old bastard. Rona is like, She just stays with him for the money. Tim, what he says about Lindsay is that some womens, when they come up to you, they usually do some signs that you know you got a chance. That you really have a chance. And some, they have the class that even if they do, you never going to know. And Tim goes, Lindsay is the type of womans you never going to know. You always going to want her, and she always going to play that game.

I was telling Mr. Jim—because I'm cool with Tim and Jim—that I met this Brazilian girl, and you not going to believe it. And he was like, What? It was this girl that I met on the Internet in a Brazilian chat room. She used to live in Florida in Miami. She's only been here six month, so she's really bored. She doesn't know anybody here besides her mother. She was trying to get to know someone on the Internet. So we exchanged pictures. I was like, Oh, my God. Twenty-four, blond, perfect body in clothes. Fabio was like, Go ahead. Try to fuck her.

But I don't want to meet a person like that. I usually try to be friends. I don't want to rush into things. I wanted to get to know her.

There's this bar I usually go. I told her, so she went there, and I went there with Fabio. She came with her mom. Her mom is really, really old, like forty-five years old, but she pretty cool. She doesn't look that old. So I ended up talking with this girl, and we kind of got with each other at the bar. And Fabio got with her mother.

After two days we went to Long Island, right next to Port Washington, because the girl, she babysit for this family. This girl to me, she was really, really normal. She wasn't a freak. She didn't look like the freak type. She got a room in the basement. I think the guy she work for is a doctor. I don't know what the lady do for a living. There's two kids.

So this girl took me there, and we on the couch, kissing and stuff. She offered me this drink that they had over there. It's like a wine, but it's strawberry. Seven dollars at the liquor store, a HUGE bottle. And then all of a sudden things start getting warm, and this girl pull out my dick and she goes fucking crazy. She was like, Oh, you like the way I suck you? And I was like, Damn. She talk really dirty. Everything she was saying, I was like, Damn. Then she was like, I'm going to do something to you. I was like, All right.

So we go to the bedroom, and she wanted to dominate. She throw me on the bed and she's just like, Shh! Shh! Shut up! Shut up! I'm like, Damn, can I do this? And she was like, Shh! Shh! Don't talk when I'm talking. I'm like, This woman's crazy. She was nice in a way. I think she was nice, like her mentality. Then she start kissing me all over. I kind of like it, but at the same time I don't like it. You know what I'm saying? I told her that. It afraid me. I'm not used to that. I'm used to kissing and hugging and whatever, but not someone telling me to SHUT THE FUCK UP.

Then you know what this girl do next? She licked my ass! I'm not lying! It felt good, kind of warm, but then when she did it, I felt fucking guilty. After she was done, I was like, Yo, you think I'm gay? She was like, No, why? Because no other womens had ever done this to me until today. And she was like, Well, it's okay. Don't it feel good? I was like, It feels weird. It makes you think, What the fuck she be thinking about me? I was like, Damn, where I meet these womens? You know, like most of São Paulo girls, they won't do that. They won't even give you a blow job. But this girl's from Rio, and every girl that I met from Rio, they all freakies. So this is the thing about these girls.

I was telling Mr. Jim, and he was like, Oh, my God. You got to tell Lindsay this story. And I was like, You crazy, man? I can't tell Miss Lindsay. I respect her. I don't even curse with her. Because that looks bad at my job. You know, the same English that I want to use in outside society, I want to use at my job. So people can look at me like, Aw, this kid is not just bullshit, he is really serious. But Mr. Jim was like, No, no, you got to tell her. She's going to love it.

I went there, and I was like, Lindsay, I don't know if I wanted to tell you this, because I don't know how you going to react, but Jim said I was okay to tell you. And she was like, Go ahead Gil, tell me. I was like, Lindsay, I went out with this girl the first time, and you know what she had done to me? No, what? The girl licked my ass! And Miss Lindsay's like, Oh, no! Oh, no! And she all shaked. Or at least she pretend. Then she's like, How you meet this girl? And she ask me all this questions, like what else we be doing that night.

Now every time I shine Lindsay's shoes, she's like, Got any stories today, Gil? And I tell her straight up, and she loves to hear it. Mr. Tim is like, Maybe that rich guy is too old to get it up, so my stories bring her a memory.

We can't talk about those stories when Mrs. Alice comes in the row. Mrs. Alice Norther is the boss of the floor. She doesn't like sex talk. At all. Whenever I'm talking about it, she goes crazy. She's like, Gil, knock it off, man! You guys want to talk about that, go to a bar! Not in here. This is not an appropriate place to talk about that. And I'm like, Mrs. Alice, look at this floor. You doesn't think this guys cheat on their wifes? She's like, Nah. So I told her, Look, you crazy, because that's the way you think . . . well, I didn't want to say about her husband. Rona say her husband cheat on her all the time. Her husband's a trader that work at another firm.

Mrs. Alice is like six feet, 145 pounds. She's really old: forty-seven.

She sits two rows away, and she comes, and then she presents herself. There's a whole bunch of rows, and she comes to this row. Then she start talking about a whole bunch of things that they don't like it. They pretend they liking because she's a boss. But the minute she turn her back, they like, Yip, yip, yip.

This lady have four kids. If you listen to Mrs. Alice this kids the best kids in the whole world. Mrs. Alice is like, My boy won this soccer match. This boy, he play soccer at his school, so Mrs. Alice thinks she knows about soccer. Another one. Because some of these peoples, they think they know about soccer. They start talking about players I never heard. Because to me the most famous ones come from Brazil, Argentina. But the peoples at the firm comes up with some British guys. Fuck man, I can't stand that British league, man. Sucks. Sucks to watch. Like watching a video game.

Mrs. Alice talks about her other son, and how he goes there to the different countries to play chess. I'm serious. A chess champion. I swear. This kid is seven years old, and he goes there, and he plays chess games with old guys, like thirty and forty. And the kid wins. I mean, this kid is some genius with chess. She never talk about her daughters, though. I don't know why.

Mrs. Alice be usually bragging, and then when she turns around, you just hear them yapping, What she comes here for? To talk about her own private life? To talk about her kids? We're not here to talk about that.

They always have pictures of their kids, though. But you think they really care? I don't think they care. This peoples is raise different. That's the way they go. Because they live under stress. If they lose someone's money, they fucked. And if you fucked on Wall Street, you fucked for life.

In summertime some of them, they send their wifes to the Hamptons, because they usually got a beach house there. The wife goes with the kids and he works. So he work, work, work, and he only see her once in every week. But what the fuck he does, he just doesn't like his wife and his kids. Because if you like her, you like your kids, you spend the time with them. Some of this guys, they have their kids just to show. It's not like they care. Because you figure, your wife is making money, you making money, you leave your house—because they usually leave their house around five, six in the morning, no more than that. So the babysitter's taking care the kids. They don't get home sometimes until ten. Sometimes they don't see their kids the whole entire week, because kids, they go to sleep early. And then when it comes to the weekend they always have this golf thing, you know, going to a country club.

Every person at that place knows the story of Mrs. Alice and her husband, because Mrs. Alice, she receive a call from a guy pretending to be the boss of her husband at his firm. He saying a whole bunch of things, not threatening her but that her husband stole money from the company. This guy was saying things that her husband is losing his job. So after that he would go to jail. Mrs. Alice didn't know what to do. She was like, How am I supposed to help you with this? Because the guy is calling the lady, how she going to know that this is not for real? She kind of went crazy.

Then the guy said it to her, the only way she could get her husband out of going to jail was if she had money, and was replacing the money back that her husband took, so nobody knew about that. But the only way she was able to replace the money was cash, because that has to be a very secret thing. She couldn't even tell no one else, just between them two. Because if anyone found out, her husband was going to jail. So she doesn't tell nobody. *Not even her husband.* I'm serious.

The guy was like, I'm going to meet you up around whatever street, and I'm going to be in a limo. You got to put the cash in a brief-case and just hand the money to me when I stop. Mrs. Alice goes to the bank and gets all the money that she and her husband have save for years to give it this guy that she didn't even know. She didn't even tell her husband that she was giving. So this guy ended up looking like he was the boss, because, hey!—when you coming in a limo and you dressing up nice in a nice suit, who the fuck is going to think that you not the boss?

And Mrs. Alice ended up going home. Then her husband came there, she didn't even know what to do. She was crying and hugging him and saying, You don't have to go to jail. And he's like, What the fuck? Because the thing was a con, and Mrs. Alice, she didn't know. She thought the guy was the real boss of her husband.

I don't know what her husband did with her. I mean, you not able to beat her for that. If it was me, I would get really mad. I would be like, Oh, my God, why didn't you call me? Is like trust, you know, between me and you. I would go bananas. I would have been depress for a month, just thinking about that humiliate. Just feeling really bad, every day waking up, looking at her face. Like, Why you do that?

Another guy that loves my stories is Mr. John Pearson. He's the boss on nine. He has his own office. You look at Mr. John, you see a little bit of finance, a little bit of cool guy, and a little bit like, Fucking I'm the boss here. But he has a naughty face.

That's the guy that I spend a year in front of his office, shining his shoes next to his secretary. The first six month he didn't used to say anything. He used to walk in, give the shoes, walk out, without even looked at me. Most times now, like Thursdays and Fridays, he's like, Hey, Gil you want to come in and share my sandwich? He give me seven dollars to shine his shoes.

When I'm there in his office, I'm like his buddy. He tells me he goes to strip bars, about the womens he gets with. They all do, but they don't tell. Everybody got someone on the side. But when Mr. John comes to the floor, he's very conservative. A totally different person. He just say, like, Hi. Just know me as Gil, the guy that shines the shoes.

Mr. John's got three kids. He live with his wife, and Rona told me she's a Russian supermodel type. Rona's like, He traded his old wife for the new wife, like a new car model. A new supermodel! Rona's like, the old wife took most his money and the new one be spending the rest. She made him get a new house. He just spent millions and millions on that. Russian girls is very materialistic. Everybody know about that.

The house is around the way of some guys here, so they know. This peoples live the same shit, they go to each other's house to visit. They usually say how it's built, that they got this inside, they got that. I don't usually know the words what the things are. Like we got a bathroom that got this, this, this, that. A room that got this painting, and this thing. I don't know what they talking about.

Last year Mr. John, he was at the Christmas party, he put it that he make $2 millions a year. He was drunk. After that he never told me no more. Only on that day he told me. I don't know what is $2 millions a year. I don't know what is $500,000 a year. I don't even know what is $100,000 a year. I don't even know how much money I make in a year.

But usually he always put it that he poor. Not poor, but his wife owes a lot from him to the men that she buys a whole bunch of things—clothes, jewelry. Money-wise, he is like, Yo, Gil, I can't take this anymore. My wife calls me up—you heard her calling now?—she want money for this, money for that. She always want more money. She got a nanny. She stay home. She doesn't work, and she still want me to give her more money, so she can spend, spend, spend, spend. This women's a bitch.

Mr. John always trying to put it that he the hardworking guy, that he there, trying to do a better living for his family. But he loves womens. He went to a bachelor party in Las Vegas. Everybody was getting stoned. Some guys doing coke. You know, all his friends from trading. They had hookers. I don't know if he fuck the hooker, but he say that she gave him head. You know, she suck his dick. But he don't consider that cheating. And from there I was like, Whoa, all right! You know, if you have a hooker sucking your dick, that's automatically cheating. You know what I mean?

This guys, they conservative about talking about cheating. But if I talk about it, they will talk, too. When I showed Mr. John the pictures from my vacation, he start talking about stuffs that he been doing. I'm there shining shoes, and he's very serious. He's like, Yeah, Gil, I can't help it man. Yesterday I had this meeting with a client, and the meeting ended up being not too long, and after that I wanted to kill some time, so I went to this bar. And I was there just by myself, and this great-looking girl came, and she start talking to me. So I bought her a drink, and we talk, and we start drinking. The next thing I see it, I take her to the hotel room. Probably left that place around three-thirty in the morning. But you know what? I think my wife is going to be happy. Because I'm going to get her something really nice today, some nice jewelry. He tell his wife he was in a meeting.

I was like, Mr. John, how come when I usually tell peoples here the stories that I have, they always trying to play it up like they don't do that kind of stuffs. You know what he told me? He was like, Hey, dude, this guys doing the same thing as you be doing. They love to hear the stories. Like when you get really out of control. They all do it.

FOUR

Greg

I LOVED THAT Gil was smarter than they gave him credit for, that he was taking it all in, remembering it all. That's what first attracted me to his story. I'm a business reporter, but I'm not a company man. I like being contrary and finding the angles other people don't see. My first time out, I wrote about a group of executives who had just taken their company private. They gave me a tour of the factory, talking all the while about caring for the workers and supporting the community, but I spotted the head of the union and got him off to one side. The tour was all just window-dressing, he told me. The executives didn't really care about the company or the people who worked there. They were already trying to scrap the pension plan and cut back on the benefits.

The people I gravitate toward are the rebels, the outcasts, the people who buck the system and dare to be different, who take risks and stick their necks out. I think I write about them for inspiration, to measure myself against them, maybe as a way to get the courage to do those kinds of things myself. Not that I ever really do.

My father, my mother, and my brother are all doctors. They actually introduce me as "the black sheep of the family." My father still asks me, "When are you going to get a real job?"

His brother was a professional investor who ran a big pension fund. Both he and my father were so competitive they didn't have much use for each other, but my uncle always went out of his way to be nice to me. It was because of him that I first set foot on a trading floor.

Actually, I was in my mother's arms, and we were getting the grand tour from my uncle. I can still see the bright fluorescent lights. I am too hot, wrapped in too many winter clothes. A huge man with a bald head and black hair on his arms and spilling over the top of his shirt talks in a booming voice to my father. Then he tries to take me. I scream. You don't need a PhD in psychology to figure that one out.

In college I spent more time working on the school newspaper than going to classes, but somehow it never occurred to me then that I could earn my living doing something I enjoyed. Instead, I went to b-school, mainly because my father offered to pay. It wasn't medical school, but it was better than nothing, and he managed to convince me that an MBA would be "good training for the mind, no matter what you decide to do later."

I was a lousy business student. I had no real grasp of the numbers they were trying to teach. The professors would show how to calculate the standard deviation or explain the difference between an asset swap and a liability swap, and my eyes would glaze. When the young hot-shots from Manhattan came to recruit, I thought they were grotesque, these guys in suits describing this life of doing deals. Who the fuck wants to wear a suit every day?

I got my MBA, just barely, but my father was right, as usual: it got me my first job, as a reporter at a well-known business magazine. Other guys I knew who went into journalism had to spend five years grinding out the police blotter in West Bubblefuck, as Gil likes to say, but I started with a major platform that important people read. Not that the salary was great, especially compared to what my former classmates were getting. I didn't envy them, though. With one or two exceptions, they all ended up unhappy, believing they were capable of better, dreaming about getting out, but trapped by the money.

Back then some people called me a junkyard-dog reporter, yapping at the heels of the big firms and the corporate-raider fat cats. Some people criticized my coverage as being overly negative, but that's the way my readers liked it, and that's the way I felt.

The story I always wanted to do was a whistle-blower story, where the underlings bring down the high and mighty. Those stories are not easy to come by. Usually the whistle-blower gets crushed or bought off by those in power, or his lawyers won't let him talk to reporters. But then along came Gil, with a story about his best friend, Eddy.

FIVE

Gil

AT TJ FRIDAY'S Eddy put it he had got fired. TJ Friday's is where we usually go, because that's where they have the special two-dollar beers. You know, from five to seven at night. I go with the guys that collect the garbage in the building, cleans the floors, the bathrooms, everything. It's like fifty floors, so they got a whole army of little soldiers that cleans that place. Each floor got to have two guys. They cool people. Simple, like me. There's two other guys that is Brazilian, some Dominicans, Puerto Ricans. A lot of them, they kind of act white because they was born here or they been here forever. There's one new guy, he has the Irish look, even the Irish way of talking. One guy, he look Jewish to me, he has kind of the Jewish hair, but they told me he's Italian.

We go there and drink our asses off, man. They usually order food from that place, but I don't like it. TJ Friday's is one of those bars that you walk in and you don't see nothing that you like, but you end up drinking, because the beer's cheap. And those guys are cheap, man. It pisses me off sometimes, but they don't make a lot of money, and most of them got families or they send the money back home. So I go there just to drink and talk to the guys.

We talk a lot of shit at TJ Friday's. Just get a group of maybe ten guys, maybe more. They like to talk about their own business, how each other usually do the work. But we end up talking about a lot of other things. Sometimes we get so banged up we don't even know what we talking. We fuck around with each other. That's what we do for fun. When we get really banged up, we start acting really stupid with the girls. Go up to girls and fucking play the worst jokes, not touching them and stuffs, just go up to them and go like, Hey, what's up? I want to kiss you. You know, saying things like that, and she says, No.

Juan, he's fucking crazy about womens. A Dominican guy, he's married, but he has a whole bunch of girlfriends. He has that HUGE accent, you know, that Spanish accent. He's like, Gil, you leeeve by yourself? I'm like, Nah, I live with my mom. Why you want to know? And he's like, Oh, man, you don't know. Have a lot of girls. *Muchachas*. Take two to your house. I'm like, Yo, ain't you married, Juan? He's like, This just between me and you, okay? But he lives too far in the Bronx. I don't want to mess with that Bronx. It's too dangerous. I don't like that place, man. You ever been to the Bronx? Drive around inside that place one day. Get up on 161st, you be like, Damn, the garbage doesn't pass around here. They don't clean the streets. They don't paint the apartments. It looks like so miserable, it's sad.

I usually chill with Fabio and Eddy. We hang out, go to clubs. Fabio, this fucking kid, he's a great-looking guy, like a superman. He goes to the gym every day. But when he goes to a bar, he will never go up to the girl. He always want the girl to come up to him. Because he think he's a super-shit. He doesn't have money, but just his body.

When Fabio was in Brazil, he met this girl that was twelve, and then they started going out. That was his first girl. The only way he could fuck her (this is the Brazilian style), he used to stay in the living room, sitting with her and her mother, and he'd be like, I'm going to go get a glass of water in the kitchen. Then he used to call his girlfriend to come with him, and they used to fuck there in the kitchen real quick. Like three or four minutes. While the mother's in the living room! From the living room to the kitchen was a hallway that if she stuck her head, she wouldn't see them, but if she got up and went straight, she would see. But she never had done that, so Fabio said that he and his girlfriend had sex a whole bunch of times. That's how he used to get laid. Standing up. That's how he took the virginity of his girlfriend. This fucking crazy Brazilians.

Fabio, he's a horny bastard. Yo, I never seen a guy like that. He doesn't get satisfied with pornos. He could get with a model-looking type, but he wants a girl that he's going to hit the first night. One time we went to China Club. I left him there, fucking three-thirty in the morning. I was like, Yo, man, I got to go. Tomorrow I got to work. He's like, Just hold on, I'm looking. There's just a few girls on the floor, with guys on top of them, but he just wanted to get *something*. I'm like, Yo, that's not the way it works, man—if you don't get anything until three-thirty, whatever's left is left.

I don't go to clubs to meet girls. You know why? Because I know they there, in a fancy place, just looking for a wealthy guy. After that night, what am I going to do with them? Tell them I shine shoes? Tell them to come over my place? Please. It doesn't work like that. I live with my mom.

I go to clubs to enjoy the crowd, because peoples there knows how to talk. I'm in the position that I want to be able to learn more English, kind of spread my vocabulary and be able to talk nicelyier. Not like the way I used to talk. Imagine I will go to get a job, and I go like, Yo, what up? I'm here to fucking get a job. Nah, it's not going to sound nice. So if I go up to the person and just say, Hey, I'm over here, I read the thing in the newspaper, so, I'm, you know, wanted to get a job application so that I can fill it out. I'm trying to talk nice here. People don't understand if you know how to talk, it's a big thing.

I hang with Eddy most times. He cleans the bathrooms on my floors, nine and ten. Eddy is a funny guy, because he never care what he says to any other person, no matter how big, even Bill Bigelow, the CEO. Eddy just walks in there, and, Yo, you haven't seen him talking to believe it. Like he cleaned all the bathroom and then this trader, one of the rich guys, walk in and pee all over the toilet. Eddy look at the guy and goes, "Yo, I just cleaned that and you peed all over it." He talks really rude to the guy, but Eddy doesn't care. That's the way he puts it. I go there to wash my hands, and I get some water on the sink, and when he sees me he's like, Yo, sloppy.

Eddy's a person that can make you laugh. The spirit is right there. I always want to do good things for that kid. Most times he's happy. With him it's very simple. We play video games over and over. We usually go to places together eating. We talk about the same things. We talk about soccer. He give me his opinions about relationships, I give my opinions. We talk about work. We talk about cars. Eddy usually gets crazy about cars and soccer. We went to a strip bar around his way. I was like, Wow, this is a nice place. He was like, Yeah, dog, and the womens was dancing. But we didn't care about the womens. We just talking to each other. I don't usually feel like that. I'm usually looking to the womens at a strip bar.

Eddy's the first guy on my buddy list. You know, that AOL thing? You know about the buddy list, this little box on the right? So you put the peoples in your buddy list and if they using the computer, if they using the AOL, the person's name is going to appear there. The person's in, so you able to talk to the person.

You can always catch Eddy any time. Because he gets home by seven-thirty, he can stay on the computer until two-thirty in the morning. He goes on the Web site that talks about Santos. People go there and usually leave their message to the soccer team. Santos, that's our team from São Paulo, the team that Pelé played for his whole entire life in Brazil. He grew up playing for that team. Now, the team's really young. Right now they got those two great kids: Robinho, he plays just like Pelé, and the other one's Diego, a midfielder. They fucking great players. They got really success right now in Brazil. They got the TV on them all the time.

You know how many times I spend on the computer? I meet peoples. There's AOL Brazil, so I go there. I go to Orkut. It's a chat room. I go there, and I just look at people's profiles. I say, Hi, and the person usually responded back, Hey, how you doing? We exchange pictures. You ask about where the person's from in Brazil, what do they like to do. Sometimes I meet girls. We talk not as a boyfriend-girlfriend. More as a friend. I try to put to her, the same way she's trying to put to me, like, if any day we even ended up meeting each other, it's not going to be like, Oh, we have to get hooked up. You got to be cool. If we like each other, we'll get hooked up. But we talk to know each other. Fabio don't use the chat room. He doesn't have no patience for that.

Eddy likes talk to womens in the chat rooms, too, but he likes more the chat rooms that is soccer. Eddy is the most soccer-crazy person that I ever knowed. Like last week he called me up crying. I'm like, Yo, Eddy, what happened? He was like, Man, you not going to believe this. I was like, What? He was like, You know Shaq? He got a Romario jersey framed in his house. (Romario is one of the most famous soccer players that ever lived.) I was like, And what about it? He was like, I was just watching MTV, and when I saw Shaquille O'Neal having that jersey in his house, man, that thing fucking touched me so much. Because they were showing that on MTV, and Shaq was pointing out all the jerseys that he had framed in his house.

I was like, Goddamn, you fucking crazy, Eddy. He's so into soccer that he buy a whole bunch of jerseys, anything from Santos. He buy tapes. He's like me, the only guy that is really into it. Some of my uncles, but they don't buy the stuffs. They like to watch on TV and discuss about the old soccer, because they don't think that soccer from today is the way it used to be back in the day.

For me to get Eddy pissed off, I just have to dis Santos. Sometimes when I get really mad, because when we lose and stuffs, I call him up and be like, Yo, you know you can stay with your soccer team, because I know they SUCK. Like on Wednesday, I was watching TV, and I was on the Internet at the same time. So he was on the Internet and watching, like me. And I was like, Yo, man. I like to tease him. I was like, Yo, your fucking team SUCK. Because they stink that night. And I was like, Yo, what kind of player we got this year? I don't even know this guy's name. And I was like, That's why I like Real Madrid. Real Madrid is the team. He's like, You fucking crazy? Why you saying that? Are you a true fan? No matter how bad our team is you got to support them.

We always argue about that. He goes like, So what you going to root for? Don't be calling me later and crying about that—you know, our team won. I'm like, Yeah, man, I'm just joking with you. I'm just playing a joke. And he goes, I know you are.

Watching soccer, that is the best orgasm for me. It's better than sex with womens. When we playing against a big rival, I'm a totally different person when I'm watching it. It can be ten guys, if they talk shit about Santos, and I'm the only one in the bar, I'm talking shit right back to them. I'm not going to go home and swallow that.

Having this guys, Eddy and Fabio, they so close to me, we say it that we cousins. Even though we not really. It's the trust that we have about each other. It's a good feeling, going out, and we all bullshitting about anything. We talk about people's lives sometimes. How stupid that kid was, just because he got hooked up with this girl that Fabio had fucked. It's fun. Even though it's stupid, it's fun. The parties we go, the barbecues we do. Just be around each other. We don't have much, just the companion. Just enjoying the time with each other. That's what make them to be part of my family.

So we there, at TJ Friday's, and Eddy's like, I got fired today. I'm like, Come on, dog. Don't joke with me. He's like, I'm serious. I'm like, What happened? He's like, Can't talk about it here. I'm like, Why? He's like, Tell you later. Then he says it that Jesus is going to clean the bathroom on his floors that is my floors.

Jesus usually do some other stuffs, but mostly the bathrooms. Jesus is really, really old, about sixty years old. He's from Honduras, black, but he's Hispanic. But the way he talks is black, because he's been here for fucking thousands of years. Jesus doesn't hang with us in TJ Friday's, because he's too fucking cheap. He's crazy. He says we all dumb. He always trying to be superior.

I never give a fuck what he thinks. I never talk to him. Whenever I see him, if he say hi to me, I say hi to him back, but if he doesn't say hi, I don't give a fuck, man. He pissed me off. I was shining Mr. Fred's shoes. And Mr. Fred was like, See the conference room, Gil, they got food left over there. Why don't you go and grab your lunch. I was like,

You know what, Mr. Turner? Let me finish your shoes here, and when I'm done, I'll just go there and grab a sandwich. Because the food sits there for hours. So, I see the people leaving, and I see this mother-fucker Jesus going inside to clean up. I was like, Mr. Fred, can you hold on for one second, so I can get just a half a sandwich. I walk into there, and I was like, Hey, Jesus, how you doing, man? Can I grab one? You know if I wanted to just grab it, I could. He was like, If you take that, you going to help me out cleaning this stuffs? And when he said that to me, I was like, All right, fuck you, man.

He got a crooked eye that goes to the side. But what really bothers me is if I'm talking to some other guy in the freight elevator, he will probably put his ears to the door, trying to listen our conversation, see if we talking bad about him. He listens to the traders' conversation. He's the type that if I talk to someone, especially a trader, he will come really slow with his garbage can, and then stop near me and listen. If I look at him, he will pretend he's my friend. He will be like, Hey, Gil! I hate that shit, because if I'm talking to someone, don't come around me. I don't like that, man.

Eddy explain me that Jesus know this girl in the Dominican Republic that he be having a relationship with her for one year on the Internet. Nineteen years old. Sends her fifty dollars every month. He think he going to bring her to the U.S. next year. He send her $100 for the visa. You know how much chance she have of getting that visa? About one in fifty thousand. Eddy asks him, Why you do this? Why you think like that? This is a fantasy. You want a fantasy, why don't you go play Lotto? Eddy is like, I'm going on the Internet and be a nineteen-year-old girl and put my sister on the phone. Then you can send me fifty dollars.

SIX

EDDY PUT IT he got fired because he was there, in the bathroom. He cleans that place, so he goes there all the time. And I'm usually washing my hands there. I stay there a good ten, twenty minutes, because I want to get all the polish off. There's a lot of polish, because sometimes I don't stop. I see my hands, like polish, dirt, polish, so I stay there and wash my hands really good. And Eddy stays there an hour, two hours. When he doesn't have nothing else to do, he will just sit there and read the *Post*. So Eddy knows what's going on in that place. I heard his stories. He told me that one time he saw a guy jerking off in the stall. But he won't tell who.

Some guys go over there all the time. Usually the big guys. Little guys, they don't go all the time, but the big guys, they do. I think it's not because they older and have to go more, but because they just wanted to kill time. Sometimes this guys stay in the bathroom forty minutes, reading newspapers. But you don't see little guys do that.

When you go in that bathroom, it's like a fucking war, man. A war. Fuck, everybody's making noise. It seem like their stomachs go bad. It gets crowded around one-thirty to two. Everybody goes to the bathroom at that time. When I go, I go to different bathrooms on different floors. I know the bathrooms that is cleaner, with a lot less people.

You know what is the funniest thing? Sometime you just don't think that a guy is going to be capable to fart that loud. They don't care, they washing their hands right next to me, and they just let go.

I'm like, Goddamn, I didn't think you were like that. So, you know, I'm kind of looking at the mirror and trying to see how they do in their face, because I'm like, Damn, yo, you supposed to be somebody out there, and you doing this next to me? And they do it loud. They don't give a fuck.

This guy Pete is the worst. Not noisy, but the worst. Whenever I go there, and that guy do fart next to me, I just get up and I walk out. Because he never tells me that he's going to. He just do, because it doesn't make any noise, but once you breathing the air you go, My God. It actually get stuck right in your throat. I know it's natural, but sometimes you just got to let people know like how bad it's going to be.

People do on the trading floor all the time. Because they animals. Sometimes you hear, but mostly you smell. It's bad. Some certain person goes by and just let it out and keep on going. They do that all the time. They don't care. If one person smells it, he will let the other persons know, though. They will go, Someone just let it out here! A big one! Nasty! Mean! Disgusting! They all go, EWW!

There's people that they got the spray and put the name of the people that usually do all the time. Like you usually go around the trading floor or you sit behind someone and it's usually you. The first time they wouldn't know, but when you start doing and doing, they go out there and buy one of those air fresheners. They get the name print out, and they put the scotch tape on it. They put something like, THIS IS PETE'S PROPERTY. They leave it right there, right on the floor, next to the chairs, then, if it happens, if they smell something, they just start spraying the person's ass. Yeah, they do that. Pretty fucked up, right?

There's not only one persons that do that. Couple people that has it. But those guys that work out, they the worst. They drink all this shakes to build their muscles. Sometime they don't know what the fuck they drinking. They just want to get big. I don't know if that mess up your stomach or it give you more gas than ever, but this guys are the worst. Whenever they fart, it's like an atomic bomb. They could stink a huge piece of the trading floor, because, imagine, there is no circulation there. There is AC the whole day or the heater, so there is no huge fan.

That happen to me a couple of times. I'm there, shining someone's shoes, and I won't hear it, but then I smell it. In the beginning I used to just stay quiet, do my job, and sucked it in. But now I get up, and I'll be like, Yo, man, I'll come back in ten minutes. I'll go shine another person's shoes. Not at that time. I'll do it later.

It's fucked up. But they don't care. Just because they went to college, and they have all this money today, and they have everything in life, they think that mean that everyone has to put up with their own shit. It's not true, though. It's not your money that's going to take you somewhere. It's your personality. But the world that they love, it's the money that's going to take them. That's how they think.

Eddy was saying the other day, this fucking bathroom is like a bar bathroom, but this guys here, they not even drunk. You know, I'm in a bar and I'm drunk, I go there, and I pull out my thing, and I'm trying to focus on that little hole right there. But some of this guys at work, they pull out their thing, and they just start peeing all over the place. The first urinal is really dirty, because peoples just want to pee and get out. The floor is really messy. You know some bar bathrooms that when you walk in, you got to step really slowly because otherwise you going to get your feet wet on pee?

The other day someone took a dump on top of the toilet! I'm not lying. Eddie had told me that.

I don't know what is the women's bathroom like. I asked the lady who cleans, I think she Dominican. I just asked her how does she feel like when she goes to the lady's bathroom? Because the womens suppose to be much cleaner. That's what I always thought. But she was like, It's a mess. I was like, How can be a mess? Women, you know, they go there, they sit. But she put it up that it's kind of like the men's bathroom. I can't imagine.

You know what's funny? Some of this womens, when they walk out of the row with their purse, I hear what the guys saying, Oh, couldn't it be noticeable the way she's carrying that big pack to the bathroom. Any womans that goes to the bathroom with her purse, the guys are like, Oh, she has her period. Yeah, they do. Because there's not that many times you see womens walking with their purse. Make-up they can do on the floor.

You know why Eddy had got fired? Because he catched Mr. Steed on his cell in the closet. I'm not lying! Eddy's closet that he usually put his clothes there, that has the sink, dirty rags, soaps, the mops. He goes there, and he open the door, and Jeff Steed is there, on his cell. It is forbidden for the traders to use their cells on the trading floor. I don't know why. I'm the only one that is capable to use the cell and the iPod. The traders is like, Gil, you the man with the real power, the only one that is capable to use the cell on the trading floor.

So, Mr. Jeff is like, Hi, I'm just here, looking for some garbage bags because we made a mess of our lunch stuffs. But Eddy doesn't care. He's like, What the fuck you doing in here? You not supposed to be here. And Steed is like, You know what? You got a bad attitude. And he just leave.

Eddy's supervisor calls him to the office and he's like, We got to let you go, Eddy. People has complain that you got a bad attitude. That you talk rude to peoples and make stuffs up.

Eddy tries to explain him that Mr. Steed using his cell in the closet, but his supervisor is just like, I don't care. I don't want to hear it.

SEVEN

I WAS TELLING Rona that Eddy got fired because Mr. Jeff was using the cell in Eddy's closet. She was pissed off. Rona's cool with the guys that do the dirty jobs. She be the one at Christmas that usually make the collection for the janitors, the guys that works in the mailroom, the shoeshine guys. She goes to the traders and gets them to give. She's like, Come on, you can afford more. Like last year I got $480. I couldn't believe it.

She's like, I don't know what this traders complain so much. They make one millions bonus a year. And they complain about the guy that cleans the toilet. She was like, Why don't they put that one millions in my account and see how much I will complain about. I will be set for the rest of my life. This guys think they like little gods, that they can do anything. Rona's like, Steed is the worst. Because he scream at her and treat her like a dog. Yeah, I heard that. That guy is like a tick bomb.

Rona had it that Mr. Jeff went to a business trip to Korea. So the hotel he stayed, the most expensive bottle of wine was probably about some two hundred and something American dollars. But in Korea, that's the top of the line. But he was like, You don't have the wine I want? What kind of five-star hotel is this that you only got a two-hundred-and-fifty-dollar wine? You know, he wanted more. And Rona's like, What kind of world that he lives on that two hundred and fifty dollars for a bottle of wine could not be enough? I was thinking, Yo, I drink a five-dollar bottle of wine, and it's going to get me high.

How many peoples did Mr. Jeff had involved? Did he ever thought about that? For me to spend that much money I want everybody to enjoy, not just me. Not only me or another person. I'm the type of person that want everybody to have a good time. If I'm able and I'm capable. If I ever had money, I never had done a good birthday party for myself. I want to rent the space that I'll be able to bring all my friends in. Like fifty peoples goes, more than that. If I had money.

Mr. Jeff look smart though. You see how he dress, he dress kind of stylish. He make all this money. And he doesn't know what to do with the money. It's a lot of money, man, for a young guy. What the fuck you think he going to do with the money? He goes out, he want to show off. It's like this at the firm: either the guy show off a lot or he's really quiet.

But they only about the money. They live in a kind of fake world. Tough head about people. They don't talk about real stuffs. They always talk about food: I went out to a dinner, and I ate this, and I ate that, and I drank this kind of wine, and I hung out until one-thirty at the most, and then I went home. That's the only thing they talk about. The thing about them is, they live that life, but they want to show that they even better than each other. They talk about things, but not like I do. If I'm saying something to you, Hey, I ate at this restaurant, Hey, I ate this, drink that, I'm saying this for you to feel good, for you to see what I am.

But they like, Look, I ate this pasta that cost me a hundred dollars, and I drink this wine that cost me four hundred, and the bill ends up coming to thirteen hundred. Some things that I hear like that makes me think in the night, Just eating—how many hours?

This guys, they do things that, it makes you think, Why is he throwing money like that? They go out to eat in a restaurant every night. Jeff went to Babbo. You ever hear about that place? He was like, Oh, man I ate so good yesterday. He was telling the names about food that I never heard in my life. It's funny, because they talking to each other, and I'm there shining shoes. And Jeff goes, I ate this, this, that. And I'm like, What the fuck is that? What kind of language is he speaking? I know that's not English. It's not like mashed potatoes and French fries. It's totally different. Goddamn, why do they have to be like this?

The thing they be asking me now is, Hey, Gil, you going to make a lot of money with tips? But they don't know. I don't make money like that. I don't get no paycheck. It's my own business. I make today, I might not make tomorrow. Last week and the week before, I just work two days and a half, because the other days were half a day. You know in the bank they have half a day, and the other days were holidays. Friday it was raining, and nobody had wanted a shine. But a lot of people wonder how much money I make. They ask me all the time. They so curious about this. I tell them, Look, no matter how much I make, I don't have benefits. They like, Oh, yeah, you don't have benefits. What about if you get hurt? I tell them I don't know. I haven't got hurt yet. When you get to that point, that's when you decide, right?

If I ever get money, I don't want to show it to nobody. Because peoples change. You know what I'm saying? If I was able to buy my own house, my own car, I just wonder how the other peoples going to be looking at me. Like Eddy and Fabio, I'd rather have no money and have the way they are right now with me. I swear. Because if I had money, the thing I see is one getting evil with each other. One wants to hang out a lot more with me because I have a brand-new car, no matter what kind it is, and my own house, so one's going to be trying to fight who can get more out of me. I don't want that. It's good to be rich, in some ways, but the friendships that I have now, I think, is stronger.

The traders probably think that I live my life miserable, that I probably don't buy as many clothes as they buy, don't live in my own house. They live in their own houses, can drink and go anywhere they want to. I think they think they kind of superior. But at the same time they like, Why this kid is so happy? You know, I'm always smiling, always telling jokes. And they see me shining shoes.

And that's what amaze me. Sometimes you see guys that make a millions dollars in one year, and this guys are crying about every-thing. That's fucked up. Because if you making a millions, what you going to cry about? This guys, they buy tons of things. It's like peoples that live their life like kings. They always have that kind of life. You never see this guys sitting in the upper level of Yankee Stadium. They got to sit down there. I was explaining to Eddy. I was like, Hey, you know, a lot of this guys, the lifestyle that they have, it's different from what we have.

Sometimes it makes me think about Leo in that movie *Catch Me If You Can*. I saw it three times. That was a nice movie. It was just nice. It gives you an inspiration about what the kid could do.

Rona is like, Eddy should get a lawyer. Rona put it that a couple years ago a whole bunch of womens at the firm had been discriminate, so they got a lawyer. The judge was a lady that made the firm give this womens a HUGE amount of money. But I'm thinking, Where is Eddy capable to get a lawyer? He doesn't know no one. He doesn't got money.

After work, I was walking, walking, walking. I like to walk because that's the only way I can relieve my stress. In front of the McDonald's, the one at Times Square, hey!—I see Mr. Greg, the guy that I used to shine his shoes at Yuri's. I'm like, Greg, what's up? Remember me? Gil? He's like, Hey, Gil, what's happening?

I wanted to tell him the story of what happened to Eddy, because maybe he could help. I'm like, Greg, I know I'm just a shoeshine guy, and I don't know how you can help, and I don't even know if you can help me, but I would just like for you to listen one minute what I have to say, sir. My cousin just got fired, and he have never done anything wrong. I don't know if you could help me out. You have so much power, that's what most people be saying. I don't know. I just wanted to ask you what can you tell me so it could help me to go at least to the right guy to try and solve this thing. My cousin Eddy heard something that a trader was saying on his cell phone. And he didn't think it was nice, because he knows the rules in that place. And the trader tells his supervisor, and they fire Eddy.

I was like, Yo, Greg, can he get fired just for complain? What is the laws in here? Can people get fired for anything just because they don't have that much power?

EIGHT

Greg

YEAH, THEY CAN, I had to tell Gil, unless there is blatant discrimination, which there didn't seem to be in this case. But was it a story for me?

I offered to buy Gil dinner at McDonald's. Over cheeseburgers and fries, he told me about his new job at the large Wall Street firm of Medved, Morningstar, and Bigelow. Gil had plenty of his own troubles—his mother had run up $11,000 on her credit card, and a debt repayment outfit to which she had been sending money for three years had defrauded her; his father, also a shoeshine guy, had gone back to Brazil after he fell on the ice and cracked his spine, and Gil was helping to support him. But Gil really wanted to talk about Eddy's problem.

I asked Gil if Eddy had heard what the trader said on the phone. Gil called Eddy, who said he hadn't. No clues to pursue there. Calling the press office at Medved, Morningstar would get me nowhere. They probably didn't even know about the incident. If I'd still been at the newspaper, that would have been all she wrote. I would have forgotten about Gil and Eddy in the rush of writing the next day's stories.

But a monthly magazine isn't so hectic, and, in truth, things were not going well for me at *Glossy*. Impressed by my newspaper work, Ed Brown, *Glossy*'s editor, had hired me with big money and big expectations. A year and three quarters into my two-year contract, I hadn't given him much to justify either.

In retrospect, it had been easy at the newspaper. The stories were mostly obvious, and since you were writing short pieces, nobody expected depth. If your copy was a mess, the editors would fix it. Sure, you had to be fast, but you learned to be fast, and at least you didn't have to be as fast as the wire-service people, who put out several stories a day.

In the beginning, the newspaper was a thrill. I remember the first time my byline got in. I sat on a bench on the Broadway median and just stared at my name for a long, long time. To see it in that distinguished typeface was almost wholly incredible to me. It conferred instant legitimacy. I knew, at last, that even my father would respect what I did, because he religiously read the newspaper every day.

From then on, each time I got a story in, I would lay out the paper next to my computer and sneak looks at my byline while I worked.

Over time, though, you realize that getting in the paper, even on the front page, is a sugar high, and it doesn't last. What's important is to write something good, but you don't have the space or the freedom to do that—even a front-page feature is only twelve hundred words. So, it becomes a grind. You have to feed the beast. At 11:19 each morning, I always thought, everybody stopped thinking about that day's paper and moved on to the next day's. It was relentless.

Your stories started to fall into patterns. You found yourself merely going through the motions. You became unhappy not only with the job but with yourself. You felt like a smoker who lights another cigarette and hates himself for it. It was time to move on, but I didn't figure that out until my friend Kevin said, "Look around. Who do you want to be at this place in twenty or thirty years? Look at all these sixty-year-old white guys in their cubicles. You want to be one of them?"

When Ed's offer came out of the blue, I jumped at it.

My friends envied my going to *Glossy*: the glamorous parties, hanging out with movie stars, book and movie offers, a discount at Prada. Not really. *Glossy* had show horses and work horses, and I was hired to be one of the latter.

Unfortunately, my previous work experience didn't serve me particularly well. For a *Glossy* story, everything is different, starting with the way you choose your topic. The magazine is a monthly, so you have to figure out if an item in the newspaper today will still be interesting in four months and if it's complex enough to be expanded to six thousand words.

For a newspaper, you explain what's news in the first couple of paragraphs. In *Glossy*, you're telling a story. It's not about hitting your punch lines up front. You have to relax and let the story tell itself. *Glossy* articles, ideally, are like "little books," Ed says. You need narrative drive, local color, and, above all, good characters. Every single *Glossy* story, whether it's about money or politics or sports, is really about people. That's all any reader cares about.

Then you've got to wrap it all up in flashy prose. Newspaper-gray won't cut it.

When I handed in my first story, Ed asked, "Who wrote this?"

I had a lot to learn, and nobody at *Glossy* was interested in teaching me, particularly the other writers—a phalanx of big guns who had been around since the Stone Age. They had written best-selling books and won journalism prizes and appeared regularly as talking heads on television. Before I took the job, people warned me, "Be careful. They're going to go after you."

Who? Me?

Newspapers are collegial by necessity. You've got to work together to get the damn thing out. But *Glossy* was a world of big egos, where treading on somebody else's territory, even inadvertently, would get you shot at. There was intense competition for the big stories, and just so much "real estate" in the magazine, as the Big Guns liked to say—that is, *Glossy* had space for only about a hundred long-form stories a year. If someone got a piece in, that was one less slot for everybody else.

Any hope of the Big Guns just ignoring me evaporated when my new salary was leaked to a gossip column, and it turned out I was making as much or more than some of them. I could see in their false smiles and over-hearty greetings that they were eagerly waiting for me to screw up. Regrettably, I was giving them plenty of ammo. Despite my best efforts, my stories continued to read "like they should be on the front page of the B section of the *Times*," according to Ed, who was rooting for me, but didn't have time for personal tutorials. I knew I was in danger of being seen as a journeyman instead of a star, and nobody needs a journeyman on a star's salary. Ed ranked stories in terms of baseball hits. At best, I'd been giving him singles. I needed a home run.

I asked Gil to tell me more about Jeff Steed.

NINE

JEFF STEED, THAT'S one guy there that used to piss me off. He always plays jokes on my hair, how my hair looks, but then walk by me and don't say hi. Mr. Jeff will be like, Gil, when you going to shine my shoes? I'm like, Sir, I got from nine till the time you leave, that is five. And you want to know what time that I have to shine your shoes. I have the whole day to shine your shoes. But this guy sees me talking, and he goes, Hey, Gil, are you here to socialize with people or shine shoes?

If I don't want to shine your shoes, I'm not going to shine your shoes. When I used to work in a store I was obligate to shine. But here I'm not forced. Kick me out of the place. But some people, when they talk to you, they really don't know how to put their words. Like this fucking guy, Mr. Jeff.

In that row it's Jeff and two other guys, and it's Fred Turner right there. I don't think they get along. Because I don't see them saying hi, bye. They do their shit. They competitors. Because you can tell when the person's friendly with the other one. They always playing jokes and little stuffs.

I went to do Jeff's shoes. Jeff was like, Oh, Gil, can you wait for two minutes, because I'm going to go grab some food in the conference room? So he goes there. And Fred was like, Can you shine my shoes? So I went to Fred. Damn, when Jeff got back he was like, Gil! Fuck, man! I thought I was next. He always wanted to be the first, and I didn't notice. I was like, Oh, shit. And Fred just looked at me, not right away, but then he looked at me, he smiled. He was saying, You know, I fucked him, I got him mad.

Mr. Jeff is fucking wired. He drinks no less than ten coffees a day. They all drink coffee in that place. It's their cocaine. The thing is when it comes around two, if they eat lunch around twelve, they send one guy to Starbucks. They take turns, so if today is my turn, tomorrow will be yours. A guy goes down and orders ten coffees from Starbucks, and he comes back with two bags full of coffee, and he hands to everybody. It's the only thing that motivates them. It gets them hyper. But their teeth are fucked up, man—darker. It's not like whiteness. Kind of yellow.

When I used to shine Mr. Jeff's shoes, he used to flip me for it. He usually flips a quarter. So he puts a quarter and calls heads and tails. I get heads, he gives me ten dollars. Tails he wins, free shine. I probably lost to that guy nineteen times in a row. That kind of get me pissed because he used to tease me every time I used to lose. He used to be like, Hey, Gil, you going to shine my shoes for free today?

Until one day that we flipped, and I won ten dollars. He got mad. You want to double that? he says. So he flipped it again, I call up heads. Twenty. He was like, you want to double that? So we flipped again. Forty. He was like, Oh, my God. You could see his face was really red. He flipped it again. I call up heads. I won eighty dollars.

Mr. Jeff was like, Holy shit, I'm paying everything that I owed this fucking kid. He just sat back in his chair. He paid me, he got on his phone. What I did was, I went to almost everybody that he knew and told what happened. Everybody was calling him on this little microphone. It's like a speakerphone, they talk to each other, they dial the extension, and it goes right through. Everybody was like, Hey, hi. Gil was telling me that you owe him some shines, and you just paid him up. How do you feel? Everybody on the floor was making fun of him.

I was going to the bathroom, I didn't see Mr. Jeff, but he came right behind me. He was like, Yo, Gil, let me tell you something. Don't you ever tell nobody that you beat me like that, because that doesn't look good.

But my relationship with Mr. Jeff got really fucked that time that he wore the Rolex. When I shine shoes, I look at the shoes and the watch. A lot of the guys at my job has Rolexes. Because that represents power to them. You know, that represents how much they make. Rolex and fucked-up shoes. But Rolex. Cartier, people has some of that too.

Mr. Jeff always wear a watch, but I never pay no attention. So this is one of those days I didn't have nothing to do, and I was walking around on the floor, and I went by him because he asked me to shine. And I saw a Rolex, a gold Rolex on his wrist. So, I play it up, like, Yo, Mr. Steed. Nice! Watch! How much does that cost? Twenty thousand? Nice. I bet the money that the watch costs if you sell that and give the money to me, I will be able to buy the car of my dreams. And he goes, Nah, this is just a fake Rolex. I was like, Oh, yeah? I bumped Mr. Fred, and I was like, You see that? He's wearing a twenty-thousand-dollars Rolex, and he says it's a fake Rolex. You think the guy that makes the type of money the way he does be wearing a fake? And Fred was like, Nah.

And then everybody start picking on him. They like, Let's see if this be the real Rolex? Looks like the real Rolex. Wow, Steed, you be able to spend twenty thousand on a Rolex? And he was like, Nah, it didn't cost me that much. I don't know if he was ashame, but he never, ever wear the Rolex or talk about it again. Since from that day, it's more than a year, he never wears the watch. He just don't wear it. That was buggy, man. I felt bad for him, because I didn't meaned to do that. It's not that I'm going to steal it.

The day after the Rolex I come around four-thirty in the afternoon. I came just for Fred Turner, because he stays there until sometimes six. On the way, there was Mr. Jeff. And he was like, Hey, Gil, what's the matter with you, man? I was looking for you the whole fucking day today. It seems that you dissing me. This is like the third time that you be doing this. And the next time that you do that, you not going to get business from me anymore. And I was like, Oh shit.

But you know what? Nobody else ever talk to me like that. Like what the fuck I'm doing? I didn't do anything wrong. Hey, this guy has my cell phone number. Everybody has my cell phone number inside my job. I have a card, I give it to everybody. They don't even call. Once in a while they do. If Mr. Jeff really needs that fucking bad, he can call. Oh man, this freaking guy pissed me off.

I went to Mr. Turner, and I was like, Sir, it's free for you today. You know why? Because you never gave me no attitude. What Mr. Jeff just said it to me, I didn't like it. I didn't curse, because I know that if I go, This guy . . . You can't curse there. Because even though they do a lot of bad stuffs outside, they take that thing really serious when they working. So, then I shine Fred's for free. He wanted to pay me, but I was like, No, no, no, no, no. But he gets a shoeshine every day, almost.

The next day I went there, and Mr. Jeff was like, Hey, Gil, come here. You get mad at me from yesterday? I was like, Yeah, sir, you know why? Because the way you approach me wasn't right. Not even my mom talk to me like that. And he was like, Oh no, I just wanted a shine real bad. And I was like, No, sir, this is not the way it goes. Look, you guys usually see me here. Everybody has my number. I gave my card out. You have my number. He was like, Oh, yeah, your card is right here. I was like, Yeah, so why didn't you call me? You know, sir, the thing is I don't care who the persons is in this firm. If you want to get me fired, what can I do? But you can't talk to me that way.

He was like, Oh, I'm sorry, Gil. And I was like, Yeah, sir, because I don't think I was ever bad to you. Because I like everybody in this place. And I say this in the same tone of voice. I say it so that everybody else could hear. I didn't care. And everybody else in the row was stopping work and looking at Mr. Jeff, and they all looked at me like, I can't believe Gil said something like that. Nobody talks to Jeff like that.

Because people, they don't usually express themselves over there. If they feeling really pissed off, they bang the phone, but they don't go to each other and talk. So, everybody's watching, and Mr. Jeff shook my hand, and he was like, I like you, too. You kind of misunderstood me. And I was like, Yeah sir, I like you too, and all that bullshit.

Now, he sees me, and he goes the day before he wants a shine, Gil, will you be able to shine my shoes tomorrow? And I'm like, Yeah, if you have them on. Now, I go there, Mr. Jeff is on the phone, he goes like, Oh, hold on, my shoe doctor just got here. Hey, Gil, where you been? I been looking for you all this day. And he gives me his shoes. And he makes this big thing. He gets up and goes, Gil, you is my shoe doctor. Oh, man, I'm so glad that you got here this time. Now, he always trying to make a big thing like this. If I just go and brush up his shoes. Or he can have his shoes that's not even able to shine. I give them back to him, he pays me straight-up six dollars. But now he always, every single day, make a big thing about it. He can't just be like, Hey, here you go Gil. My shoes. He got to stop whatever he's doing and pay attention to me. I'm like, Well, whatever. I'm not into that. It's weird to me.

Mr. Fred was telling me today, Jeff's voice makes him crazy. I was shining Fred's shoes, and Jeff was kind of talking loud on the phone, and I was laughing, because the thing he was saying, I don't even remember, but I think it was funny. And Fred was like, he was shaking his head, and he was like, I can't stand this guy. You don't have to be this loud. So I asked Fred, He's kind of annoying, right? And he was like, Yo, every fucking morning I hear him talking loud. And when Jeff do that, Mr. Fred bang the phone on the desk and turn on the TV really loud. But he doesn't talk to Jeff about it. If I was him, I would go up right there and be like, Hey, sir, would you be capable to be a little bit quiet, not that loud. There's certain things we don't need to know.

But Jeff always got to be on top, taking advantage, the guy that makes the fun. When I used to flip for it and I lost, he would be like, Hey, Gil, every time he pass by me. Thanks for the shine. You know, like, he fucked me. I knew what he was saying. That he won. It was free. So he don't have to spend his money.

To Greg, I was like, I will never shine that guy's shoes no more. Because he got Eddy fired.

BUT I TOLD Gil, No, I want you to do just the opposite: be friendlier than ever, keep an eye on him at all times, ask the secretaries and janitors and copy-machine guy if they notice anything unusual about his behavior lately. If we can catch Steed doing insider trading, I told Gil, I'd write an article for *Glossy* that would embarrass the firm into giving Eddy his old job back.

Gil loved the idea of being a spy, so much so that I had to warn him not to attract attention. In the meantime, I would do some background-checking.

An Internet search turned up society-page pictures of Steed with models and B-list actresses at charity galas. There was also a profile of him in *Palm Beach Now!* magazine, which featured his pink stucco mansion, renovated and decorated in gaudy taste, with gold-plated bathroom fixtures, monstrous Venetian-glass chandeliers, and cheesy white gilded French furniture. He also owned, according to the article, a Manhattan townhouse that probably cost upwards of $15 million, and lots of bad but expensive art bought at auction. He was on the boards of several nonprofits, meaning he gave away serious money. His lifestyle seemed lavish to me even for a star trader.

I had a source at Medved, Morningstar—and a good one: my college freshman roommate, Isaac Moser, who worked there in private-wealth management. Isaac achieved college immortality when he lost his entire food budget for one semester in a poker game the week before classes began. His solution was to buy himself a hundred-pound bag of dog food. If it was merely a ploy to get the rest of us to buy him real food, it worked.

Isaac and I came to New York around the same time, and for the first couple of years we spent a lot of time bar-hopping together, but I saw him less when he started dating and then married Cheryl, a woman I didn't much like. When they had a kid, Isaac fell through to a parallel universe where everybody was a kid or had a kid, and everything was about kids. We would still make dates to play pick-up basketball or meet for a drink, but more often than not he'd cancel at the last minute because the kid was sick, or the kid had given him a cold, or he'd been up all night because the kid couldn't sleep, or Cheryl was in a bad mood from being with the kid all day. We managed to get together only once or twice a year, but Isaac was always happy to hear from me and to reminisce about the old days when he was a carefree drunk, gambler, and playboy.

I called him to make a date for one of our elusive get-togethers and slipped in, "Hey, Isaac, I was at a party where I met some of your people."

"Oh, really? Which ones?" I could tell from the distracted tone of voice that he was looking at his computer screen.

"Fred Turner," I said.

"I know him. Nice man. Went to Harvard. I think he was a Rhodes scholar or something. Real rising star here, part of a special proprietary trading project where they gave a dozen young guys $50 million each to trade with, and the winners get to keep their jobs."

"Will Turner be one of those?"

"Who knows. It's three-quarters luck, especially in a big firm like this where the stress is so much on beating benchmarks."

"What about Alice Norther?"

"Oh, my God. You met her? She's a managing director. Real piece of work."

"How so?"

"I can only tell you this because I know your legal department would never let you use it if you ever decided to write a piece about us."

"Oh, yeah? Don't keep me in suspense."

"Word is she got ahead here by giving head to old man Bigelow in his private bathroom." Bigelow was the CEO of Medved, Morningstar.

"Oh, come on! How would anybody know that?" It certainly didn't fit in with Gil's description of her, at any rate.

"And then there's the story of how she got swindled by a guy pretending to be her husband's boss . . ."

"That one I heard. But, you know, anybody could be taken in by a good scam." I had no idea why I was defending Alice, whom I'd never met.

"I know, I know—but, honestly, if someone you didn't know told you your wife was a criminal, wouldn't you at least call her to check?"

"I don't have a wife."

"Well, that's another story," he said, laughing. "How's Annie?" Annie was my girlfriend since college. She and I were functionally married, if not legally—a source of endless annoyance to our friends, some of whom were already on their second go-arounds.

"Fine, fine. Working too hard. There was also this guy, John Pearson."

"Jesus, who the fuck gave this party? Why wasn't I invited? You think they're easing me out?" He sounded as if he was only half joking.

"I wouldn't worry about it. It was just a boring benefit given by one of Annie's clients." Annie was a corporate lawyer at a big firm, where, in her spare time, she did pro-bono work for nonprofits and charities.

"Pearson's the risk manager. Right under the head of equities. Gorgeous, young Russian model wife. Did you meet her?"

"Uh . . . no." My palms were starting to sweat. I'm not good at telling lies, and I felt I was getting in too deep.

"That's another famous story here. She's wife number three. Pearson met her on a business trip to Russia. Wife number two was also a Russian model he met on a business trip, but one day he came home early and found her fucking the Russian plumber. She said she was homesick!"

"No secrets around there, I guess."

"The system works!"

"You know Jeff Steed?"

"You met him, too? At the same benefit as Pearson? He was in my training class. Real kiss-ass. He knows Bigelow's wife. Steed didn't have to scramble like the rest of us for a spot. Nan Bigelow set it all up for him."

"You don't sound like a fan of Steed's."

"I don't really know him that well. I'm just going by his reputation. Supposedly, he got blackballed when he tried to join the Young Lions."

"What's that?"

"This club of young stock-jockeys, mostly hedge-fund equities traders, who meet once a month to blow smoke up each other's asses. If one member blackballs you, they don't let you join. Somebody did that to Steed, which is pretty embarrassing. Didn't seem to affect his performance here, though. He's one of the top earners."

"The poor kid made good?"

"Poor? Are you kidding me? Not poor. His parents were L.A. jewelers or something. Oh, oh . . . I got some action here. Got to run. See you next Tuesday."

ELEVEN

Greg

I DON'T HAVE one recurring dream about failure. I have two. In the first, I discover that I forgot to get a profession. I just plain forgot. I have to return to live at my parents' house. In the second dream, Annie has dumped me, and I am living, surrounded by empty liquor bottles, in a fleabag hotel on the Bowery, where my few remaining friends bring me food and beg me to pull myself together.

After two pieces of mine in a row didn't run, Ed put me on a celebrity profile for the cover. The hacks love cover assignments, which are short on prestige but long on perks—a stay at a four-star hotel and dinners on the expense account with L.A. friends—and, since you can finish them in a week or two, they are a ridiculously easy way to fulfill your contract, which requires you to file a certain number of articles a year. For a serious reporter of the kind I fancied myself, though, it was slumming. Humiliating, even.

I'd never done a celebrity profile, but it didn't take a genius to figure out how. You spend an afternoon or two with the actor, bowling or playing golf, in order to pretend he's doing something other than talking about himself. Then you solicit flattering quotes from the director and the other actors who worked with him on whichever picture he is flogging that month. Then you go home and trick it all up with writerly bells and whistles, which is like trying to freshen up a corpse with rouge and lipstick, because at least half a dozen profiles of any given actor have already been published.

And the material is trivial to begin with, because actors don't have interesting lives. They spend most of their time on location or traveling to location. As for their personal affairs, they don't want to talk about it, and who can blame them? I could try to get some new, juicy bit out of Ms. A-list, I suppose, but the idea made me queasy. Not that I'd succeed, anyway. Actors are drilled by their flacks to deflect prying questions from nosy reporters.

The details for my meeting with Ms. A-list were arranged by her flack, Marci. All I had to do was show up at the pool of the Beverly Hills Hotel at two o'clock on Tuesday. Which meant I had to stay on location in that pink-and-green fantasia of Hollywood luxe—even if in one of the smaller, sunless rooms that overlook the tar roof out back. It didn't matter. The room was still swell, and I would spend most of my time having martinis and steak tartare in the Polo Lounge or eating club sandwiches by the pool, anyway. Maybe being a celebrity whore wasn't so bad, I decided after a day of doing just that.

Ms. A-list, like most celebrities, allocated media access in inverse proportion to her box office, our celebrity wrangler Nina Jerske told me. That meant no bowling or golf. For Ms. A-list, two hours with me was an eternity. So was Tuesday, which came and went without her showing. Ditto Wednesday and Thursday, on each morning of which Marci called me to say, "We have to resked for same tomorrow."

I figured I'd use the dead time to do a little background checking on Steed, who had grown up in L.A. The idea was slightly seditious—spending Ms. A-list's time to research a story Ed hadn't assigned yet—but I was up against the wall.

I called Kevin, who had quit the newspaper shortly after I did, when a book he wrote that won the Pulitzer became a best seller. Although he looked and acted like an East Coast preppie, he grew up in L.A. and moved back there as soon as he could—i.e., after Spielberg paid him an unbelievable sum for the movie rights to his book. He bought a Neutra house with walls of shimmering glass framing a spectacular panorama of the city, and, as if that wasn't grand enough, he put in an infinity lap pool at the edge of the terrace.

Kevin's father, a producer, was old Hollywood, and his mother was old Los Angeles society. If Kevin didn't know somebody in L.A., he knew somebody who did. As it turned out, he and Steed had gone to the same prep school. Steed's father was a minor entertainment lawyer, Kevin told me, and his mother operated an estate jewelry business, of which Kevin's mother was a customer. Jeff had evidently been a goofy kid, the object of considerable teasing, not least because he carried around a briefcase, which his classmates threw out of windows at every opportunity. His popularity was evidently not enhanced by his composing of Barry Manilovian songs, performed by himself at the piano.

Kevin recalled that in eighth grade he had been briefly best friends with Steed—"I felt sorry for him"—and, as a result, had just missed getting rich a lot sooner: Steed's piano teacher passed on a hot tip to buy stock in Mitgo Electronics, a small Alabama company nobody ever heard of. Steed's parents wouldn't let him act on the tip, so he forged his mother's name on a letter authorizing the bank to let him cash his bar-mitzvah bonds. With the money, he bought two thousand shares. He also passed the tip on to Kevin, whose father bought ten shares as a joke.

Week after unbelievable week, over a period of about six months, the two boys watched the stock soar four, five, six points a day, from around three to a high of over three hundred. Kevin got cold feet at a hundred and fifty. His father, he says, is still kicking himself for not buying more shares. Steed sold out just below the peak and was not punished by his parents for his forgery. After the stock collapsed, it became known as a textbook case of stock-market manipulation.

TWELVE

EDDY CALLED, AND he's like, Let's go to the beach. I'm like, Dog, I got bills to pay, and what will you do when the rent comes up, and the Internet, and the phone, and the cable? Because you not making. Did you ever thought about that? But he just wanted to chill. Mr. Greg has it that he will help Eddy, but I don't really know if he will. He's in California, and I don't know how long he stood there.

What is the most funniest thing, I go to my place today, it's like I'm an FBI agent because Mr. Greg put it I should be a little spy on Mr. Jeff. I will go there. I will act like this simple Brazilian kid that shines the shoes and doesn't know any better about anything. They won't know. They don't pay attention to peoples. They just think Gil is a little stupid kid that shines shoes. They think Gil only knows about shoes. I do know a lot about shoes, but I know about a lot of things now than I used to.

I went there, and Mr. Jeff was stressing. He was with Fred Turner. Fred was supposed to do a trade, a favor for a trade, I think, and he didn't end up doing. And then Jeff start fighting words to Fred, but smart words. I don't remember what they were. They fighting with smart words, back and forth, back and forth, until Fred was like, You know what? Forget about it. Jeff was really pissed. His face was all red. Everybody else was just quiet, doing their own thing.

Because Jeff, unless he's making that money, he's going crazy, fucking forget about everything. He will even forget about his own friends if his friends doesn't make him a good trade that day. The way he talk, like, yo, he will scream at them, usually just numbers. Sometime he will go back there, and he will say sorry just because at that time that he wanted to do that thing, he was so nervous about the money, he forget about the other person.

Then this intern was screaming at Jeff, telling him the numbers really loud. He gets up, and goes like, Look, I'm sick and tired of you screaming at me. Can you come here and tell me? He didn't curse, but I knew he felt like cursing. Why does he have to say this to the girl? Poor girl, she was young. Fucking make somebody traumatized. I would leave if he talked to me like that. Like a dog, man. Whenever the big guys say, the followers do. Like go down there, and get me a coffee. All right, sir. Fuck, you the boss—not that you the boss, but you the guy that make money. Everybody knows that for them to be on that level, they got to go through all these shit. I'm like, It's okay, Mr. Jeff, I will come back later.

I went to the other floor to shine Mr. Tim's shoes and he's like, I'm losing a lot of money today, Gil. I could use a laugh. So, I tell Tim the story about this two uncles of mine in Brazil. They married, but they wanted to have a good time. This both guys get drunk, and they end up going to a whorehouse. They were there, one choose one girl, the other choose this other girl. And my little cousin was there, too. My little cousin was sixteen at the time. He choose another girl. I think it was the first time he go to a whorehouse. In Brazil fathers don't be like fathers here with the sons. Here, the father always is like, Don't look! Don't look! But in Brazil they like, Go over there and grab that women's ass. And they take them to a whorehouse for the first time. I'm not lying.

So, one of my uncles, he was in this room, and he was fucking this girl, and the girl was like, Harder, harder. Then she was like, Spank me, spank me! And he was spanking, and the girl was still going, Harder, harder. Then she stop and look at him, and she was like, Damn, I can't feel your dick. Your dick is too small.

My uncle run out of that room. Man, he was pissed off. He started knocking at the other rooms. He was like, Yo, let's go, let's go. This fucking bitch said that I had a small dick.

Mr. Tim is like, Your uncle tells the story on hisself?

Mrs. Alice come over from the other row, and she's like, I hope you guys not talking dirty again. Tim's like, No way, Alice, we just making *small* talk about Gil's uncles. Right, Gil?

I was cracking up.

I shine Mr. Pete's shoes. He give me six now, but he's a cheap man. I got to stay a long time on his feets for him to give me six. If I don't spend at least a good fifteen minutes on his both shoes, he will give me four. But if I spend fifteen, and I talk to him, he gives six.

It used to be that Pete was four guys sitting next to each other. I used to go there on a Monday to shine this four guys' shoes and, let's say the first one would start paying, he used to give twenty dollars. Then the next time I used to go there, it was the next guy that used to pay. Twenty. The next guy. Twenty. Then I used to come to Pete. Twelve. Everybody used to give me twenty, except Pete.

I told him, Pete, it's not about the money, man. I always came back to you, because you a funny man. But you usually used to piss me off. I used to go there, shine everybody's shoes, and when it was your time for you to pay, you used to give me twelve dollars. That used to be eight dollars I was losing. And I had to do the same job. Pete start laughing. He was like, Now the six is making it up for all the money you lost.

Pete, he's fucking psycho in the head about money. Everybody knows that he's cheap. He buys cheap clothes. He doesn't spend money with food. Tim was telling me, Gil, can you believe this fucking guy goes to one of this little carts they have on the street and buys coffee? That is a dollar for the two, fifty cent donut, fifty cent coffee. You know how nasty that shit is? Tim is like, God, I can't believe it, that guy is my boss.

Pete's a cheap motherfucker. That's the way he put it: I'm a cheap motherfucker. He doesn't care if I'm there every day. He cares the much effort I put into his shoes. The fucking guy can be on the phone, busy, busy, busy, but he knows. I don't know how. He knows. He's like, You took enough time with my shoes today?

Pete doesn't buy nobody a lunch. People spend money on people there. They buy each other lunch. Eight, nine, ten guys order in $200 worth of food. They only touch it if they know each other.

They like to order fucking sushi that I hate. When they give me that stuffs, everything goes into the garbage, because I don't take a piece. Yecch!

They order hamburgers. You know what is funny? When they order those big hamburgers, they take the bread and throw in the garbage. Just eat the meat. I'm thinking, Next time when you call up, tell them not to waste their bread. I would like to say it to them, It makes no sense, man. Just tell the guy: No buns.

Some days they have Chinese or ribs or chicken. Juice chicken. And mash potatoes, salad, pasta. Sometime they have this HUGE cheesecakes. When a group do a really good thing, they get shrimps and fucking nice fish.

I just go there, Hey, how you doing, guys? Oh, Gil, help yourself. Yeah, all right, later. Let me shine one shoes. Then I'll go around, Can I take a piece? Because they going to throw in the garbage, anyway.

Thursdays and Fridays the best. The other day they had lobster and steaks. I was like, Let me try this lobster. Never had that before. Jim was like, Gil, how you like it? I took one bite, threw it away. I was like, Yo, man, I don't know. He was like, Tell me something—that thing smells like pussy, right? And not clean pussy, but really dirty pussy. I was like, Shit, how you know?

Some days they got pasta, calamari. The food is so great. They have a whole bunch of food, sodas, drinks, juices.

But Mr. Pete, he never get other people food. He only buy his own stuffs. Sometimes he bring his food in little luggages, a lot of them, in all this little plastic wraps. I always want to ask him, What kind of food is that?

One time Mr. Pete, he didn't have no choice, he had to order lunch for everybody. I don't know why, because he don't usually do that.

We already know this guy's cheap. So he order from across the street. When I saw the food, I was like, Holy fuck. There was just a few sandwiches, and the sandwiches was turkey. The turkey was not roasted, it was turkey turkey. That's the only thing he have it. Come on! Who's going to eat that? Because they usually like different stuffs, ham and tuna. Just one or two of them that ate his stuffs. I looked to Mr. Jim, and he was like, Holy shit, I knew he was cheap, but not that cheap.

I went to Mr. John's office. Man, his face is fucked up. He got those dark places under his eyes, like he not getting no sleep, and a HUGE cut on his head, like he banged it. I was like, Mr. John, what happened to you? You fighting? Your wife hit you? He was like, Nah. I went to a dinner with this guys in my job.

He got pissy drunk, that's the way he say it. And after dinner he was like, Aw fuck, let me go home, so he was going to the garage to get his car. He's walking to his car, an Explorer pull over and the windows roll down. When he saw it, it was two ladies. One was kind of dark and another one was white, and the ladies was like, You want to do us? And he was like, Yeah. And they was like, It going to cost you. He was like, How much? And they like, Three hundred each. So what he did was run to an ATM machine and took them to the hotel. He got up at like three and the ladies was gone, and he couldn't find his cash and his credit card.

He call the limo to take him to his house in Jersey. And the car comes, and they get there, and the driver was trying to wake him up, wake him up, wake him up. But the driver couldn't. You know what the guy did? He left Mr. John on the curb. The guy just left him there. Mr. John slept on the curb. He ended up waking up like seven in the morning right by his house.

He was like, Oh. He didn't even know what happened. I was cracking up. I was like, Mr. John, are you serious? He was like, That's how bad I was, Gil. I was like, Damn, that's really bad. What your wife be thinking? And he was like, Are you kidding me? She doesn't know. She doesn't never get the fuck up until eleven, because the stores doesn't open.

I went to see Mr. Fred Turner. He's a person that everybody look at him with so much respect. Everybody has him as a God. He the main man, the man that has the finance. The classic six foot three. He got the look of all the bosses over there.

I'm like, Goddamn, he's not the boss. People treat him better than the boss. People treat him with so much respect. It's more than the money he make. I wish I could be like that. I can't. I can't be as quiet. He's the type of guy that when he say things, he's sure, and he knows what he saying. He knows how to act. It's funny and weird, but it's good, because he make hisself look good.

Mr. Turner doesn't usually talk to me, but he comes when I'm shining shoes, and I'm sitting on the box, and he slap me right on my back. Like he's passing, he's going to the bathroom. He's not doing that hard though, but he just tap me on the shoulders and things like that. Like, Hey, Gil, just to tell that he's here. I think that's fucking cool.

That guy has so much money, but he simple. He only owns two pair of shoes. I don't like that Johnston & Murphy shoes, man. But it looks good. The leather is good. Mr. Turner's very to hisself. He doesn't talk. Everybody's playing jokes, and he's over there concentrating on his own thing. He's young though, thirty-one, thirty-two. I think womens probably love him. They jealous of his fiancée.

This guy, he's always flying. He travels a lot. Getaway for the weekend. California. South Beach. Aspen. He's a rich guy, but he doesn't show as much, but he's a very generous man. Very, very, very, very. Because a lot of them, they have money but, you know, when you have money, some people just like to show their money. He doesn't like to show. But when it comes to be generous, he's very generous. Like when he tips me.

Today, he give me fifteen dollars. I was like, Hey, Mr. Turner, here's your change. He was like, No, keep the change. I'm like, Okay, thank you very much. I don't have to say anything. Ten dollars is the minimum he give me now.

I know he's going to get married this summer. I would love to go to his wedding, though the girl not supposed to be that pretty. I would love to go. I know those are dream weddings. Nothing like a Brazilian wedding.

After two hours I'm on the floor, and Jeff sees me on the phone. He just goes, Hey, Gil, what the fuck you doing? You always on the phone. That's true. I stay sometimes more than a half hour just on my cell with my cousins. Call back and forth. That's why sometimes my bill comes up so high, because I have nobody to talk to, so I'm calling. I just want to call and talk. Sometime I'm on the phone, going around to pick up people's shoes. I'm the only one that can use it in that place.

So Jeff is pissing me off. I'm like, I know you not capable to use the cell on the floor, Jeff, but are you capable to use in the bathroom? He just look in my face like I'm fucking crazy.

Then he start laughing. He's like, What are you, the CIA?

Jeff is kind of joking, but kind of not joking. He's like, Gil, you trying to turns us in, our trades and stuff—to get some money? Like they have someone in the firm who is a spy.

I just start laughing. What can I say it?

He's like, Gil, you a spy, right? You a spy.

I'm like, How can you say that?

He's like, I know you a spy.

I think he's fucking around. But at the same time he doesn't know he's telling me the truth. He's like, Gil, I know you got the fake accent. I don't believe you. Are you an American? I was like, Yeah, Mr. Jeff, my father got us the citizenship thing back in the day.

He's like, Gil, stop lying. Who you work for? The FBI? The CIA? I think he's fucking with me. He say that just as a joke. He's like, Gil, I know you be smarter than this.

He knows, but he doesn't know.

THIRTEEN

Greg

KEVIN OFFERED TO put me in touch with people who knew Steed in the old days. I told Kevin, Okay, but I had to be careful. I didn't want it getting back to Steed that I was asking questions about him—not yet, anyway. One source Kevin mentioned seemed safe: Vergil Peterson, a character actor who had steadily worked in World War II movies and Westerns before hitting the jackpot as the rootin' tootin' sheriff on a television sitcom that ran for a decade. Before he retired, Peterson lived next door to and was best friends with the late Amy X, widow of the famous producer Abe X. She had hired Steed, straight out of high school, as her personal assistant, and over the four or five years he worked for her they developed a close relationship. According to Kevin, she bought him expensive watches and designer clothes, took him to Hollywood parties, even spent vacations with him, aboard her yacht.

"You mean, he was her boy toy?"

"More like a surrogate son," Kevin said, and explained that Amy's real son had joined a cult that forbade him from contacting her.

Kevin got a phone number for Peterson, who was by this time raising horses outside of Palm Springs. I called and said I was writing a story about Jeff Steed.

"How is that boy?" Peterson asked, his voice full of affection. "I haven't seen him in years." Peterson didn't read *Glossy* magazine, but he was delighted to talk to me. "Call me Vergil," he said.

I offered to come out to his "little pony farm—nothing fancy," but he told me he didn't want yet another city boy getting his shoes dirty walking through the rocks and buffalo grass on the banks of the "Rio Vergil."

"Anyway, Mrs. Peterson and me wouldn't mind getting out for a night on the town, especially if you want to buy us a couple steaks and a few good martinis," he said. (When I later mentioned "the little pony farm" to Kevin, he hooted with laughter. "Little pony farm?" he said. "You know what he's raising out there? Arabians. They go for $200,000 a head.")

Vergil gave me directions to a hotel near Joshua Tree National Park. About four and a half hours later, I was checking into a concrete box in the middle of nowhere. (I got a room for the night because I didn't want to drive back to L.A. after drinking and in the dark.) The only other building within sight on the vast desert horizon was a Western-wear emporium, across the dusty, empty highway. Since I had an hour to kill before I was supposed to meet the Petersons in the hotel restaurant, I went over to check it out. The place was filled with chaps, Native American pots and trivets and dolls, a lot of turquoise jewelry, boots with spurs, and the main attraction: a world-class collection of cowboy hats. I bought a bolo tie, just to fit in.

The Petersons arrived on the dot at five. In his late seventies, Vergil was a big man, dressed in a denim jacket, snakeskin boots, and a Stetson with a brim so big you could hold a hootenanny on it. His wife, a decade younger perhaps, was Winona, or Wi, for short. Smiling and mostly mute, she wore a buckskin vest with about a mile of fringe, and a bright blue blouse that set off her dazzling aqua eyes.

Vergil dug into the pocket of his shirt and pulled out a photograph. I thought it was going to be an autographed publicity still of him in his salad days, but it was a snapshot of a formidable, late-middle-aged woman, encased like a sausage in a brocade ball gown and hung with a truckload of big jewelry. Standing next to her was a grinning, skinny, curly-haired kid in a tuxedo. "That's Amy," said Vergil, pointing. "Quite a gal she was. Too bad you never got to meet her. And that's Jeff. Very sweet kid. So musically talented."

I explained to Vergil that Steed was now a big success on Wall Street. "Well, that don't surprise me, at all," he said. His Western accent waxed and waned.

Maybe because of the early hour, there were no other diners in the restaurant. We ordered steaks, and, while we tucked into them, Vergil told me about the late Amy—the charities she headed, the parties she gave, her far-flung travels, her beautiful home and incredible taste. This was all merely a warm-up for his stump speech about Amy's deceased husband, Abe, and his legendary sense of humor: a collection of knee-slapping howlers that invariably started with Abe getting shit-faced drunk and ended up with him falling off a boat, or taking off his clothes, or peeing in public, or making some terrifically rude remark to an important person. At each punch line, Vergil and Wi threw their heads back like two horses in heat and hollered with laughter until tears came to their eyes and they started coughing and choking. Vergil actually had to hold on to his belly once or twice. Since the stories were all of the you-had-to-be-there variety, I had to do a lot of fake laughing.

When Vergil finally took a breather long enough to order a fourth martini, I asked, "So when did Jeff start working for Amy?"

"Let me see . . . that would be about twelve years ago, right when Amy found out she had the cancer. Jeff was like a gift from God . . . a gift from God. Gave her the courage to go on living and fight, when her own kids could have cared less. Them two never even came to the hospital at the end." He looked like he was going to dispatch a rattlesnake with a six-shooter. "'Course she and her daughter never got along. The son, he was just crazy, poor kid."

"I heard that Jeff was more like a personal companion than personal assistant."

"Well, you heard wrong. I mean, he was a wonderful companion to her, but the kid was a financial genius. By the end, he was managing all her money—and she had a lot of it. Abe was a very successful producer. But Amy told me that Jeff doubled the money Abe left her."

"Was she the type who was helpless with money?"

"No, sir. Amy was no dope. She knew what she was doing when

it came to investing, or at least she knew how to find people who did. She only let Jeff play with some small sums at first, but that kid had the magic touch. I tell you, he'd pick a fucking stock and you'd just sit back and watch it zoom to the moon. He made a fortune on that dot-com shit, and he got her out before it collapsed. I even made a little money, thanks to some of his tips. 'Course from time to time he got a little . . . uh . . . overenthusiastic, and Amy's lawyer would have to step in and say no. Like one time the little rascal ordered some duplicate stock certificates and was going to sell them, even though Amy had used them stocks as collateral." He chuckled.

"Did she pay him a commission or just his regular salary?"

"I don't really know what their arrangement was. Until the end. I do know about that because I was the executor of her will."

He pulled out a manila envelope with the word CONFIDENTIAL stamped across the front, and slid it across the table to me. "I thought you'd be interested in seeing this, so I brung it along," he said, "but I can't let you have it—even if you was a lawyer." Huge stage wink. "But, you can take it up to your room and read it for fifteen minutes. You can't copy it, though, and you better be back in fifteen minutes, or I'm sending a posse up after you," he said, giving me the evil eye.

As soon as I got in the elevator, I tore open the envelope and pulled out Amy X's will. There was no way to photocopy it and not enough time to copy it by hand, so, once I got to my room, I ran to the bathroom, closed the door, and read it at breakneck speed into my tape recorder. Fourteen minutes later, I was back in the restaurant, handing the envelope back to Peterson.

Vergil glared at me like I was a punk Mexican caught with a crack whore in the back of a stolen Lexus SUV. "If you copied one word of this, I'll have to kill you," he said, pulling a giant gun out of a shoulder holster and pointing it straight at my nose. I must have turned ashen, because soon enough he and Wi were doubled over in hysterics. "Guess you was too young to see my show," Vergil said, wiping the tears from his eyes. "I used to say that line on every episode. It was sort of my tag line: 'I'll have to kill you . . .'"

I used up the one fake laugh I had left. "Fuck, you scared the shit out of me. Pardon my French, Winona."

"Honey," she answered, in the only sentence she'd uttered until then, "that's 'how d'ye do' where I come from."

"So you're wondering why I showed you the will," said Vergil.

I was. Amy had left the bulk of her estate to her son and daughter. What did this have to do with Steed, who got only $10,000 and a few personal effects?

"Well, here's the really interesting part, and I don't think there's any harm in telling it now, because it's ancient history, and the kids signed off on the will. When Amy knew she was dying, the two people closest to her was Jeff and her estate manager, Ken Strand. She wanted to leave a good bit of her money to them two, and her kids didn't need it because their father set up trust funds for them. Amy even figured leaving them any more money would be downright destructive, but she figured if she left it to Jeff and Ken, the kids would challenge the will out of sheer greed. So, Jeff came up with this scheme to form a shell corporation in Panama that he controlled. You know about shell corporations?"

I did. In Panama, for about a thousand bucks, anybody can hire a lawyer to set one up. The corporation pays no taxes, and the person creating the company does not have to provide his real identity, which exists only on a single bearer share, held by the bearer. If the Panamanian authorities are asked for information, they will release only the name of the local agent, unless a crime has been committed in Panama.

"So, Jeff had Amy sign promissory notes to purchase mining claims and oil leases from the Panama corporation. When she died, the estate had to pay off the notes before her kids got anything. The money she wanted to go to Jeff and Ken got to them, and the kids was never the wiser for it."

That explained how Steed had gotten so wealthy so young. The scheme, while it didn't seem either illegal or immoral, was nothing if not precocious for a kid just out of high school.

By this time we were all dead drunk, so I ordered coffee for everyone.

Vergil eased into a new topic he'd clearly been waiting to broach: "I bought a copy of your magazine, and I got to tell you, I was very impressed. *Very* impressed. And I was thinking, Why not do an article on *me*? Your readers would be very interested in seeing how Sheriff Billy Bob is raising horses, especially since they watched him riding them for so many years."

"Vergil, you know, that's not a bad idea." At this point, I was so wasted that I barely knew what I was saying.

He toasted me with the dregs of his sixth martini and then announced that, aging prostates being what they were, he had to pay a visit to "the little boys' room."

As soon as he was out of earshot, Wi piped up, "Me, I never liked that kid too much." By this point, she was a poster child for the sorrows of gin: blue eyes red, makeup and hair wildly askew, speech slurred.

"You mean Jeff Steed?"

She'd obviously been waiting for the chance to give her version. "Yup. Slick as snot on a doorknob, always working some angle. He almost got Amy into some serious trouble on account of some so-called investments, something to do with some insurance company in Ohio. Of course, she didn't need no help from him. She was money-mad, that Amy. That's why the son didn't have nothing to do with her. And Amy and Abe got hauled in by the feds about five years before Abe died. Insider trading, they said, some tip Amy got from her sister. They could never prove nothing, but I know because she told Vergil about it and he run to his broker like he usually done. It's a miracle they didn't all end up in the clink."

"Wi, what are you cackling about?" Vergil was back.

"About the time Abe fell off the boat in Avalon and they found him the next morning washed up in the dinghy with the fish in his pants."

"Aw, shit."

FOURTEEN

Greg

BY FRIDAY, MY $395-a-night room was about to become a $695-a-night room, and even drinking in the Polo Lounge started to get old. Ed had given me the cushiest assignment in the universe, and I was about to fuck it up, like everything else. We'd have no November cover, thanks to me. After Ed fired me, I'd be lucky if I could get a job as a book reviewer for *Modern Bride*. My e-mails to Marci started to get increasingly desperate and dishonest: "Need interview ASAP or mag goes with Angelina."

At the last possible moment, Ms. A-list came swanning through the bougainvillea, which perfectly matched the Birkin bag dangling from her elbow.

"I'm so sorry about the scheduling bullshit," she said, leaning close, making eye contact. "Night shoots," she explained, sinking into a chair. "I hope it hasn't been too big a pain."

"Not at all. There are worse places to get stuck."

She laughed. "Still," she said. "I'm sure your real life's better. New York, right?"

I nodded. "How did you know?"

She smiled. "Just a hunch."

Over the next two hours, precisely, she talked breezily about her life, from her days at Juilliard—the "back story"—to her Big Break to her determination not to "let the material dictate my choices." As instructed by Nina, I waited until the bitter end before asking the only question anybody cared about. (Not that Nina had to tell me—it's the Golden Rule of journalism: save the touchy questions for last, otherwise you risk stopping the interview in its tracks.) By that time, a few drinks had lubricated my tongue and hopefully hers as well.

"I'm kind of embarrassed to ask this," I began, wincing, "but are you dating Colin Farrell?"

Ms. A-list reddened slightly, feigning surprise that anyone would care about "my pathetic love life."

"Ah . . . but they do."

"I'm single." She grazed my hand with hers. "Will you marry me?" She graced me with that breathtakingly sexy, low laugh that turned strong men to jelly.

A day later, I came out of the hot Hollywood canteen du jour to find her waiting for her car. "Hi," I said. "We have to stop meeting like this." She smiled and handed me her parking ticket. She thought I was the valet.

FIFTEEN

I PUT IT TO Eddy that Mr. Greg will help. Eddy's like, He will get a lawyer? I'm like, Eddy, this things doesn't work like that, but Mr. Greg has the power. He is a very important man. He will write all this article, and the firm will have to pay money. To you. Eddy is like, How much? I'm like, Eddy, be cool, man. This articles takes time.

I'm trying to give Eddy a good mood, so Friday night we go to Flow, and I was the one that pay for the drinks, everything. Flow is a cool place, man. I saw Lil' Cease, the guy that used to be best friends with Biggie. (Biggie was a guy that died, a heavy guy. Notorious B.I.G. Lil' Cease used to hang with him and Lil' Kim before.) So I saw Lil' Cease. The fucking guy is five foot four. I went up to him and was like, Hey, how's it going, man? Because I read in the magazine that he came out with only one album, I think in '99 or maybe 2000. The album sold 138,000. That was nothing for a guy that had his name before. You know, he used to hang out with the coolest guy in the whole hip-hop industry.

He look not the way you see him on the video. He look so poor. He didn't look flashy. I went up to him, and I didn't talk ghetto at all. I was like, I bought your last album, and I think a couple of songs there was really nice. And he was like, Oh, thank you very much, fam. Fam is like family. That's what they use. You ever heard that word? Yo, what up, fam?

Eddy is talking with this Colombian girl, Natalia. A very beautiful girl. She lives in the projects. Eddy knows her. I was like, Eddy, How the fuck this girl gets into this club if she coming from the projects? He was like, Oh, she knows the deejay.

She dress real high-class. Yo, you see this girl, you never going to be able to tell where she comes from. Even the way she talks. I never met her, because she doesn't hang with Brazilians. She look to me about twenty-two years old, same as me. So we talking, and this girl only drinks Hennessy. But she gets Hennessy for free, because the jay's her friend. He gets a ticket, and she goes there, and drinks for free the whole night.

I'm drinking Red Stripe. And we just there, drinking, drinking, drinking. So Natalia was like, Oh, let's go down the basement. There they be playing funk and old-school rock 'n' roll. She was kind of banged up. She was going down the stairs, and she had her glass of Hennessy. Going down, I was behind her. Eddy was right next to her. When she was eight steps for her to go, she fucking slipped. You know when you slip, and you go down the stairs with your butt? Oh, my God! Her drink spills over. Yo, Eddy, this kid was going bananas, just cracking up on this girl. I looked at him, I laughed, but I was like, I don't think this is nice to do with a girl. But Natalia was cracking up, too. She was like, Oh, my arm and my butt hurts. She was drunk, so it didn't hurt her.

We just stood there, downstairs, until four. All of a sudden Natalia kiss me, a French kiss. But I knew this girl was wasted. Yo, I don't know if she was on drugs or she was drunk. I just didn't want to mess with her. I will talk to a womans if she be sober, but once I see the womans drunk or took drugs, that's enough for me.

We leave that place around four. Natalia is too drunk to get home. I put her in a taxi with me, and we go to my place, because my mom had visit her friend in Boston. We ended up sleeping together. Nothing happened. In the morning she woke up. She was like, I bet you never did this before in your life. I was like, Something like that.

So we went into the city, and she was the one that pay for my movies. You know, a lady never pays for a guy's movies. But she pay.

She wanted to pay. Because we went to a place to eat, a pizza place, and I was the one that pays. And then she felt that she had to pay for my movie, and I was like, All right.

Sunday we hung with Fabio. We drove in Fabio's car by Home Depot in Yonkers, because Fabio, he had to fix some stuffs for his mom. He went inside, and it was just me and Natalia outside. She was like, You know, this is what I like: Sunday. My husband waking up really early, you know, fixing the house, whatever has to be fixed. That's what she wanted if she was married. And I was just listening to her story. You know, my husband has to be very caring. I'm like, Yeah, okay. And she's like, You know, my husband doing everything for me. Oh, this would be a perfect marriage. I was like, Yo, you know when you going to find a husband like that? Trusts me: like never.

And she was like, You know, that's why you don't get no girls. I was like, Yo, you know how many girls I get? You don't even know. And she was like, You guys all players. I was like, I wonder how long this motherfucking husband's going to put up with you, because if it was me, and I know that I'm marrying a girl like you, I would have dumped you right away. And she was like, Yeah, whatever.

You know, people usually, when they date each other, they have this imagination how each other is going to be. Natalia say she always had this thought about a guy that she wants to control the guy. Because she is a Scorpion. I know because my mom is a Scorpion, and she is the same fucking way. Oh, my God, man. Scorpions. When a person tells me that it's a Scorpion, I'm like, Yo, that's my mom. Walk away from this person. I'm Aquarius. We has to have our freedoms and be capable to hang with a whole bunch of different womens.

But when I tell Natalia I shine shoes for a living, she is cool with that. She was like, You don't need no shame on that. You make a good living, doing. Because that's the thing, when I talk to them, they usually ask what I do. If the womens doesn't ask me what I do, if they don't care, if they just like me for what they see it, and they talk to me, and see that I'm capable to go from one level to another, that's what I like in womens.

I want things to start me knowing the person, me talking to the person. The person liking me not for what I do or what I have, but for things we say. She say things that I like it, and I say things that she likes it. And we are kind of like each other.

If I was rich, and I buy an apartment and end up buying a car, and end up dressing better and going places better, and if I meet a girl, what the fuck's the girl going to think? Oh, he has a nice car. Oh, he has his own place. She not going to like me for what I am.

I always have that in my mind, if I ever end up making money, I will marry someone from Brazil. I'll pretend that I'll go there poor. I'll spend like a month, two month there. And I'll see if this person really likes me.

SIXTEEN

Gil

TODAY I GO see Mr. Jeff. He's like, Here come the CIA! That's what he usually call me now: the CIA. He usually used to call me the Shoe Doctor. Whatever. What is wrong with that fucking guy? I think he's a clown. Too overrated. Maybe he's trying to hide his true self.

Mr. Jeff is sitting with Matthew. Matthew is a intern from Texas, and Mr. Jeff was the guy that usually teach Matthew a lot of things. When the interns come, they has to teach them a lot of stuffs. So Mr. Jeff's the one that take the time in the afternoon and teach Matthew about everything.

Most of the interns that goes there this fucking goofy types. All this fucking kids. I don't know where they get this kids from. They look at you and they be like, Damn, there's a shoeshine boy here? But they don't talk, you know. They just walk and stare at you like they seen something out of the planet. This kids probably go to school in All-the-Way and West Bubblefuck. That's how Fabio put it like when it's far. He's like, Yo, man, we going to West Bubblefuck. This is like the end of the world.

I think this kids, they usually go to school that is like only going to school and parties. But they don't know what the real city lifestyle is. They don't think there can be a guy that shines shoes inside the building. They probably think, Can he make a living out of that? And when one of the traders is like, Hey, this is Gil, they don't want to shake my hands, because they think my hands is all dirt and that it dirt their nice clothes if they touch me.

But Matthew is the one intern, though, he cool with me. He always shake my hand. He doesn't worry about dirting his clothes with the polish and stuff on my hand.

Matthew dated one of George Bush's daughters. I'm serious. He messed with her. George Bush used to call him "that little fuck," when Matthew call her up at her house, because George Bush hate him. Like Matthew knows him. I'm not lying.

Matthew's twenty years old. One of those guys that have the straight hair that goes on the side. Really well dressed. He dress not fancy, not Gucci, but he know how to dress. His father was rich. He wasn't in the whole Enron thing, but he went to jail for that same similar reason. For stealing money in the legal way, not like putting a gun to a person's head, but a lot of people lost money because of his dad, and his dad was in the federal prison.

Matthew was the one that told me, and I was like, Yeah, right, this kid wanted to be tough, so he be telling me that his dad went to jail. He doesn't even look like the type. I was like, Yo, Mr. Turner, you hear what Matthew said it to me, because he was there. Mr. Turner said, Ah, that's true, though. But his dad is in one of those—How you call it?—white-collar jails. Fred was like, Gil, you really think he went to jail? This guy was in a jail that you were able to drink champagne and play golf. I was like, For real? What kind of jail is that? Fred was like, That's when you have money. I was like, Damn.

I went to see Mr. Damien. He's in the rows that peoples makes really big money. You just got to watch. I think it's the merger market, something like that. I know the peoples there that makes money, and I know who doesn't make that much money. I just know.

Mr. Damien's the funniest guy. He's black, but he has power. He smart, the classic businessman, all dressing up, shoes that cost $700. He's the kind of brother, old-fashioned, but he knows how to talk to the white guy. He's smart in the job and street-smart. He's the boss. He is. He talks really smooth and cool. We always talk about womens.

I'm like, Yo, Damien, how come you always go out and talk about girls, and you married. He's like, My wife is a lawyer. I'm like, Yeah, you don't like her? He's like, Nah.

Yo, he got the best fucking view, the view to the pantry, where they sell the candy bars, gum, chips, where they have the machine that makes the coffee, the microwave and the water, and a little refrigerator. So they got tons of girls going in there.

Damien, he sits there, and he just look at the womens passing by, because every womens got to go inside to get a soda, this and that. He sit there, and I'm there shining his shoes, and he's like, Aw fuck, I'm only capable to look, Gil. If I touch it, I'll get fired. That guy is fucking hilarious. I love him. Sometimes I'm there for an hour with this guy.

I'm there shining his shoes, and I see the womens coming, because sometimes he can't see it, the way he sitting. So I tap on his shoes with my finger, because I'm shining. I'm like, Yo, yo, yo, look right, look right. He goes like, Damn, dude! What you think about her *ass*-ets? I'm like, Hey, Damien, damn. Sometime when he see a white, American skinny woman, he grabs a piece of paper and goes like, Gil, look through this. Do you see anything in here? You know, like when you put the paper to the side, you can't see anything. You can just see a thin line. I'm like, Yeah. He's like, This is the girl's ass.

Mr. Damien ask me, Dude, I know a couple of Spanish girls, but I just don't know what to do. So I try to make it seem like I kind of know what Spanish womens likes. I'm like, Hey, if you tell them you want to be their boyfriend, they'll give it up in the first night. They do. I been with two Spanish girls, so when I talk to them, and I see they don't want to do, but they do, I'm like, I'm looking for a girlfriend and stuffs like that. They like, whoosh, straight up, give it to you.

Then I stood there for about an hour just talking to Mr. Jared. He was wearing Allen Edmonds. He dress conservative. There's a lot of kids like that, they like twenty-three but trying to put an image on themselves that they old, so the other peoples will respect them. But Jared don't work. I don't know what the fuck he does, but he don't work. He's just like a rich guy. This guy loves to shop. The other day, he went out and bought a thousand dollars' worth of DVDs. I'm serious. Most of the time I see him, he playing a video game on his computer. He pull out a Web site and sometimes he play pool, or baseball, or this little games that they have sometimes from Snickers, the chocolate. This guy, he bets through the Internet. He usually do that. He bets on baseball, any fucking thing. That's what he do.

I'm like, Yo, Jared, you got the nicest job. Because even myself won't be able to do it. He's very cool. That guy is cool as hell. I was like, Hey, Jared, what is the insider trading, something like that. Because I heard that from Greg. I didn't want to ask the big guys, because that would be so obvious. Jared's like, Where you hear about that? I'm like, I just heard it from a guy here. Someone got arrested for that. So, Jared turns to me, and he goes like, Gil, it's like I know someone that I really trusts for a long time, a friend of mine, and we both work at different firms. But no one knows about it, except his little group. And he calls me up, and he tells me that, and I go ahead, and I just buy the stock before anyone. Because I know that that going to make me a lot of money. But the thing is he's the one that give me the tip, but he's not suppose, because he's the guy that be dealing with this stocks, so he know everything about it. That's not legal. I was like, Oh, all right. You could really get arrested for that? He's like, Yeah. I was like, Wow, this days you could get arrested for anything. I got arrested when I hop on the turnstile. He start laughing. Sometimes you got to play stupid. You got to tell somebody something or ask them a question, and then you got to play a stupid joke, so you can put this image that you really stupid. So they could just be like, Yeah, this kid is dumb, so whatever I said it doesn't count.

Today Lindsay asked me to shine her boots, and I don't know why I said that to her, but I went like this, Miss Lindsay, I got to tell you something. She was like, What? I was like, You know why I like you so much? She kind of looked at me like maybe she thought I was going to say something to her like, I want you. But I was like, You know why I like you so much? Because when I first start working in this place, you never look down on me. You always look at me like I was a human being. And that really touched me. I really liked that. That's why I respect you. When I say that, she didn't have tears under her eyes, but she was surprised. She looked at me like, Wow. She ended up giving me $20, but I didn't say it for that. I said it because I meaned it.

SEVENTEEN

Gil

MONDAY WE WENT to this bar on Ludlow Street. So we drink, Natalia was kind of fucked up, I was kind of fucked up. I was like, Yo, Fabio, can you chill here for a while? He was like, Yeah. So, I took Fabio's Subaru with Natalia to Roosevelt Island. In Roosevelt Island, if you go to the end, where people usually smoke weed, it's a really dead zone. We went there, and I showed her the view. It's a beautiful view. You can see everything in Manhattan. The buildings are very beautiful, and the lights are twinkly.

I show it to her, and she was like, Yeah, it's really nice. We walking back to the car. Then we started kissing with each other in the front seat. She looked so beautiful. Everything was with passion, with love. I really liked this girl. It was like, Wow. I didn't need anything else, just her. This girl looked so beautiful. She looked like Cleopatra. She got straight hair, she knows how to dress. She stylish. This woman to me was perfection. And she loved to be with me.

But this girl fell in love now. It ended up me and her on Tuesday again. She ask me if I had a girlfriend, this and that. And then she went like this to me, I really like you. I was like, Why? She's like, You're not ghetto, you don't sound ghetto. I was like, What do you mean by that? Then she say it, You sound kind of gay. I was like, Are you fucking serious? Yo, you want me to bring the ghetto over here now? I can be ghetto as you fucking want. She was like, Nah, I just like the way you are. You have a different style, your hair, you know how to dress, this and that. I was like, Yeah, but why you calling me that? She was like, Nah, just the way you talk. Most of this gay guys very polite. Now, if you be polite with a girl, they like it, but if you talk ghetto, they like it, too. I tried to be ghettoer, and she was like, Nah.

Then she asked me, We are? I was like, What do you mean, we are? She was like, You still going to see me? And I was like, Yeah. But she wanted me to be her boyfriend. I was like, Wow, I don't think I'm ready. The thing about her is that she going to want to dominate, and I'm not going to like that. Right now I just want to meet peoples.

Damn. This girl kind of drove me crazy. We went over to my house, but nobody was there. It was a sneaky-sneaky sort of thing, for two hours and a half. But I know nobody was going there. My mom was working. So Natalia came, and we drank some. Yo, but this girl got on top of me. She goes, You like the way I ride you, huh? I was like, Damn. She kind of grabbed me by my neck. I was like, Damn, this girl's going to fucking choke me. I grab her in her arms, and I asked her why she was doing after a while. And she was like, Wow!

I got to be careful. I know this girls, they catch feelings. I heard that on a hip-hop song. They want you to fuck first, and then you to be the boyfriend.

You know, Fabio, he was telling me, You can go with Natalia, but don't you ever, ever, ever let her catch you with another girl. He's like, If you fuck her up in the relationship, go with another girl, and she find out, she's going to make your life miserable. Super-miserable. Because he listens to Spanish womens radio in the mornings, so he hears their stories, like what they do to the boyfriends that cheat. He's like, Yo, don't you ever, ever go and cheat, or don't you ever try to lie to her, because if she thinks you lying, you fucked. She's not like the Brazilian type of girl that's going to cry. This Colombian-type girls don't cry. They act.

That's true, though. If Natalia catch me looking at another woman, she fucking goes bananas. She will punch me right in the arm. She will be like, Why you got to look at this other womens?

I was in the Brazilian nightclub in Astoria, it was me and Natalia on Thursday. We fought before we went there. Me and her, we weren't even looking at each other in the club. Brazilians are kind of like that. If we fight before, when we go to the place, we don't even stay near to each other. Everyone goes in their way, because we trying to show each other how tough we are. Like we don't have no feelings for each other. When we got there, me and the guys, we started drinking like maniacs. Natalia had a couple of drinks, but she couldn't drink like us, so we probably had about six Coronas and shots, and we fucked up already.

There was this blond girl, yo, that I liked it. I was drunk out of my mind, and I start talking to her, and she like me. I'm like, Come here, let's go. I got to talk to you outside. When I came outside, and it was just a block away from this little corner that I was going to take this girl to kiss. When I was two steps away from the corner, I swear, I just heard someone screaming my name at the top of their lung. A-GUI-LAR. I froze at that time, I swear to God. I was holding hands with the blond girl. I let the hand go, and I was just like, I'm . . . so . . . sorry, that's my ex-girlfriend. I'm not going to turn back, but if I was you, I would either run or go up the street, because I'm going to try and control her. Because she is going to fuck me up. And you, too. The girl look at me like, What? I was like, Yeah.

When I turn back, I saw Natalia down on her knees—you know when someone's praying? I swear to God. She's crying. She had both of her hands close tight, tight, tight and she breathe so heavy, I thought she was going to have a heart attack at that time. When I saw that, I didn't know what to say. I was caught in action. Then she got up, and we had this girls grabbing her, the girls that came with us. She was trying to punch me. The girls are holding her up to stop.

We had to go home in different cars, and we had our friends to talk to us. We ruined the whole night for the other guys. We went home, and she didn't wanted to do anything with me. She was just asking me questions: Did you get hooked up with her? Did you like her? Why you do this to me? I know you like blondes. She was crying the whole night. I was like, I'm sorry, Natalia. I didn't meant to do that. I was drunk. You got to be really calm in those moments, yo, because when you fucked up, you can't say anything.

"DID YOU FUCK her?"

Annie was joking, but also dredging my eyes for a glimmer of guilt. She isn't usually the jealous type, but I'd never spent a week supposedly interviewing a movie actress by the pool.

"She's not that kind of girl . . . but she did ask me to marry her."

"What are you talking about?" Alarm bells now in her voice.

"You know. We were just fooling around. She finds New Yorkers refreshing. She thinks we're more intellectual and serious." I left out the part about her mistaking me for the parking valet.

"Are you going to see her again?"

"Come on, sweetheart. Just kidding. She has no interest in me. She's dating Colin Farrell, I hear, but I couldn't get her to admit it. Did I not chop those scallions small enough?"

Annie was mincing furiously. "No. They're fine."

Annie is head chef when we make dinner. She picks the recipes, mixes the ingredients, does the spices. I'm the prep man and dishwasher. We were making tofu with *mabo* sauce. Annie's parents are Korean, but she was born and raised in Georgia, where her father worked as a chemical engineer. One of the things that kills me about Annie is this southern accent coming out of her beautiful Asian face.

"I had some time in California to check out that Medved, Morningstar trader I was telling you about—Jeff Steed. He's from there, originally."

"Oh, really?"

"I'm thinking this may be a pretty big story. It turns out Steed had a criminal mind even as a kid."

"How did you manage to figure that out by the pool with Ms. A-list?"

"Come on, Annie, I'm serious. This could be important for me."

"Sorry. But you really think a story about one trader breaking the rules is that big?"

"One trader breaking the rules usually leads to a bunch of his friends. Remember Dennis Levine, the Drexel Burnham trader from the early eighties?"

"Vaguely."

"When the SEC busted him it led to a ring that reached all the way up to Ivan Boesky and Michael Milken. As I recall, at least one lawyer was involved, a Wachtell, Lipton hot shot."

"Oh, yeah. That *was* big."

She stirred some *gochi-gang*—Korean hot-pepper sauce—into the tofu, and I put out a dish of *kim*—seaweed sheets toasted in sesame oil and salted. The idea is to pick up the tofu and rice with a piece of *kim*, but I usually eat the *kim* on the side, like potato chips.

We make a lot of Korean food now, which is ironic, because Annie didn't eat any when I first met her. Being the only Asian—actually, the only nonwhite person—in her school was hard, and she still gets upset when she talks about it. The other kids made fun of the kimchi in her lunch box and the way her parents mangled English. Her house smelled strange because of the food her mother cooked. The other kids would tell her she wasn't showering enough, because her skin was darker, and when she went to their houses they would ask if she was going to eat their dog.

Being different causes some people to dive deep into themselves, but it made Annie stronger and more extroverted. She studied magazines and TV shows and made her mother get her the same clothes the actresses wore. She insisted on peanut butter and jelly in her lunchbox, and when her mother made her bring some *sundabu jiggae* (spicy tofu stew) to a potluck tasting party at school, she threw it out on the way and told the teacher she forgot.

She was valedictorian of her class and the first person from her school to go to Harvard. When the Asian kids approached her there to join their group, she put them off. Having spent her entire life trying to get away from being a foreigner, why would she want to join an Asian group? All her friends were white. Sometimes I think she chose me because I was the whitest guy she could find.

But, at thirty-two, Annie was trying to discover her cultural identity—backward, as she put it. Dissimilating to figure out what she lost.

"Steed was barely out of high school when he was forming Panamanian shell corporations to fool a rich woman's heirs and inherit the money himself."

"How did he manage not to get caught?"

"It wasn't actually illegal. The woman wanted to leave him the money, because she felt her kids didn't deserve it."

"So, how does that make him a criminal?" Annie is a lawyer, after all.

"It's just part of a pattern of sneaky behavior. There were other stories about him getting duplicate certificates to sell stock that was being used as collateral. *That's* illegal. And he forged his mother's name on a bank document. Fast forward to now, when he's caught by a janitor using his cell phone in the bathroom supply closet. Why would he bother to do that unless he was trading on inside information?"

"Maybe he's cheating on his girlfriend." Annie bugged her eyes. "Seriously, though, if it is a case of insider trading, how are you going to get the story?"

"If he broke the rules once, he'll do it again. These Wall Street guys equate net worth with intelligence and omnipotence. The richer they are, the smarter they think they are. They think the rules don't apply to them anymore. They get away with it for a while, but then they get careless."

"And you're counting on this shoeshine boy . . ."

"Gil."

". . . to inform on him to you?"

"Not just Gil. There's a whole network over there—janitors, secretaries, copy-machine guys. The traders aren't careful around them. They barely even see them."

Annie got up to brew some *poti-cha*, the woody-tasting tea served after Korean meals. "If you can make it work, it'll be a great story."

What I love about Annie is she's so supportive of everything I do. If somebody that intelligent doesn't think I'm a fuckup, then I must not be.

"Maybe they'll even make a movie out of it," she added, "and if she plays her cards right, Ms. A-list can play the sexy secretary."

"I think someone is jealous."

"You love it."

Supposedly, the only reason we hadn't gotten married yet (and still kept separate apartments) was her relatives in Korea. They knew she was dating, but they thought I was Korean. If they found out I was white, they would be scandalized. What they believed was national pride struck me as similar to the racism Annie had experienced here, but according to her, it also had a lot to do with the presence of the American military in Korea. Some Korean women marry soldiers, but the soldiers tend not to be the highly educated ones, and the women are mostly lower-class (there is a rigid class system in Korea). The perception is you would date a white boy only if you weren't right or proper for a Korean man, and none would have you. The next best thing is a white boy.

To be honest, the Korean relatives suited Annie and me just fine, because neither of us was ready to have kids. Annie especially had issues, which were making her more and more anxious as her biological clock neared high noon and her spare time devolved into an endless round of baby showers. She talked about pregnancy as some kind of college science project, with an alien growing inside her, doing things she had no say over. An avid runner who has done a couple of marathons, she had managed to convince herself for a while that giving birth would be like running wind sprints, something she's good at. But then a friend of hers had a baby and described it as like having your body broken in half.

Annie worries that after having a kid she'll turn into a lumpy, sagging old crone. She wonders whether I'll still be attracted to her. I've pointed out how many hot MILFs there are in the city, but she says she keeps hearing from her friends how they can't lose the last ten pounds of "baby weight."

She worries if she'll be a good mother, if she'll nag too much, if she'll try to micromanage, and the kid will end up hating her. Will she be a good role model? Will she resent the sacrifices she has to make and then subconsciously take it out on the kid? What if she gets a kid that she doesn't like? She says she'd just want to hit the reset button and start over, which makes her feel terrible.

And how would it affect her career? She says her firm doesn't mind if you have a kid, but then they want you to pretend it didn't happen: back to work in six weeks, no reduction in your billable hours. If you want to take more time off to be with your baby, they put you on a different, lesser track.

What did I think about having kids? Well . . . everybody else was doing it. I figured we'd have to, sooner or later. There were even parts I looked forward to, like doing a better job than my father had and seeing a little piece of myself running around. But the troubles I was having at *Glossy* had spooked me. How could I think about having a kid if I wasn't sure I'd have a job tomorrow? True, Annie made a good salary, but being a househusband did not interest me. There was one of those in my apartment building. While his wife went off to her high-powered job, he scrounged for pocket money by babysitting other people's kids along with his own, and illegally renting out our community room for birthday parties. I could just hear what my father would say if I turned out like that.

NINETEEN

Greg

GIL INVITED ME to a Yankees game, with tickets he got by trading a free shoeshine every day for a month to one of the traders. He didn't ask Fabio or Eddy, he told me, because they didn't understand the game. "What is the fucking rules in here?" they always asked him when baseball was on TV.

On a blazing, hot afternoon we sat right over third base, with a superb view of the home team getting slaughtered by the Red Sox. We ate the chemical-laced stadium hot dogs, and drank too much beer, and got rowdy along with everyone else, hurling insults at the ballplayers.

Gil's espionage efforts were not producing much, so I told him to approach Rona. "Tell her you met a guy who can help Eddy, but don't tell her I'm a reporter at *Glossy*—that might scare her away."

"I don't think she will care," said Gil.

"Trust me. Just play it my way. You said she told you she knew enough to put some of those guys behind bars—quote, unquote—right?"

"Yeah, she did. She knows everything about this guys. Yo, once I was there shining Mr. Bigelow's shoes . . . "

"You shine Bill Bigelow's shoes?"

"Yeah, all the time."

"I can't believe you never told me that. What's he like?"

"He cool. He got this HUGE office."

Bigelow was a legend on Wall Street. I'd written a profile of him years before, for which he would talk to me only about his hobbies—playing bridge and growing antique roses at his estate in Connecticut. I had to rely on others to fill in the basic biography: he didn't start out in a gold crib, as Gil put it, but poor, in the South, where he attended a state university on a football scholarship. After serving in Korea, he came to New York, but the white-shoe firms weren't interested in anyone without an Ivy League degree or a family pedigree. He had to start out as a Merrill Lynch–type broker, then moved to a small, boutique firm, where he managed to charm the notoriously slippery and foulmouthed founder by learning his passion: bridge. When the founder retired, Bigelow took over, cleaned up the firm, and grew it. Over the years, he had transformed himself into the kind of patrician WASP who once wouldn't have given him the time of day.

Bigelow prided himself on being a man of old-fashioned values, which his employees claimed was just a euphemism for being cheap, especially when bonus time rolled around. (One of his notorious homespun memos advised limiting the use of company cars because "walking is good for you" and "costs only the price of shoe leather.") He was on his second wife but only because the first one died. There was a grown son, who had worked as a bartender when I wrote the profile—a pale carbon copy of a carbon copy of his father.

Despite his genteel affectations, Bigelow was an astute corporate infighter, and he survived the earthquaking takeovers and mergers of his era to hold on to his job.

TWENTY

Gil

MR. BIGELOW'S THE CEO. He's really, really old, like seventy. The first time I go there, Rona was like, Hey. You never know. He might like you, and he owns the company. So I was like, Well, if he really like me, and I talk to him, maybe I'll get a job there. Because he is the guy that hire everybody, everybody who makes above whatever. If he want to put a dog in there, just to fucking walk around the floors, he can. Because Mr. Bigelow is worth no less than $250 millions.

The first time, I was freaked out, man. It's in a different part of the building. They got their own special elevator that go there. In the thirtieth floor, when you get off in the elevator, it's two doors, two glassy doors on each side. If you go to the big bosses, where Mr. Billy sits, you going to walk in this HUGE hallway, but really nice, with that stuffs they got in the bathroom on the wall. It makes you look like you in a fucking movie. You know *The Matrix*? Everything's really nice.

Then you see a nice front desk with a secretary. Puerto Rican girl, she look good. She cool, though. She smile at me and say hi. Because some of them, they don't even say hi. So, I walk there, and she got to call up this other secretary that is connected to Mr. Bigelow. And this other secretary, I think she check it out with him. And he made me wait. I was waiting for ten, twenty minutes, man. I don't like to wait. Twenty minutes for me is a lot. Then she has a security guard, black old guy, come up to me, pick me up, and just drop me right at the secretary. I'm like, I thought he was going to drop me in his office.

All right, I walk into the office. His office was HUGE. When I got there, I was like, Shit, man. HUGE windows, a whole wall of windows. Once you walk in, you be like, it's a different world from every part of the whole building. Man, the carpets. You know, when you step on a carpet and the foot sink down? I was going to take my shoes off, when you step, because I don't know. I didn't want to dirt on this carpet. Imagine the dirt, the polish, and stuffs. I get this thing dirty, man, and I'm going to get fired. I know once you piss people like that off, they fucking disappear with you. They get mad at you for the rest of their lives.

I saw the plate that they bring him on for lunch, covered with a metal thing. They make the food inside that floor. He has a shelf full of books, pictures, whole bunch of stuffs. I think he has a bathroom inside his office. Because there's this little secret door, so I think that's the bathroom, because that's what I see him coming out. Because when I walked in, he wasn't there, and then he came out of that door. The furniture is old, woody. He has a HUGE desk, that's where he do all the business and where the phone stays. There's another rounded little table with a sofa. And old-fashioned chairs. Everything's woody.

Right in front he has this big flat-screen TV that has all the stock exchanges. He wasn't watching no other channel then. I thought he was going to be watching ESPN, because he has pictures, a whole bunch of pictures framed of sports things and people playing cards that I didn't recognize. One was signed on this thing, but I didn't ask him who the person was. I just saw it. Rona tell me that before he work finance he usually used to play football back in the day. Until today he plays cards all the time.

So he was like, Hey, how you doing? Good, sir. All right, you ready to shine my shoes? Yeah. They were Gucci, but old-style Gucci that have the Italian flag, green and yellow, right on the buckle. Old-fashioned Gucci that have the styling. Not stylish Guccis, brand-new. He was dressing up really nice with those things that hold up the pants, and nice tie. His shirt was kind of white-and-reddish-striped. This guy know how to dress. His hair, slicked back. I'm there, shining his shoes, and he's on the phone. He was like, Hey, George, what's up? The deal . . . buhbuhbuhbuh. When they start talking about deals, man, I'm like, Huh? Then he grab the newspaper, read it, Wall Street. He light up this HUGE cigar, he's smoking, smoking. Man, that thing stink.

I was thirty minutes over there, just killing time, looking around, but I was shining shoes less than five minutes. He give me three dollars. He didn't even ask me how much. I was going to tell him, four dollars, sir, so he can give me six. But he was like, Thank you very much.

Everybody used to think that when I shine his shoes he gives me twenty-five dollars, thirty dollars. But he used to give me three. He makes 50 millions a year. I'm serious. Rona told me that he made that last year. She say he got his house that cost about 10 millions, a HUGE house in Connecticut. They usually buy stuffs in Connecticut and Westchester. In Jersey, just a few of them.

Nobody likes Mr. Billy in that firm. Because last year nobody got their bonus, just a few people. Everybody hate him. They like, this fucking guy taking my money. Because he gets a lot of money, and nobody got shit last year. So everybody was pissed at that guy. Nobody think that he's good.

The thing is: for me to go to his office, this wait can be five minutes to a half hour. That's money I'm losing. And he usually used to give me three dollars! Sometimes he didn't even have money to pay, so he tell his secretary to pay. She used to go like, How much he usually give you? Three? So I used to hate him. Because I used to spend time on his shoes. No matter what I used to do, for one year, he give me three dollars. And I'm thinking, this guy got the money to give it, but he doesn't.

So every time his secretary used to call me, I didn't answer. I didn't want to do his shoes. It was not even that. He didn't used to treat me nice. He used to be kind of mean, you know. His cigar really stink.

Then he see me in the lobby, and he ask me, So, what is the difference? How come you don't come around and shine my shoes no more? And I was like, Ain't no difference. And I went to tell his secretary to tell him what was the difference. She told him straight up.

Then you not going to believe what he do. He was like, You know what, Gil? What I really like is foot massage. I don't care if you shine my shoes. I like foot massage. He goes, I'm going to give you twenty-five dollars, but you cannot spend no less than a half hour on my feets.

Now I got to stay there for half an hour. It's funny, right? I just go the way I'm shining shoes. I stay there with the brush. He goes like, Ahhhhhh. And then he usually used to sleep. This guy makes 50 millions a year.

I keep going there, and now he usually starts telling me his little stories. He says he doesn't talk to his father before his father die. I never got to that point with my father. I told him about my father, like me and my father didn't used to have a good relationship, but now we do. He was like, You know, my father never care about his sons. He was saying that he didn't talk to his father for twenty years, something like that.

He says it to me to finish high school. Go back to high school, and go to college, son. Because he went through the same process. He said he was just like me when he was younger. He says he had to work, so he worked hard, went to school. But I don't think he tells me the truth. I don't know. To me he look like just a regular one of this rich guys, but he's the only one that says something like that to me.

I don't know for him, but the other ones, I think, they always had that easy life. It's not like they work hard, it's the schools that they went. You know everybody over there's like that. They never came from a really fucked-up school and been in that position. They always come from nice schools, in the country. They usually tell some of the guys, I'm from Syracuse, Georgetown, NYU. You'll never hear a guy that's from fucking LaGuardia College. You never hear a story like that.

I think they got into schools, you know, because their parents were there. It's like you building a house. You got to start from the bottom. They send their kids to good schools since the beginning, so the kids are always going to like it. They go to good schools, good places. That's how like most of the people at my job is. That's how I see it.

Every time I go there now, Mr. Billy is like, Gil, you got to go back to school. Because let me tell you a story about my cousin. He was a orphan. That's how Mr. Billy always start. Yo, I'm shining this man's shoes, and I start cracking up, because this man tells me this same story that I heard from him fifty times. He already told me this story over and over: So, my cousin was a orphan. One day my uncle adopt him, and he start going to school and stuffs. Then he graduate four years from this and then four years from another thing. Back in the day he used to do the job in the mailroom, and then he became the manager of this firm, something like that, and when he was eighty-three years old—that's the age he has now—he has 3 billion dollars.

I go like, Damn. So what the heck your cousin do with all this billions? Buy a Rolex? A Denali? He have a flat-screen TV? And Mr. Billy's like, No, I'm not talking about that. I'm talking about if you want to, you can go to school. And *save* all your money. My cousin had his whole life saving his money. And I'm like, Why? Why he do that? You can't take that 3 billions with you in the grave. Then Mr. Billy close his eyes, and I brush his feets.

But how many guys that is worth $250 millions is going to notice a little person like me? And care. Not that many. The fact that he cares—that's big. Now, if he asks me to do a favor, like go there, get laces, whatever, I will do it right away. Because I have the respect for that guy.

TWENTY-ONE

TODAY I WAS like, Rona, this guy I know put it he can help Eddy. She's like, Who? I'm like, This guy that I usually used to shine his shoes at Yuri's. He's a very important man. She's like, A lawyer? I'm like, I don't know, but he's big. So Rona goes, Okay, I got stuffs to show him. Then I call up Greg, and he's very interesting to see it. He's like, Where? When? He's like, Bring Eddy over there, too.

There is this club I go in Queens—Carioca Finest. I go there because I feel like I'm at home. It's my own culture—most of the people there is Brazilian, but we have Spanish people, Greeks, Irish people. It's a mix. Everyone is dressing okay. People in my culture, they don't usually like to dress up. But that's nice when you dress up and look different. I go there to drink and look at womens, and I'm trying to talk to them. That's what I do for fun. I usually meet up with peoples that I haven't seen in ages. Brazilians go to the same spot if they don't have nothing to do. Sometimes I bump into peoples that I haven't seen in three years. Four. Then you just gossip. Oh, what have you done? And what have you done for your life? They always like to know. If you doing good, they envy. If you doing bad, they criticize you.

I want Mr. Greg and Rona to like it. I just felt like I got to please them. I want them to feel my culture. I want them to be happy. I want this night to be just like every regular night that I come there, and everyone is there, and peoples jumping, having a good time, all this beautiful peoples. It's fun. Because sometimes when you talk about a place and you bring your friends into the place that you were talking about, you want the place to be exactly the way you were describing. But I think that Mr. Greg's not used to seeing a club that big, that many peoples, and those type of music that they usually be playing.

It's not like I want to bring him there so he could look at the place and just walk away. I want him to have fun, enjoy hisself, and nothing bad to happen. On Sunday, I'm so nervous. I'm so freaking nervous. I'm like, Please, please, just for tonight. I want this to be good. It's big for me that he will come over. He's a different individual. I have a lot of respect for him. Since that day that he used to come to Yuri's I always had that respect. When Mr. Greg usually used to come, I thought it was nice of him, because he would sit there and just pay attention to whatever I had to say it. The time that I worked there not that many peoples would do. Some of them would probably talk to you and give you the tip and bye. He used to take his time and talk.

Then I told him about Eddy, and he respond me, Hey, look, I got this great idea. I can write this articles. I was like, This guy's full of shit. He just want to get rid of me. It's all right. He always been nice to me. I didn't believe on him. I thought he was just telling me this, that. That he going to put Eddy's story in the magazine. I was like, Aw, man. He probably think I believe in this. But let's see what's going to happen. But now I think he will do it.

Mr. Greg doesn't know Queens like I know, so I put it that me and Natalia will meet him in Manhattan at Brazil Grill, this restaurant I go. When I first start working in the firm I didn't like to go to a restaurant, because my parents never took me. I remember going to a restaurant with them like three times in my whole entire life. I really didn't know how to act. To me, not knowing how to pick it up a fork, how to cut the steaks, because my mom always did that for me. It's really weird when you sitting around peoples that know how to do stuffs and you don't know how to do. You just don't feel part of it.

From the minute I put my feets inside a restaurant, I always thought that everyone was watching me, watching my moves, watching the way I was eating, and just listen to what I was going to say and that bothered me. If you drop a knife and the way you pick it up and the way you chew the food, this things used to bother me a lot. That's why it make me so uncomfortable. It's like you going to a place and, Wow, I'm an outcast here. I don't look like them. I don't talk like them. I don't dress like them. It's really frustrating. That's how I usually used to feel. But then I used to observes a lot that people didn't care. They all like my way. They come there with jeans, sneakers, book bags, fucked-up hair. Some of them looked they didn't have money to pay for the whole plate.

Last week I took Natalia and Fabio and his girl to this Italian restaurant. We go there, and they didn't even know what's on the menu, because it's all in Italian, and they couldn't even pronounce right. I was the one that had to tell: This is good and this is not good. I felt— I'm not going to lie—a little bit not above, but like when you know everything, and they don't know and you got to teach them. It make me feel really good, because I had peoples now watching me, how I act, and how I do the stuffs.

Natalia loved the restaurant, but she thought the way I was acting was kind of snobby. You know, this three didn't even put the napkins in their laps. They don't give a fuck about that stuffs. They don't pay attention to this little things. I was trying to teach Natalia, but she say that's bullshit. I know I made her feel really uncomfortable, but I was trying to help her out and teach her stuffs. But she doesn't care.

She's kind of like my mom. They always think the way they do is the right way. And if you trying to teach them something, they think you trying to be superior. I'm not trying to be superior, it's just that I want them to feel the way I am. It's going to make them feel good—because if they go out with someone else to a restaurant or someplace else, they going to know how to act without a person looking at them weird.

TWENTY-TWO

Greg

I MET GIL and Natalia at Brazil Grill, just off Times Square. Natalia was pretty, zaftig, very shy. I tried to get her to relax, complimented her blouse (gauzy, colorful) and her earrings (elaborate, dangly), kept her plate full from the family-style platters of *bacalhao* (cod cakes) and barbecued sirloin ("sir-lee-on," Gil called it). We drank many caipirinhas (which means "falling down" in Portuguese, Gil explained), a sweet-tart mixture of limes, sugar, and *cachaça* (sugar-cane liquor), but Natalia never looked me in the eye and would respond, very softly, only with a word or two.

She was nervous about making mistakes in English, Gil told me later, and because a man had never served her food before. In Latin America, real men don't serve food. They get served. I probably should have figured that out, but I'm used to being the waiter at home.

Natalia shot Gil a withering look when he told her to put the napkin in her lap. She told him in Spanish (Gil translated later) that he "would never be on that level."

After dinner we got Fabio's car, borrowed by Gil and parked nearby—and we were off, weaving, dodging, swerving, flashing our high beams at any car that dared get in front of us. My stomach felt like carnival in Rio, and by the time we crossed the Queensboro Bridge into Astoria—a Greek neighborhood that had more recently become mixed with Arabs, Brazilians, Italians, Serbs, Polish, Chinese, Koreans, and Indians—I was wondering whether Gil actually had a driver's license.

We arrived around eleven at the club, a large, dark loft, with lots of smoky glass, three or four bars, and a dance floor. The place was practically empty. Fabio was there, though, with his date and another girl, introduced as a cousin, which, I eventually came to understand, are to Brazil what generals used to be to tsarist Russia. Fabio was a good-looking guy with a gym body he showcased in a tight black T-shirt and pegged pants. His date was small and pretty, with masses of dark curls. Cousin Vera was a big girl with a mane of bleached-blond hair and a mannish face. So massive were her delts and shoulders I kept looking for an Adam's apple. No sign of Rona the secretary, yet.

Gil had told me that people "dressed up," so I wore a jacket and tie. People were dressed up, but not in monkey suits. The men affected either gangsta or Latin. The women busted out of tight, colorful party clothes. Vera was just barely contained in a shiny gold halter. Despite her monumental appearance, she was even shier than Natalia. I was going to take off my tie, but Gil seemed proud I looked like a big shot, so I didn't. He led our group to the "VIP section," a roped-off area on a riser. All you needed to be a VIP, it appeared, was 125 bucks to spend on a bottle of champagne, which Gil insisted on paying for. The eager host (the party promoter who put on this shindig, Gil confided) led us to a low table with couches on either side. Gil ordered a bottle of Veuve Clicquot. And there we awkwardly sipped, as Gil gabbed in English, Spanish, and Portuguese, like a juggler trying to keep too many balls in the air.

Finally, Rona arrived. I knew who she was the minute I spotted her across the room. She wore Manhattan black, but with more gold jewelry and more cleavage than you'd expect to see across the East River. Undoubtedly a knockout cheerleader type in high school, she was ruining her skin with too much tanning.

"Rona Bakalar," she introduced herself, putting out a hand after Gil greeted her. "You a lawyer?"

"Uh . . . a reporter, actually."

"Oh." Long pause. "We're not supposed to talk to reporters. I can lose my job."

"Don't worry. This is strictly between us. Gil asked me to help out with this friend of his who got fired. So, I said I'd try. My girlfriend is a lawyer, and I know a lot of important people because I write for *Glossy* magazine."

"Oh, *Glossy*. That's a different story. I love *Glossy*. I wait for my copy every month. The ads are really outstanding."

"Gee, thanks very much. So . . . Gil says you've got something to show me."

"Yeah. Take a look at this." She pulled a piece of stationery out of her pocketbook and gave it to me. It was imprinted with a coat of arms and a motto: *"Traihaat, Secherheet, Virdeel."* I couldn't translate it, even though I do know some German. I guessed it was archaic. The handwritten note, in French, asked Steed to call about transaction #6713 and was signed "Lucien Thissen."

"It was mixed in with some receipts Jeff Steed gave me," said Rona. "I do his expense account."

As the note was in French, but the motto wasn't, I guessed that Thissen was Swiss, some kind of aristocrat or banker.

"May I keep this, Rona?"

"Yeah, but if you do, just please, please, don't say you got it from me or use my name in any way. I have four cats to feed."

"I promise. I take it you don't like this guy, Steed, much."

"That would be an understatement."

"Any reason in particular?"

"He's a screamer. Throws his expense receipts at me. Never says thank you. But if you want to know the whole truth, I'm also getting a little revenge for a friend."

"Oh yeah?"

"When he first got there, he dated one of the other executive assistants. She fell for him pretty hard and broke up with her boyfriend. Then, like two weeks later, Jeff dumped her. Said he had trouble with intimacy. I think Jeff was just using her to get gossip about the boss. She works for Bill Bigelow, the CEO."

"What a creep," said Vera unexpectedly.

"I doesn't have no trouble with intimacy," said Gil, making goo-goo eyes and grinning lasciviously at Rona, who ignored him, while Natalia's eyes blazed.

"And him getting this kid fired . . . it's just *beyond*. It's one thing if they want to fuck with each other, but to go after a poor kid who barely earns enough to live on. Is that champagne? Do you mind if I have a glass?"

The club was filling, and Gil moved us out of the VIP section and down to the dance floor, where we switched back to caipirinhas. Fabio's date very sweetly offered to teach Rona and me how to samba. Rona was a natural (she used to teach dance aerobics, she told us); I was pathetic. But with the booze suddenly hitting me hard, the music cranking, and the crowd hopping, I didn't care. I called Annie, who was having dinner with a client, and told her to come out to the club after she was finished. I knew she wouldn't, but I was feeling guilty about having fun without her. "Just don't drink so much you can't get out of bed tomorrow. We're supposed to have brunch with your parents," she said in a stern voice.

Gil nudged me in the ribs. "You like Vera?"

Vera was sitting by herself on a bench. It dawned on me that Gil had intended her as my date.

"Gil, I got a girlfriend, and Vera is much too young for me."

"You don't like her?" He looked hurt. "You don't understand. Brazilians don't look at womens from here up," he said, drawing his finger across his neck.

"Get out of here." I went over and asked Vera to dance. It took a lot of persuading. She clearly felt as idiotic as I did over the setup. Mercifully, our group was soon sucked into the crowd. Women shimmied on chairs and tables, couples were grinding as smoke poured out of a machine, hit the colored lights, and shrouded the room with a garish mist.

I told myself I should get out more. I'd forgotten how fun it was to be a drunk, dancing fool.

There was a break in the music. "Wow, that's great, an old guy like you, dancing, Greg. You don't see that very often," said Fabio.

"Thanks, Fabio."

Gil chimed in, "Yeah! Greg! Bring back the nineties!" and he imitated my arm motions.

Rona came to my rescue. "These kids think they know how to dance. We'll show them how to dance," she said. And off she spun me into the smoke.

Around two-thirty, Eddy showed up from his new, temporary job as a dishwasher in a restaurant, where he earned $250 a week and got no benefits for working eleven hours a day. His coworkers were all undocumented Ecuadorians, the newest underclass of the underclass in the city. Willing to work for less than anyone else, they were pushing out other immigrants from the lowest-paying jobs. Eddy was smaller and skinnier than I expected. He seemed so vulnerable in his little green-and-yellow soccer jersey. Gil and I hung out with him at one of the bars, and I heard his story.

He was a farm boy from Minas, the state to the west of Rio. His mother was only thirteen when she had him, and his father had never been in the picture—Eddy bristled when I asked about him. His mother moved to the U.S. and remarried when Eddy was ten, leaving him to live with grandparents. From that time, he had to quit school and work at hard jobs, twelve hours a day—construction, stringing barbed wire, heavy-duty cleaning—for $2.50 a day. He shook his head sadly as he remembered his childhood. "I worked too hard, too hard," he said. "My mother was poor. My father was poor. My grandmother, poor. My grandfather, poor."

Eddy moved to the U.S. when he was sixteen, but his stepfather wanted no part of him, so he had to support himself from the first day in this strange, new country. As a janitor at Medved, Morningstar, he had sent a good chunk of his salary home to his grandmother, the one person who had cared for him.

"Eddy, I hope I can help you get your job back," I said. I was pretty toasted at this point, on the verge of getting maudlin.

"Thank you so, so, so much, Mr. Waggoner," he said.

"But, listen, guys, don't get your hopes up too high, okay? This is going to be tricky."

"We know," said Gil, but the look on Eddy's face said the opposite.

TWENTY-THREE

Greg

THE NEXT DAY I had lunch with Harry, a retired law-enforce-ment guy who keeps ties to the SEC and the state attorney general's office. When I was at the newspaper, I often talked with him on back-ground. In his late sixties, Harry is a straight arrow. He once told me that the big guys on Wall Street got away with highway robbery all the time, and it gave him ulcers he could never prove it.

Harry insisted on meeting at the back of a dark, Garment District restaurant, Ludwig's. As if it wasn't odd enough that a Conservative Jew like Harry would want to go to a German restaurant, he ordered fried shrimp and a whiskey sour, so WASPy a drink that even WASPs don't drink it anymore.

"Harry, are shrimp kosher?"

"I was going to suggest the Carnegie Deli, but they told me they'd have to sprinkle kosher salt on you before they let you in the door."

I am constantly persecuted by ethnic types. Annie's mother used to look at my pallid skin and ask if my health was okay.

I don't usually drink at lunch but I ordered a martini, to keep Harry company, and a schnitzel. As soon as the food came, I told him what was up: "I'm reasonably sure that a guy at a prominent New York firm is trading on inside information, and I got hold of this document I need your help in figuring out. But, the deal is: if your old bosses decide to start an investigation, you give me an exclusive on it—after the guy's indicted, of course."

Harry carefully picked the tails off his shrimp while he let the idea marinate. "We don't do deals with journalists," he said cautiously. "But maybe we could work something out—as long as our finger-prints were nowhere on your story."

"That's doable."

"What do you have?"

"A janitor caught the trader on his cell phone in a supply closet in the bathroom. The next day the trader got the janitor fired."

"Did the janitor remember any of the conversation?"

"No, unfortunately."

"Well . . ."

"But, I did a background check and turned up some unbelievable stuff on the trader. Right out of high school he was involved in form-ing a Panamanian shell corporation for a woman who wanted to hide money from her kids and leave it to him. He forged his mother's name on a bank document. And he tried to sell stock being used as collateral by getting duplicate certificates. This was all before he reached the legal drinking age!"

"I'm impressed."

"Here's the clincher," I said, pulling Rona's paper from my pocket. "The guy accidentally mixed this in with his expense-account receipts. It's a note, I think, from a friend he's using in Switzerland to execute his illegal trades."

"May I see it?"

I hesitated for a moment. The note revealed Steed's name, but at this point, I had nothing to lose, and I handed it over. "I read German," I said, "but I can't really translate the motto. I couldn't find the words in a German dictionary. I'm thinking they're archaic or some regional Swiss dialect."

"It's not German, it's *Letzebuergesch*," Harry said, examining the paper. "It means something like 'Loyalty, Security, Advantage.'"

"*Letzebuergesch*?"

"The official language of Luxembourg. I have to admit, you're probably on to something here. I'm guessing this is a note from an account manager at a bank in Luxembourg."

"Wouldn't that be a typed letter?"

"The IRS does spot checks on correspondence coming from certain countries, but they're not allowed to check handwritten correspondence, so some foreign banks will address and write your correspondence by hand."

"Why Luxembourg and not Switzerland?"

"Since the mid-eighties we've had a lot of success getting Swiss banks to be more transparent, mostly by threatening to fine their branches here. No fishing trips, but if we go to them with convincing evidence of criminal activity, we'll usually end up with the information we want. They also monitor their customers pretty closely now. You can still use a Swiss account for tax evasion, but if they notice a pattern of suspicious-looking profits in your trading account, they're going to start asking questions, and they'll close you down if you don't have good answers. Luxembourg, on the other hand, has been going in the opposite direction. They saw an opportunity when we started to crack down on the Swiss, and since their banks have a lot less exposure here, we can't put much pressure on them."

"Everything you're telling me fits in with my theory about this guy."

"Even if it does, nobody in Luxembourg is going to be giving us the details."

"What are you saying?"

"I'm saying that as suspicious as all this is, it's not enough for us to open an investigation."

I was dumbstruck. "Seriously?"

"Look, we have our hands full going after outright fraud. Less than ten percent of our resources go to insider trading. In the eighties we got tough for a while and had some successes with Dennis Levine and a few others, but you know *why* we got tough?"

I shrugged.

"Because John Shad, the SEC chairman back then, got pissed off when *Business Week* published an article that said basically everybody was doing inside trades and he knew it. Even then, nailing Levine was pure luck—because some guy in Merrill Lynch's Caracas office wrote an anonymous letter about their brokers piggybacking on a New York broker who was piggybacking on Levine's trades. Until then we had no idea. We were inviting Levine to be on ethics panels in Washington. I'm serious."

"But, I thought your enforcement capabilities had made some kind of quantum leap with computerized monitoring . . ."

"We get better, they get better. Especially with these new hedge funds and private-equity firms, we have no idea what's going on. If you're cautious at all, we're not going to catch you. You'd have to be pathetic amateurs, like Bacanovic and Martha Stewart. The big Wall Street guys, forget about it. Most of them don't even think insider trading is a crime. In some countries, it isn't."

We ordered dessert—pecan pie for him, key lime for me— and coffee. "This is all very depressing," I said. "Basically, we know my guy is breaking the law, and there's nothing we can do about it."

"That's not what I said. What you have to do is give this note to his firm's compliance department. They'll have access to him and his trading record without court orders, and they'll have a lot more leverage over him than we would at this point—simply having a trading account outside the company, let alone one in Luxembourg, is probably enough to get him fired. If they find what you think they will, they'll come to us."

"That sounds like letting the fox investigate the chicken-coop massacre."

"Not really. The big firms are always figuring out new ways to push the envelope, but they don't tolerate rogue traders. Listen, though, if they do turn up something and come to us, I won't forget you."

"But, that could take a while, right?"

"These investigations are never easy."

The martini and the coffee were sloshing around in my stomach like carbolic acid. This story was not moving as fast as I needed. If I wanted to save my skin at *Glossy*, I'd have to look for something else and put this article on the back burner. I was letting down Gil and Eddy, though. As a reporter, you're not supposed to get emotionally involved with your sources, but in this case it was hard not to.

TWENTY-FOUR

Greg

O N E O F T H E traders got the bright idea of inviting Gil to join the Medved, Morningstar soccer team, although when they introduced him to opposing teams they said he was an intern, not a shoeshine guy. Playing with the traders gave Gil props, big time, and he kept repeating what the team captain said after auditioning him: "You play like butter." Since the players split the rental cost of an indoor field at a gymnasium complex, Gil had to scrape together $500 for his share.

From the first game Gil played in, he was the ringer, and he wanted me to come watch, supposedly so I could see the traders firsthand, but I think he really just wanted me to see him play. I arrived early and hid in the empty balcony of the bleachers. I felt more like a father than a spy. The traders started to show up, chatting and joking as they got into their expensive soccer shoes and ratty athletic clothes left over from college days. There were two young guys who looked Latin, but most of them were white guys in the thirty-to-forty-five range, who could have walked out of a Cheever story. Bones were creaking as they stretched and warmed up. Finally, Gil arrived in a bright green-and-yellow jersey with Ronaldinho's name on the back. He spotted me in the balcony and nodded coolly in recognition. Once the match started, Gil and one of the Latin guys dominated, although a few of the old white guys were surprisingly good. Gil was the smallest player by a long shot. He zipped up and down the field, and scooted between and practically under the big guys. His control of the ball was so amazing that he seemed to wrap his foot around it. I noticed he passed more than did the traders, who tended to grandstand and make showy, hail-Mary shots doomed to failure.

Gil kept his head down most of the time, but no matter where he passed, a teammate would always be there. When he jumped to go after the ball, his limbs would shoot off in every direction, dissolving into a jumbled blur, a cubist painting, and then, miraculously, in midair, he'd coalesce with the ball. He scored three goals, including the game-winning one, and his teammates were high-fiving him and slapping him on the back.

I loitered outdoors while he changed, and we met, like two CIA agents, in the dark alley behind the gym. Flushed with exertion and excitement, he went for beers with me, and we dissected the match and his performance.

Then I gave him the bad news. "Gil, I think this article is going to take a little longer than I thought."

"Oh, yeah?"

"Unfortunately. Maybe Eddy should try to get a better job than the dishwashing gig for the time being, at least until I get this thing nailed down."

"I don't think he can. His boss won't give him a reference."

"I'm sorry. These things always take longer than you think. In the meantime, what I need you to do is give this piece of paper, the one Rona found, to the compliance department at Medved, Morningstar."

TWENTY-FIVE

Gil

BUT I DON'T know what is the compliance department, so I will take the paper to Mr. Billy. Mr. Greg, he disappoint me so much, man. He put it that he could help. I thought he could help. Maybe he was just saying to make me feel better.

I go there, and Mr. Billy's like, Gil, let me ask you a question? When you planning to go back to school? I'm like, Sir, it's kind of hard for me right now. I'm helping my mom pay the bills at my house and my daddy's not working. Because people think I pay no bills. Mr. Billy is like, So you not going to college? Let me tell you a story about my cousin that he was a orphan. And I'm thinking, Can't you believe it, that this guy is going to tell me this story for another time. And he's like, My cousin went to college, like eight years for college, and he studied hard, and he went to a company in another state, and became the CEO, whatever. At the age of eighty-three, he had 3 billion dollars. And I'm like, What the fuck does that thing has to do with me?

He's like, If you want to have a good life, if you want this womens to like you, you got to go out there, go back to school, and make money. You got to be able to take a nice lady to a nice restaurant. You know, a girl you probably work with, or a client, or whatever beautiful peoples you went to school with and stuffs.

I'm like, Mr. Billy, all right, I got your point, but I got something to tell you that is very important. And he's like, What?

I'm like, Well, sir, I never came here to ask you for nothing. I just wanted to ask you one question. My cousin Eddy that cleans the bathrooms on nine and ten just got fired, and this might sound really strange to you. I know you don't have time to listen to this, but if you give me just one minute, I can explain to you. I don't know how can you help me out, but I wish you could save him up or give him a different job. I know that a lot of peoples ask you for this, but I don't think this would be that hard for you. You don't even have to fire the person that report him.

Mr. Billy is like, Report? For what? Who reported him?

I'm like, Mr. Steed. Jeff Steed, I think he be the person.

Mr. Billy's like, Oh, yeah, my wife knows that guy. But what had your cousin done?

I tell Mr. Billy that Eddy caught Steed using his cell in the little closet.

Mr. Billy is like, Gil, I'm going to look into this. My employees, some of them think they can do anything because they make the money, but that is not the case.

I'm like, All right, sir. And just one more thing—this paper that I had found it.

Mr. Billy's like, What's this?

I don't know, sir, but I wanted to give it you.

Where did you get it?

I found it on the floor in the bathroom.

And Mr. Billy is very interesting in it. He's like, We going to see about this, Gil.

TWENTY-SIX
Greg

I GOT A call from Ursula Uze, the number two at *Glossy*. She handled the business side of the magazine, including writers' contracts. Ed had no stomach for being a disciplinarian, so that job fell to her, as well.

"Greg," she said in her slight German accent. "I vould love it if you'd stop by for a chat in my office tomorrow afternoon. You know, your contract is up in a month."

Her tone was crisp. Too crisp.

Ursula was forty-something, with the body of a twenty-five-year-old—rail-thin and taut, with gorgeous, long legs and perfect breasts. The younger guys in the office, the editorial assistants, fantasized about being disciplined by her. Some of them misbehaved on purpose just to get called down to her office—to be chastised, as they put it. One twenty-three-year-old preppy got drunk at a *Glossy* party and described to me a detailed scenario that featured Ursula as the head-mistress of his private school and a hairbrush.

Ursula wore beautiful clothes that emphasized her figure but not in any obvious way. For our meeting, she was dressed in funeral black. My funeral. "Greg, how are you?" she asked in a soothing, musical voice, perfect for such inducements as "Don't worry, it's not going to hurt very much," or "It vill all be over with very quickly. Just don't scream, *bitte*."

She sat down behind her desk and leaned forward sympatheti-cally. All I could think of was how good blondes looked in black.

"Great. How about you?"

She smiled, but there was no warmth in it. "I've asked you here today because I wanted to see you before I talked to Ed about renewing your contract. How is it all going?"

"Great," I said again, like an idiot.

"Oh, I'm *so* happy to hear it. Because I was worrying a lot about you lately: are you happy here?"

"Yes, of course I am."

"Oh, good, good, because some of the other writers have told me they think you are not so happy."

"That's ridiculous. I'm very happy here. Unreasonably happy, you might even say."

"Oh, lovely. But, frankly, I am still a little worried. I was checking your numbers, and I see that you are two stories behind on your contract."

"Well . . . uh . . ."

"And I couldn't help noticing that two of your last four stories didn't run."

"Well . . . It has taken me a little longer than I'd hoped to get the hang of a *Glossy* story, as opposed to a newspaper story."

"Yes, yes, the two are *so* very different. But, also—I don't know if you were aware of this—we had a terrible time with Ms. A-list after your cover story. It seems you confused Ms. A-list's mother with her stepmother, whom she hates. She accused us of trying to dishonor her real mother, and she says she will never appear in our magazine again."

"Why didn't the fact-checkers catch that?"

"Well, it seems they did, but they tell me you insisted you were right, and so they let you go with it."

Did I really do that?

"Then there was your Media Corporation story. That was rather an embarrassment for us."

A bad fuckup on my part, I admit. The CEO had granted me exclusive access, wining and dining me and flying me on his private jet while he outlined his brilliant new strategy for the future, as opposed to his not so brilliant strategy for the past, which had almost bankrupted the company. Unfortunately, everyone else in the world, more or less, knew he was about to be fired, but somehow I'd allowed myself to be snowed, and I was on such a tight deadline that I didn't bother to talk to the doubters. *Glossy* ran my glowing piece about his radiant future the month before he was fired.

"You see," Ursula continued, "I wish I would have a stronger case when I go in to see Ed about you."

That was a nice way of putting it.

"I understand," I said. "But, you and Ed have to know that this has been a very hard transition for me, coming here, but I'm finally getting the hang of it. I apologize for whatever mistakes I've made."

"No need to apologize, I'm sure. But maybe we should be asking ourselves, are you missing other opportunities by staying here? You know, *Glossy* is not right for everybody."

I had to admit that was good: me leaving was an opportunity.

"Ursula, I know I've been a little slow off the starting block, but I'm working on a huge story right now, one that will take the roof off this magazine," I said, improvising.

"Oh, really?"

"I haven't told Ed about it yet . . ."

Ursula arched a lovely reddish-blond eyebrow. "Really?"

". . . but I'm on the verge of nailing it!"

"Do you think it's wise to wait to tell Ed?"

"You'll have to just trust me on this. It'll be worth it. You'll see. We're talking major front-page headlines here, the magazine blowing out of the newsstands. Just give me three weeks, and let's postpone any discussion about my contract until after New Year's."

"That would be unusual, but Ed can decide. Why don't you tell him about the story, though."

"I will. I promise." Undoubtedly, she would beat me to it. But she didn't know what it was about.

So, that was it. They were sending me down to the minors, the magazine equivalent of double-A in Greensboro. I wasn't going without a fight. How many days did I have left until Christmas?

TODAY, PETE'S JOKING about his own suit. He's like, Gil, you know what kind fabrics this suit made? Bird cloth. I'm like, Are you serious, Pete? He goes, Yeah, it's cheap, cheap. Man, he was cracking me up.

There's a guy that sit right next to Pete. Pete wears Florsheim, and this other guy had a pair of Prada. Florsheim, they kind of comfortable, kind of casual, but they look cheap. They *do* look cheap. So, Pete wanted a shine, and the guy next to him wanted, too, but the guy next to him was wearing the Pradas. I was like, Wow, man, you got some great shoes here. And Pete was trying to put the guy down. He was like, This shoes is not made for work. Because some of them there look at Prada, and they like, Wow, you want attention? It's too expensive. That's what Prada means to them.

Pete's like, Oh, this shoes is not made for work, this and that. The other guy was quiet, because he doesn't want to talk about his Prada. I went to Pete and was like, Damn, Pete, I think if he sell his shoes, he can get three pairs of yours. Pete was like, Nah, you're wrong Gil, you're wrong.

They don't like that when you put them down. Pete was like, I bet you my shoes are expensiver than his. I was like, Aw, all right. You talking to the guy that knows about shoes. Pete goes like, Yeah, but you don't know how much I pay. I was like, All right, cool.

I kind of felt bad, so I was like, Aw, Pete, you got nice shoes, I was just kidding with you, this and that. When I brought the shoes back, Pete was kind of busy on the phone, so I went to the other guy. I was like, Man, sometimes I got to be fake. I love Prada. Yo, I love your shoes. If I had the money. I never had owned a pair of Prada, but if I had money that would be the shoes I would get: Gucci, Prada, Ferragamo.

I was shining Mr. John's shoes when his wife call him. He was like, Damn. He was talking to her about the kids. She was supposed to buy stuffs for them, but she didn't do, and when he hung up, he was like, Aghh. Gil, my wife costs me a lot. She stays home in bed. She never do nothing. When I show him a picture of a girl, he always like, Gil, they hot. You got to hook me up with one of this girls.

He was like, Yo, Gil, I can't understand this girls I meet. Whenever I go to places, I try and talk to this girls, they always want money. He's like, Gil, let me tell you something. You go to a bar, you sit on a bar, you trying to chitchat with the girls, make them laugh. You buy them two drinks. And you just go, Let's go, I got a room. That's what he told me. He might be fucking around. I know they fuck around with me sometime. He's like, After a half hour, you be like, Let's go. If she say no, you go, Yup, next. I was cracking up when he said that, man.

I go see Mr. Jim and Mr. Tim. Jim wanted to get a Camry. He was trying to get the Camry on the Internet. And then he got it for $12,000 and change, 2001. He was going to buy that car, 36,000 miles. I was like, Jim, you buying a girl's car. He was like, Aw, Gil.

I tease him. I was like, Yo, Tim, your boy over here wants to get a girl's car. What is this? He is going to get this car for his girlfriend? And Tim start making fun of Jim. He's like, He doesn't have no girl-friend. He's like, I'm starting to wonder about this guy. And, can you believe it? Jim change his mind. Now he will get an Acura Integra. Really nice car. I was surprised that he change his mind because of me.

Tim and Jim, today they throwing a football on the trade floor, a little football. The other day Jim shooting a little plastic gun, one that he buys in Toys"R"Us. And they have plastic balls in there. He and Tim is shooting it on the trading floor at each other. They like little kids. I think most of them do to get attention from other people. But they don't even see how stupid they could be.

Then Natalia calls, and I tell her to come there to my job. Everybody was just staring, really nice. Some guys were like, Wow, she's beautiful. They like, Oh, you going to take care of her, this and that. The black guys loved her. She got a big ass. She's kind of light-skinned. She's got a beautiful face. I think she's a beautiful girl.

But the white guys was like, Gil, don't marry her. That will be the biggest mistake of your life. Because if you get married, and your wife ever caught you cheating, if she wants to get a divorce and she got proofs, she is capable to get 70 percent of what you make, and you only get 30 percent. They tell me how much money divorce costs. Most of this guys at my job, they would never get divorced, because if they do, they would lose everything that they making. We're talking big money.

They be like, Hey, Gil, you don't want to just look at just one womans. You're only twenty-three, man. You got a lot of things ahead of you to do. They not like brainwash me, but they kind of open up my mind.

We go see Mr. Jared, and I'm telling him that Natalia got a job babysitting for this Colombian woman in New Rochelle. Natalia take care of four kids, and the kids weren't raised here, so they have different manners. If you say something, they'll curse you back, and you can't do nothing with those kids. For Natalia, it is miserable. It's $300 a week. She working her ass off every day, from eight until eight or nine at night. Sometime the lady tells that she is going to come home at one time, and then she comes three hours later. It's fucked up.

Mr. Jared was going that he pay the lady who takes care of his kid $600 from nine to five. And he even pay the fares. Six hundred a week from nine to five. That's perfect. One kid, a little, tiny baby.

Then Mrs. Alice comes to the row and is saying her babysitter quit, and she is asking, Do you know any nice girls for this job? I'm like, Yeah, Natalia, my girlfriend. This is her. And Alice is like, Hi, are you experience? And Natalia's like, Yeah, I work for a lady in New Rochelle until today. So Alice says, Well, come to my place and you can meet my husband and my kids.

TWENTY-EIGHT

Greg

THEN TWO THINGS happened: the story moved, and I caught a lucky break.

"What did you say the name of your guy at Medved, Morningstar was?" Annie asked, calling from her office.

"Aguilar Benicio."

"No, not the shoeshine boy. The other guy. The trader."

"Jeff Steed."

"Yeah, I thought so. There's an item about him in this newsletter for arts administration professionals I get. He's resigning from the boards of Big City Modern Dance and Save Rome, because of, quote-unquote, 'his hectic personal life.'"

"Wow. Sounds like a bullshit reason. What do you think really happened?"

"Maybe, they found out about his insider trading and asked him to leave. They wouldn't want to be associated with that. Imagine the newspaper stories: 'Jeff Steed, a trader at Medved, Morningstar and a member of the Save Rome board, was indicted today.' That doesn't look good."

"How can I get the real story?"

"I know somebody who works in the office at Save Rome, but they might not even know. You'd really have to get to somebody on one of those boards, and they're not going to be too eager to talk about it to a *Glossy* reporter. There might even have been some kind of legal settlement prohibiting them from talking."

"You think you could get to anybody informally?"

"I'd have to look at the board lists. But isn't Dede Fulton one of your fixers?"

Fixers are people employed by *Glossy* for the purpose of passing on gossip and hooking up the writers to sources in various spheres of influence. We have a movie director's daughter who helps with Hollywood, the husband of a famous designer for fashion, a former White House staffer for the Republican Party, and so on. Most of the fixers are no help whatsoever. Ed says he isn't sure if some of them are even still alive. But Dede, a stunning blonde of a certain age, is the exception, a crackerjack with her portfolio of New York society.

"Why would she know about it?"

"Her mother is Nan Bigelow, married to Bill Bigelow, the head of Medved, Morningstar. I believe Nan is also on the board of Big City Modern Dance."

"Dede is Bill Bigelow's daughter?" I recalled when I'd interviewed him he told me he had only one son.

"No, Dede is Nan's daughter from a first marriage."

"Oh, my God. Fortune smiles. Isaac told me that Nan is Jeff Steed's protector. She got him his job at the firm."

I googled Nan and found that *W* had done a profile of her. Annie was right. Nan was on the Big City Modern Dance board, according to the article that recounted her life: she was formerly Nan Butney, a nurse from Houston, where she married and divorced husband #1, a wildcatter whose wells failed to gush. She met Bigelow in Connecticut while she was tending the first Mrs. Bigelow during her final illness. According to the gossip at *Glossy*, people still snickered to imply that Nan had nursed her last patient into an early grave. But Nan was evidently well liked in society—a high-spirited dame who made the unavoidable encounters with her stuffed-shirt husband more bearable.

"Sure, why not. She'll *love* you," said Dede, when I asked her to set me up with her mother. "I'll take you to lunch with her at Jock's on Thursday. But, I won't tell her why. It'll be easier to get her to be indiscreet once we get a few glasses of wine in her. If we tell her what's up beforehand, she'll call the other board members, and they'll tell her not to talk."

If they don't know you, it's impossible to get a reservation at Jock's, more a club for society ladies who lunch than a restaurant. When I showed up a little early on my own, Jock glared at me as if I were a pus-oozing leper applying for a job as a sous-chef in the kitchen. "Do you have a reservation?" he demanded in a voice that implied I couldn't possibly. I explained I was with Mrs. Bigelow, causing his granite façade to dissolve into fluttering obsequiousness. He led the way to "her table," the one with the best view of the door and vice versa. Dede and Nan arrived ten minutes later, both heavily armored in couture and makeup. Nan couldn't have been more excited to meet me, and she mugged and batted her lashes shamelessly.

As we checked out the menu (Cobb salad, popovers, a lot of soft, white, and pink things with cream and cheese sauces), the banquettes filled up with ladies, all variations on a theme. Each time a new one appeared, there were squeals of recognition and bad French. Nan, I noticed, did not make eye contact with any of them. No way was she going to let them horn in on her new discovery. As a result, they were wild with curiosity and made no attempt to disguise it. I could hear them twittering behind my back and across the way: "I think I met him at Carry's," "They're getting younger and younger," "That must be the NYU professor. She took his course on Renoir."

Even though Nan never looked up, she supplied a running commentary: "She's fucking her fitness trainer," "The daughter of so-and-so, who's in prison for price-fixing," "She's the only person in the city who doesn't know her husband took a black male prostitute to opening night at the Met. And you'll never guess what the opera was. Can you? No? Well, let's just say it's Tchaikovsky's *second* most popular opera. I am *not* kidding."

After the food came, I was trying to figure out how to steer the conversation around to Jeff Steed, but Dede beat me to it: "Mother, how is the new season at Big City shaping up? Greg, did you know

Mother was the head of the board of the Big City Modern Dance Company?"

"*Really,*" I said. "A seminal company." Whatever that meant.

"You know," Nan said modestly, "I used to be a modern dancer myself. With Martha Graham." She was summoning the ghost of that long-ago, lithe, young girl for me to admire.

"I'm not surprised. You obviously have a dancer's body." I should have been sent to the electric chair for that one, but Nan was beaming, so what was the harm? "What does being head of the board involve?"

Dede was making sure to keep her mother's wineglass filled.

"Oh, fund-raising, mostly. And checking to see they don't spend more money than they have. But I get involved with some of the creative aspects—scheduling and casting. Would you be interested in helping us with a little volunteer work, Mr. Waggoner? I'm sure we'd be honored to have you write a short feuilleton or two for our program."

"Just say the word. You know, I just noticed recently that something peculiar happened on your board . . ."

At that moment, an old dragon sitting opposite couldn't stand it anymore and charged our table. "Nan, were you in Venice for the Biennale? I haven't seen you forever." I could have killed her for wrecking my painstaking setup.

Nan wasn't any happier. Her eyes narrowed into pinpricks of hate, but she knew when she was beaten. "Hello, Arlene," she said wearily. "You know my daughter Dede, and this is her friend Greg Waggoner."

"Didn't we meet last summer at Carry Foster's barbecue in Southampton?" the dragon asked, fiercely inspecting every inch of me.

"Uh, that wasn't me, I'm afraid."

"Greg Waggoner is a writer for *Glossy* magazine," Dede explained.

"Oh God, my *favorite* magazine," said the dragon. "I read every issue cover to cover. The ads are *outstanding.*"

"Thank you," I said, waiting for the usual questions about what I did there.

"What do you do there?"

"I'm one of the writers," I mumbled, trying to indicate I had no interest in talking about it. But then, to my surprise, the dragon lost all interest in me and turned to Nan.

"Nan, I've been dying to ask you. What in God's name happened to that nice young man you always used to bring here? That Mr. Steel, the one you got to join the board of Big City Dance?"

I couldn't believe my ears!

"What do you mean, 'What happened?' Nothing happened," snapped Nan.

"But I saw he quit your board and Save Rome's, as well."

"He had personal commitments," said Nan firmly.

"Come on. That's *all* there was to it?" The dragon was toying with her prey. "But there is talk, you know."

"No, I didn't know."

"There's a story that he got you people into some bad investments."

"Well, it's just that, Arlene: a story. Now, you'll really have to excuse us. Mr. Waggoner and I are talking business."

"Oh, yes, of course, darling. Sorry. Sorry," said the dragon, withdrawing in triumph. She didn't get three feet from our table before making a general announcement, *"C'est un ecrivain du journal Lustre."*

"Mother, what did happen to Mr. Steed? He seemed so nice," asked Dede.

"I'm not allowed to talk about it," said Nan, depressed. The wine—everything—had suddenly turned on her.

"But, you can tell *us*," said Dede.

"No, I really can't . . . Okay, maybe I can. But not a word to anyone," said Nan. "Especially *you*, Mr. Waggoner." She gave me a stern but flirtatious look.

"You see, Jeff—he works for my husband—gave us a lot of money, but with a string attached: we had to invest it in a hedge fund called Persimmons, run by a friend of his. He was very upfront about it, but it still sounded fishy to us. We had our lawyers check into it, though, and they found it's unusual but perfectly legal, especially as Persimmons wasn't charging us any fees for handling the money. So, we did it, and suddenly, that part of our endowment is getting 30, 40 percent returns while the rest is getting 6 percent. The board had an orgasm"—she locked eyes with me—"and put a good chunk of the rest of our endowment into Persimmons. We were making money hand over fist. Our financial worries were over. Jeff is a genius. Our savior. They dedicated the annual school recital to him. They're going to name our new theater after him.

"And then, the fund sank like a stone. In one month it was down 58 percent! Jeff explained it to me, but I don't really understand, something about one position Persimmons took didn't cover some other position because something happened they didn't anticipate. The board flipped out, withdrew all our money—which was still more than we'd started out with, I'd like to point out—and kicked Jeff off the board. I hear the same thing happened to him at Save Rome."

"My God, what a mess," said Dede.

"And the worst part," said Nan, "was they were blaming me for introducing Jeff to the company. How do you like that? I offered to resign, and that shut them up, I can tell you. When they voted to invest all our money in Persimmons I told them not to put all our eggs in one basket. Even I know that hedge funds are notoriously risky. My husband won't have anything to do with them with his own money. By then, I'd started to distance myself a bit from our Mr. Steed, anyway."

"How come?" I asked.

"Things were never the same since I had him to dinner with the Greenwoods and the Morrises, and he brought that Russian girl."

"Which Russian girl?" asked Dede.

"The one that was sixteen, at the most, and getting paid by the hour. I mean, her skirt was half the size of an Hermès scarf. And she barely spoke a word of English, so you can imagine what *that* was like. Especially as Harry Greenwood spent the entire evening trying to communicate with her in sign language. I don't think Susan will ever forgive me. Especially the part about how Russian girls are willing 'to defend the motherland with their breasts,' or some such nonsense."

"How did you meet Steed?" I asked.

"He was a protégé of my sister's, and he was very good to her when she was dying. One of her last requests was that I should help him out, and I must say I was quite charmed by him all on my own. I recommended him to my husband for a job."

"At Medved, Morningstar?"

"Yes. And Jeff is quite a star there, they tell me."

Suddenly Jock materialized with chocolate soufflés.

"Oh, my God, Jock, I can't eat that. I'll turn into a blimp. But, thank you," said Dede. "Mother, I've really got to get going."

"That's all right, dear," said Nan, licking her chops, at me or the soufflé, I couldn't decide which. "Mr. Waggoner and I will wallow in all this chocolate, won't we, Mr. Waggoner?"

TWENTY-NINE

WE GO IN the car with Mrs. Alice to Greenwich, Connecticut. We drive on the highway that is dark and it's nothing but trees. Trees, trees, trees, trees. On the sides there's deers, the little ones. I'm freaking out. If it's in the beach, it's different. I can be in the beach by myself, but I just couldn't be in a place with a whole bunch of trees. A place, one house here, another house there, it makes me wonder, Yo, doesn't nobody comes around here and fucking try to steal? I don't know—this is my mentality that I have. I live in my house, and I know I have neighbors. I scream, I have fifty thousand people that is going to be capable to hear me.

I'm very, very careful to see where we going in case the car break down, so I know how to get out of that place. In Brazil the street gave me a lot of things that if I grew up here, I wouldn't know. Like how to be street-smart when you walking. It's not that I owe people money, but I always like to know where I am and where I'm going. I'm the type of person that if you take me from here to whatever place, I'm always going to be talking to you, but observes where I'm at and what direction I'm going, what the name of the streets—I always got that in mind. Some people just go. Fabio, he goes. You call him up, Where you at, Fabio? He's like, I don't know. He gets to the place, but he doesn't know. I was never like that.

It's two hours, and we leave the highway, and we drive in all this little, tiny streets with no peoples, and I'm like, Where is all the peoples?

This is creepy, man. I'm looking over at Natalia, but she doesn't look at me. Mrs. Alice describing her the kids, how the other one win all this soccer match, and the little boy win all this chess prizes. And I'm thinking, I can't wait to see this kids. They probably little brats.

Then we hit the driveway and it's all this tiny, little crunchy rocks under the wheels, and I'm like, Damn, we so far out in West Bubble-fuck, the driveways don't be made with cement around this way.

You got to see Mrs. Alice's house—my God! It's HUGE. Like ten bedrooms. From the outside, it's crap, it's from the seventeenth century. It looks not nice, but old from outside. You know, like a castle, a little castle. Not stone, but kind of. Mrs. Alice say that she cannot touch the house from outside. She cannot change the model. In Greenwich it's like that. I don't know why. Because that's the way they made. But inside you able do anything.

I'm like, Whoa, I can't wait until I see the inside. We go there, but inside everything was old, too. Even the dogs. Like old-style dogs that you don't usually see it. You know, the really big, HUGE ones, and smart—not the black ones. There's a hallway with steps, and a room with all this couches. I think it's just for people to look on. Because I'm the type if I sit on your couch, I'm not going to put my feet on it with my shoes on. There was a HUGE chair that kind of look relaxing. You sit in that chair, it probably makes you feel like a king. The carpet was flowers and different colors. That cost them a lot of money that you invest in the carpet. A lot of money you throwing away. Because you got to clean it, and then it gets old and dirty.

The paintings, very old. One I would describe about someone that's lost in a mountain and trying to look for something, and there is a river over there. That's the only thing I see it. There is another that remind me of *Lord of the Rings*. Or Pamela Anderson, if you watch the porno tape that she and Tommy Lee fuck on the boat, and there's a lake and mountains. It's like that in that painting. If I owned that house I would get real pictures of Brazil and the most beautiful parts of the world.

Damn, in the kitchen this table they have to eat on was old. I don't know how much they pay, but it's the type of table that even if I see it in the garbage, I wouldn't take it. I know it's heavy too, because it's that old, woody kind. It matches with the carpet. There was a desk that would be like one of the ones that probably one of my grandparents usually used to sit to write letters. You know, back in the days that people used to use a bird feather to write, this is what it reminds me. The desk was not my style, because it was so old. I like the computer one, the brand-new one that peoples usually buys at IKEA for $150. Mrs. Alice's desk probably cost a lot more, but that's the way I see it.

Then the drawers. They remind me a lot of Brazil. We have drawers like that in Brazil. Old. Because some furniture we used to get from time to time was from grandparents. You don't have money to buy furniture the way they do here. It was really old furniture from someone that gave it to you. I'm like, Mrs. Alice, this drawers is from your grandparents? And she is like, Nah, they from Christie's in New York. Because it's from back in the day from George Washington. And she had to compete with all this other guys that wanted, and she ended up paying eighty-some thousand! Yeah, she told me that! Fuck, man, when I heard that, I just start laughing. Mrs. Alice is like, What's so funny? Natalia is like with her eyes, Shut the fuck up. I'm like, I don't know, it's just funny. You want to tell how much I would have paid for this drawers if anyone would sell it to me? I wouldn't pay no more than maybe fifty dollars at the most, if I really needed.

I don't like that old stuffs, because we live in the future. We don't live in the past. On *MTV Cribs* the basketball players always have everything brand-new, from the future. Hip-hop guys, the same thing. If I ever get a house, I will get a flat-screen TV, something I will be able to watch it. I'll get surround sound, because I want the music to be blast. And a bar. Not with that many liquors, only the liquors that I like it. I will get things that I will be able to bring all my good friends. When you get just the closest friends, you don't want to have anything HUGE, because you don't want to make the impression that you have a lot. Because then people going to be like, Wow, you have a lot. So what's next?

Natalia is like, Oh, Mrs. Alice, this so beautiful, and this and that . . . buhbuhbuhbuh. Like she wanted it. Like she would buy that stuffs in a million years. Trust me, she wouldn't.

Mrs. Alice's husband come in the kitchen. Big guy, six foot four. Bill. He shake my hand and ask me, What do you do for a living? And I tell him, I shine shoes, sir. He was like, Oh, that's really nice, you make a good amount doing that? I'm like, it's okay, sir. Some peoples are just, Oh, you shine shoes, and they look at you like you nobody. But he was like, Oh, you really do that? That's pretty good, though. You make good money? All right. Are you taking good care of her? He seemed like a pretty decent guy. And I was like, Yeah. Thanks, sir.

And the daughter Willa and the son Carter is in the kitchen. Willa's like nine, all this braces on her mouth. Mrs. Alice is like, Willa and Carter, this is Natalia. She might be coming to take care you kids. Willa just listen to the CD, she don't even take the phones out. The girl, she think she's a teenager—the lipstick, dressing like Britney Spears, wearing boots, tight jeans, and the top that show the stomach. But what's really weird: she almost bald! Like a Ronald McDonald's kid that got the cancer. I'm serious. Natalia is asking her questions, and Willa is saying like one word. Hi. Bye. Yes. No.

Carter's a normal boy, like fourteen or fifteen. He's like, Ma, I got to go meet up with my friends. She's like, No, you stay for dinner with Gil and Natalia. He's like, Fuck that, I'm going. She's like, Don't you be using that language, young man. You think Mrs. Alice tell him he can't go? Nah. You know what she do? She's like, Leave the credit card on the counter. I'm serious! That's what she say! Leave the credit card on the counter. This kid, fourteen, and he got his own credit card! So he leave it and slam the door.

We go to the little boy's room. Oliver. This kid's only seven. What kind of person is going to name a kid Oliver? You call a kid like that, the other kids going to beat him on the playground. That kid never going to have lunch money once in his life.

We go there, and I'm like, Whoa. I didn't say anything, but I'm thinking, Did you see the size of this kid's room? It's the size of my house, man. It was so HUGE, and the ceiling was all the way up there. And the big-screen TV, and the woody table that was so fucking heavy you couldn't lift it once. Brand-new computer. HUGE chess board. Chess, I never played that game. It's very complicated. I think it works only for smart motherfuckers. That's a genius right there.

This kid, Oliver, is with this thick glasses. He's reading this HUGEST book that I ever saw in my life. Natalia and me, we go hi to this kid. He seem like a nice kid. Quiet.

The baby girl is two, two and a half. She tiny, a little one that doesn't stop talking. This little girl doesn't stop. Talks, talks, talks. Like a machine. To herself. All the time. Her name's Jenny, but Mrs. Alice calls this little girl Lucifer, like the devil. Yeah, I'm serious! Her mom goes, Hey Lucifer, this is Gil and Natalia.

Lucifer! How can you call your kid something like that?

So, Natalia got the job for Mrs. Alice's kids. Six hundred dollars a week. She going to work Monday night to Saturday night. Stay for the week, then Saturday night she will come back to the city and has it free until Monday night. But when she's up there every night she will call me up.

THIRTY

Greg

"WE NEED TO talk about something important tonight," Annie said.

"What?"—even though I had a pretty good idea, because a week or so before Annie had told me she'd missed her period and was going to buy a pregnancy test.

"I don't really want to talk about it on the phone. I can probably get out of here by seven tonight, so I'll meet you at your place. We can order take-in."

Holy shit. I was going to be a father! Had the test results been negative, she would have told me so over the phone.

"Okay," I said, trying to sound cool, even though my heart was trying to claw its way out of my chest. "Take-in. Sure."

"I love you," Annie said significantly.

"Me, too."

For a long time after I hung up, I sat, staring at the phone, taking deep gulps of air. Annie was on the pill. They tell you it has a failure rate of .05 percent, but you don't believe it can ever happen to you. Even after it actually does.

Working was impossible. I needed to take a long walk and think. I willed my feet over to the park, where I took paths at random, staring at my shoes and adding up how much it cost to have a kid, a subject I'd heard my married friends talk about all too often.

Annie and I would have to move in together. A two-bedroom

apartment in Manhattan these days costs around a million dollars. A really nice two-bedroom with a view is a million and a half or more. With both of us working (that is, if I managed a miracle and kept my job), we would need to hire a full-time nanny: $30,000 a year, and that would not be for some fancy Irish nanny. Our kid would have a Jamaican accent. Nursery school, $14,000 a year, and private school after that, $30,000 a year, plus they expected you to make donations to the "capital fund," minimum $5,000 a year per kid. Then there were piano lessons, swimming lessons, gymnastics, summer camp. By the time the kid got to college, tuition would probably cost around $100,000 a year. It all added up to somewhere north of three million. By this time, my legs were shaking so hard, I had to sit down on a bench.

More deep breaths. I had to pull myself together. I thought about all the reasons why I loved Annie. She's the smartest person I know. She never gets depressed or down. She is a lawyer for the right reasons—because the law fascinates her. She keeps me on the straight and narrow. Unlike many intelligent, dynamic people, she actually listens, and doesn't talk unless she has something to say. She loves sex, and she has an amazing body. She thinks I'm the greatest guy in the world.

I had to be the strong one. Annie had enough fears and doubts of her own about having a kid. Other people managed to afford it, somehow. So would we. There never was a "good" time. We needed to get over it and get on with it. We would have a beautiful child together. It was what we both wanted. It was the start of a wonderful, new life together.

I would be more responsible, work harder.

I started focusing on the imminent realities: Who would this baby look like? Would I mind changing diapers? Would I get any sleep at night?

That helped.

I decided to make a celebratory dinner. I went to the seafood market and got oysters—Annie's favorite. She likes them raw, but I remembered hearing somewhere that pregnant women weren't supposed to eat raw fish or shellfish, so I would fry them. I bought a bottle of good champagne and some flowers for the table. Shopping, setting the table, making the food, and drinking quite a lot of wine while I was making the food made me giddy: I was going to be a great father! I was in command of the situation! I was going to make it work! I was an adult, a man, at last.

I heard Annie's key in the lock. I raced over to meet her and take her in my arms.

"I'm pregnant . . ." she said and burst out crying.

"I know, I know," I said. "It's going to be wonderful. We're going to have a beautiful child together."

"But my hormones . . ." She was alarmingly pale.

"What about them?"

"They're high."

"Is that bad?"

"Twins."

"Don't fuck with me."

"Or maybe triplets. They won't know for eight weeks."

The room started to spin. "Greg, oh my God," I heard Annie saying far away. "Are you all right? Should I call 911?"

THIRTY-ONE

Gil

THE MAIN SECURITY for Mr. Bigelow call me up, because that's the guy usually call me up when Mr. Billy wants a shine. Every time I go to that place I wish I could live there. If they be like, Hey, Gil, you want to come and just live here, sleep in one of these office, that would be my biggest dream.

Mr. Bigelow's office so HUGE, you got to be kind of sick to have it. Did you ever stop and thought about that? It has to be sick, because you can do anything, you fucking run the place. What is to be to run a place like that? You become your own little god, you walk around and people go, Wow! There, he's bigger than a movie star. People talks about it, they know that he has money. This is a guy that got his own private jet, the jet from the company, he eats for free, he wants to go to a strip bar, he could spend $20,000 in a night. If you can do that every other day, it would be like nothing.

That guy, he ask me every single time if I was going back to school. I can't say it, but I want to say, Look, I pay rent at my house. Fucking wake up! They think that you live that easy life, your parents pay for everything, you never pay no rent, you just study, because it's easier. You don't have nothing else to do than study.

The guard kind of escort me to Mr. Billy's office. I got to go through the first secretary and then, when I get there, Mr. Billy's on the phone, like always. I wait, and when he gets off I start shining his shoes.

He looks very sad and disturbed. He look right into me and say,

Gil, I got to tell you something. You got to keep a secret between me and you. I know you is one of the persons that I can trust in this company, because everything that I say in here, you never went outside and told peoples about it. So this is the thing. I been looking into this things you had told me and found Mr. Steed be doing stuffs that is not allowed.

Mr. Billy's like, I'm going to call Mr. Steed up, and I'm going to try to talk to him about this, and see if we can get a deal, like if he can leave the company, and I wouldn't do anything to him, just leave at that.

Mr. Billy, he wants me to stay there and see, because he wanted me to see what is the right and wrong of this business that he do. He's like, Big guys think that they can do whatever, but it's not like that. Gil, I know you a very honest person. You always here on time, you always do your job. You never complain about it. I wanted to show it you that honesty pays. But, most of this guys that make all the money, that's the only thing that they do. They always complain. They don't know that they having a position of being right and wrong. They always think that they Mr. Right.

He wanted to show it to me how bad things could get inside the company. Because the way that I see it, everyone's perfect in that place. They don't cheat. But he show me a totally different world that I never expected to see it.

Mr. Billy goes and have his secretary call up Mr. Jeff, and Mr. Jeff comes there five minutes later. I'm behind Mr. Billy's desk shining his shoes that Jeff doesn't see me. So, Mr. Billy starts telling him the situation.

He is like, I'm very, very disappointed that you had done some stuffs in the company that I had found out. Look, I kind of found out through some sources that I have in the company that you been doing a whole bunch of stuffs that is not allowed with this and this and that. So, I think that you no longer supposed to be in this company. The stuffs you be doing can get me fired, because I'm the main boss in here. And you can get the company in serious trouble. We all going to look bad. So, what is best for you to do is leave the company.

Look, you had made a lot of money for us. But meanwhile you had not been truthful. What I would like you to do is fire your own self.

And Mr. Jeff don't say nothing, he so shock.

And Mr. Billy is like, I hope that this experience had teached you what is right, and how to do better in your life, and you being more careful in your next job.

Then Jeff go fucking crazy, because he never expected that thing, and he doesn't want to fire his own self. He gets really pissed. He start getting red. He's not like screaming, because he know he cannot scream inside the office, because if the secretary hear any screams, she will call up the security right away. So he goes very quiet, Go fuck yourself, Bigelow. Fuck you, fuck you, fuck you.

I can't believe he's doing to Mr. Billy.

Then he goes, You know, I cannot get fired. You got to give me some money to leave the company. We can leave at that.

Then Mr. Billy get really mad, because he wanted this guy to leave on his own self. He is like, Look, I'll give you an hour to decide this.

Then Mr. Jeff look at Mr. Billy's eye, and he goes, Look, asshole. That's what he say it to Mr. Billy! I'm not lying! He's like, I know everything about you. Does St. Joe's ringing this bells in you? I know all about that and what you did it and this and that. I even know it which bank in Swiss that you be using and how many millions you stole it. Fuck you, fuck you, fuck you, you big steaming pile of shit. If you don't give me the money, we both going down.

When I heard that thing, I was freaking out! I was shining Mr. Billy's shoes, and I continue to the point that the things start getting really bad. Then I just stop. I never thought that I was going to hear those stuffs. I'm thinking, Holy shit, I'm not supposed to be in here.

Mr. Bigelow is fucking choking like it seems that he lost the air, when you breathing and something goes into your throat, and you choking. And Mr. Jeff is like, I want fifty millions, or I'm going to the feds. They already knows about what you be doing. You know they already been asking peoples. YOU got one hour, Mr. Bigelow. One hour to decide if you giving me the money or going to prison. I'm glad to be out of this shit-hole.

And Mr. Jeff, he just leave from there.

And I'm there behind the desk! I was almost crying, because Mr. Billy forgot all about me. Everybody forgot about me! And I'm there listening to these whole thing. When they start talking about those millions, the millions that Mr. Jeff wants, and the millions that Mr. Billy stole it, I was going, Holy shit, now I know things about both this two guys. *I'm fucked! I'm going to die!* They going to kill me, because it's all about the money. And if they kill me, nobody's going to notice! Because when you big like that, and you get a small guy like me that has no money at all, it doesn't make no difference. Not even the police would go after the incidents or try to see who I am.

Mr. Billy doesn't move for five minutes, and then he look down. He's like, Oh, Gil, you still there? I'm like, Yeah, I'm here, fixing some shoes. He's like, What did you hear? I'm like, Nothing, man, nothing. I was too busy concentrating shining the shoes here. Changing the laces. I'm listening my iPod. I didn't understand what you guys saying.

I finish the shoes, and Mr. Bigelow ended up giving me a hundred dollars! He's like, You a good boy, Gil. Keep that, son. Don't tell no-body about this. That guy, Mr. Jeff, he just crazy. Getting fired made him crazy. He doesn't know what he says. He just trying to defend hisself, saying anything that had come to his mind, making up all this stuffs.

I go like, I know, I know. Here's your shoes, Mr. Billy, and I walked out of his office.

But now I know all this thing!

PART TWO

HOW TO SHINE

THIRTY-TWO

WHEN I WAS younger, my daddy taught me the whole shoe-shine thing at the health club he used to work. I had that as a part-time job with him that I used to shine three or four pair of shoes, and he used to give me ten dollars for the day. To me that was fun. That wasn't like somebody was watching me. Nobody knew I was doing. I could lie to peoples.

The first time at the club my daddy was like, Sit here, and I'm going to teach you. The first thing is the rag. You take the rag, you know, the thing you blow your nose. He used to give me that, and he was like, Yo, here you go, you open it up, you fold it in half, not in the middle, but right on the little point you put your two fingers and make a little doll out of it. Then you twist the end around the back part of your hand, and grab with the other three fingers, so it's tight over the top of your two fingers, but not too tight or it'll hurt. You got to make your fingers feel comfortable. If it's too tight, you going to be breaking your fingers after five minutes. You got to have the end kind of loose. It took me a couple of hours. I seen people trying to do that for the whole day, get the rag right on your hand.

First thing I brush the shoes to get the dirt off. Then I'll get this thing that we call spot remover. It's like alcohol, to take off all the old polish. Then you get the rag and go in the polish with it. You got to know the color. It's a difference from oxblood to mahogany to cordo-van. You got to look at the shoes. There's a difference from tan to mid-brown to brown. Black is black. Blue—sometimes people don't know what's the blue shoes. They usually use the black polish to shine blue shoes, because they think just because it's dark, it's going to be black.

After that you get a little bit of polish with water on the rag. You never know how much polish. You got to feel it. It's not like you going to dig your finger into the polish can. You just got to get two and three touch, just a little bit, and then you throw a little water, and then you go around the shoes really slowly. It's like you polishing a car, you got to go in circles. Slowly. You got to feel the leather, because some leathers, when you do it real fast, it peels off.

Some guys think if you do it really fast, the job's going to get done in seconds. But they don't know. It's not like that. You got to feel the shoes. You can't just be there, do everything so fast. You got to work the whole shoes time by time. If you see that the shoes getting dry, you got to throw a little bit of water, then get more polish. Then you go all around the shoe, and the shine comes out. When the leather's too soft, it doesn't get as much shine. When it's kind of hard though, like Alden, Allen Edmonds, they get a really high shine, because they made of horse leather.

It depends on how you do your job. Some of this guys, they don't know, so they put a lot of polish, brush it, that's it. A lot of people shine shoes like that. Polish has to go in time. You can't put too much polish at once. You put a little bit, a little bit more, work on the shoes. If you put too much polish, you got to brush them up. Some people take their time and do it really good. Those guys that work in the building the way I do, they usually go like, You got to spend eight minutes on every pair of shoes.

If you put a really nice coat, you don't have to do five, six coats. Just one or two. You got to get one time really good, and then the other time you go really slowly to burn the polish on the shoes. That's where I really use the water, to burn the polish, like a mix. Going around and around and around. After that you look, you see it, the way the shoes look, and just put a little bit on the front.

Sometime you use not polish but crème. Crème is different than polish. Crème doesn't shine, it brings back the natural color of the leather. With crème we never use water. It treats better the leather, but that depends on which leather. Not every leather takes it. Horse leather won't take it. But very soft leather, I tell you, like Gucci shoes that has a very soft leather that's losing the color, it's kind of scraped-up white, you put the crème on that shoes, it's going to turn the shoes brand-new. Not shiny, but the way the shoes came from the store. A dull shine. If the person asks you put crème and then polish, it gives you a little bit more shine, but it ain't like putting straight-up polish. Because when you mix one to the other you never going to be as shiny, shiny.

This guy Roberto I used to work with at Yuri's, he used to look at the shoes that was really beat up and he's like, This piece-of-shit shoes. I'm going to fucking use crème on this. He goes to where the crèmes are, and he's like, Fuck it. He just don't care. He gets a little brush and go around real quick because that's a quick job. It gets the shoes to look kind of okay, because it gets the whole shoes. Like the polish, you don't usually get the whole shoes, but crème you usually get the whole shoes. Because when you polishing, you get the toes, but not the back, because it's hard to reach there with polish.

The white crème you use after you polish is different. They call it the delicate. They say that it treats the leather and usually gives you a better shine on the front, on the toes, makes it brighter. It does a little bit. It might do, but I don't see no difference. That's more to bullshit the client. It's just to show the customer, Oh, I'm here to show you that we doing a great job. Sometimes you do a fucked-up job, and you put that thing on, and you go with the towel.

With crème I usually brush them up, and that's it, sir. With polish you buff with a towel, but the towel got to be clean. You get the towel, put a little bit of water, put a little bit on the shoe, and go up and down, left and right. Not a lot of pressure. You got to go on the back and sides, too. You don't get the shine with the towel, you get the shine with shining and shining and shining the shoes. The towel is to clean it—like after you wax a car, you usually have to get a towel to wipe the extra polish off.

Sometimes right on the side it will be kind of scrapey. So you got to rub on the side. It's really hard though. The front and the back's going to be perfect. The side is the hardest. The sides are not straight or flat, so for you to get this part shiny, it's really hard.

My shoeshine box costs about a hundred dollars. Inside the kit we got to have two brushes, one for brown, and one for black shoes. But I usually use the brown brush for lighter shoes, and the black for cordovan-brown, dark brown, shoes like that. You got to have black polish, brown polish, blue polish, tan, neutral, mahogany, oxblood . . . You know, you got to have that whole nine yards. Then it comes the crème. Because a lot of people picky with the shoes, so they want you to use crème. Crème comes in the same colors—I got to have brown, dark brown, cognac, mid-brown, neutral, black, cordovan.

I got to have my towel, the thing that you usually buff them up with. This is how we do it: we go to the store and get a brand-new towel, and then we cut it in pieces, and then we throw them in the washing machine, wash them. That's the way I make it. A towel I usually use for a day. I have a spray bottle. I have two toothbrush. I usually use the toothbrush on the side of the shoes between the leather and the sole, right on the edge; sometimes the shoes get really dirty right there, so the only way we able to clean it is with the toothbrush, because the toothbrush penetrates on the area. Besides that I have the shoe dressing for the sole. It's a liquid in a bottle. That is not that important, but a lot of people want it, if you work in a store.

I look at the shoes, I can tell what kind of shoes they are. I know from Gucci to John Lobb. They usually make John Lobb in England, so they cost about $1,200 and up. You never heard about those?

Some shoes is expensive—I'm not going to mention the name—but going to last you for just a little while. I really don't like that. Fucking piece-of-shit $300 or $400 pair of shoes. The leather is messed up. I don't like the leather. There was this guy, he had a brown pair of shoes. After six month these shoes start peeling off, because the leather is so soft. When you rub them some, it starts peeling off. Same thing when you go to the beach and start rubbing your skin, and it starts peeling off, your whole skin. When I start shining those shoes, I was like, Oh, shit. I went back to the guy and gave it to him, and I was like, Yo, sir. I'm cool with this guy. I was like, Hey, sir, this shoes. I don't know what to say. He was like, Yeah, this shoes are felling apart.

Gucci shoes are nice. It's my favorite. The style. The buckle, the metal thing, makes it look really nice. You have a pair of Guccis on your feet, I think even better than if you have a pair of Versaces or any other shoes. Versace shoes are more for people that wants to show off. Guccis makes you look like you the man. You wear a pair of jeans with that shoes, and you be like, Damn! The leather's good. It lasts you, if you treat them good, for three or four years.

Ferragamos are good though, really nice leather. Manolos, nice. Really nice. They not the type of shoes that last forever. It's more for stylish. That's how I see the shoes. It's just to tell other womens that you have a pair of Manolos. You know what else I love? Paul Stuart. I think those fucking shoes are classic. The way they shaped, really nice. The way the leather—very durable, soft but durable. The way they look. Those shoes are perfect.

THIRTY-THREE

WHEN I WAS about six, my daddy came to the U.S. His relationship with my mom wasn't going too good at the time. I used to see fights all the time. He used to drink and come back, because he was always the type that used to go out and have fun, and come back real late, and my mom used to go argue with him.

He had this friend of his since he was little, and this guy had gone in America before. This guy told him, Look, we can go to America and make a lot of money. That's what my daddy came for. It's not that he was hungry for the money. I think he just wanted to try the American thing—you know, everybody comes here for the land of opportunities. My dad first came, and we didn't hear from him for the next six month. Because we don't have a phone in our house back then. He finally call up his dad and told us to be in some certain place, like a family's house, because he was going to call there at that date, at that exact time, because back then it was really hard to get that connection.

Like after years, I heard what was the real story of my daddy when he came here. He came with $90. I'm serious. He didn't know how to speak the language. His friend said they were going to stay at this nice place, they had a nice job ready for them. But they go there, no job. His friend was like, Look, we don't have enough money, so I don't know what we going to do now. That's his friend from childhood. Then his friend went his own way, and my dad was alone. He used to live in a pension, a lot of Brazilians in one big house. This guys who usually used to live in the pension said, We shine shoes for a living, so why don't you come and train with us. That's how my daddy started.

But he said he suffered a lot. He had people who beat him up at the pension. He use to wake up really early, and one of the days he went out, and there was a lot of noise in the house. And he went there, and he was like, You know, you guys got to be quiet. Don't talk too loud or be playing music at this time, because it was in the weekdays. And one of the guys beat up my dad just because he said that.

They taught him how to shine shoes. It was funny, because when I used to live in Brazil, it was just that people used to ask me, What does your daddy usually do in America? Because Brazilians, we don't even know what's life in America until we come here. We think it's another planet. We think that it's a planet that people live different, live that wealthy life, drive nice cars. Because that's what we see in the movies, right? We see people driving really nice cars.

That's what I used to think before I first came here. I thought that my daddy had a really HUGE house, a nice car. But I didn't really know. I thought with my daddy shining shoes that he used to make a lot of money. But I didn't know. He used to tell me that he made okay money. And he used to send every penny that he made back to me and my mom in Brazil. That was a lot back then. When my daddy started sending money over there, we got our house all fixed. We got a car. I used to go to a really nice private school. My daddy never came back to visit. He never wanted to go back again.

Then my daddy wanted to bring us to the U.S. It took him a long time to get the money, because you got to pay for the passports, and you got to prove that you have money to come to this country. If you want to do it in a legal way. We tried a visa four times at the American consulate. First time, they didn't give us the visa. The second time, they gave me the visa, but they didn't give my mom. So my mom went there to try and get her visa. She brought my passport and her passport, saying, Why did he get the visa what I didn't have? So they cancel my visa, and they didn't give anything to her. We haven't seen my dad for five years, and we're like, How we going to be living this life? My mom used to say, Yo, we got to be really down to the earth. Your dad might find another womans there and leave us with nothing here.

She didn't used to have a job then. The life we used to live was because of my dad. He used to send $300, $400 a month to Brazil, sometimes more. He used to work at a really wealthy club on Park Avenue. At that place you were able to make $100 a day shining shoes back in the day. This guy that sold him the job, I think my daddy pay about $1,000. There's a huge mafia in this thing. For me to get this place that I work now, I pay $3,000. Not all at once, but $300 a week. You can't just walk in someplace. You got to know someone.

If there's a shoeshine guy there, and the guy is going to leave for Brazil or whatever, the guy is going to ask you for money. He's going to be like, Look, this is a spot that I made, it's my business. It's like selling a business. But if I got a better job, and I don't need the money, I would never charge the same amount. I'd just give it to the person. But a person that I trust.

My mom was desperate. She wanted my dad to come back. She used to talk to me once in a while. She never taught me you got to lie to your dad to get money out of him. No, she used to be like, Don't you ever say that. When I got kind of sick, you know, when you get the chicken pox and stuffs, my mom never, ever made me tell it to my dad. Because my dad was working over here, and she didn't want him worrying about it, so I always make my dad think that the life was perfect for us in Brazil.

My mom was like, Your dad's going to come back, so we not going to have the same life that we be having now. They were talking about that. He couldn't take the life anymore, because he missed us so much. Because Brazilians are not really attached to material things, but more to family type of stuffs. That's how we see it. Most of the Brazilians that work here, they never have their minds in here. They always have their minds back in Brazil, because that's our family and friendship. Over there the people, they don't like material things. Because people over there usually don't have it to give. Even the rich people—they never tell that they have money.

But then my dad met this guy in New York that his brother work as a doctor in Brazil. There was a congregation here, a doctor thing—buying stuffs for his doctor's office and all that. So, the doctor was coming here for that, and he went to the visa office, trying to fake it out that he was my mom's husband. My dad pay him $1,000 to do that.

We're all praying. You don't even know. It was really big to me, because I always wanted to see how it was. I always had that dream: the United States. My daddy used to send pictures to me, and toys.

My mom told me what I had to say in the interview. We just met the doctor at the consulate, and we talked. And then we lied. It was the first time we lied. So we lie about everything. The doctor didn't have to show a marriage license. Back then it was more talking than anything. He talked to them like he was going to come here for this congregation, buy some stuffs that he really needed, but he wanted to bring the family over to show them how New York was. This and that. The lady was like, Let me see your passports. It was like that then: when she got the passport it was boom, boom—canceled or not. But she got the passports and said, All right, you can go. Come back here in three days.

I never seen my mom that happy. She didn't even know what to do. She was so shock, I had to pull her up, Let's go, let's go. We walk out the American consulate with this guy, and we say thanks and my mommy just started crying, crying, crying, crying, crying. And I was like, What you crying for? You don't have to cry. I was young, but I was telling her you don't have to cry.

We walking, and my mom was like, I can't believe it, how we going to call your dad from here, how we going to call your dad from here? She didn't even know what to do. So she called up my grandpa, and he called up my dad, and my dad call us up later that night.

When we got the visa, my mom got the last four numbers so she play the Lotto. That was the first thing she did. She play it only if she have a high expectation that she dreamed a number or if she find a dollar in the street, she'll play the last four numbers of the dollar. She didn't win, though.

Then we went to eat good, like eat out. We never ate out. To eat in McDonald's in São Paulo, it's a luxury. We went to this really nice place, it wasn't that expensive for me to eat there today, but if I was a regular Brazilian, middle class, it would be expensive. Then the next day, my mom got in the car, we drove to the church that you got to walk up the 365 steps. That church is so beautiful at nighttime, it's up in the hill. Weekends, they put the lights on that goes up and down the roof, like they do the houses here at Christmas, but the church is up in the mountain. It's beautiful. Everybody loves it. My mom made a promise to the saint of the church that we go there if we got the visa. We walked up the 365 stairs for a half hour. Then we go inside and pray.

In three weeks, we sold everything that we had in our house. The funniest thing with my dad was he was always like, We never going to tell people what we do. He thought it was bad luck. So, we keep it as a secret. We told everybody we were going to move to another state in Brazil, and we couldn't bring our stuffs in a truck. It's not that dangerous, but if you're going to move to another state, you don't want to bring all that stuffs. My mom took me out to buy some really nice clothes. In Brazil I used to go to weddings and dress like shit—not like shit, but jeans and sneakers. In Brazil we couldn't spend a lot of money to go to a party. But to come to the United States my mom got the whole outfit—the jacket and stuffs. Clothes I never wore before, shoes that I never had put on in my life.

All the time I was in Brazil, I never had shoes. Only sneakers. Never had shoes.

I put the shoes my mom got on my feet, and I was like, Whoa! Whoa! You know like Bally's shoes? The skin was just like that. You could feel it! And I was like, Yo, the sole is made of leather. I never seen a sole made of leather! It was funny to me at the time. It was hard walking in them, because it was hard right in the front, you know, not like sneakers, with the heels and stuffs. I loved to be dressing like that. It make me feel really big. Like when you big. Like, Damn! You succeeding in life!

The last day, I went down and I told all my friends, We going to the U.S. The little girls, I remember, that hated me until that time, they started kissing me. I don't know why they were doing that. They were like, Oh, you going to the U.S. We going to miss you, this and that. Hope you send us pictures!

THIRTY-FOUR

WE WENT TO the airport. It was a couple right behind us, kind of old, forty-something years old. It was a really tiny plane. If you going to fly international, it's got to be a HUGE plane. But we had to get the tickets and everything in two weeks, so we got a cheap flight. A really cheap flight. We came through Miami. First time we ever took a plane, though.

My mom got onto the plane, and she was okay. But when the plane start taking off, she start freaking out. She took her seat belts off, and she was like, We going to die! We going to die! We going to die! And the couple behind was like, No, sit down, put on your seat belts. No, we going to die! We going to die! But my mom finally puts the seat belts on, and starts holding my hand, and the plane was in the sky.

My mom, the whole fucking flight, she was freaking out, especially when the plane started shaking, because, you know, the turbulence. Oh, my God! Oh, my God! she was going. She started to pray and pray and pray. That made me nervous. I was like, Damn. Until today I don't like the idea of being on a plane. She freaked me out. She freaked everybody out.

We got to Miami. My dad said he was going to pick us up in the airport. We got our luggages. We didn't know how to speak Spanish or English. To me, I was looking at everything like, Shit, this is just like in the movies. Everybody was talking English. I was like, Damn, if we tell our friends this, they *never* going to believe us.

We start looking for my dad, but he got there kind of late because he was on a plane from New York to Miami. For us to go through immigration, we couldn't carry no papers in our pockets, because if the immigration stop us, if they found any phone number from the U.S., anything, they'd deport us right away because we came here on excursion with a whole bunch of people that was going to visit Disney. That's what everybody usually do: they say, We going to visit Disney, and we going to stay there for a week, and then we going to go back, but they end up staying. At the airport we left the group, and we started trying to look for my daddy. That airport was HUGE! It was fifty times bigger than the Rio airport. The Rio airport is just one entrance. I was like, Mom, this airport doesn't look the same. This airport is like, yo, *humongous*!

We want to go to the same hotel where my daddy was supposed to be there. Ramada. But we don't know the name because we had to keep that in our memory. My mom knew this Brazilian singer, her name is El Bajamario, and from there we got to remember Ramada. My mom was freaking out. She was like, Oh, we never going to find your dad. I was like, Look, we got money, we can go to New York. But my mom, she was always the type, if she cannot get one thing, she's not calm. She freaks out. I'm not like that. If I cannot get it, I'm going to stay quiet and try to think. Even though we didn't have my daddy's address in New York, I thought, We get to New York, we get there. We just go there and wait for my daddy. He's going to show up someday.

We found some lady in the airport that was sitting, waiting for someone. She was speaking Spanish, and my mom is trying to communicate with her. You know, because Portuguese and Spanish are really different. We could understand the lady, but she couldn't understand us. My mom knew the name of the hotel, and she was like Ramada, Ramada, Ramada. And the lady put us in a cab and spoke with the guy that was Spanish. When we got into the Ramada Hotel, we went to the receptionist, and we ask my daddy's name: Claudio. And lady at the desk was like, No Claudio. Because in America you usually go by the last name, not by the first. But in Brazil you usually go by the first name, not the last name. And my mom was like, Oh no, he's not here. She starts freaking out again. She sat on the sofa and she started crying and crying. She went all over her purse, took everything out.

Then she went back to the lady again, and she was like, Claudio. And the lady was trying to speak with my mom, who was like, CLAU-DEE-OH. And the lady was like, Claudio—oh, Claudio Benicio. And my mom was BENICIO, YES, YES, YES. And the lady was like, Mr. Benicio, yeah, he just went to the airport, he's going to be back. So sit down. My dad got there a half hour later.

We spent a week in Miami. To me it was a great time. Damn. Miami. My dad got me some sneakers. Not Nikes, I was kind of disappoint in that. But I was like, Damn, I'm living the life here. Everything was different to me. The food was different. In Brazil you don't eat McDonald's the way we eat here. To me that was a paradise. Over there we eat most rice and beans. We don't drink soda every day. And here I was drinking juices and soda all the time. I was like, Whoa!

The beach is so fucking quiet, man. You go to the beach in Brazil, it's crowded. Damn, you go in Brazil, you not even able to walk on the beach there is so many peoples. And why there's no waves? In Brazil you see a seven-foot wave in front of you. Over here, you don't see waves. It was totally different. The sand of the beach was totally different. It seemed so natural in Brazil. In Miami it seemed fake to me.

We flew to New York. My dad had a friend of his that drive a limo. So we had a limo—one of those old limos, old-school ones, like the first Lincoln. We had this guy picking us up, and I was like, Wow.

God, it was cold. It was in February. We inside the limo, we taking pictures, we like, Oh, this is great. We went to where my daddy used to live. It was him and two other guys that used to share rooms. It was a tiny apartment, two rooms in the house. We ended up all sleeping in the one room. To me it was like, Shit. He said he was going to rent another house, and my mom was going to have a job.

He ended up renting this small studio in Astoria after two weeks. We went there, but it was suck, because we used to stay inside for the whole day, watching TV that we couldn't even understand. Just stay, trying to kill time. It was like you in a prison. Trying to kill time in a prison. We just used to stay there. What am I going to talk about with my mom? I don't want to talk to my mom. We didn't know New York. Now I be able to walk for miles. I know New York like a lot of peoples doesn't know. But back then I didn't know.

I remember one time when we first got there my mom wrote letters. We go to the post office, and this lady who was standing right next to us ask my mom some questions. And my mom didn't even knew how to say, We don't speak English. My mom was shaking her head, no. So I look at the lady and say, No speak English. I knew, because my daddy taught me how to say that. No . . . speak . . . English. The lady made this big thing: Ahhh, ohhh, they no speak English. I didn't even know what she was saying, but I look at my mom, and I saw her crying. To me it was like, I speak the language, I speak Portuguese, but I don't know how to speak this goddamn language. I felt so mad at the time, because I wanted to learn.

It took me a month to go to school, because you got to take a whole bunch of exams. I remember we went to the clinic in Corona, Queens. I had to stay the whole day there. Blood test, this, that. Man, they do the whole nine yards there. I got there at eight in the morning, and we didn't leave until three.

I remember the nurse, when she tells you to get on your underwear, and I was laying down on the bed, and then she comes in trying to see my penis. I was like, What the fuck you trying to do? What do you want to see? I think she was trying to see if I was a guy or a girl. But she knew that I was a guy. I don't know why she wanted to look at it. I got out of there, and I was like, Yo, Mom, this fucking lady just did something, I didn't like it. But my mom was like, Don't be mad, it's normal.

I started going to school. There was Hispanic kids in my class. And I was like, Goddamn, I don't know English. And now this peoples speaking Spanish! Because in Brazil I didn't know what Spanish was. I didn't know African. Yo, I didn't know French. I just knew Portuguese. I thought Portuguese was all over the world.

I'm there the first day of school, and I was like, Wow, it's like in the movies—the hallways. And I got in the class. I was like, someone here has to speak Portuguese. But no one speak Portuguese back then. I was like, Wow, man. I didn't know how to say hi, bye in English. The only thing I knew how to say was "hot dog." It was not even "hot dog." It was "hotchie doggy"—the way you say it in Brazil.

I was trying to get my way around the first day. Then in the lunchtime the teacher tried to introduce me to some Brazilian kids, but they like, Okay. They weren't cool. They were from some other state. They didn't want to help me. Since then I had this thing, if you're from São Paulo, I'm going to help you; if you're not, I really don't care.

In my class you used to get Korean, Chinese, Mexicans. Yo, it was like United Nations. Forty people in class and no one spoke a word of English. I used to sit there like a fucking dumb. I was having a lot of trouble with not learning. There was this one kid that spoke Portuguese and English. But he was always being an asshole. He used to tell me to curse at the teacher so I can get in trouble. He used to be like, Tell her, will you suck my dick? So I was like, Yo, will you suck my dick? And I thought I was asking her for something nice. I thought I was doing something good. But I was cursing at the teacher. I didn't even know. It fucking got me in trouble, and I didn't know how to explain my own self, that this kid taught me how to say that. There was no translator at that time.

I got beaten up by some kids that used to want my lunch money. If you new in this country, in a new school, you had kids to beat you up for money—all the time. Not beating you up really bad, but punching you, Give me your money. Kind of intimidating you. I used to get that.

First I learned Spanish. That got me around pretty well. I used to have Colombians, Mexicans, Dominicans in my class. I used to learn English from them. That's how I learned English after a year and two month.

THIRTY-FIVE

SOMETIMES I HAVE nightmares. I wake up in Brazil and I'm like, Holy shit, how the fuck am I going to go back to America?

I see all this peoples that I grew up with, and I'm living by them—you know, me not coming here, not being successful, not being able to speak my own language right. And not having anything. It's crazy. I just go crazy. I start seeing things that I don't want to see, like shooting and stuffs, getting robbed. I know it's not the life in Brazil that I usually used to see it every day. That used to happen once in six month. But those days I wake up pretty stressed out in the morning. I don't want anybody to talk to me. It makes me think so much.

When I was sixteen, I left back to Brazil with my mom. Her relationship with my dad wasn't that good. I got down there, and I was like, Brazil is different, man. I didn't know how to cook, but down there you got to cook if you want to eat. Sometimes we used to starve in our house. It's not like you have money and you go into McDonald's. They don't have McDonald's around my way down there. They don't have cheap stores selling junk food and stuffs, like the deli store. You got to go to a place that you going to buy a homemade hamburger or cheeseburger, but it will be kind of expensive.

I lived the life over there, doing simple stuffs that used to make me really happy, like play soccer. If you go out in Brazil being poor, it's not like you going out in Times Square being poor. You go out in Times Square with no money, it ain't no fun, because you not going to be able to go into any of those places. There's so many places for you to go here, but you got to have money. In Brazil, it's so many people that doesn't have money, you end up doing a lot of other things.

We usually use a lot of imaginations, like playing with kites. Over there you see more than a hundred kids playing with kites at the same time. Over here you don't see that. Over here you might see one kid in the park. But over there they make this thing on the kite called *ceroll*. They break glasses, you got to bang them with a hammer, and it got to be really thin, like a powder. You put it in a can, and then you mix it up with glue. Not a regular glue—we got a form of glue that you can melt it, so we could mix that with the glass and put it on the line of the kite. With that my kite would be able to cut your kite, and your kite would go loose. It's very dangerous. Because at the same time if a persons passing by with a motorcycle, and that line gets in the persons' way, it can cut, not the whole neck, but it can cut the neck. I heard stories like that.

Sometimes a whole bunch of us used to go to the beach. But it isn't like here you go in a bus that have AC. Over there the buses that have AC you got to pay four times the time you pay in the regular buses. So we used to go on the bus wearing just bathing suits—no shirts, no shoes. Because if we surfing and leave that stuffs on the beach, it's gone when we finish. Peoples steal it.

There's a lot of other things that you don't spend money at all. To me everything was a very new and simple life. Very simple. I used to love it. Love it. The temperature every day was seventy. Sometimes it used to rain, but not every day. Just in seasons.

But I used to think, Damn, what kind of life I'm going to live here in Brazil? I always had that thing in my mind. I used to see some of my friends, really young, with kids already. And I used to think about what the fuck I'm going to do for myself. I'm not Brazilian. I'm Brazilian, but I'm not Brazilian. Peoples used to call me American when I was down there just because I had live in the U.S.

They don't know what is America, what America is all about. To me that was very fun. Sometimes I used to go to the rich part of São

Paulo, and I used to see them talking about stuffs that I already lived over here, and they didn't know.

In São Paulo the rich peoples always had money, so they could get any shoe they wanted in the store. Imported shoes. Because over there Nike and stuffs, it's imported. It's always very expensive. Here you have the mentality everything is easy. You go down to Brazil, you be like, Oh shit, things so cheap. But with the peoples that live down there, it ain't cheap. Peoples over there, they got to do miracles to survive. The minimum wage there is, I think, $140 a month. For $700 you going to live good. A single person, you going to be able to go out and do a lot of stuffs. But you have to have a great job to get that.

I ended up living that chilling life. Chill, just live day by day. Most of the time I used to have a lot of fun. We used to go on the street. I used to play basketball, after that I used to chill. Girls used to pass by, we used to call them over and start a conversation. Over there, they very outgoing. They not like here—Oh, what do you have? What are you wearing? The conversation we used to have with the girls there, they used to love it. I used to get girls like crazy in Brazil. I was very calm, and I used to talk and tell them I was raise in the U.S. I never had sex with no girls in Brazil, not because of disease, but I always had this thing in my mind, if I ever ended up making any one of these girls pregnant, I'm going to stay there for life.

I used to cry to my father every other week, saying that I want to come back. He used to respond me, No, you not coming back. I don't have the money. But I'd cry and cry, so he say, Okay. I was going bananas. To me that was a dream come true. The life over there, I didn't want to live day by day, be like, Oh, today I'm going to have food, tomorrow I'm not having. When I want to buy sneakers, I want to buy it. You don't know how the peoples buy sneakers in Brazil? It's the same thing you buying a car here. You finance it. You know that? Peoples in Brazil finance the sneakers in ten times. Yeah, they do. Per month. I'm serious.

I wanted to be something. I didn't want to be just a regular person down there.

THIRTY-SIX

I GOT BACK here. My daddy was sitting on the couch. He was like, Have a seat, son. Because my daddy, he knows how to talk, I swear. I don't know if he got his ass whupped when he was younger, but he grew up in the streets. It wasn't like my mom. My daddy's very street-smart. Like very. He is capable to tell what people do drugs and stuffs. Or when a person's kind of lying.

He go ahead and told me to sit next to him. He was never aggravate. He never hit me—never, ever in his life. My mom would fuck me up, but he would never touch me. He was like, Look, we got a situation here. You got to work.

Five days later I was working at Yuri's Shoe Repair shop. I was seventeen and a half at that time. My daddy said he had a friend was going to quit that place, so I went there, and I trained for two weeks. When I started, Yuri didn't want me there, because I was too young, he thought. I had to lie to him and tell him that I was eighteen.

First, it was kind of hard for me. My first day was like, Wow, what the fuck I'm doing here? I was so ashame, I just want to hide my face, so nobody see me. I felt like a prostitute, like I was doing something really wrong. Not wrong. Stealing is really wrong. But, to shine you have to have a lot of confidence, not be ashame at all about yourself. When I shine shoes with my daddy, I work in the back of the club, so nobody see me. But if somebody walk by Yuri's they could see me right there in the big window.

I just want to go back home and sit there and tell my dad that I paid the rent, paid this, I'm just going to chill, go back to school, just have the simple life. But I was like, Man, I got to do this. Because I promise my dad I was going to come back to the States and work, no matter what.

I was in a different world. To shine makes you feel that you are your own kind. You don't care how peoples going to feel about you, but you got to care about how yourself feels. You know, because it's different.

Yuri's was miserable. You had to be in the store by seven and know that not that many peoples goes to shine their shoes until eight-thirty. It's awful. I had to wake up really early in the morning and see shoes, shoes, shoes, shoes, shoes. In my place now with the traders I probably shine no more than twenty, thirty pairs a day. Now, I take my time. But when you in a place where you see one shoe after the other, and a lot of them, you just doing and doing.

Those shoes that the customer brings to get full soles, we don't get paid at all, but we work in the store, so we have to shine them. We got eighty bucks a week from Yuri. So, if we work from seven in the morning to six in the afternoon, how much will we get an hour? It sucks.

How can I say this to you? You work like that, you wake up, and you don't want to do nothing. You don't want to be in that life. You just play the Lotto. You dream. It's good that you make money, you make great money. I used to make about $180 a day. Now, I make a little less, but I don't have to work as much. Right now I work maybe 20 percent what I used to work there.

Me and the other guys at Yuri's used to fight for one dollar. We used to get really mad at each other, because we used to go by turn. When you not doing anything for half an hour, you just sit. And you see somebody walking in, what you going to do? Hey, it's my turn. Right? So then it was somebody else's turn, and you would fight with the guy.

You shine there, it's like a lottery. Most of those customers give two, three dollars tip. But the guy who shines doesn't know if you going to give him a dollar or two dollars. He's like playing with the lottery. I seen it a week ago, I was in the store, talking to the guys that used to work with me. This Hispanic kid give a really nice job to this lady. The boss charge her four dollars, and she gave a fifty-cent tip to this kid. Yeah, I'm serious.

If a rich guy come in, we was like, Look at this guy's shoes. He fucking got a nice suit, nice shoes, nice watch. We used to say, Damn, this guy must have money to give it. He probably have more than two dollars to give. But he might give fifty cents.

There were some peoples, we used to call them dummy peoples. They knew, but they didn't want to give it. They act stupid, you know? They make themselves look stupid, so we can believe that they were giving us fifty cents because they were retarded.

You know who usually give fifty cents? Old peoples. Roberto, he used to be crazy if an old guy used to give it fifty cents. The store could be packed with customers, he would be like, sir, sir, hey. He would be really mad. He'd go, This right here, it's for you to save for when you die, so you can pay for your grave. He usually say that same phrase all the time. I'm not lying. When Roberto used to say that, I used to crack up. I used to be like, Goddamn, why you got to say those things, Roberto? He was like, This fucking peoples make money. They just stop in time.

I'm the type of person, this is the way I used to judge peoples—if it was an old guy, an old lady, I used to see that as my grandparents. I'm serious. I used to tell this guys that all the time. If you grew up the way I did, come to this country, haven't seen your grandparents. You know, until today, I love grandparents. They know how to treat you well. Grandparents are cool.

No matter how much an old guy was going to give it me, if he need help, I would do it. Until today I'm on the street, I see someone old, I'm going to help them. In the store it was the same thing. An old person who usually used to give it fifty cents used to come down off the chair and the other guys were like, Let this motherfucker break his head. He's going to give me fifty cents, anyway. I was like, Man, I don't see it like that. I always try to talk to old peoples, make them feel good, because, look, if you seventy years old, eighty years old, what else do you expect from life? You been through everything.

I start working at Yuri's, man, and I prove myself. Time by time I start having a lot of clients, because I used to talk a lot of crap about sports and stuffs. Was peoples that used to go there to just talk about the Yankees, Mets, Knicks. With some peoples that used to go there just to hear stories about Brazil, because they been to Brazil.

Was this one guy, I know he's big-time, because one time I saw him on TV. This guy first time started giving me two dollars tip, and before I leave there, he used to give me fifteen dollars. He gave me a pair of tickets to a Knicks game. He gave me $150 for Christmas. Nobody ever gave me that amount before that time. A really cool guy.

This other guy, I thought this guy was a lawyer, the way he dresses. Big guy that had a moustache. You know, because you judge peoples with the way they dress, so I fucking give him the best shine, and he give me a dollar. That was me, investing. Usually you invest in customers you don't know. But he didn't say anything to me, he just sat there. He read the paper. So after two times he went there, I was reading the newspaper, and I saw his face in a picture in the newspaper. He was the fucking boss of most magazines. I was like, Shit, this man has money. He's cheap. So when he came really early in the morning, I said, Hey, I know you. I saw your face in the *Post*. And he was, Yeah. So from that day he started giving me three dollars.

I shined Senator Kerrey's shoes for four times, man. I didn't know who he was. So he come in and for the first time I shine his shoes he give me a two-dollar tip. Cool. Regular customer. And then after the second time, I read in the newspaper. I was like, Oh, my God, this is the senator of some state. I keep it to myself. You know, when you buff the shoes, I was going hard on one, the right one. He was like, Don't go too hard, because I don't have a leg. I went easy. He kind of pull up his pants and show it to me. Weird. Someone told me that he lost it in the war. Vietnam.

This other guy came, a doctor. He was real nice to me, and the other guy that shine there, Phil, used to be like, in Portuguese, He's trying to take you home. He used to play me all the time with that thing, because Phil was gay. He used to play those jokes every fucking day. He see this guy walk into the store, and he used to be like, Look at his eyes, they like the stars. Like when you see a girl and you like, Damn, that girl. So he used to be like, Look, look, look at his eyes. Here come Gil's boyfriend.

I used to think it was funny when he say it. He always say things about gay things and things like that. And he was like, How much you wonder this guy's gay? He used to be like, A gay person always know the other gay person. And one time this guy bought me a sweater for Christmas, and Phil was like, Damn, he's giving you too much present. I think he's expecting too much from you. Are you going to give him anything? I was like, Damn, I'm not really down and out for this stuffs. Phil used to fuck around with me. You don't even know how much I used to hear from him.

When a womans come in, that's when me and Roberto used to talk. We like, Damn, yo. I would say in Portuguese, Yo, Roberto, are you able to see her underwear yet? Yo, man, are you getting hard over there? Roberto's there, he's shining her shoes, taking his time. And he's trying to look at the girl. And I'm like, Yo, are you getting hard, man? Are you going to masturbate after this?

Once it happens that a girl comes with her boyfriend, and I'm shining the boyfriend and Roberto's doing her shoes and taking that time and trying to see her underwear, and I'm like in Portuguese, Yo, man, I'm already finished with this fucker. What the fuck, are you going to take long there? He's like, Yeah, let me look a little bit more.

The first thing Phil would say when a womans come in was like, Would you fuck her? Would you fuck her? One day he say that, the lady was Brazilian. The lady was like, What do you mean, fuck her? I was like, Oh my God. No, we be talking about some other fuck. Fuck, I mean some other womans. She's like, But you just said it to me, right? If you would fuck me. I was like, No, no, no, not you, no. It was this

HUGE mess. My boss, Yuri, got involved. He wanted to know what we were talking about, because we always talking Portuguese, and this woman was really mad.

Now I feel so happy when I walk to the traders every morning, and I see the same peoples. And the peoples always talk to me nice. It's good to have that kind of environment. If anybody treat me bad now, with no respect, that is not the rich guys. The guys in the mailroom, they like shit to me, but not the traders. These are the great guys, I tell them all the time. They ask me how I feel sometimes. I'm like, Guys, you make me feel like a real person. It's not like I have to work at the shop and be treated like a slave.

They treat me like sometimes I'm The Kid.

PART THREE

TRUST ME

THIRTY-SEVEN

Greg

ISAAC, MY BUDDY at Medved, Morningstar, called to say he couldn't get out unless he brought along Cheryl, five months pregnant with kid #2, so could we make it a foursome, or "a fivesome, as it were?" Normally, I would have found an excuse to cancel, because Cheryl drives me nuts, and Annie, who went to law school with her, likes her even less than I do, because Cheryl treats her like a traitor to motherhood and family. It wasn't always that way. When Cheryl and Isaac were dating, there was endless talk about Cheryl's brilliant future legal career, but about six minutes after they got married she quit working, to have babies. The old bait-and-switch.

But I needed to pick Isaac's brains. Persimmons, the hedge fund that had torpedoed Steed's social climbing, was run by a guy named Joe Cantone, previously a big shot at Medved, Morningstar, and Isaac would be able to connect the dots for me. Annie reluctantly agreed to come along ("What am I supposed to do? Trade recipes with her?"), but only if I promised to go to a benefit for one of her nonprofit clients, a theater company. Which meant the performance and then dinner. In Brooklyn. Six hours, including travel time. Not a fair trade, in my book, but I had no choice.

"Who picked this restaurant?" asked Cheryl, a big, bosomy blonde. Isaac, a small guy with a cowlick and bad skin, thought he had won the lottery when she agreed to go out with him.

"Actually, Greg did," Annie said. The big joke between Annie and me was that I ate more Korean food than she did. A lot of American food had started tasting greasy and heavy to me. More and more, I found myself wanting to eat *gaewoon*, a Korean word used to describe simple, healthy food, a little bit salty and sour, like fish and pickles, that cleanses your palate and your system.

"The one thing about Korean food I don't get is it seems every dish is laced with the same hot sauce," announced Cheryl as we sat down at the table. She had a point.

"We can go someplace else," said Annie, who couldn't have cared less what we ate, as long as it was fast.

"No, no, I'll be all right. I'll find something. Although I can't eat any raw fish, because I'm pregnant"—an unnecessary announcement not only because Korean cuisine does not feature raw fish, but also because Cheryl was as big as a house. Following her to the table, I had noticed her eyes narrow as she checked out Annie's size-zero figure. (Annie wouldn't let me tell Cheryl and Isaac yet that she was pregnant.)

"Look, darling, short ribs. Your favorite," said Isaac, pointing at the menu. I couldn't tell if he was still infatuated with her. Little digs had crept into his phone conversations—that she ate too much, that she wouldn't give him blow jobs anymore.

We ordered barbecue (marinated beef, shrimp, and chicken grilled in a pit in the center of the table), and the waitress brought the *ban-chan*—the little dishes of appetizers that precede Korean meals.

"God, I'm really thirsty," said Annie, taking a big drink from her water glass.

"You just think you're thirsty," said Cheryl. "It's the spices in these pickles."

"No, actually Cheryl, I *am* thirsty."

I gave Annie a look, and she obligingly began to ask Cheryl questions about her and Isaac's two-year-old son.

I turned to Isaac. "Hey, you ever hear of a guy named Joe Cantone?"

"Oh, man, did that hit the news already?"

"Did what hit the news?"

"Jeff Steed resigning to go work at Persimmons."

"Holy shit. You're kidding! When did that happen?"

"Yesterday. You know Jeff Steed?"

"Not really. I met him at a party." Why hadn't Gil called to tell me? "Was Steed in some kind of trouble there?"

"Nah, just the latest one out the door to a hedge fund—although, in my humble opinion, this seems like a stupid time to do it, with everyone and his brother starting one. There's something like eight thousand of them now all chasing the same alpha pool."

"Any idea why Steed picked Persimmons?"

"He and Cantone were very tight when Cantone worked at Medved, Morningstar."

"In what?"

"Emerging markets, and Cantone was good at it. There were a couple of years there when he shot the lights out. Did particularly well with Korean equities, I recall." Isaac glanced around the restaurant to note the coincidence. "They promoted him to managing director, and he was running that entire side of the business, but then one day about two years ago he went to Bigelow and announced he's going to start his own global macro fund. I think he started with something like $125 million, which is not much for that kind of thing, but he was doing pretty well there for a while."

"Didn't I read in the *Journal*, though, that he ran into a rough patch about six months ago?"

"Worse than that. Word was he was facing a huge margin call. Dead man walking, investors stampeding for the door. I think they were mostly funds of funds, which panic at the first sign of trouble. He was down something like 40 percent. And he had a lot of expenses—high rent in a fancy building, a dozen employees, a Barbie-doll second wife spending his money faster than he made it—the works. Supposedly, he had a nervous breakdown, locked himself in his office with piles of newspapers, and magazines, and research. Nobody could get him to come out for a month except to take delivery of pastrami on rye."

"You mean he's not sleeping?" Cheryl was on her cell phone to the babysitter. "Well, put him on the phone . . . Hi, sweetie, it's Mommy. Why are you crying like that?"

The rest of us awkwardly stared into our plates, while Cheryl ostentatiously managed the domestic crisis.

"He had a temperature this afternoon," she explained after hanging up. "It's hard to understand these things if you don't have children yourself."

There was a hard glitter in Annie's eye. I gave her another imploring look.

"When is the new baby due?" Annie asked Cheryl. I'd have to get her flowers tomorrow. "Are you going to use a midwife again? Didn't you have the first one in a bathtub?"

I turned back to Isaac. "So, how did Cantone pull it out?"

"I don't know. Probably just got lucky. That's the nature of macro— you've got to have the stomach for volatility."

"You think Steed had anything to do with rescuing Cantone?"

"How would he have done that?"

"I don't know. Maybe, he gave him some hot tips."

Isaac laughed. "Do you know something?"

"No, no, just playing 'what if' in my head."

"Steed may be slippery, but he's not a moron."

"Okay, to be honest, I heard that he was caught doing something improper at Medved, Morningstar, but I couldn't pin down what it was."

Isaac gave me a long look. "There have been some rumors," he admitted.

Cheryl's cell phone rang. It was the babysitter again. Fuck! "Is that *him* screaming? Oh, God. Please put the phone up to his ear. Right. Now. Melissa."

Annie was staring into space with extreme annoyance.

"Hi, sweetheart, it's Mommy. I know. I know. I know."

"Can you tell me the rumors on deep background?" I asked Isaac over Cheryl's din.

"Are you writing a piece about this?"

"I don't really know. But even if I do, I can't use rumors."

"Oh, sweetie, Mommy misses you too." Cheryl was giving us dirty looks for continuing to talk over her maternal star turn.

"I've heard a bunch of things—I don't know if any of them are true," said Isaac. "That he was trading for a friend, that he was caught in the stairwell with one of the interns giving him a blow job, that the management committee voted to fire him, five-four, with Bigelow's being the deciding vote. One thing is pretty unusual that I do know is true: they're letting him leave with his bonus. Some people say Bigelow's wife made the old man do it. She got Steed his job in the first place. Greg, you absolutely can't use any of this unless you confirm it elsewhere, and I know I don't have to tell you to keep my name out of it entirely."

"Isaac, don't worry, man."

"Honey, put Melissa back on. Melissa? We'll be home in twenty minutes."

"So, did you hear about Steed's girlfriend, too?" said Isaac, obviously embarrassed by Cheryl and trying to ignore her. "Russian. Beautiful girl. Looks like she's about nineteen."

"Oh, yeah, I guess I did hear about her." I remembered Nan Bigelow telling me about Steed bringing her to a dinner party.

"They say he met her at a strip club. I mean, she was a dancer there."

"Really!"

"I hate to interrupt you two old gossip hens." Cheryl was off the phone. "But we've really got to get home."

They made a fast exit, and Annie and I were left in peace to drink our *poti-cha*.

"Oh, God," Annie said. "People like that make you not want to have kids."

"But *we* won't be like that."

"How do you know? People change when they have kids."

"Sometimes for the better. Did you hear what Isaac said?"

"I was too busy talking about the joys of breast-feeding with Cheryl."

"And thank you for that!"

"Well, I'm going to be doing it soon myself. One on each teat!" The doctor had confirmed she was having twins.

"Steed quit today. Isaac pretty much said he was forced out, but the CEO, Bill Bigelow, let him leave with his bonus, which is strange."

"What do you think is going on?"

"I have no idea, but I'm going to find out."

ASHTON KUTCHER, I love that guy. The guy is simple. The guy look good. He's a handsome guy. He was a model. He knows how to dress well. He's a funny guy. He got all that looks. What I read in a magazine, he's kind of like me. He was a guy that was living, making a day-by-day, and one day he make money. And today he just trying to help peoples, trying to make peoples from the industry look bad with the *Punk'd*. I like that. Because they show that this peoples are not always like gods. Some of them, they just think they can do anything to anybody. Like Michael Jackson. I think that motherfucker's crazy because he think he's like God. But Ashton, he's a happy guy. Because he always got that respect.

Mr. Bigelow always give me respect. Even when he come to the trading floor, which he doesn't usually do, he will say hello to me, ask me how is my day. That's big. When he walk on the trading floor, he is like God. I wouldn't like nobody else to know what the guy went through with Jeff Steed. I don't care what is the situation. Even if this guys killed each other I would be like nothing happened, because that is not my business.

In Brazil we see something bad happen, we never talk about it. We just keep it to ourselves. There is a thing that they usually say it in hip-hop: Keep it real on the streets. That means you don't get no one else involved. No police, no detectives, nobody. Mr. Billy and Jeff Steed, they have money. They capable to pay off people to tell them who was the person that rat on them. They can send guys to kill me. Because they have that power, and the cops wouldn't protect my ass.

I was thinking I should pack my shit right away, try to get some money, book the first ticket back to Brazil. Because everything they said it in there, they don't want peoples to know, and there was only our three in the room, and if anyone hears this, they will know the loudmouth that it came out of. And from there I will suffer the consequences. I don't know what is the consequences, but talk and I will find out.

Thanks God, this guys don't take me serious because they see me doing the job that I do. They probably think I'm not intelligent at all. They just have me as a kid. They don't think I understand what they are and who they talking on the phone and the things that they say it to each other when they have a conversation. Most of them don't care if I hear or not. They think I'm ignorant, yo. They think, What does this kid has to offer? He came from another country. He can barely speak the language.

So, I will keep my mouth shut, do whatever I usually do it, put my iPod on, just walk around the trading floor like nothing happened.

I go over there with Tim and Jim, and I'm like, I got a good story, guys. They like, Oh man, we got to hear this one. So, this is the thing: My friend Murilo was going to have sex with this girl, and he call me up and was like, Look, go on MSN and log on for the camera thing, and you going to watch me fuck this girl—LIVE. So Fabio and me go and log on from my house. Murilo goes and set up the camera and everything, and the girl goes take a shower. You plug that into your computer, so you can be at your house, and I can be at my house, and we can both see each one the same time. They have that at my job—they can see each other from the floors.

So Murilo hide up the camera—this is the camera that moves. When the girl came out the shower, she gave him head. And then he start fucking her in the natural way. What you call it English? Not chicken style, but in Portuguese, it's *papa-mamey*—mother-and-father style. Just the normal way that you usually face the person. He goes and fuck her in that way. You know, he always told with us that he was so good in bed, this and that. So, this kid goes and when he start doing, I told Fabio, Let's mark how long he going to take. Then all of a sudden he turn this girl on the side and start doing really fast. Came. Hugged the girl, and he was just there. And we mark on our watch how long he took.

I'm like, Jim, Guess how long he took. Jim goes, Six minutes? I'm like, No, two minutes and nineteen seconds! Tim and Jim were cracking up. They love to hear crazy stories like that. I shine their shoes and Jim gives me twenty.

I'm like, Jim, I'm not going to lie to you, this money going for a good cause.

He's like, What?

I'm like, The Aguilar Benicio Drinking Foundation. They love that shit.

I go see Fred Turner, and he's like, Guess who doesn't work here no more? I'm like, Who? He point to Jeff's desk. Empty. All the stuffs that Jeff had it, his laptop, his papers—gone! I'm like, What happened? Fred is like, He got a new job. I'm like, Are you serious, Fred? He's like, Yeah, happiest day of my life. Now, I don't have to listen to that fucking guy no more.

But you know what is the funniest thing? I bet that Mr. Jeff had got fired by Mr. Billy for the argument that they had it.

I went to see Pete. I'm thinking he's changing. Mr. Pete used to be the worst dresser. Then I start saying things like that around people, that this guy fucking doesn't know how to dress. Sometimes I just talk to peoples about the way other peoples dresses. I don't know if somebody talk to Mr. Pete or he hear something, but this guy's changing, man. I can't believe it! Now, he buy Ferragamos, nice shirt, nice pants. Today, I was like, Wow! What made you change? He was like, Nobody. Why, Gil? I was like, Oh, sir, because you look very nice today, like fashion. He was like, I always dress like this. I was thinking, Yeah, right.

Then Pete is like, Wow, Rona look great today, doesn't you think?

I saw him showing off to Rona before. He would work and then show it to her how much he made it. So, I kind of knew that he was going to get that. I walk downstairs where the smoking area is, they together. Pete is smoking, Rona's just chilling, because she doesn't smoke. I was talking with Jared, and he's like, Haven't you notice, dude? They go get coffee together. They go get lunch together.

You know the funniest thing? I told Rona, I think Mr. Pete is your boyfriend now. She's like, How you know who is my boyfriend? I'm like, You figure it out. I go to rows, and I hear what people say every time. And it was very easy for me to fake that one out, because you guys always together. But Rona just laugh.

THIRTY-NINE

Greg

I CALLED UP Gil and asked him why he hadn't told me about Steed leaving. He said he himself just found out because there was no going-away party. I asked if he gave the paper Rona found to the compliance department.

"Yeah, just like you said it."

"Were there any repercussions?"

"What is repercussions?"

"It's like, did anything happen to Steed after you turned the paper in?"

"Not that I heard it."

"Is anybody gossiping that Steed got fired instead of quitting?"

"Not really."

I called up Harry and asked if they had heard from the Medved, Morningstar compliance department about Steed.

They hadn't.

I had no choice now but to approach Steed directly. I figured I had a pretty good chance of getting him to talk to me. His new company was small enough not to have a PR department to prevent him from doing so, and who wouldn't want to start a new job with a feature about himself in *Glossy*?

I never ask for an interview. It sounds too formal. I say, I'd like to drop by, and maybe you could offer me some guidance, or I'd love to hear what you have to say about this or that. People let down their guard if they think they can steer you.

Steed's secretary at Persimmons put me through. I congratulated Steed. Would he possibly have time to chat with me about his new job and the trend of valuable people leaving the big firms to work at hedge funds? He would be delighted. He loved *Glossy* magazine. He was a subscriber!

I met him at his new office, in a plush town house off Madison Avenue. The geeky boy from Vergil Peterson's snapshot had grown into a handsome man, deeply tanned, with broad shoulders, and a head full of curly premature salt-and-pepper hair. The décor was overwrought and cheesy, with an Oriental carpet, Tiffany lamp, and a partners desk.

Steed offered me a sherry. "I keep this for guests," he explained, sounding as if he were impersonating Cary Grant. *Glossy* does that to some people. He was drinking coffee, so I told him I'd have one of those. After settling us into big leather armchairs, he rang a little silver bell. The secretary brought more coffee and a plate of little tea sandwiches, with the crusts cut off. Incredibly, Steed gobbled them all down, without offering me any.

I'd brought a pen and notepad, because I figured a tape recorder would make him nervous. For half an hour I played softball: tell me about Bill Bigelow ("Very old school. I learned so much from him. And his wife, Nan, is so charming and cultured. Have you ever met her? *She* would make a great profile for *Glossy*."), your hobbies ("I play the piano and compose music in my spare time."), how you got interested in finance ("My grandfather, who came to this country with nothing and made a fortune in the stock market, gave me bar-mitzvah money to invest."), your first job ("A lovely lady, Amy X, took me under her wing.").

I nodded and smiled a lot. "Why did you take this new job?"

"The big firms are run by businessmen and lawyers, not by investors. So you don't get the opportunity to be creative there. They put you in a box, and they never want you to go outside it. But some of us are in it for the love of the game. We think outside the box. Like my old friend Joe Cantone, the fund manager here. We've always wanted to work together, and the time finally seemed right."

"Yeah, I've heard many good things about him. How do you guys work together?"

"Well, Joe is into global macro and emerging markets; I'm basically a global stock-picker."

"I see."

"I know some people say this is the wrong time to go into hedge funds, that there are too many people trying to feed at the same trough, and I grant you, plenty of us are not going to make it. There is going to be a vast winnowing. But, the right hedge funds are going to be crucial in the new economy."

"I hear you."

"Because hedge funds are more nimble. They're not just about the quick trade anymore. They're becoming more activist with the companies they invest in, part of the process, creating value. I don't know if you happened to hear this, but just a couple of weeks ago, Joe got a seat on the board of the Korlux department store chain. So, you see, we're starting to give the private equity folks a run for their money."

Right, I thought. Meaning, you drain all the money out and leave the companies swimming in debt. But I wasn't in there to argue or make a point or prove I was smarter. When I was at the newspaper, I occasionally did co-interviews with a reporter who would challenge sources and get into arguments. I would come out of there and say, "What the fuck were you doing?" Because all you want to do is make a source feel as comfortable as you can and get him to think you're his best friend, so he'll go on and on and on, even when you start asking the tough questions.

"Jeff, I noticed that you recently resigned from a few nonprofit boards. I think I read you said it was because your personal life had gotten so hectic."

"Well, at the time I had to say that, because I hadn't announced my new job yet. But at Persimmons, it's just Joe, me, and two other guys, and we're responsible for over $400 million. That's not going to leave me much time for pro bono work. Once I get my feet wet, I'm going to get back into charitable work and supporting the arts. It's certainly my intention to do that, because I think it's important that we who have so much give back to society. We lead such privileged lives," he said, sweeping his arm to indicate the opulence of his new office.

"Jeff, we got to talk about one thing, though. I hear that you were advising the nonprofit boards about their investment strategies and suddenly things hit a rocky patch."

His smile vanished. "They knew about my expertise and asked for my advice. Unfortunately, I didn't fully appreciate at the time that nonprofit boards are forever fearful of being accused of mismanagement by the donors and government watchdogs. They don't really have the stomach to ride out rough patches. They panic at the first hint of a loss. My mistake, I guess, but nobody was complaining when I was getting them 20 percent returns."

"Just walk me through this in a little more detail. What kind of investments did you recommend?"

"It was an aggressive strategy. Big City Modern Dance, in particular, is trying to raise money for a new theater and school building, and their endowment is not huge."

"In particular, did you give them money on the condition that they put it into Persimmons?"

"Yes, I did. And there is nothing illegal about that. Persimmons was charging them no fees, and at the time, I'd like to point out, I was not in discussions to come work here."

"But, did you yourself have money in Persimmons?"

"Of course I did. Are you saying that's a conflict of interest? I call it putting my money where my mouth is."

"So, what went wrong?"

"Unfortunately, there was an anomalous situation with a synthetic CDO that a lot of other people besides Joe got caught in, too. The foundation boards freaked out—please don't use that phrase in your article. Just say, I think we're talking about a difference in style, really, and I admit I probably should have been more sensitive to the fact that nonprofits have a duty to be conservative and to preserve their assets."

"Have you always been a fan of modern dance?"

"Ah, yes. My mother was a great supporter of the performing arts, and she used to take me to all the famous dance companies when they came to L.A.—Martha Graham, Paul Taylor, Merce Cunningham."

I took notes, but not about Steed's devotions at the altar of Terpsichore. I was writing down what he'd said just before. It's an old trick: if you take notes while they're telling you sensitive material, they get nervous and stop talking. You wait to let them answer an innocuous question, and then write down the good stuff that came just before.

"Jeff, I want to bring up something else I heard. This is a little troubling, but I thought I should be upfront with you and get your side of the story. I've been hearing that a janitor lost his job at Medved, Morningstar because he caught you using your cell phone in a bathroom supply closet."

Steed stared at me in shock. I think his mouth actually fell open. "Listen, Mr. Waggoner, exactly what kind of profile are you writing here? I thought this was supposed to be about my new job here."

"It is. But I have to follow up on what people have been telling me about your background."

He softly whistled, to indicate time out. "Look, I think I need to go off the record here."

"I don't think I can let you go off the record. I have this account of you using your cell phone in a bathroom closet nailed down pretty tightly. All I really need is your comment."

"You don't understand. Trust me. The real situation here is much more complicated than you know. You're not going to feel good about yourself if you go with what you've got and then find out what really happened. It's a much more complex situation, not a simple black-and-white thing."

"I'm not here to judge you, Jeff. Or say you did right or wrong. I just want to get the story right. It's going to be a much better story and much better for you if I can put your side in, but I can't really do that if you go off the record. Because other people are on the record."

He stared moodily into his coffee cup as if he was trying to read his fortune in the dregs. "Let me give you a hypothetical situation," he said.

I had to give him credit: that was good. With a hypothetical story, he could make up all or part of it, and it would be tricky for me to use any of it.

"Imagine a guy who advised people, including some charities and nonprofits, to invest with a friend—not because the guy is a friend, but because he is the best. Everybody makes a lot of money, and everybody is happy. Then the friend makes a mistake nobody saw coming. His fund may even go under, taking some of his nonprofit investors right along with it. So, the first guy stretches the rules to help out. He's not doing it for himself, he's doing it for some good causes."

"If that's what really happened, my readers would be very sympathetic, I'm sure."

"But some other people may not. I don't think you quite understand what's at stake here, Greg. What if telling your story means twenty dancers will end up on the unemployment line? I admit I don't know much about being a reporter, but I'm guessing that personal responsibility and good judgment come into it somewhere."

"You're asking me to believe you did it all for charity?"

"No, not all. As I said, it's a complicated situation." He hesitated for a long moment, turning over in his mind whether to go further. Finally, he said, "There was also this girl."

"The Russian girl?"

"How did you know?"

"You weren't exactly shy about introducing her around town."

"Do you know her background?"

"No."

"She grew up in an orphanage in Siberia and came over to this country completely on her own."

"How old is she?"

"Twenty-two. She has a six-year-old son, a beautiful little boy, Sasha."

"Where did you meet her?"

He hesitated. "This is still all hypothetical."

"Whatever."

"I met her in a strip club. She was dancing to support herself and her son. That's the best-paying job you can get if you're an immigrant without a green card. She could earn $500 or more a night with tips and lap dances. She's been stripping since she was fifteen."

"What kind of relationship did you have with her?"

"She is the most beautiful woman I've ever met. I fell in love with her at first sight. I would even say I became obsessed with her."

"Why didn't you marry her?"

"I would have. At one point. Lucky for me, I didn't. She's a very disturbed person. I mean, I don't want to judge her. She's had a very hard life. But, she has a serious drug problem, among other things."

"Cocaine?"

"Yeah, mostly, and other stuff, too, including the Zoloft her doctor has her on, which turns her into a wild animal when she drinks on it, which she does a lot."

"Did you ever try to get her help in getting clean?"

"Yeah, I did, but a person has to want to quit an addiction. With her it goes a lot deeper than the drugs. When you've experienced the kind of pain and deprivation and abuse that she did, I don't think that can ever be cured. The drugs help her to forget for a little while, at least."

"Are you still seeing her?"

"No. I can't. She's too crazy. She still calls, but I don't answer. I want to emphasize that we're not talking about normal-type lovers' quarrels here. We're talking about scary stuff. She was seeing other men in my apartment, my own bed, for money, while I was at work."

"Oh, man." I couldn't help but feel sorry for the guy. The pain was all over his face and in his voice. "Why are you telling me all this? Did she take you for a lot of money?"

"No, not really. I mean, I spent a lot of money on her. I gave her expensive gifts and cash, too—anything she asked for, actually, but it was all willingly, on my part. The thing was she had saved up $50,000 on her own. Do you have any idea how hard that was for her? How many hours of stripping? How many men pawing at her? She asked me to invest it. People like her always dream of some get-rich-quick scheme. She'd already lost $20,000 by putting it in a travel Web site some friend of hers started. So, I really wanted to do right by her. I wanted for once in her life that something would turn out right, that she would have some kind of financial cushion for herself and her son."

"So, you put it all in Persimmons."

He just looked at me.

"And when the fund collapsed you called Cantone with some hot tips so he could recoup."

Steed seemed shocked. "You're putting words in my mouth, Mr. Waggoner. I said I bent the rules, not broke the law."

"Then, why was there an internal investigation at Medved, Morningstar on you just before you left?"

"Where did you hear that? Did somebody at the firm tell you that?"

"I'm hearing that from people."

His expression tightened into a sneer. "There's a lot of people at the firm who were very jealous of me."

"I'm sure."

"They make up all kinds of crap about me. You can't believe anything these assholes say."

"But *was* there an internal investigation that you know of?"

He looked at his watch. "I'm sorry. I have another appointment, and I don't really want to continue with this until I talk to some people at my old firm to see what's going on and who is spreading these rumors about me. Let me get back to you on this."

Right, I thought, and I'll never hear from you again. "I'm telling you, it's always better for you if I can put your side of the story in."

"Mr. Waggoner, I think you have entirely misrepresented this interview to me. You came here claiming you wanted to know about my new job. In fact you think you're going to do some juicy little exposé.

But you'd better be very, very careful. I know a lot of important people in this town. One word from me, and you might find that your career is in a tough spot."

"Are you threatening me?"

"You'll be hearing from my lawyer, Mr. Waggoner." He stalked out of the room and slammed the door.

When they start talking about lawyers, I always think, Gotcha, you bastard.

MY CELL PHONE rings and this guy is like, Gil, is that you?
It's Saturday morning, and I'm thinking, Who the fuck? Because this
guy doesn't have the Portuguese accent. But the guy is like, This is
Jeff. From work.

I'm thinking, Holy shit. I'm fucked! He knows *I* was there shining
shoes when he had the argument with Mr. Billy.

Jeff is like, Gil, you got plans tonight?

I'm like, Why you want to know?

Jeff goes, Matthew and me, we going to the Knicks game. Knicks
and the Clippers. You want to come?

I'm thinking, Should I care? Mr. Jeff will take me to a place that's
a lot of people, so I don't think he would do something.

Jeff explain me that we going to sit down on the floor. I'm like, Are
you serious, Jeff? I been the Garden about twenty times, but I usually
sit in the middle. I never got that close in a basketball game. You feel like
celebrities. I like to feel like that. I don't like to get noticed—to be a
celebrity is fake. You always surrounded by fake people. But just to go
down there to see how it feels. One time. I'm like, Wow, Jeff! Hell, yeah!

Jeff's like, Come to my crib tonight, seven-thirty. We leaving here
for the Garden in a limo, and he tell me his address.

I was really big into basketball until they had the all-star game
in New York. All this basketball players was staying in the Hilton
on Fifty-third and Sixth. I went there, to the lobby. I was able to see

everyone. Kobe was a rookie. Motumbo, he speak five languages—he speak very bad Portuguese from Portugal. I got pictures with Tracey Murray. But the guy that I was waiting for, he disappoint me so much: Shaquille O'Neal. He walk out the elevator and there was a whole bunch of peoples, more than thirty, all around him, asking him for autographs, asking him to say something. He didn't say nothing. He just ran into the peoples like he was a truck, and the peoples was little cars. He didn't care. He was taking over the whole thing, just walking through peoples, got into his limo, didn't say hi, bye, didn't even wave. I remember that. Man, from that day I stopped everything. I watch basketball once in a while today, but not like before.

So, six o'clock I go to Mr. Jeff's. It's not an apartment—it's a whole fucking house, and here comes Matthew and Jeff out the door, and we got the limo, and the driver goes to the Garden. There was a bar in the limo, so we drinking on the road. Matthew is there, just chilling, drinking a HUGE glass of tequila. Mr. Jeff, he's there, drinking coffee like he usually do it. The bar got Alizé passion fruit, like that song that Biggie sang that I was sixteen when I first heard it: "Alizé keep me dizzy. Girls used to dis me."

I used to drink a lot Alizé. It used to make me in a fast mood, like, Oh, I'm in heaven. When you drink it, you feel really calm, and that's how most human being want to feel. Nothing in your mind. No family, no fucking problems, no, never, never, nothing. We got to the Garden, I ended up having four Alizé. Yo, the last one, I grabbed that and just drink like water. You know, when you kill the drink in one minute?

Man, the seats in the Garden was off the hook. Front row. That's where Jay-Z and Beyoncé, Puff Daddy, they all sit. But they usually go when there's a big attraction. They don't go when there's Knicks and L.A. Clippers. Knicks and the Lakers, they will go. I think they usually go to show off. So, it was nobody I knew in those seats. I didn't even watch the game, to tell you the truth, I was just watching the guys throwing the ball. I was so banged up, man, and Matthew and me got beers. And the game was not even over, hey, and Mr. Jeff wanted to leave five minutes before the game finish.

Jeff call up the limo, the guy was around Penn Station, and we catch this guy, and Matthew was like, You know Gil, now we going to really have a good time.

We went to this guy's apartment that belong to Matthew's friend, right on Madison Avenue. We went there, and this guy had coke. We talking, the guy offers us a drink. But the main reason that Matthew go there was to do coke. He never done. His friend that own the apartment was an intern, too—a big white guy, really dirty. Look like he do a lot of drugs. The guy got a frame with a picture on the wall, put it on top of the table, and then he put lines of coke for each one, for me, him, Jeff, and Matthew. Matthew's like, This is the first time. I'm like, Me, too. Because I never had done.

Matthew did. He's like, Oh, my God! Wow! My head is all this little lights, man. Then he's like, All right, Gil, your turn. I was like, All right. First time. I was like, Oh, shit. That stuffs was really good. It got me fucking so hyped up. I was like, Fuck, fuck, fuck.

Then Matthew asked Jeff if he wanted to do, but Jeff was like, Nah. I don't know if Jeff really do, or he just didn't want to do because I was there. I was like, Aw, shit, I made a mistake of doing. I thought Jeff was going to do, too. But then Jeff ended up not doing. Now he got something on me. Maybe he going to get me fired.

Then we went to this new club in the limo. I don't know what the fuck it was called, I was so banged up. Matthew and me was high and drunk at the same time. We went there, and the guy at the rope see the limo and Mr. Jeff, and he just skip us whoevers in the line and tell us to go right in. When you get skipped like that, everybody looking to see who it is, like you some celebrity. Aw, man, once I sat down everything started spinning. I asked for a glass of water. Crazy night.

That place is nice. VIP. They have a HUGE fireplace by the wall. It's ten feet long. They even have a little place, like when you go to a movie theater, and you go inside the little booth to take pictures. They had that thing over there. I was like, Goddamn, I never seen a club like this. Inside there was beautiful womens, nice bar.

I see the menu and beers seven dollars and drinks twelve dollars. A bottle is $300. I'm like, Jeff, I don't think I be drinking much tonight, and he's like, Don't worry about it, Gil. Everything's on me. So, we drink for free because Jeff gets two bottles. A bottle of Belvedere vodka with juices and a bottle of Dom. But Jeff just drink coffee. Yo, I bet that guy doesn't never sleep.

Jeff sits there with his coffee, and the womens, they come. Like nine. Russian, black, white—supermodel types. But I think it's more to show peoples what he is. Because I don't see him dancing with girls that much. He don't get with them. Some of them are models and wealthy girls. I can't even tell. You go to a place like that, you don't know who is who. For you to be in there is not easy. This places you got to know someone to be in. You just cannot walk to the door and be like, Hey, how much is it?

Three, four of this girls is Russian. They fucking freaky. I look at them, and I can judge people like that. I know how to look at them. They look really nice, but I know they very materialistic. Very. Very. They wearing sexy clothes. Sexy and expensive. Gucci, Prada. Russian girls love that shit, I don't know why. Fendi. Everything that is really expensive. They not wearing Banana. Why Russian girls like that? They smell so good. Throw a whole bottle of fucking cologne on.

They some black girls that look real good. High class. Wearing jeans and fancy coats. Fancy stuff. Not like this ghetto girls. Nice boots, nice shoes. One girl was wearing a Von Dutch hat. Aw, I love it. I'm like, Damn, this girl got an attitude.

American white girls there, too. Some of them look like real top executives, this girls that probably dress up for the whole day, then just put the jeans on and go out at night. But they look good. Like they went to good schools. They don't look dumb.

I'm wondering who the fuck I'm supposed to talk to. About what? Because I know that womens like that usually like to talk about what they do in their own business. And I don't have nothing to say to them. I'm going to be like, Wow, I'm a trader, I trade stocks. I cannot go with the lies. It's too much.

I can go to a club, and I can probably find myself a pretty decent girl. A nice, good-looking girl. She going to look at me, she going to see the way I'm dressed. She going to be like, Damn, he be dressing pretty nice. He might have some money. He probably do something that he makes money. Because that's the way peoples look at you. If you dressing all banged up like a gang-banger, you ride in a nice car with nice rims, people going to think either you sell drugs or you a hip-hop superstar. That's the way the society judge you today.

When I go to clubs and a girl ask me what I do for living, I never tell her I shine shoes for a living. I say I work in the bank. What do you do? I'm a computer technician, I fix computers and stuffs. Why? Why should I tell them? I know I'm not going to get more than that.

Brazilians know what peoples do. They always know what peoples do. That guy dress like a fucking king, but he shine shoes. They know who works in construction and who's a stripper. That's why I don't want to live in that world no more. I don't hang out with peoples like that. They don't want to grow in life. They just want to live their lifestyle.

This Indian guy comes up in the club, and he was like, Hey, can I ask you a question? He was like, Um, do they let you in with sneakers? When that guy asked me that question, I look right at his face, and I was like, Well, that depends who you are. He walked away. I was like, Yo, what kind of place is this, man? This is not the usual place that any person can just walked in. I don't know if the guy really was interesting in that. Maybe he wanted to know the reason. Maybe he was saying that for the fact that he had a friend that probably went there and wasn't able to get in.

In this place you don't see a guy approaching womens like when you go regular clubs. Because in regular clubs you see a guy just go behind a woman and start dancing, even if the women doesn't want. That's what they do. But in this club it's more like talking and the way you present yourself. You can see the way peoples talk. We standing and then this guy came and talked to this woman next to me. And I was just looking at the way the guy was talking to her. The way he use his hands. I was like, Wow.

It was beautiful girls everyplace. I was trying to talk to this girl. She was from Brooklyn. I was like, Hey, how you doing? She was like, Hi. I was like, Where you from? She was like, Brooklyn. I was like, So, what you ladies going to do right now? And she just went, Well, we going to go home. I was like, Why? She was like, I got to work tomorrow. I was like, Cool.

Then I went to this other girls. I was like, Hey, so what you all ladies usually do on Sundays? She was like, Why? I was like, because me and my friend Eddy, we usually go to Flow. Flow is this hip-hop club by the Holland Tunnel. She goes like, Flow, what's that? That ghetto club? Dissed me. Fucking bitch. If I buy her a drink, she will be talking to me.

Then this girl starts talking to me. She's telling me that her father know Jeff. She's like twenty-four. Beautiful face, an American white-girl face. Kind of highlights hair. She's probably about five foot nine, but kind of chubby. Her stomach, when she sits, it goes in waves. She's wearing fancy clothes. She was wearing this Gucci bag, and when I saw it, that was the real Gucci. Because I know the leather, and I saw it inside. She was just showing to me all the things she had it. The boots she was wearing—Prada. She was wearing all black, black pants, black shirt. Because that kind of hides her fat.

Me and this girl, we start talking. First, she start telling me who is her father. Her father's a lawyer, her godfather's this, her uncle's that, her mom make this much money. Then she told me what kind of car her father drives. She said that he had a Lamborghini. I wasn't believing this girl. Then she put it she got a HUGE house, but she haven't found the right person. And I'm like, All right. She showed me some of the pictures of Gucci shoes. She has a camera on the phone. She takes pictures. She was like, This is me in my house. I'm like, All right. She kept tell me about her material stuffs—money, money, money, money—and what she had it.

I was like, Can you just hold here for a second? I got to say something to Jeff. I was like, Jeff, who is this girl? Because I think she be lying to me. She told me that her father's a millionaire. She makes money, she's rich, this and that. You know, why she have to lie to me? I'm just there because I like her personality. She seem kind of cool if she stop talking about those things. And Jeff is like, Well, it's true, though. She is rich. I'm like, All right.

This girl seems like a very lonely girl. I think she said those things to make peoples like her. For what she have, some peoples will be like, Wow. She's beautiful, if she lose a little bit of weight, she look perfect. I think she a cool person. It's just that I don't like it when peoples talk about money. It bothers me a lot. It does.

I danced with her, but she wanted more. She wanted me to stay there, dancing with her and kissing her like I never seen a women in my life. I don't like that when I go to a place. I like to go there and chill, and Natalia would fucking kill me if I got with this girl. I was like, Hey, we got to go back to Jeff. She was like, You not going to stay here with me and dance? I was like, No, I got to go find my friend, Matthew. She was like, I'm going to get with guys. I was like, Go ahead. So, she went there and got with two different guys. She kissed them and danced with them. I was like, All right, I don't care. Fuck it.

I go back to Jeff and Matthew. Matthew, he's getting with a Russian girl. He been doing more coke in the bathroom. There's little pieces on his nose. He is so banged up, man. Jeff sees me, he's like, Gil, come on over here and sit with me. I go there. The music's really loud, so nobody can hear what we saying. Jeff is like, You okay, Gil? You having a good time? I'm like, Mr. Jeff, tonight I be living your life. It's perfection, man.

Jeff is like, I got to ask, though, why you tease me about the cell a couple days ago?

I'm like, You know, Jeff, I'm just joking with you.

He's like, But why the cell?

I'm like, I think it's funny. It doesn't mean nothing.

Then Mr. Jeff wanted to know if I hear anything that him and Mr. Billy said that I was there shining shoes behind the desk, because Mr. Billy explain him I was there.

Jeff was like, Were you listening to us guys' conversation?

I was like, Sir, I don't even know what you guys were talking, because when I work I usually have my iPod on, and you can see, I'm always listening to music. When I get hooked in my iPod I don't want to know what everyone else is saying. I love music, so I just concentrate too much into the songs that that's the way I learn how to rhyme, because I usually listen to hip-hop. That's how I start a rhyme, listen too much to one song that you get used to that and the words. Because in hip-hop they usually speak too fast, that's how you get the words and the whole phrase that they are saying.

Jeff's like, But we were talking pretty loud.

I'm like, When you guys talk there I know this things not interest to me. I can barely speak the language. As you can see I have this HUGE accent. For me, I'm not interesting. I've been doing this job for three years. I was listening to hip-hop. You know how high the bass usually go? I didn't care. I seen you guys going crazy all the time. It's not only you. You go on the trading floor and you see a guy going after the other and just cursing the other guy out and walk away, and then ten minutes later one goes over to the other and they just start talking like two fucking bitches, say sorry to each other, and they do some stupid joke and laugh at each other.

Jeff is like, Well, that's good, but you got to be very careful. Because this guy is coming around and ask questions, and Jeff didn't like it. He's like, This guy is trying to bring me down. And Mr. Bigelow, too. If anybody ask you that we had argue, you don't know nothing. Okay?

I'm like, Okay.

Then Jeff put it he was working with his friend that run a hedge fund, and he ask if I wanted to work for them.

I'm like, But, which work, though?

He's like, Driving the customers to the airport and maybe do copies—just be there to do every little work that is need.

I'm like, That would be great. Hell, yeah.

Mr. Jeff is like, I will pay you $30,000 a year. I'm like, How much is that a month? He's like, maybe $2,000, after taxes. I'm like, Wow! Are you joking with me?

Jeff's like, Well, Monday, I want you to go to Bahamas, live the life for a while. You ever see that place? It's beautiful. Beautiful beach.

Jeff, I can't go no place. I don't have no money at this time.

Just write your name, your address, and your girlfriend's name and address.

My girlfriend babysits the kids for Mrs. Alice, so she is not capable to go.

I will call Mrs. Alice.

You will? For real?

Yeah. I'm going to send you guys. All expenses paid.

Jeff, are you serious?

He's like, Gil, you and your girl going to have the time of your life.

But I'm thinking, Come on. I'm not going to believe anyone until I see it. I'm like, Jeff, can I ask you something else?

What?

I don't think it was nice for you to get my cousin Eddy fired.

Who?

Eddy, the guy that cleans the bathrooms. He put it you got him fired?

I didn't get nobody fired. I don't even know who is this guy you talking about.

I'm like, Jeff, Could you help Eddy get his job back, though? Just talk to his supervisor, put it that he's an okay kid.

Jeff is like, No problem.

Sunday I got up so late, man. Everything kind of spin. I feel like shit. There come flashbacks the things I said to people and how I act. I'm like, Damn, I can't believe I said all this shit to peoples. It's pretty suck.

I tell Eddy that Mr. Jeff will talk to his supervisor, and he is capable to get his job back. But Eddy doesn't care. He bought a plane ticket. That guy surprise me so much because you know what he say? He will go back to Brazil next week. He say the peoples here is cold, and he doesn't get the same love that he had it in Brazil. He doesn't like the foods and the cold and the loneliness, not having family around. He's missing Brazil. Missing the weather that we usually have it in Brazil and the womens.

Eddy's like, Dog, you going to come down there, you and Fabio, we will go to the stadium. Aw, man, that would be my fucking biggest dream: just be in the stadium with Eddy and Fabio, and fucking drunk. Our team's scoring, and we just going nuts.

Yo, I will miss that guy so much.

FORTY-ONE

Greg

"ARE YOU WRITING an article on a trader named Jeff Steed?" It was Ed calling first thing Monday morning.

Damn. Ursula must have told him. But who told them what it was about? "Uh . . . well . . . I have been looking into the possibility of an article."

"Did we assign it yet?"

"I didn't want to tell you about it until I was sure there was a story there."

"Oh, good. I thought I was losing my mind, because I couldn't remember us talking about it."

"Did Ursula mention it?"

"No."

"How did you find out, then?"

"Mr. Steed just left my office."

"Oh, shit." Outsiders, especially irate ones, never got past the barriers designed to protect Ed. Steed must have blasted his way in with an Uzi.

"Quite an unpleasant character, your Mr. Steed. He threatened me. Implied he could get me fired because of all the important people he knew." Big mistake on Steed's part: Ed did not get where he was by being a coward, and being a New England WASP, he was deeply offended by bad manners. Threatening him was a sure way of getting him to do the opposite of what you wanted.

"Why didn't you tell me he was coming in? I might have been able to help."

"I didn't have a chance. He ambushed me. I don't know how he got past security downstairs or reception, but he was waiting for me at my office door."

"Oh God, I'm sorry."

"Not your fault—although it would have been nice if I'd had some idea what he was talking about. I had to fake it."

"I hope you told him I had a sterling reputation for fairness and accuracy."

"Of course, I did. Which is also what I told Al." Al Lieberman owned *Glossy*, along with several other magazines.

"Oh, no! How did he get involved?"

"Bill Bigelow, the chairman of Medved, Morningstar and Bigelow, called him to say you were doing a hatchet job on one of his former employees. I guess Al knows Bigelow socially."

"*Fuck!* Was he upset?"

"Bigelow—yes. Al—no. He gets this kind of thing all the time. He isn't trying to interfere. He just wanted me to know what was going on."

"Oh."

"You probably should come in and bring me up to speed."

"When do you want me?"

"About an hour ago."

Ed's office is sleek, with modernist, blond-wood furniture and wall-to-wall windows that frame an unobstructed view of the spire of the Empire State Building. A bit incongruously, Ed tends to dress like he's about to go trout fishing. Or at least sit by the fire with a scotch and fantasize about trout fishing. This day, he had on his favorite dogwood-pink corduroys.

"Start at the beginning," he said. He seemed amused.

I told him all, from meeting Gil to my interview with Steed.

Ed loved it. "We've got to get Bruce to shoot the shoeshine boy. Can you get the piece ready for the next issue?"

"How much time does that leave me?"

"Three weeks."

"I don't know. That might be tough. I don't have all the specifics yet."

"How do you plan on getting them?"

"I don't know."

"Whatever. I'm not worried. This piece will write itself. I'm putting it on the lineup. I need a big story for the issue. Greg, I knew you could do it. I never lost faith in you."

I was grinning so hard I thought my face would crack. It felt good. Having the big story. Pleasing Ed. There is something Ed does that makes you want his approval. I've never been able to put my finger on exactly what it is.

Please God, let me not disappoint him, I prayed as I was going down in the elevator.

FORTY-TWO

Gil

MONDAY, JEFF'S LIKE, Come to my new office. I go there, and he's like, Look, this plane tickets for you and your girl, leaving three o'clock this afternoon. I call up Mrs. Alice, so your girl can go. He was very busy, so he just went like, Oh, you know, when you get there, take a cab to the Royal Cay Hotel. He kind of explain me what was the place about, Madonna stays there, Jennifer Lopez, but it's not like you going to see them. I thought I was going to go there and see. I didn't even know how it was. It was all new to me.

Jeff is like, there is just one little favor that you got to do me. The last day you go this bank—and he write it down the name—and the man will give you a luggage to bring it back to me.

You think I will do it? Bring back a luggage?

No. I will fucking open that shit first before I get on the plane. I don't know if there's any drugs in there, if there's a gun. Imagine if they give me a close luggage. You know where I will put the thing? Maybe in the first thing on the plane, and I will just walk away to the back. Not under my seat. I will always open. You never know what the other person be giving you, so that's what you got to do it. And if I see that there is something really different, I wouldn't report to the police, but I would put that somewhere that no one will find. It's my risk. It's like I give you a car to drive, and you don't know I do drugs, and I forgot some bags of cocaine or marijuana inside the car. You get pulled over and the police are like, Let me search your car.

Come on, man, I don't want to get locked up for the other person's stupid shit.

Jeff is like, Okay?

I'm like, Why not? But, Jeff, what is in the luggage?

Business papers.

Okay, if it's just papers. But, Jeff, is illegal to bring papers from Bahamas? Can you go to prison for that?

Oh, no, nothing like that.

Then why you doing this way?

He's like, Sometimes you just want to do some certain things that ain't nobody's business. It's kind of a privacy thing. Not illegal, but you don't want the men to find out. So, Gil, you got to guard the luggage with your life, because you know how much this papers is worth?

I'm like, How much?

Fifty millions.

I'm like, Holy shit!

Then Jeff handed me a envelope. He's like, Have a good time!

I didn't want to rip the envelope right there in his face, so I stay cool. When I get out of there I take the envelope and open. There's bills and bills. I count $2,000 in hundreds. I'm like, Fuck, man, it's like we hitting the lottery.

Natalia and me got the plane. I fucking hate to be in a plane. I just hate to be in that little thing when it takes off. But we going first class. First class is really nice when you up in the air. I think every moment I step into a airplane, I think I'm going to die. But first class, this is fucking amazing. You just sit on that HUGE chair, and you have that beautiful stewardess coming to you and asking what you want all the time. You just press the button and they right there. They take care your jacket. The way they treat you, it's not like flying economic.

This one stewardess, so beautiful, man. Green eyes, black, shiny, shiny hair. But Natalia is right there, so I can't even look.

We got to Bahamas. Wow! Eighty-some degrees. We got in the cab. It was like this is a good dream. We could see this whole view.

That ride to the hotel, it's really amazing. You can see all this beautiful buildings. We got to the hotel. It was a fantasy place. That building all white, it looks from the 1960s the way the whole design is made. I kind of had an imagination how it looked, but I didn't know what was going to be inside and all that treatment.

I didn't even know how to dress to that place. I was wearing Diesel sneakers with jeans. I didn't know that you had to dressed up. Me and Natalia, we not with the crowd, the accents, the clothes. It's classic made for rich peoples. A person like me, I got really uncomfortable when I went there. When you not used to a hotel, you don't even know what is a lobby. And people usually trying to figure out who each other are. They look at each other's face. That bothers me a lot.

When we got into the desk, that was really messed. You cannot book something for someone else. You got to be present at that time. I had to show either Jeff's credit card or ID to get approve it. I gave the girl my name and Jeff's name, she told me, Oh, he has to be here. I was like, How can this be, man? Why does this always have to happen to a poor guy like me that can barely speak this fucking language.

She was like, Oh, do you have a credit card? I was like, Miss, I have no credit card. A checking account? No. Do you have any cash on you? All this questions that was kind of putting me down in my own ways. You know when you get to the time that you really nervous, you just want to cry? So, I was getting to that.

Natalia and me got out the hotel. We walked around and try to stay calm. I call up Jeff. I was freaking out on the phone. I was like, I'm going to get on the next flight back to New York City. I don't care about this anymore. Because I like to feel comfortable most times, and this peoples down in the hotel, they not make me feel comfortable. They like, You don't belong in this world. Go away. That's kind of like they put it to me.

But Mr. Jeff is just like, Wait. He call up the hotel and have his secretary fax in the credit card and license. Jeff was like, I'm so sorry for whatever they done it to you. You don't have to be nervous. We go back to the hotel, and everything was solved.

We got up in the hotel room. It was on the tenth floor. We had the whole view to the beach. It was beautiful. I open up this little refrigerator, and it had everything inside there from peanuts to champagne to beers to snacks to Swiss cheese, candies, chocolates, wine-bottle opener. I was like, Wow! The room was all white. Beautiful bed. The shower have two heads. I took pictures of that!

I call up Jeff to thank him. I'm like, I'm here. Finally got in. He's like, Look, there is a card up your drawers that has a name and account number. Go take a look. I'm like, Oh, okay. What is this for, sir? He goes, Don't purchase anything outside of the hotel. I don't want you to be spending your money. Anything you have to get, just order. I'm like, Are you serious, Jeff? He's like, Yeah. I was like, So, what should I order? Beers? He was like, Why don't you order a bottle of champagne? What is your favorite champagne?

They have this little menu inside the room that has fucking millions of things. They has bottles in there that cost $1,500 to $2,000. You ever heard about Louis the Thirteenth? I think it's a whiskey. A little shot was $200. Jeff's like, Get some Dom.

I hung up with him, got on the phone, and called up the service-room guys. The guys when I answered the phone were like, Hey, how you doing, Mr. Benicio? I stop, and I went, how you guys know my name? They went like, Every customer in the hotel has a last name, and that's how we have to respond them. I was like, Oh, yeah. Cool. I would like a bottle of Dom. He was like, How many glasses? I was like, No, I don't need no glasses. I want the whole bottle. Because when I go to nightclubs, you go up there and go, Let me get a glass of Veuve, because they don't come with the bottle, they just give you the glass. So, that's what I thought. I thought they were going to bring me the two glasses. I'm like, No glasses, the whole bottle. They like, No, no, no, how many people you have with you? I'm like, Oh, just me and Natalia. They like, All right, so there is two glasses. I was like, Oh yeah, okay. I was so stupid, man.

This guys came up with the Dom. We ended up drinking the whole thing. But then Natalia, she really, really bad throw up. She too excite. I was like, Oh, I wanted to go out, I wanted to do something, but Natalia is going to bed right now. I was trying to wake her up. But she has this HUGE headache. She couldn't get up.

You know what I did? I got dressed up kind of well. I thought like, Oh, this is the hot shit. I put on my Armani Exchange T-shirt, my jeans. I went down to the lobby. When I got there, everyone is wearing a jacket. In the eighty-degrees weather. There is something wrong in here, man.

I was like, you know what? I'm just going to go and grab myself a fucking cigar. So, I got me a twenty-five-dollars cigar from this little boutique, because everything was paid up to the room.

I go outside. They got a HUGE pool. Little bungalows right next to the pool. I went to the bar in the back at the beach. I'm like, Yeah, I'm in room 1025, hand them the card. Let me get a piña colada. I sat all by myself and just watched those peoples. It was really fun to me because it was beautiful peoples.

When you don't experience, and you just want to learn so bad, and you don't know how, it's like you a fucking wild dog. You go out there, you want to be like those civilized dogs. I was like the wild dog, and those are the civilized dogs. They knew how to drink and how to act. Because I was so used to go to that club scene and see everyone talking loud and acting aggressive, like they had to show something to each other. And this peoples over there, they so cool, well dressed-up, not screaming, all talking in a one-to-one voice. I was like, Oh my god. And the whole scene was unbelievable. The stars, the palm trees. Everything was so perfect. That was my little adventure that night.

The next day we woke up, and we order the breakfast. It cost about $56. I was like, This shit must be like fucking lunch. This guy brought over in the silver cover. I was like, Holy shit, what the fuck is under this thing? When I looked it up, it was just scrambled eggs with toast bread and bacon. It was just simple, the same thing that I usually make it at home. It won't cost me no more than $2 to $3. Come on! I can make that on my own. This is what they call VIP. Same shit if you go to that fucking diner on the corner, you just got to put the silver thing on the top.

We had our breakfast. We were so excite. We went to the beach and just sat there for two, three hours. Natalia was amaze. It seem like she never seen the beach before. Meanwhile, I was calling up all my cousins on the phone. You know, when you just want to brag about your life: I'm having this wonderful life. I'm over here, drinking champagne, drinking beer. This guys are bringing me fucking beer right on the beach. Because at the hotel those guys serve you right down on the sand.

I think I spend more money on the phone than the hotel room cost. I don't know why I was doing that. There was this one day that I got a little drunk in the afternoon. I was in the water, walking toward the ocean. And the ocean was kind of rough, and they were having little waves. A wave came and just caught me. Meanwhile, I was talking on the phone with Fabio. A wave went over me. I was like, Hello? Hello?

This is the most incredible life. I didn't know that rich peoples live like this. They don't have to do shit. I think they probably have someone to wipe their own ass if they want to. Because everything you wanted, you just raise your hand. This guy used to come, and I used to be like, Can I get a towel? I felt so bad that every time someone used to do me a favor I used to give $5. Because I didn't pay anything to go in there, so the money I used to carry, it was just to give it away to the peoples that work there. The guys at the door, they used to open the door for me. So once a day I used to give the guy at the door $5. Everyone used to love me at the place.

I talk to everyone. The guy at the door, the guy that give the towels, the bartender. They see my tattoos. I look really ghetto. They probably thought I was a rock star from Brazil. Which I wasn't. They didn't know. Natalia and me was just always acting cool. Going from the beach to the hotel.

We were so afraid to eat with everybody downstairs with the lunch tables that we usually used to order our food in the room. And most of our food used to be either pasta or hamburgers. Because we didn't know anything else on the menu. It wasn't written in English. It was all like in fucking French, so we didn't know. We used to look at the prices. Some of that shit used to cost forty-some to fifty or sixty dollars. Me and Natalia used to think about to each other, Wow, what the fuck this supposed to mean? It's not written in English. That's how we used to think most times. It was tough.

We didn't even went inside the pool, we were so afraid. What the fuck people's going to think if we go inside the pool? The pool was there, we took pictures and everything, but we didn't put our feets inside that pool. We were so uncomfortable. We just this two wild dogs. We always want to be away from peoples, because we always thought peoples was going to start judging us.

One day I looked out from our window, and I see this HUGE groups of guys on the beach and a motorcycle, and they all black. I was like, Yo, Natalia, that has to be something going on down there. Let's go. We went down there, and it was Puffy shooting a video for one of his protégés, Loon. When I saw Puffy, it was like me seeing God at the time. But I didn't know how to act when I saw him, because when you see celebrities, peoples don't usually know how to act.

That guy was my idol. Because he was the one that brought Notorious B.I.G., and to me that made my vacation. Seriously. That's the only guy I wanted to take pictures and talk about when I get home. I didn't care about taking pictures of the hotel. I wait for him to do this whole video thing. I saw that he was heading back, he was on his cell phone. He had two bodyguards next to him. There was not that many peoples around him asking for autographs, so he stopped and I went up to him. I was like two feet away, and I was facing him. I was like, Mr. Puffy, could you take pictures with me. He's six foot one. He look down on me, and he just went, Not now. And he walked straight back to his hotel.

I was like, Wow. Here's a guy that I support him buying all his fucking CDs for years, and that's the way he be treating his fan. That's pretty fucked up.

The next day I saw the guy that sings with him, Loon. Natalia was the one that spot that guy. She was like, Oh, that's Loon, because she knew who that guy was. I was like, All right. Let's go talk to the guy. I was like, Loon, would you take picture with us? He was like, Cool. I was like, Wow, man. I'm pretty impress. Because yesterday when I asked Puffy to take picture with us, he dissed us. Loon was like, Oh, yeah, Puffy's always like that. Don't mind. The guy is always busy. But Loon is from Holland. He asked it where we staying, where we from. He took pictures and pictures, not only one. He was really cool.

After three days I start to get comfortable. I hang out at the bar. I was just feeling like one of those guys, like a big shot. I was like, Wow. I was feeling like a important person. I think that's what I wanted to feel. I knew how to talk. I knew how to express my ways with nice gestures, using your hands.

I was playing pool, and this other two guys came in and was like, Can we play pool with you? I was like, Cool. When I looked, I was like, Oh, shit! It was unbelievable. The guy was Jake Smith that used to play for the NBA. I almost ran up on my room and got my camera, but I didn't. I kept playing. I was like, No one else is doing. Why should I do? So we playing. He probably thought that I was a hot shit. Right in the middle of the pool game one of his friends comes with five gorgeous blond, brunette girls. He was like, Hey, Jake, come here. This girls were jumping on this guy. I was just acting cool. One of the girls ask me what I'm doing there. I'm like, Oh, I'm here, working on a big deal. I don't know how it's going to be. It might be good, it might be bad. She wasn't that impress because she probably hear this bullshit all the time.

But then Jake is like, Oh, what do you do? I'm like, I used to work at Medved, Morningstar and Bigelow, with Mr. Bigelow, the boss over there. But I just got a job at a hedge fund. He's like, Wow. Who your clients? I'm like, Who my clients? Well, my clients can be just like yourself, anyone that has the money and is into making a lot more money. He's like, What's the minimum amount that you need? I'm like, Five millions or more. He's like, What stocks you buying lately?

I'm like, Well, iPod is making a lot of money. The technology is growing so fast. But you should probably invest in the new PSP. You ever heard about the PSP? It's this new videogame from PlayStation. Everyone's getting it. You can download music. You can see movies through that. It's the hottest product out there. The fever is worse than the iPod. He's like, What do you think the stock has the potential to go? I'm like, It's going to double your money in three or four month. He's like, Fuck! What else you invest in? I'm like, Medical, real estate. Real estate's a good thing for you to invest. He's like, Where? I'm like, There's a couple places. Hamptons. You can make a lot of money. A lot of people is moving over there. Your money can double from night to day.

He's like, The guys that manages my money, I'm not too satisfied. I'm like, Cool. Call me. He give me his card. I will give it to Mr. Jeff. Who knows? Maybe he will invest his money. NBA players, hip-hop stars, they got money, man, money to invest. I know how to talk and they will understand it.

The last day I heard something going right under the door around seven in the morning. I drink a little bit the night before, because we used to get fucking hammered. I was like, Oh, what is that? You know when you just half-awake, half-asleep? I just grab the whole thing and sit down on the toilet. I just went like, What the fuck? Four thousand dollars. I didn't know that room service costs that much. I was like, How come Jeff didn't give me this money? I could have got myself my own apartment. TV. Sofas. Whatever.

I call up Jeff. I was like, Jeff, I got to talk to you, sir. I know you did it what you did because you like me. But the bill came up too high. Look, I'm here to at least pay half of it. I'm sorry. I don't know what to say. I didn't know that this place cost me so much.

He respond me, Gil, don't worry about it. What you spend there, I think I will probably spend it in one night. You just got to pick up the luggage from the bank and bring to my house when you get here.

FORTY-THREE

Gil

WE TAKE THE taxi to Bay Street, where the bank stood. You ever been to that street, man? It doesn't have nothing but banks: Citibank, Bank of America, HSBC, and a whole bunch of them that I never heard. We go there, and the manager comes, a white guy that's not dressing for the tropics: Gucci loafers, blue jacket, white shirt, red tie. He's like, Oh, you the guys that work with Mr. Steed? He has this accent that is European. European or German. He brings back this luggage, nice leather, kind of heavy. He's like, There should be no problem.

He drive us in his car to the airport. Beautiful black Mercedes S-Class. Probably cost no less than $100,000. I would love to drive that car, but I don't think he will let me. They drive left-side down there. It's crazy. I don't know why they do. We get there, and he knows the guys that is airport security. We like VIPs that they just skip us right by the security. The guy is like, Have a good flight. Give my regards to Mr. Steed. I'm like, I will, sir. Then he leave, and Natalia's like, What's in the luggage? I'm like, How the fuck do I know?

The luggage is kind of heavy. When I sit on my seat, I put that luggage right in front of me, so I wouldn't put on top. I'm thinking, Wow, what if it's money in there? Money that I never seen in my whole life. Cash. Greens. This would be it—every person's dream come true. I would ask the stewardess if they got a parachute. Open up the shit and let me jump. I will jump from the aircraft with that fucking luggage. Or I would just go and tell Natalia that I have this money, and we will both go back to Brazil, marry each other, and that will be our little secret. But then I will have to live like a soldier down in Brazil, because they will track my name down easy.

Natalia wanted to go to the bathroom, so I was like, Okay. Then I got the cover that they usually put when you sleep in the plane, and I block it up, the luggage, and I open it up—just to see. But it was just papers. A whole bunch of them. But come on, you think that's all? You think Jeff is going to send me to Bahamas just to get some papers? No way. There must be something hid up in the luggage that I'm not capable to see it.

Natalia comes back from the bathroom, and I put the luggage back. We take off, and what I was most worry about was being on the plane. I didn't think about nothing else beside that fucking plane. I think that when I'm on the plane, my life is in danger. Seriously. That's how I think. Because until today I can't have that on my mind: how can a plane be in the air? I don't believe it. I'm one of those. I get really nervous about it. I don't trust planes. I trust more my own driving.

I didn't even think about immigration until the plane landed. But in my head there's still something wrong. Maybe, the papers inside the luggage is not legal. Maybe, they will think I stoled the papers. A guy that big like Mr. Jeff would never, ever ask me for a favor that was just the usual stuffs. You think he make me carry the luggage just because he too busy? Come on! I'm pretty tense. I don't tell Natalia. Because the more people you will let them know, the crazier you will get. There's two people, so you don't want that.

We get on the line that you usually do to get checked. When I got into the immigration, it was tough, though, especially when you see that guy in the booth. It was this guy, I don't know if he was in the Navy, but he was wearing a white uniform. I look at the guy, take a deep breath. That guy was really serious. I was like, I just hope this person will not even look at my face, just let me go, let me go. Every little detail, every little way the person looks at you and the words that you say it, I just want to be accept. Please, please, let me go. Don't ask me too many questions. It was one of those situations. The heart was going really fast, my hands were kind of shake, my palm start feeling sweaty, I felt all cold. I'm not focusing on nothing else. I don't even know what the person be saying to me.

There is no way I can stay calm, because I don't know if I'm doing wrong. If this papers is not legal—I don't know how serious this thing could be. If they find this other stuffs, like drugs, I don't know what they will do. I was like, Wow, either I will be really nervous, and the Navy guy will know, or I will just stay calm, but there is no way I can stay calm, so I just pray for the best.

He's like, Why you go to Bahamas?

Just came back from my cousin's wedding, sir. It was a short trip. I kind of enjoy it. All the money that I had I spent down there, man. That place is unbelievable. They got casinos. I love to play poker. Poker's my thing. I ended up spending a couple of thousand dollars down there, but I'm pretty happy. Some people get their orgasms having sex. I get my orgasms playing poker.

He's like, Oh, yeah, what kind of poker you play?

I don't know much about poker. I don't know how they play. I don't understand that game. But I'm like, Every kind, my man. You get the cards now, we will play.

Oh, my God, I could see them put this handcuffs on me. Maybe they will put handcuffs on my feets.

He ask me if I had food or if I had drugs. I'm like, No, sir. He point at the luggage, What's in there? This is business material. Papers. You wanted to take a look? Feel free if you want to. Open it up.

Then he start to open the luggage.

I just start to shitting in my pants. I'm trying not to look down, just look straight, and breathe and let go . . . breathe and let go . . . breathe and let go . . . and just thinking what could be the next question.

But he see just the papers and he doesn't read them. He doesn't find nothing else.

When I got through, it was the best fucking feeling. I jumped around. Me and Natalia walk on the airport outside. I was just looking at everything like it was a paradise. We get this cab, and I leave Natalia at her mother's crib in Queens and bring the luggage to Mr. Jeff's house that is in Manhattan.

FORTY-FOUR

OH, MAN, THIS house is perfection. That's the thing about that house, everything is separate, like has doors to go in. The living room has glassy doors. It's all white. The kitchen is HUGE. Two refrigerators, HUGE ones. A little glass table right in the middle.

I didn't went to the bedrooms or anything. I just went to the main floor. There's three other floors up. This English lady that works for Mr. Jeff comes there, and she's like, You wanted to see the rest of the house? I was like, Nah. I just don't want to be too crazy about it. Not crazy, but some people just don't like when you go over to their crib and go, Wow! and you act like you never been to a place like that. So I was just acting normal. She's like, Mr. Jeff will come in a minute. So, she take me down the game room. In the basement.

In the game room there was a real bar, and I saw like, Yo, beers. She open up the refrigerator—all types. They even have that Jamaican beer I like, Red Stripe. I couldn't believe it when I saw it. I was like to the lady, Who drinks this? And she was like, Mr. Jeff's hairdresser drinks it when he comes here. And there was rows of champagne, ten of each one. Ten of Dom P, ten of Cristal. I was like, Wow.

There was a HUGE flat-screen TV, and there was like—you know when you go to a movie theater and you see these things outside that they have a picture of the movie. So Jeff has the same size, the HUGE ones, with autographs. He has one by *The Terminator*, with Arnold signed on the left side. When I saw that, I was like, Yo, this fucking thing right here doesn't cost no less than a thousand dollars. And then was another one, *Scarface*. I don't know who was the other persons that signed it, but one was Al Pacino. And then the other movies, I'm not too familiar with them. It was right next to each other, just five pieces. I was like, Wow.

There was a pool table. I'm like, Yo, this just like *MTV Cribs*.

And the funniest thing, there was this HUGE bear. A real one. It was there just to be there. I was like, All right. Maybe Mr. Jeff shot this motherfucker, but the English lady was like, Nah, he just bought it.

And I ask the lady to see the cars. In the garage it was a HUGE Yukon Denali, like GMC. And there was a Range Rover, the new one. There was a Jaguar. The English lady say Mr. Jeff drive a Denali, with spinny rims and a system that blows the whole house. She say he doesn't like no other cars. He just have them when he goes to places. But he just like that one particular car, the Denali. I think most of the rappers usually have it. You never heard about that car? It's a beautiful car. Sixty thousand.

And the English lady showed this thing, but she's like, Don't touch. It's a Barbie-doll box not with a Barbie inside, but it was Snoop. Replica. Snoop gave that to Mr. Jeff. Snoop Dog. He don't let nobody else touch it. She was like, You can probably hold it, but don't shake it or anything. And don't tell him.

You know about Snoop? Snoop Dog's a Crip. The ringer of my cell phone, that's a Snoop song. Snoop went to Rio. You never seen the video? Snoop Dog is the biggest thing out there. Everybody loves Snoop. He's the one that say, fo' shizzle my nizzle. He's the one that start with that.

Then Mr. Jeff comes in his bathrobe. I give Jeff the card that I got in Bahamas for Jake Smith that used to play for the NBA. I'm like, Jeff, I put it that I know this guy that was really powerful that works in a hedge fund. This NBA guys and hip-hop stars, they worth a lot of money. There is a whole bunch of them. Like Puff Daddy and Russell Simmons, they worth close to a billion. Master P is worth half a billion, maybe more. Jay-Z is like half a billion. Fifty Cent, he probably worth half a billion. So, Jeff, I can talk to this guys. For me, growing up around poor people, I kind of know how they think when they start making the money. They just wanted to go out there and try and to buy things they never had it. They won't go out there and buy themself a book and learn. They will buy themself a car and nice jewelry. Because that's how you usually get the respect from peoples.

I'm like, I can talk with this guys on that level. Like street ways: Yo, my man, let me tell you something. I'm over here, believe it or not, you know what I'm saying? I work for this hedge fund. There's not a lot of people from the hood that made it. You know how we talk to the white boys, it's differently. Dude, you could see how much money we making for other people. We got a list. If you invest like a millions, my man, I will get you 20 percent. We got a lot of ways.

I'm like, I can talk to this guys and get them to put that money with you. Did you ever thought about that?

He doesn't care. He just thinks I'm bullshit, an ignorant kid that is not capable to do nothing.

He's like, Let's see what we got here. And he put the luggage on top of the table. He ask if I open it up. I'm like, No. You think I'm going to touch it? This is my job: going there, picking up, and coming back. That's what you wanted me to bring it to you. That's why I went there.

I'm like, Sir, can I just ask you one question: What is the papers in there?

He's like, This papers from Mr. Bigelow to invest in the hedge fund that I work now.

For real, Jeff?

Yeah, and we got to keep it a secret because it doesn't look good if the men at Medved, Morningstar find out that he do.

I'm like, Is this papers legal?

He's like, Most of them! That's how he put it!

I'm thinking, Shit! Now, I know. I'm like, Jeff, this is the first time I'm doing for you, but on the next time, I would like to know. Because who will know what will be the next thing that I'm bringing without knowing. Because I don't want to get locked up. I don't think I need this job for this. I'm here to do you favors. Otherwise, I'll just quit from here. I don't need this job.

He's like, Gil, don't worry about it, you can't get locked up for carrying this papers.

But something is not right here. Mr. Jeff is very ambitions and he knows how to explore other people's weakness side. But money is not everything. In the beginning it will be nice, but then I will start seeing other things. I will be living a fast life, but I think the time I wake up until the time I went to sleep I will be living with fear. It's like a little mice when you put the trap. The mice got to be smart enough to kick these cheese out of the trap, and the trap will go off without it catching him. But then when he thinks he has it, the trap is going to work and *splat!* I'd rather be poor for the rest of my life than locked myself in a mice trap worth millions.

Jeff is like, You did good, Gil. You can start working for me on Monday.

I'm like, Jeff, I can't go there until after Christmas because I got Christmas tips and I usually wait the whole year for that.

I will just pretend that I'm taking the job, so Jeff can let me go from there. I just want to live life calm—not go crazy, you know? Not party hard, not drinking every day. Try to do a little better, the way I dress, the way I talk. I'm more concerned about this than I was before. The way I present myself in places. Just live a normal life. The peoples at my job, this peoples made me change a lot. Because when you dress ghetto and you act ghetto, you never going to get anything out of it. But the way I act right now. It's so nice, cool. People usually see the difference. They see me as A-OK kid. That's what I think.

So, I leave Mr. Jeff's place, and I call up Mr. Greg. He be leaving a lot of messages on my cell.

FORTY-FIVE

Greg

ANNIE AND I were reading the Sunday newspapers when Gil called. "I've been a little worried about you," I said when he showed up at my door a half hour later.

"Oh, yeah. My bill came up so high, they cut my service off."

"Where you been?" I asked. He had a tan.

"Bahamas."

"You're kidding. You didn't tell me you were going."

Annie came over to shake his hand, and I got him a beer.

"I've heard a *lot* about you," she said.

"Me, too," he answered.

"What were you doing in the Bahamas?" I asked.

"Just chilling."

"How's Eddy? Did he go, too?"

"Nah, he went back to Brazil."

"He did?"

"Yeah. Hey, you Japanese?" he asked Annie.

"No, my parents are Korean."

"Oh, because in Brazil, we see a person from over there, we always think the person's Japanese because there is a whole bunch them in Brazil. *Japa*, we say. We see that, we always think the persons a genius."

"Koreans are pretty smart, too," I said.

"I know that." He was starting to relax a bit. "What is like the womens in Korea?"

"Submissive," said Annie. "The men call all the shots, make all the decisions. My mother had to bow to her father when she met him on the street."

"I got to go to that place!"

"It's a very traditional society," explained Annie, warming to one of her favorite topics: how women are treated in Korea. "When a woman marries there, they say she presents her new husband with three keys: the key to a new car, the key to a new apartment, and the key to a new job. It's the idea that you marry a woman for her family, her property, and what she brings to the marriage."

"Hey, Greg, when you get married with Annie what kind of new car will you get? A Jaguar or a BMW?"

"I was thinking more a Porsche."

"Good luck," said Annie, which got Gil giggling.

"See, Gil, Annie's not really a typical Korean woman. When she walks into a store in Korea, they speak to her in English because she looks the store clerks straight in the eye. Your average Korean woman would look down, at the floor."

"You ever been to Korea, Greg?" Gil asked.

"Uh . . . no. I'm too white."

"Koreans don't like America?" Gil asked Annie.

"Oh, yes, they do. It's the dream, the lack of a class system, the idea that if you study and work hard enough, you could be president, no matter who you are. Is that how Brazilians see America?"

"Not really. We don't even know," he said. "It's just what we see on TV and movies. America is like, wow, I'm going to have a house and a whole bunch of Nike sneakers. I'm going to be able to go places like Disney. So stupid."

Gil got quiet again and gulped down his beer. I got him another.

"Gil, you look kind of upset," I said. "You want to tell me about it?"

"Not really. I don't know if you going to keep a secret or not if I'm going to tell you."

"You don't trust me by now?"

"I think I will find a way to solve this thing on my own, even if it's not that great, though."

"Is it about your job?"

"Yeah."

"Are you scared to tell me?"

"Dude, that's one thing that I really don't know about it. Because the human mind is so unsure that people could become crazy for little things."

"But you know, I'm there for you with your problems."

"I know you are. But this thing is really, really serious. It is not like some certain stories I told you. It's really crazy. I don't think it's good for me to tell you."

"It's worse to keep things all bottled up inside yourself."

"But, what benefits I'm going to get?"

"I might be able to see it a different way than you do. I have more experience. I'm older."

"That sounds like my mom, what she always be saying to me."

"What's the point of having friends if you don't trust them?"

"I don't know." He thought about it for a while, and killed his beer. I got him another.

"I told you a lot of things. I don't know if I should. But it makes me feel better," he said finally. "It makes me have this confidence that I have in myself these days. Like in Bahamas. I went there and I behaved right. I never used to feel comfortable."

"What were you doing in the Bahamas?"

"Mr. Steed pay for me to go over there."

Holy shit! Then he told me the rest: witnessing the argument between Steed and Bigelow, going clubbing with Steed, flying first-class, staying at the fancy hotel, bringing back the briefcase.

"Were you scared?" asked Annie, who had stopped pretending to read the newspaper.

"Oh. My. God. When the guard open that luggage, and he ask about playing that poker that I don't know nothing, I was shitting my pants."

"Just tell me again: what exactly did Steed say to Bigelow?" I asked.

"He said that Mr. Billy had done something bad, and he had accounts in Swiss, and Jeff wanted fifty mil to fire hisself or he will report Mr. Billy to the feds, so Mr. Billy could go to prison."

"Are you sure he said fifty million? That's a lot of money."

"Fifty mil, that's what he said it."

"Who are you more worried about now? Jeff Steed or Mr. Bigelow?" asked Annie.

"Mr. Billy, he cool, but I got that fear of Jeff. I don't know what is true and what is not with that guy. It's a weird feeling. I lose the trust in the person. I just don't want nothing to do with them."

"Gil, are you sure all this is completely true? You didn't make up any of it?"

"You think I'm lying?"

"No, no. It's just so crazy."

"I don't think it was nice, what Jeff said to Mr. Billy."

"Yeah, well, on Wall Street it's survival of the fittest—you ever heard that before? That means you, too. You've got to be very, very careful now. Do not attract attention to yourself. If these guys knew how smart you were and how much you understood and that you were talking to me, and I was writing this article, they would flip out."

"I know that. But, Greg, you don't got to do this article now."

"Why not?"

"Because Eddy doesn't care no more. He's back to Brazil."

"Yeah, but this is still a great story, Gil."

"You think it's nice, though?"

"No, but these people aren't nice."

"They nice to me, some of them. Mr. Billy is nice."

"They're doing things that are bad. Steed is breaking the law, for sure. He's trying to blackmail Bigelow."

"You think it will help Mr. Billy if you write the article?"

"Maybe it will. Listen, I don't want you to worry about any of this. Just go back to work and go about your business as usual."

FORTY-SIX

Gil

I GO SEE Tim and Jim. They like, Gil, you got a tan! Where you been? I'm like, Oh, I just went to the tan salon. Because I didn't wanted to explain them about me and Natalia going to Bahamas. The traders, they always like to know about a person's life. They love that shit. I don't know why. They love to ask me how, what I did through the weekend. When I ask them, they just tell me something that I know is not true. I ask them, So what did you do? They like, Oh, I sat at home, watched football, took care the kids. I'm like, That's it? They like, Yeah, had a couple of beers. You think that's true? Hell no, man. They tan. They think I can't see? They go on vacation, but they don't want to tell me. Either South Beach or California or ski in Sun Valley. When I'm passing by and shine someone's shoes, I hear them talking to each other.

Tim, he's not going through a good time right now in his job, though. It's like his boss trying to fuck him over. He was really tired. He had a red eye. I was like, Yo, Tim, come here, man, go put some eye whiteout, because your eyes look really red. And he was like, Gil, I don't give a fuck. I'm tired. I want them to see that I be working here, that I'm not bullshitting. That's what they think that I'm doing. I'm like, All right, Tim. It's a new boss, changed. So this guy, I don't know what he thinks, but he doesn't know Tim. Tim doesn't explain it, but that's the way he put it to me, that they think he not doing the good job there.

Matthew came up to me and he's like, I have a friend of mine that's coming from out of town, Gil. Do you know where to get the good stuff? I'm like, You mean smoke? But it's kind of illegal if I bring it to you in here. He's like, No, no, no. I want good coke. I'm like, Oh, I don't mess with that, Matthew. I'm sorry. I wish I could help. He's like, You don't have any friends in New Jersey? I'm like, No. If I was doing this in here, I would never shine shoes because imagine how many people I probably know in this place that fucking do the same thing you want. I just don't want to lose my job, and I don't want to mess with this.

Because a lot of them do. Everybody, I think, tried that. Friday mornings you see it. Because peoples usually go out on Thursday. They come there and they tired, but not tired. You can see they have a runny nose. And they go like, Wow, Gil, I was up until four, and I just came into work. They didn't slept, and they hyped. You got to have something on your fucking system for you to act like that. I don't think you just act like that out of the blue. If I go around every Friday there will be at least five or six.

Mr. John come back from vacation, too, and told me they had a bachelor party in the Dominican Republic. It was like eight guys. All this guys that went there knew each other. One of his friends went there first to set up—this is the guy that knew about this whole thing. They wanted to make a surprise for the bachelor. So his friend went there, went to a so-called casino. A white guy, never had that before, started gambling. He first blew out his first credit card, and then he blew out his second credit card. And then he had money, blew out all his cash.

The Dominicans were like, White guy, over here! American! They brought him into this room. They were like, We going to lend you some money, if you want to continue playing. So, this guy goes and play for the whole night. I don't know if he was on coke, or what. But he was fucked up, John say. He play for the whole night. Then it was a period that they stop. They were like, Sir, you owe us $200,000 American dollars. And the guy was like, Holy shit. The guy went crazy. He was like, I can't pay you—this and that. I got friends coming over, you know, we going to do this bachelor party, whatever.

John say that they hold the guy and they call up the cops, the Dominican Republic cops. They haul this guy in. When his friends got there the next morning, they had to chip in ten thousand dollars—they gave to the casino guys, so they could let the guy go. But the police got all his information, where he lived in the U.S., every little thing that you can imagine.

It's all right. After that, they went there, they had more money. They rented out this house. Eight rooms. HUGE swimming pool. Thirty American dollars a day. They got some fifteen girls, the first day. Some girls were just there for the pizza, some girls were just there $30 a day, some girls, the high-class ones, $200 a day. One of this girls look like Britney Spears, blonde, blue eyes. I'm like, Dominicans look like that? Mr. John say he couldn't believe it when he saw it.

When Mr. John first walk into the house, four girls, four naked girls jump on top of him. And he's not used to that, he say. Jump and start kissing him and start grabbing him. And then he just went crazy. He say most of the time he just stood with one girl. He say he stood with this girl for three days. He used to look into his side, and it was his friend making out with two other girls, and the girl used to call up more girls to come. It was a party thing, a HUGE orgy.

If the girls weren't having sex, they were free. You could get the girl now and fuck her, and if you feel like fucking again, you just go get her and fuck her again. John said that one of his friends just fuck all of them girls. That's how they were doing, switching around, like a big circle. John said his friend got head from this girl inside the pool. How crazy is that? Never heard such a thing like that.

He said there was sex all the time. But he just wanted to stay with this one girl—he the type that he get attached to one person. He asked this girl questions like, What is the hardest thing when you meet a guy? Because he said that most of them, they were just doing because they had kids. It was hard, single moms and stuffs.

John said it was a great and crazy thing. He said that it was the thing that you got to do once in your lifetime, and that's it. But he say that when he come out of there, he couldn't look in peoples' face. I was like, Why? He was like, Because it was so crazy. Just thinking about people doing that.

At the end they driving back to the airport, and they go to buy antibiotics. They all fuck with condoms, but they lick this girls, went down on them, and they don't know what kind of diseases they had. John say there was this down-the-road pharmacy, and they ask this guy. They didn't have the antibiotics, but they have shots. And one of the eight guys was a doctor. You know what he did? He got everybody lined up on the road, seven guys lined up on the road. Told them to take their pants down. And the needle was not small, tiny needles, because they didn't have there. It was HUGE. Everyone had his own needle, and he said his friend give each one a shot in the ass, and people were passing by on the road, and they didn't even know what the fuck they doing. Because everybody's on the line, and his friend was giving shots, a whole bunch of shots, for a whole bunch of different things.

This is not the end of the story. His friend that gamble all that money came back. He wasn't going to pay, he wasn't never going to go back to the Dominican Republic. He thought, What the fuck, this guys never going to come over here.

The thing that happened was, he ended up finding out there was a mafia here, too. A Dominican mafia connected to that mafia down there. They knew where he lived. This guys keep on calling his house and make him threats: If you don't pay us, we going to get somebody to kill you. They call him up, they were like, Yo, you got to pay, you got to pay.

He had to hire a lawyer to know about this whole thing. Because he didn't want to pay the Dominicans. They made a deal that he had to pay $75,000, after everything.

I'm like, Oh my God, are you serious, Mr. John?

I went to shine Pete's shoes. This guys were talking about how this other guy was supposed to go to his college reunion. Mr. Pete was like, You know, I'm going to my college reunion, and I'm feeling so good about myself. Man, he look really good, now. He's dressing so nice, nice suit, nice tie, Ferragamos. He wanted the guy who sit by him to notice that he dye his hair, but the guy didn't say nothing until he make the comment, What do you think? You think I look younger? The other guy goes, Nah, you look the same. Pete goes, I dyed my hair. The other guy was like, Oh, you dyed your hair? They never pay attention to those stuffs. They would probably pay attention if there was a booger in your nose, but not that you had dye your hair.

When Pete goes to the bathroom, they ask Rona how many guys there that she have noticed that had dyed their hair. And the other guys listens to her, and she was like, There's five guys that dyed their hair, and she start pointing it out who it was on the floor. And then Rona goes, But, down there—she points down there—it's probably three out of one, like two pubic hairs will be white and one will be black. I was like, What the fuck is that?

I went to this bar after work that Pete and Rona were there, and I just pretend I don't see it. They drinking and talking, but then you know, come on! That's no business shit. They're not there to do business. Because if they want to do business, they won't go to a bar. Then he just kissed her. I think he had everything all planned out. It was a long-ass kiss. I felt like, What the fuck is this? It was like going back to ninth grade. Then they just went off on each other. They kissed each other for no less than an hour. After they leave, I follow a little, just to see. They walking on the street, and Pete would just stop and kiss Rona, but it seem he try and respect her always. He wasn't that aggressive.

FORTY-SEVEN

I CALLED BILL Bigelow's office, and his secretary put me through.

"Mr. Bigelow," I said, "this is Greg Waggoner. My editor Ed Brown tells me that you called our owner, Al Lieberman, with some concerns about an article I am writing."

"Yes, Mr. Waggoner, I did. I'm very worried that you have been getting some faulty information."

"If that's so, I'd like to come in and talk with you."

"I was hoping you would. I'm going to put my assistant on, and you can make an appointment with her."

She scheduled me for the next morning. Steed must have given Bigelow an earful about my interview with him. I didn't care so much about Steed anymore. He was now just a supporting player. The real story was Bigelow, his Swiss bank account, and the illegal trading Steed was blackmailing him with. It would have been smarter to wait to approach him directly until I had more information—the name of a stock or an accomplice, some detail that would make Bigelow think I knew 75 percent instead of 25 percent—but I had no time. My only hope was to bluff him.

The next morning, Bigelow's assistant led me into his office, with its thick pile carpet, sports memorabilia, and pictures of what looked to me to be bridge tournaments. Carrying a *Wall Street Journal*, Bigelow entered from the door to the private can.

A big man, bulky in the way of an athlete gone to seed, he had a jowly face with blue veins around his nose and milky, blue eyes behind thick lenses. He was wearing an English bespoke suit that had seen better days. I couldn't help but notice the high shine on his new Gucci loafers. Gil had told me that Yuri finally refused to work on the old ones anymore, for fear they would disintegrate.

"Mr. Waggoner, so nice to meet you," Bigelow greeted me warmly. "My wife is such a big fan of yours, reads all your articles in *Glossy*. She tells me she even met you recently at lunch. Would you like some bottled water or a cup of coffee?"

"No, thanks."

"Unfortunately, I don't get much time to read magazines myself."

"Oh, well."

"But, a lot of people I respect read *Glossy*, and they tell me it is a fine, fine publication. Al, your owner, is a neighbor of mine up in Connecticut. Nan and I play bridge with him and Sarah." He paused significantly to let that sink in.

"Is Nevada Jones a friend of yours?" I said, nodding toward the wall where an inscribed photograph of the legendary quarterback hung.

"No, but he likes money. A lot!" said Bigelow, chuckling. "So, tell me, what is all this I hear about an article you're writing about that fine young man Jeff Steed?"

"I heard from various sources that Steed was a colorful personality, not your usual trader."

"I think genius is the word I might use if I were writing your article, Mr. Steed. I've seen a lot of bright young men come and go in my time, but Jeff is in a league of his own, a trader of true genius."

"How did you let him get away?"

"I offered him a huge bonus to stay, but I couldn't compete with a hedge fund. There is a compensation structure here, and we have to be fair to everyone. Frankly, it's not even the money with these young guys. They don't want to work at the big firms, anymore. They think we're dinosaurs. They don't want to deal with the red tape and the bureaucracy. They don't want to go to management meetings. It's all different from when I was starting out. Then we knew we had to work our way up. There were no shortcuts. I think there was precisely one hedge fund at the time, run by . . ."

I didn't want to let him get started waxing nostalgic about the old days. "Mr. Bigelow . . ."

"Call me Bill, please. I feel old enough as it is without you young bucks mistering me all the time."

"Okay. Bill. I was wondering if you were aware that there is an impression out there that Steed's departure was not entirely voluntary."

"Where on earth did you hear that?"

"I've been talking to people."

"And that's the kind of lousy thing they've been saying?"

"That some impropriety was involved, something that was discussed in the management committee."

"Now, why would you want to go and write something like that about a fine young man like Jeff Steed, the kind of thing that could ruin a promising career?"

"I don't want to ruin anyone's career. I just want to write what actually happened. So, tell me: Was he asked to leave?"

"Poppycock! That's what I say to that."

"Bill, there are probably reporters out there who that would work on, but you and I know that word is meaningless. I need you to make a statement that means something."

"Okay, Mr. Waggoner . . ."

"Greg."

"Okay, Greg. I can't make it clearer than this: Jeff left of his own accord."

"Bill, I can't print that. You and I both know it's not true. You're one hand clapping. I have too much information, so don't even go there."

"Well, if you already know everything, why are you bothering to ask me about it?"

"What I need is for you to help me understand the factors that forced the company to make the decision it did." It was always good with guys like Bigelow to get them to assume the corporate mantle.

He thought for a minute. "All right, but this is way, *way* off the record."

"If 'off the record' means I can't know what you're telling me—no way! I have to be able to know what you're saying. What I can do is not attribute the information to you but to a source close to management, or something like that. I'm aware that this is a very sensitive matter, and I want to handle it correctly."

"Greg, I am trusting that you will do just that and that you will also protect me totally. Yes?"

"I will."

"Mr. Steed was asked to leave because he was found to have committed an infraction of our corporate policies."

"Such as?"

"I'm sorry. I can't discuss that, even off the record."

"Was this infraction related to an incident in which a janitor discovered Steed on his cell phone on the trading floor?"

"What sort of nonsense is that? Who told you that?"

"The janitor. His name is Eduardo Silva. Evidently, the firm fired him after he reported finding Steed on his cell phone in a men's room utility closet." Since Eddy was back in Brazil, there was no harm in naming him.

"We subcontract out the cleaning and cafeteria work to an independent company, so I don't see how we could get one of their employees fired."

"Evidently, you did."

"I'm a detail-oriented man, Mr. Waggoner, but you'll forgive me for not keeping track of the janitorial staff. I'm sure there is a logical explanation for this man being let go, and I'll check into it for you."

"When you investigated Steed's infraction did you discover any illegal activity?"

"If we had, we would have turned the information over to the SEC."

"Bill, I am also hearing that the firm allowed Mr. Steed to leave with his bonus, which seems to me highly unusual under the circumstances."

"I'm afraid I can't discuss that. There is a legal agreement that prohibits me from doing so."

"I also understand that you personally made the decision to let him keep his bonus."

"Whoa, there. Time out. I do not want to be in your article in any way. I simply *will not* be in the article."

"Bill, you're in it. It is unavoidable. That train has already left the station. The question is how you're going to be portrayed." He began to look very unhappy. "Now, my understanding of what happened, and it is a pretty clear understanding, is that you shared a mutual interest with Mr. Steed. There were things that you could do, let's say, to harm Mr. Steed, and things that he could do, I gather, to harm you, and so it was convenient that you both leave this negotiation with smiles on your faces."

"What in hell are you talking about, Mr. Waggoner?" His jowls were set and hard, his blue eyes fierce.

"I think you know."

"I have no idea what you are talking about."

"Look, there are any number of theories floating around out there, and I have a good sense of what Mr. Steed's interests were, but what I need to understand better are yours, because I'm forced to discuss them in the article. I have some concrete information, and I can engage in a lengthy speculation, but I'm looking for some guidance from you."

"Guidance about what?"

"It's pretty apparent that there was concern over a certain transaction." When you were dealing with an investment firm, you couldn't go wrong with the word "transaction."

"Oh?"

"Look, Bill, I understand the situation that you believe you're in. You have to understand, though, there are a lot of voices in this article, voices that you can reasonably expect are going to be discussing what you did. All I'm asking you, and we're way, way off the record here, deep off the record, is to add your voice, so that I'll have an understanding of what occurred from your point of view. It's in your interest that I know every fact that can be mustered in your favor. I know that this was an unusual transaction, involving foreign banks, but how did you perceive it and your role in it at the time?"

"Which transaction are we talking about, exactly?"

"The same one that Steed knew about."

He flinched ever so slightly. My heart started to race. "Look, Greg, there are many gray areas in finance."

"There are, indeed."

"Especially when we're talking about what is nonpublic information and how one hears it. Even the regulators are not really consistent about it."

"How did you hear this particular information?"

He started to say something, but then stopped and studied my face. For too long. "Mr. Waggoner, do you know what psychic bidding is in contract bridge?"

"When you get ESP about your partner's hand?"

"No."

"I'm sorry, I haven't played bridge since I was fourteen."

"A psych is used to bluff your opponents into thinking you have a stronger hand than you do in a certain suit."

"Oh?"

"Beginners get excited when they learn about it, and they tend to use it at every opportunity. Serious amateurs might use it once in a great while to liven up a dull game. Expert players never use it."

"What's your point?"

"That I'm quite surprised at you for trying. I thought you were better than that."

"Bill, I admit that I don't have the full story, if that's what you mean. That's why I'm giving you the chance to present your side of it."

"I think you are on a fishing trip here, Mr. Waggoner. You'd better be extremely careful about what you write. Jeff and I have the best lawyers in the city—arguably in the world—and we won't hesitate to unleash them."

"I've been sued six times, and my record is six-zero, so bring it on."

"We have other weapons in our arsenal. You're playing in a pretty big league here. If I were you, I'd be very, very careful. People could get hurt."

"Is that a threat?"

"Let's just say my hand it too strong for a simple overcall."

MRS. ALICE CALL me up on my cell phone to come to shine her shoes. She never do that before. It was around midday. She always have her shoes shined off, so I go there to get the shoes. She's on the phone, but she goes, Wow, Gil, you look great with the tan! Can you shine my shoes on the feets today?

Couple of people there sitting on the desk, but she sits, when you start a row, almost at the end by the windows. She was facing me and nobody else, just me and her in this little hallway that goes by the window, so nobody sees it. I'm there, she was talking on the phone, with this little earpiece, and looking at the computer screen. I had my head down the whole time. And she had on, not a miniskirt, but it was a little bit up to her knees. I didn't look up, because some peoples watch me when I'm doing that, especially womens. Guys, they don't care as much. But, when I look up, Alice had no panties. I was like, Holy fuck. There was her pussy, no underwear, no nothing. Just thick, brown pubic hair. I was trying to figure out, What's up with that?

I kept on shining, I took my time there. It couldn't be a mistake. Fuck that! Hell, yeah! She had to fucking know. Because when she did, she had her legs open. What she think? I'm not going to look? She didn't even try to close. She looked good, though. She didn't look that bad. Her body's kind of strong. You can see her legs are strong. They not huge, but they okay size. She got tiny feet, baby size, five and a half.

I went to switch, I kind of tap on her foot when I was done. Same thing. I took my time, another ten minutes. She gave me a good tip, ten dollars. When I finish, she just went, Thanks a lot, Gil, and she smile at me like we have a little secret.

I was home around ten, and a women call me up. First, she was like, Hey, hi, do you recognize my voice? I was like, No. She sounded a little bit drunk. I was like, All right, I can't guess who it is, because the persons that usually call me at this time, they usually Brazilians, they never an American. I don't have American friends that call me that late. I'm cool with Americans, but it would be a fucking surprise for them to call me late, and I don't have it.

She sound kind of old, too. She didn't sound that young. Then when she told me who it was—Mrs. Alice—I was shock! I was like, Is Natalia there? Alice is like, Yeah. Downstairs. Taking care the kids.

We start talking, and she said that her husband went on a trip again, and in the job she's got to pretend that she's a happy person, but deep down, she's a really unhappy person. We kind of talked about everything. She asked me if I was happy with Natalia, and if we will get married. I just told her I'm too young. Brazilians, we don't usually take marriage that serious when we young. In Brazil we don't have that marriagey lifestyle that you guys in America has it. We got to enjoy life a little bit.

She start to laugh. She kind of play it off that she was a nice woman, but at the same time kind of dirty. She say that she did stuffs before, but right now she doesn't do. One time, right after she was married—that was maybe fifteen years ago—she got with a young guy. He was a intern at the firm. And he was a fun guy, but he had to go back to wherever he came from, because those interns, they usually come from different states. She start telling me about this young guy that she did, and that was a hint from her. I was like, All right.

We start getting open with each other. She asked if I ever cheat on Natalia, and I didn't, but I told her I did it twice. She's like, Oh, that's not nice. I told her, Well, it's not nice, but until I'm old, I'm going to enjoy life. She kind of laughed at the same time when I say those things, but she kept to herself. She didn't say anything.

I'm like, What this womans want to do with me now? Is she fucking real? Because this is kind of unbelievable. You never going to imagine this is going to happen to you. I already know that she wanted to do it. The way she sounded, like, duh, if you know how womens is. If they say something that they done it, they want to do it. They like that.

When I see Alice the next day at work, I went to talk to her, say hi, whatever, ask if she was feeling better. She was like, No, no, I'm cool. She was trying to be very professional. She didn't flirt or anything. I was like, Whoa, this woman's kind of crazy. One night, she was talking to me all sweet, and today she's really serious. I went like, All right, I got to go, bye. She was like, Hey, come here. Wait for my phone call tonight. I was like, Cool.

So I went home. Alice call me up around eight thirty. She was in the bathtub, that's how she put it. She was like, Hey, how you doing? I was like, Wow, this womans changed her voice. She was like, Well, I'm here, I'm laying in the bathtub. I'm kind of drinking this wine. And, you know, I feel comfortable when I talk to you. I'm starting to getting to know you and stuffs. We start talking about things, like how I kind of live my life. Like I go there, and I work. And she always deal with this big business things. And she told me that even though I kind of experienced some of this stuffs, that sometimes I go to places that rich peoples goes, I'm never pretend to be a rich person, and she like that.

Because she's like, Most of those guys at the job, they always trying to pretend that they something, but sometimes they not even that. They have money, but they don't have no class. Because they all about money. They don't care about their own family and stuffs. She was telling me those things, and I was like, Whoa, cool.

And then she got really emotional, and she was asking me about my sex life with Natalia. I'm feeling kind of funny, because I'm thinking that Natalia is over there, taking care the kids. But I was like, Well, I really have good sex with Natalia, but I enjoy doing with older womens. And then I told that one time I was at the barbecue at my uncle's house, and there was a whole bunch of peoples over there, at least fifty, my aunt's friends. We stayed there the whole afternoon. And this old lady, she was over there. She was kind of old, she was like forty-three, blond, skinny, probably about five foot six. We start talking. I was drinking like crazy, probably had about four, five Coronas. I had that little buzz. This lady just got divorced, that's what my aunt told me. Because my aunts usually talk around peoples, and whoever's not married, they usually talk about.

I went there to talk to her, and she saw that I was not that dumb, because some of this Brazilian guys, they can be pretty dumb, really from the countryside. But I'm from the city, and I have a lot more interesting things maybe to talk to her. She kind of liked me, whatever. And then she invite me to go outside in her car, and we went. We drive around the block, and we stop right next to this park, because they live in Westchester. And over there we did it. We did everything. I told Alice how I got this old lady, and I was fucking her doggy-style in the back inside this tiny little car. This lady had a Neon, it's not that big of a car. It was hot that day, and we couldn't open up the windows. She didn't want to leave the car on, the AC, so all the windows got foggy and we got hot, hot, hot with all this sweats on our bodies.

Mrs. Alice was like, Whoa! I kind of heard her making noise through the phone. I was like, Okay, so what you doing? She was like, Well, you not going to get mad at me if I tell, and you not going to tell anybody? You know, I can either lose my job and you can lose your job. I was like, Trust me, I know a lot of things than you think I know, and I never say nothing to anybody. I always kept to myself. A lot of peoples when they say some stuffs around me they think that I'm that fucking dumb, but I ain't that dumb, though. I just pretend that I'm dumb.

Alice goes like, All right. Then she told me that she was masturbating herself, that she was into the story that I was telling her. She was like, Well, I like the way you did it in the car.

FORTY-NINE

Greg

IT WOULD STILL be good, I kept telling myself, the article I'd described to Ed, but it wasn't a home run. More like a double: the tale of Jeff Steed, rogue trader—his teenage financial capers (on the record from Vergil), his friendship with Nan Bigelow, the Luxembourg bank document, getting caught "stretching the rules" in the bathroom, his friendship with Joe Cantone, his love affair with the Russian stripper, his foul-ups with the nonprofits, being asked to leave Medved, Morningstar (on background from Bill Bigelow), going to work at Persimmons.

That story seemed so pale, though, now that I knew about Steed's blackmail attempt, charging Bill Bigelow with insider trading. Unfortunately, I didn't know enough to write that story. I couldn't even go with the blackmail scene—Gil was the only witness, and I couldn't compromise him.

There was no time to worry. I had to start writing.

Nothing came, though. Knowing there was so much more than I could write paralyzed me.

I stared at my computer screen. I went on the Internet. I read my e-mail.

I drank coffee. I took a nap. I drank more coffee.

I wrote the first sentence forty-seven times. I kept reviewing the notes and tapes of my various interviews.

I was listening to the tape of my drunken dinner with Vergil and

Wi, when something popped. Wi was saying, "And Amy and Abe got hauled in by the feds about five years before Abe died. Insider trading, they said, some tip Amy got from her sister or somebody. They could never prove nothing, but I know because she told Vergil about it and he run to his broker like he usually done. It's a miracle they didn't all end up in prison."

At the time, I hadn't paid much attention to this little juicy bit, because I didn't know that Amy X's sister was Nan Bigelow. But now I realized that Jeff Steed had probably heard about Bigelow's insider trading from Amy X! She must have told him about it!

I dug out the Petersons' number from my notes and dialed, praying that Vergil didn't answer.

"Rancho Vergil." It was Winona.

"Wi, this is Greg Waggoner, the guy from New York who took you and Vergil to dinner a few months back."

"Oh, yeah. Thanks for nuthin'. The waiters had to *carry* Vergil out to the car after you left. He was out cold. Didn't get up for three days, the old fool."

"I wasn't in such good shape myself the next day. I don't know how I got back to L.A. in one piece. But, hey, listen, I just had one question about a little thing you mentioned then."

"What?"

"Remember you told me that Amy X got a tip from her sister about a stock and that she and her husband got into hot water with the government for acting on the tip?"

"I surely do. And Vergil bought some, and the feds hauled his tired ass in there, along with Amy and Abe."

"Would you by any chance remember the name of the stock?"

"Not likely to forget that one. St. Joe's Mineral Corp."

"Wow! Wi, thank you so much. Anytime you're in New York, I'll buy you another steak."

"Not much chance of that."

An Internet search revealed that in the early eighties, the day before the Seagram Corporation had made a tender offer for St. Joe's, there had been massive trading in St. Joe's stock and options, causing the share price to jump 50 percent. An SEC investigation uncovered that Edgar Bronfman, who owned Seagram, had discussed his plans with a friend who was a European banker. When Bronfman canceled a dinner date, the banker had deduced the tender offer was imminent and bought a truckload of St. Joe's call options. He also leaked the news to several clients, who took advantage of the tip. The SEC successfully prosecuted the banker, but never succeeded in getting the Swiss to release the names of the secondary layer of their clients who had profited.

I called up Harry to ask about St. Joe's. "The longest investigation in our history," he explained. "Over ten years of my life. We just closed it down a few years ago, and we never nailed the American side, even though we pretty much knew who they were. We could only get the Swiss to cooperate so far."

"Any possibility that Bill Bigelow was involved?"

Long silence, then: "What do you know?"

"I have some strong circumstantial evidence."

"Man, if you can prove that . . . We believed that Bigelow and a few other Medved, Morningstar execs were the red-hot center over here. We had them in for questioning at least a half dozen times. But we couldn't get them to crack."

St. Joe's was my trump card, but I needed to go see Bigelow again to play it.

FIFTY

Gil

AFTER WORK WE driving up to Greenwich to see Natalia because this kids is driving her crazy.

Mrs. Alice tells it that she love the kids. Well, she does love the kids, but she never gives no attention to them. They only see the kids and play with them a little bit. At the same time they don't want to be around.

The Latino usually raise the kids different. The parents always there. The kids do something stupid—BOOM, smack them. It's not like the Americans. Raise the kid, if the kid do anything wrong, they trying to talk to the kids. And the kids talk back to the father. And the father just forget about it, and just let it die. Because he doesn't want no aggravation. But Latinos, the kids talk back—BOOM, you get smacked in your mouth. So you never do that again.

Fabio and me, we went there. To me the kids, they very quiet. The little boy, Oliver, stay in his room playing chess at the computer. Willa sit in her little corner with the iPod. She get up and change her clothes no less than three times in one hour. Natalia show me Willa's closet that you can walk in. It's no less than five hundred outfits. It was like a little store. I'm serious!

Willa's going bald because she picks her hair out. Her hair is like no hair, just little hairs. She looks ridiculous, like a Ronald McDonald kid. They took her to the doctor, and they say because her mom doesn't give her no attention, so she goes crazy. That's how Natalia put it.

Alice doesn't care, that's what Natalia says. It's fucked up. The Latino usually stays home to take care the kids. Now, the American way,
they don't give a fuck. They'd rather pay someone to take care, and
only have the kids on the weekend. That's how Natalia usually explain
me: the mother comes home, kisses the kids, and puts them to bed.
If the baby girl gets up in the middle of the night, Natalia is the one
that gets up from her bed and goes to take care. Natalia got to stay on
weekends, too. I don't know why they have a babysitter if the parents
home. It seem like they can't take care their own kids.

But the kids nice to Fabio and me. Very quiet. Natalia say the kids
see a different person they don't know, they try and act nice. But to
her they nasty, when no one else around. Everything that they make
a mess, and Natalia can't leave a mess around the house. That really
gets her stressed out all the time. She was like, I can't believe it, this
fucking kids. When the mother's around, they listen to me, but when
the mother wasn't around, they fucking want to destroy the whole
house.

I was like, Yeah, but don't hit them, because once you hit them,
you go to jail. She was like, It's not my house, I don't care. They can
break the whole fucking house. I was like, Yo, Natalia, don't hit the
kids, please. Because she doesn't know. She's Colombian, and that's the
way there: whatever you do wrong, the parents usually hit.

The baby girl, Jenny, the one that Alice call Lucifer, the devil girl,
the worst. Since from the time that she gets up until whatever time,
she talks to herself. Two years and a half! This little girl talks, talks,
talks, talks.

When Natalia comes, Jenny is like, When you going back to Colombia? Natalia is like, Why? And then she was like, Because I see
your luggages, and you don't live here. And Natalia was like, Yes, I do.
And the little girl was like, No, you don't live in this house. You live in
Colombia. Why don't you get your stuffs and go back there.

The parents offer Natalia more money—like $20 more—so she
can have this kid up the whole afternoon. You know, because kids usually take a nap in the afternoon, they usually wakes up in the middle

of the night. Natalia had this kid up the whole afternoon until seven at night, so the kid sleeps when she go to bed.

This little girl goes and asks for cereal, right? And Natalia goes there, fills up the dish with cereal, and the little girl goes, I don't want that. So, Natalia puts the dish away, and the girl goes, I want the cereal. And then when Natalia goes back, the girl goes, I don't want that.

That little girl plays mind games, man. She's crazy. Natalia goes with her in the supermarket, the little girl was inside the shopping cart, and she was throwing everything, like when she could grab some, inside the cart. Natalia was like, Stop. But the girl doesn't listen to her. Two and a half. And the little girl bites her, hits her if Natalia doesn't do the things that this girl wants to do. This girl got no manners. She hit Natalia on the leg, on the face.

You know what the little girl said to her mom, she be saying things like, Let's see titties. Always about titties. And, Let's go in the bathroom and see daddy taking a shower. Stuffs like that. Isn't that crazy?

The thing is the parents don't hit the kid. The kid goes on top of the table, and steps on the food, and Alice goes, Oh, don't do that. Oh, get down. Natalia looks around, and she goes like, Fuck, if that was my kid, I'd be slapping the shit out of her. I keep telling Natalia, Look, don't you ever hit this kids. You can go to jail for life. Because this kids are so spoiled, they never get hit.

I'm there with Natalia and Fabio in the kitchen. We see the car light arriving to the house. Park the car, and there was Mrs. Alice. I was like, Wow. I'm not that great of an actor, but I'm pretending nothing happened, like everything was cool. Mrs. Alice comes, and she say hi. She ask how my day was, how Fabio's day, how Natalia's day was, how was the kids behaving. She say that she got to go use the bathroom and the bathroom is up into her room. She goes there, and five minutes later she comes back down, and she ask me help her out moving some boxes that is in her room, and she wants to put up in the attic. Fabio's like, I can help, too. She's like, Nah, it's just one box.

To me it was fine. I took that as a job. I walk up the stairs, and I didn't even think what she was going to do to me. I just thought she really want my help. Once I got to her bedroom she look at me, she kind of smile. I didn't even know why she smiled at me that way for. I asked her, Are you smiling because of the phone talk that we had it? You think it was funny? She's like, Nah, that wasn't funny at all. I'll show you something that is not funny, but it will make you smile.

She throw me on the bed, pulls down my pants, and start going down on me. I was like, Whoa, I can't believe she's doing. And I told her, Look, Natalia can come here anytime. She's like, I don't care.

She kept on doing, doing, doing for the next five minutes. I was like, Aw, shit, this womans really crazy! I was like, Oh, my God! I came. She look at me with this HUGE smile and just ask me if I was satisfy. I was like, Wow, what am I going to say now? She was like, You don't have to say anything. Just get down there and kiss your girl and pretend nothing happened.

I looked at her, and I'm like, I'm not an actor, but I'm going to try. I went the bathroom and throw some cold water on my face, trying to be calm. I get down there, and Natalia asks me if the box was heavy. I'm like, Yeah, it was pretty heavy. And I just keep on trying to do whatever I was doing. Fabio's like, What was in the box? I'm like, Books.

FIFTY-ONE

Greg

I CALLED BIGELOW'S office. His secretary wouldn't put me through, so I told her to give him a message: I had some important new information, and I was certain he would want to comment on it.

There was no time to wait for the interview, though. I had to write around it and slot it in later.

Now the article flowed out of me in a torrent. Usually it's torture for me, getting the paint down on the canvas. Not this time. I drank a gallon of Mountain Dew and blasted through.

It didn't take me long to realize that I couldn't avoid including the big scene between Steed and Bigelow. Steed's accusation was the only thing that connected Bigelow directly to Wi's tale of insider trading in St. Joe's. To use the scene I had to get Gil's permission, because it meant outing him. But, I reasoned, if I nailed Bigelow on St. Joe's, there would be no risk to Gil in revealing his role in the story: he'd be a hero, the shoeshine boy who brought down the crooked CEO!

A problem was that Gil actually liked Bigelow. I would have to explain to Gil how insider trading was a crime, how in the end it hurt people like him and his friends. That was not going to be easy. I'd have a hard enough time explaining it to my readers, most of whom would probably act on an illegal hot stock tip in a heartbeat. Gil was a smart kid, though. I knew I could make him see that when rich people sucked all the money out of companies, the little people were the ones who got hurt.

It took me twelve hours to write twelve thousand words. I barely stopped to wolf down the food that Annie brought me. When I couldn't see straight anymore, I took a sleeping pill, passed out for six hours, woke up, and spent another six hours editing and revising the piece.

I gave the draft to Annie. She won't read my articles while I sit there and ask, "Did you get to the part yet where . . ."—so, I waited in the bedroom.

After an eternity passed, she came in and pronounced it "the best thing you've ever done." She is a tough critic, so I believed her. I knew it was that good, anyway.

"What's the missing part with Bigelow that you've still got to write?" she asked.

"I need him to respond to the St. Joe's stuff. I don't expect him to break down, blubbering, and admit everything, but I've got to get him to acknowledge some kind of involvement, no matter how obliquely. Then I can let the reader judge. Otherwise, we'll be open to a libel suit, and the lawyers won't let us run with it."

"When are you seeing him again?"

"I have a call in."

I e-mailed the story to Ed, who read it in an hour and pronounced it "the best thing I will ever publish. When are you going to write that last chunk to tie it all together—the interview with Bigelow?"

"As soon as it happens! Don't worry."

In my heart I believed it would be a piece of cake: knowing about his wife giving the tip to her sister, I would be able to unhinge him enough to say something indiscreet, something that would show he was as guilty as hell.

I called his office again. Trying to make my voice as bold as possible, I said to his assistant: "Tell him I want to ask him about St. Joe's Mineral Corp."

FIFTY-TWO

FOR CHRISTMAS, I usually used to get good tips, but they don't remember I got no benefits. When I'm not working, I'm not getting paid. And it's nobody at that place from Christmas to New Year's. They go to St. Bart's, Miami, ski. Mr. Fred usually go up to Sun Valley in Idaho. They love to ski, most of them. But that's two weeks when I'm making no money. They give me Christmas tips to buy presents, but I got to used that money for the rent and the phone bill.

Mr. Tim, he give me a bottle of Dom for Christmas. Rona was like, The traders cannot get presents that is super-expensive. I think the max is $150. Because that's the way they do it. This is how it works. So probably some client give the Dom to Mr. Tim, but he can't keep it, so he give to me. Me and Natalia, we going to drink it on New Year's.

Then Jim start going off on Pete and Rona. He put it that Pete kind of have low self-esteem in a way. Jim's like, Someone, which I'm not going to say the name, and the person knows for sure, say that Pete doesn't have a big dick. And he goes, That's why he's like that with womens. Whenever he gets a womans, he fell in love. He wants to have that woman, because he's afraid that he's not going to get accept. But you know what is funny? His brother, which is gay, has a bigger dick than he is, because this guy I know that is gay told me.

This fucking peoples gossip the whole fucking day. This is little fucking trading-floor shit. What they going to do to pass the time? They gossip. They fucking talk to each other, and it's like little secrets.

You hear them, buhbuhbuhbuh. Yeah, don't tell anyone. It's between me and you. And they fucking say something crazy. Jim's like, don't tell anyone, when he said that thing about Pete's dick.

Then I see Rona. The thing about Rona, she be having health problems, I think. Because yesterday I went up to her, I was like, How was your weekend? Did you drink a lot? Did you get drunk? She was like, Nah. To me that was the answer. I was like, All right. Now, her face looks kind of miserable. Either she got into a depression, because I think she just turned thirty-six. She doesn't seem happy at all. She doesn't talk to me like before. I feel bad. Right now she will barely talk to me. Before she used to come, stop, Hey, Gil, how you doing, how's your day, what'd you do for the weekend? Now, she sees me, she goes like, Hi. She's not the same. She changed completely. She don't even look at my face. It's like she looks at me like she's kind of pissed.

Yo, man, you see this womans, I don't know what the fuck. I was like, So what happened to you, Rona? It seem like that you not getting enough sleep. And she just went like, I'm kind of unhappy right now. She didn't want to talk about it. Like her face, when you have that place under your eyes dug in, like it's getting black in her eyes.

She asked me for a shine today, and I ended up forgetting. I got there really late, about five ten, that's the time she was leaving. She looked at me, she was like, You know, you dissed me. She looked at me kind of pissed. And I didn't like that.

I didn't want to talk to her. I was pissed at her. Because she never respond me that way. I went up to her, and I was like, Yo, Rona, you think I dissed you? She was like, Yes you did. I was like, How can I dis you? How can I dis a woman that always treat me like one of your coworkers. She looked at me, and she was like, I'm sorry, Gil. I was like, You didn't hurt my feelings, but I'm never going to dis you. She kind of liked it. I don't know, Rona is going through some things in her life. I don't know what she's going through. She look a lot older. I don't know if it's her skin, because she used to go tanning all the time. She got a lot of freckles on her chest. She looks really depressed.

I think that she and Mr. Pete argue a lot now because you don't see them together like they usually used to be.

Then Rona call me inside of the copy-machine room, which there is basically no one there most times. She's like, Gil I got to talk to you. Come here. This is really serious. I want you to think about this, mostly to help you out. I don't want nothing bad to happen to you. You know that guy, Greg, from *Glossy* magazine that he was asking questions about the firm and stuffs? Well, I don't think you should talk to him no more. Or anyone. Because whatever happens in this trading floor, a lot of things are secret. Peoples not supposed to know. You could get in trouble if you say something about the trading floor. And who knows what can happen to you. I hope you never ever talk to that guy no more. Because I told Pete that we had talked to that guy, and he is very, very, very upset that we been doing.

I'm like, Oh, yeah? You think it's bad?

She's like, Yeah.

I'm like, Okay, Rona. But I think Pete is just making her say that.

I went to see Mr. Pearson. I'm like, Mr. John, you know Mrs. Alice? He's like, Yeah. I'm like, You think she likes sex? He's like, Dude, are you kidding me? I was like, Because I think she like me. He was like, Oh, dude, that's awesome. Let me Bloomberg her. He was going to say something really crazy about me, that I like her and stuffs. But then, when he did, she wasn't there. So he goes, You know what? She's a freak. You know what she really likes? She loves to give blow jobs. When she goes to a dinner and they having dinner on the table, and if it is like a restaurant that has a hotel, she will take one of the clients, and she will go up to the room, blow him, and come back down like nothing happened. She loves that. That's pretty crazy, right?

I was like, Wow, I never heard a story like that.

I went to shine Mr. Bigelow's shoes. Mr. Billy's like, I got to ask something very serious. Gil, I know you a good kid, and I have that trust in you. But did you ever tell any persons about the argument I had with Mr. Steed?

I'm like, No, Mr. Bigelow. No, I didn't.

He's like, Are you sure?

I'm like, Yes, sir.

He goes, Because we got a leak in this firm, and some peoples have ask Mr. Steed and me questions that they not supposed to know it. So, Gil, you got to think really, really hard. Are you sure that you doesn't tell no one? Maybe just as a little secret?

I'm like, No, Mr. Billy. I don't think I ever say something like that.

He's like, Has anybody ask you any question about the firm? Anybody?

I'm like, Not that I know. No one have asked me any question.

He's like, I know you a good boy, Gil. But you got to be careful. You can't talk to nobody about the firm. If you talk, that is a very, very bad thing. Because you don't understand what bad stuffs can happen.

I'm like, When I hear things that sounds like trouble, I rather keep it to myself because that's the way I was brought up: you don't hear, you don't see things. Like in São Paulo, if you see someone getting shot, people fear for that. Because if you talk to the cops, turn the murderer in, they going to go after you, then they going to kill the whole family.

He's like, Okay, Gil. I knew I can trust you. Just be careful.

Now I'm very, very confuse about talking with Greg for all this article. You think it's bad?

FIFTY-THREE

Gil

TODAY EVERYBODY WILL go to the Christmas party. I usually look forward to that thing every year. I like to be around peoples and see how everyone acts when they drink.

On the trading floor they do push-ups with guys. At the end of the year, they usually do. They get two guys, whatever think they are strongest. It's like show-off. This year they get Tim and Jim. Then they get a group of guys, and they face this two guys to each other. And they put a stapler under their chest. For them to do the right push-up, they got to hit the stapler every time they go down. Whoever do the most push-ups, they win. But you got to bet. Tim and Jim that do the push-ups, they don't win anything. They doing for free, just to show off. The only persons that usually wins is the peoples that bets on this guys. They get like twenty peoples from the one side that bet on one guy and twenty peoples from the other side that bets on the other guy. Then Tim and Jim, they do a crazy number of push-ups, but Mr. Jim the winner.

Rona is like, Come here, come here! She holding this envelope. I'm like, What's that? She goes, I made a collection. The traders are happy to give it you for Christmas. I'm like, Wow, thanks, Rona. She usually do that every year, but this envelope is HUGE, full of cash. I can't hardly believe it. I don't look too close, just put in my pocket. I don't want it like I'm greedy to open too fast. But I go around the corner, and I like RUN to the bathroom. I tear that fucking thing open.

There's $800 and change in there. I'm jumping up and down, I'm so happy. Now, I'm capable to get presents for everybody, perfume for my mom, clothes for Natalia.

Mr. Fred Turner came and he was like, Today is my last day! I'm like, Are you bullshitting me? He's like, Nah. Got a new job. Hedge fund.

I will miss that guy so much. He is the man! Fred put it that he has to buy this new clothes, and he's like, Gil, why don't you come with me right now, and I will buy you shoes. A gift from me to you for Christmas. We walk to the store to see the shoes. Well, I don't care, it's a fancy store, whatever, fucking peoples here looking at me. I don't like the way they looking because I'm not dressing for the occasion. Most people, they want you to follow the code. You got to dress up pretty nice so you can be in a place. I went in that place, and I was like, Wow. I was looking at the shoes with Mr. Fred, and I felt cool.

But then this guy that works there was like, Oh, no, I'm not going to serve you. Oh, no, we doesn't got this shoe in your size. Oh, no, you should go to another store, you should go to another store where they got that shoe. When he kept saying on that, I was like, Yo, I'm getting the picture here. Let's go, Fred, let's go.

I didn't felt as secure. I was just like, Wow, this person doesn't want me here. I felt down. Right now I would know how to respond him, but at that time, I didn't know. No one ever taught me that. Then Mr. Fred went to the counter and he ask for the manager and the manager came, and Mr. Fred give his card to the guy. And the manager was like, Oh, my God, can I do anything for you? And this guy help us out to find some black Ferragamos. Beautiful. With that really soft leather.

When I saw the manager kissing Mr. Fred's ass, I was like, Wow. That was fun. I was like, Crazy. Never had that. It felt great. I felt like, See, Fred, this is what I experience most times. I couldn't believe it. It was like me seeing a movie star right in front of me, someone I never expect. Wow! I wish I could call up everybody and tell that story, but I like to keep it to myself.

You know, because I wanted to be accept in the world, but I never thought I was going to be capable. By accept I mean just when you say something to someone, the person doesn't turn their face on you. Or treat you in a different way. But they always make you feel comfortable. Even though if I'm doing something wrong, they smiling and saying everything's cool. Like you make me feel important. Sometimes peoples want to feel important.

I didn't used to know anything. It's all about your head. You got to know how to control the way you think. If you capable to control your brain, just a little, you capable to go far. And that's what I'm trying to do now. Hanging with the traders in the beginning was really awkwards for me. Just seeing things that I wasn't used to see. Talking on some certain level that I wasn't used to. Being polite. Sometime it was a drag for me to be polite with peoples. Because if they do something I didn't like it, I wanted to get even. Today I don't think like that.

What I learned more how to communicate. I went from a scale of three to maybe an eight. If I see that somebody don't like what I'm talking about, let's change the subject. Just talk about something else and not getting mad. I change the way I dress, the way I talk.

Respect. This is the way I see it. I want to be able to walk in anywhere and be able to feel good about myself. I'm not there to bother anybody. When I go to a Brazilian place, peoples don't usually look at me like he's another bum—because they all the same thing. That's respect to me. But when you go in an American place—let's say I walk into a club, and I wanted to tell them what I do, but in the same time if I tell them, they going to look down on me and be like, What you doing over here? You don't belong to this place. Respect means you walk into a place, and peoples don't have to ask you or do anything to make you feel uncomfortable.

I'm there maybe to socialize, maybe to hang. That's what I like to do. I like to talk. But I don't want to feel guilty. That's the way I feel, because sometimes the peoples at my job have things to say it that I don't even know what they saying. And I'm like, Wow, why they saying this things? And I feel guilty because I'm not able to be on that conversation. You know, like be in the same world. I want to improve my English. I'm doing a lot of reading right now. Every day I buy the *Post* or the *News*, and I read it. I try not to communicate the way I used to. I try like hear the words. Sometimes I used to usually think that a phrase was something, something, something, and that's the way I used to pronounce it, but I was wrong. Right now, I'm trying to pick up things a lot more.

Knowledge is the main thing. All those years I went to school as a kid, I don't think I learned nothing, until I started hanging out with the traders. They taught me how to talk. Present yourself in the right way even though if you not dressing right.

The traders, they treat me like I was as good as anybody. That's when I begin to respect myself. Because anybody can learn to dress nice, speak nice, but the difference between a person that shines the shoes and a rich guy is not how the person behaves, it's how the person treats you.

BACK AT THE office everybody leave to get ready for the party. Everybody got to go button-up shirt. People dress nice. I can go whatever, but I want to dress nice, so people, when they look at me, they don't have the same impression that they have at my job, you know? This kid looks dirty. You know, Look, Forrest Gump. Not Forrest Gump. The Castaway. I'm going to try and look really neat, so when they look at me, we can't recognize Gil. I got to leave early, go home, wash, be dressing nice with my Ferragamos. I go home, come back.

First, when I got there, it was a shuttle bus that took from the firm to the place, this HUGE club by the Javits Center. There was one bus leaving every other fifteen minutes. Fabio and me went there, took the bus. Fabio ended up sitting on the bus, the guy that sat next to him was Mr. Medved. Mr. Medved is the other big boss with Mr. Bigelow. Mr. Medved be even higher than Mr. Bigelow, I think, but he's kind of old. I don't think he do the day-to-day. He just come in to show hisself, that he still be alive. I never shine his shoes. I only seen that guy one or two times in my life. He start the company back in the day. I couldn't believe he goes not in a limo, but the bus. So, Fabio is talking to this guy like he knew him, talking kind of slang. Fabio was like, Yo, so where you from? And Mr. Medved was like, I'm from New York. And Fabio was like, What part of New York? Mr. Medved is like, Park Avenue. Man, I was cracking up. When we got out the bus I was like, Yo, Fabio, come here, man. You know what the fuck is that guy? He's the boss of Mr. Billy Bigelow, the boss of the whole company.

Fabio is like: Oh. My. God.

We were in the door, and it was a table when you walked in. They check the name with the invitation, your name and ID. Me and Fabio, we doesn't get no invitation, so we took someone else's that wasn't going. We there, and the lady wouldn't let us in. I was about to go back home. I swear to God, because I don't like it to go to a place and just be shot down right there. It looks really bad to me, I think. If I'm not invited, and that happens, to me it's the worst thing.

But then we there, and Jared wanted to get me in, but he was only able to get *me* in. He was not capable to get Fabio. They were going to leave him out, and I didn't think it was fair. If I came with him, either way we going in or we go to some other place. Right?

Then Mrs. Alice comes and she's like, Well, what is the problem here? The lady who was sitting on the table, the lady who was looking at the guest list, was like, I'm not going to be able to let them in, because their names not on the list. And Mrs. Alice was like, What are you doing with my employees? They employees of this company just like I am. And the lady was like, Well, miss, we not going to be capable to let them in unless if you want to sign for them, and if it's overcrowded, we got to charge you $150 each.

Alice was like, Look, you making my employees embarrass over here, because you holding them up. And that doesn't look right. You see all those peoples going in are looking at them. She had the attitude, she kind of put the other woman look bad that was like, Do you know who I am?

Oh man, when she said that. Fabio was like, Yo, Gil, ain't she the lady that Natalia babysit the kids? But for her to say that, he was like, Who the fuck is she? Then I was like, Yo, Fabio, she's the boss from ten. He was like, She's the boss? Oh shit. So, the girl at the table wrote our names and was like, All right, guys, just go.

Fabio and me got into the party. I saw everybody. When you go to a party like that, you going to see different groups. The peoples that make a little talking to themselves. The peoples that make a lot talking to themselves. The black peoples in the one corner. The Latin peoples in this other corner. It's funny, you know? You don't see nobody mixing it up. The only black peoples that was mixing it with the bigs was those that make money in that place.

You know what surprised me? Mr. Tim. He was talking to some big guys over there. He saw me, shook my hand. The second time he shook my hand. He was like, Hi, Gil. He was surprised to see me. Because in the morning my beard was huge, my hair was kind of big. So nobody was able to recognize me in that place. Because I went there really dressed up: gray pants that I have, and a nice button shirt from Banana, with my hair slicked back. The Ferragamos that Mr. Turner had bought me.

Mr. Tim start to talk to me, ask me how my life was, so I tell him straight up. I think he looks at me, and I think he kind of feels bad for me. Because the way he looks at me, like maybe he wants to help me out, but he doesn't know how. Mr. Tim was like, You know, Gil, I would like to pay for your scholarship if you ever end up going to college. If you need my help, I'm here. I'm not a gay, I just want you to do good. He want to sponsor me. That to me was nice, man.

I started drinking Heineken, Heineken. I probably have four Heinekens. I started dancing with one of the secretaries there. This girl was like, Ain't you got a girlfriend, now, Gil? I was like, Yo, not for tonight. I was like, Just keep it between me and you. So, I ended up dancing a little bit, and then I went back to the bar, drank, ate.

I went to talk to Miss Lindsay. It was her, Mr. Jim, and this other guy that sit in the row, this other Marine guy. Like he was an ex-Marine, this fucking guy. He knows me, but nobody recognize me with that hair. I was like, Hey, Lindsay, how you doing? I tap her on the shoulders. She turn around, I think she kind of had on a buzz. She was like, Huh? Gil? And she hugged me, and she kissed me on the cheeks. The ex-Marine guy was like, Hey, what is this, Lindsay? You making out with this guy, now? I was like, Oh, shit. Is he for real? This guy is not making no sense. I don't know if he was playing a joke with me, because he know me even though he doesn't get his shoes shine, or he was saying that for me to get the fuck out of there. I stood there only to say hi to these people, and I ended up going back to the bar.

Then I see Matthew. He's like, What up, Gil? You having fun yet? If you hang out with Matthew on the regular now, like every day, you know that he got very into coke when you observes the way he react. Like he do in the bathroom at work.

You can see he's skinnier and skinnier. He's very hyped up. His eyes are popped. The way he breathe is not the same. He breathe a little faster. He breathe in up his nose every other second. He talk only about hisself and material stuffs. His clothes all messed.

He was doing coke at the party. His nose, instead of boogers, has little pieces of coke, because he was snorting. I was like, Yo, Matthew, you got something on your nose. He's like, I do? He wipe his nose. He's like, Is it gone? The mouth, he won't stop chewing. You never notice this? I don't know why people chew when they on coke. From side to side with their tooths.

Then Mr. John comes. He got so drunk that he was doing the cross on Matthew's head, like when you go to St. Paddy's for the Catholic holiday, and they have that ashes. The black cross. He been doing on all the interns. He just do that to fuck around, I think. He like to show off. I don't know why he do. He was trying to tell them, I'm the boss. All you got to respect me. Because that's the way they think.

When Matthew leave, I'm like, Mr. John, why you doing that? Mr. John is like, Look! Then he show it, this stuffs were right on the palm, so people couldn't even see what it was. He would go up to each intern and be like, Come here, son. This is from me to you, a tradition from the firm. The kid didn't know what the fuck was in his hands. It was sperm! And he was doing the cross! He had went to the bathroom and jerked himself off and kept the sperm in his hand. I'm like, That is disgusting, Mr. John! Why you do that? He just laugh.

There was Rona. She was so bad, they put her in a chair. She was over with the coat checks. I was going to the bathroom, and I went up to her, Hey, Rona, how you doing? Man, she was so banged up, I couldn't almost understand nothing she said, like her words so slurry, but I think she put it that she and Mr. Pete not going to see each other no more. I was like, Oh, Rona, I'm so sorry. I was going to pay for her for the whole cab to Queens, because she was bad. I felt bad. She was looking like she was fifty-five years old.

This other couple was standing there, and I was like, I know her. And they like, We know her, too. I never seen this peoples. It was a lady and a man, two old peoples. I was like, I'm paying for her cab. I think they thought I was going to take advantage of her. They were like, Nah, nah, nah, we already have this thing taken care of. Like, All right.

After that I start drinking cranberry and Bacardi lemon. A lot. I was kind of fucked up already when Mrs. Alice come up to me. She was very quiet in my ear, Meet me outside, Gil. I got a car. I wait ten minutes, and then I go out, and she wave to me from this limo. I get in, and we go.

FIFTY-FIVE

Gil

WE GO TO this restaurant that was kind of fancy. It was in SoHo, you know one of those little cozy restaurants that they have candles and stuffs. It was trees right in the front door. The floor was made of woods, and there was a really old bar. There was this little table by the window, and we got that table, because it was really quiet. There wasn't that many peoples there. I was like, Wow, Alice, this place is cool. There was not that many other lights, it was not one of those bright restaurants. I didn't even know what to order. She ended up ordering a bottle of wine. It could be any wine, it could be a $10, $20, $50 bottle of wine that to me it wasn't the difference, because it taste good, though. That wine to me was great.

She ordered some salad. I was like, Wow, man, I don't eat salad like that, but all right. I was trying to put it myself that, it's not that I have class or anything, but I was trying to act that I was kind of educated. And we start talking. She asked me how it was to live in the U.S. She says that she thinks I'm kind of smart, because I speak more than one language and not that many peoples is capable to do that. And that I was a nice person. We ended up eating and getting a little banged up because we drink that whole bottle of wine. And she ended up ordering another bottle.

She ask me if Brazilian guys usually do cheating on their girlfriends. I'm like, Cheating? Every guy in Brazil do. Everyone. America is a free country, right? I see this as a free country, but I think Brazil is a lot more freer than this. Because over there you could do whatever. You could bribe the fucking cops, that's free. You could shoot guns in the street, and no one cares. They would be like, That's normal. If a guy go with lots of womens, they call the guy a *garanhao*. That means, he's the man. He will get with any womans anytime that he feels like.

She was playing with her foot on my leg under the table. The first time she hit me with her foot, I was like, All right, it was by mistake. That's how she start it: foot to foot. Then she kept on hitting me, and she put her foot between my legs, and laughing in my face at the same time. I was like, Man, this woman's pretty wild. I didn't think she was like that, to do in a restaurant. Then she grabbed me on my hand and look into my face. And she was like, Let's put it like this—if you don't feel comfortable, just pretend that you met me on the street, and we don't know each other at the firm. We don't know what each other do. We don't know where each other came from. I thought you were cute, and you liked me. I was like, All right.

From there she asked me if I was into her. I was like, Well, right now, I am. Damn, I was pretty banged up, and I was horny. She was like, Oh, so, what are we going to do after this? I was like, Well, you want me to tell you the truth? And she was like, Yeah, go ahead. I was like, It might not sound too nice for you. She was like, Why? I was like, All right, I'm going to tell you. She was like, Okay, go ahead. I was like, I feel like going to a motel with you. She was like, I was going to say the same thing. I was like, Whoa, all right.

Then she got the check, and we ended up leaving. When we got in the hotel, it was really nice. Everything was class, the elevators were crazy, with different color lights. She open up the door of the room, and she threw me on the bed, and I was like, Wow, this womans crazy. And I was like, Okay. Then we start making out over there. This womans ended up pulling a weed from her purse. I was like, Whoa, I can't believe it. Alice was like, You going to smoke with me? I was like, All right.

We smoked. And I was like, This is fucking cool. Now I know a lot more things than I was suppose. We were doing again. She kissed great. She gave a great blow job—she was like a little animal on my dick. Then I fucked her. She was kind of tight for an older woman.

After that she asked me questions. She was like, I heard that Mr. Bigelow had an argument with Jeff Steed. Were you there around at that time? I was like, Umm . . . kind of. She was like, Somebody told me you had been in the office when that happened. I was like, Who? She was like, I can't tell, it's a secret. I was like, All right. She was like, Do you want to tell me? I was like, I don't feel comfortable. She was like, Well, you had done this whole thing with me, and you don't feel comfortable? What about me? So, I kind of ended up telling her. The whole thing. Everything. And I tell her about Mr. Greg, how he wanted to write in the magazine about all this things.

Alice is like, Oh, my God, Gil. What did you did? This is very, very bad, that you talking to a guy from a magazine. Gil, if they find out, they going to fire you. Maybe they will put you in prison. She's like, you can't never talk to him again. Everything at the firm is very confidential. You got to say that you made all this stuffs up. This and that. She is really, really, really upset.

Then she dial up a number on her cell. She's like, Bill, you never going to believe it. Gil is the leak. Yeah, he's the one that's been talking to the *Glossy* guy . . . No, I know . . . Don't worry, he's here. He's not going anywhere . . . Yes . . . Yes . . . Well, I think we can still turn this around . . . No, don't worry . . . He'll do whatever I tell him.

I'm thinking, Oh, my God, I could go to jail for talking with Mr. Greg, and at that minute he's calling me on my cell.

FIFTY-SIX

Greg

I NEEDED TO talk to Gil about going on the record with Steed's blackmail attempt, but I kept getting his voice mail. The next morning, too. I assumed he was nursing a Godzilla-sized hangover from the Christmas party, which he'd been talking about for weeks.

Finally, Bigelow's assistant returned my call. Showing my hand had worked. I was summoned to his office immediately.

This time he didn't bother pretending to be cordial. My finding out about St. Joe's had obviously pissed him off. Intimidation was the name of the game.

"Mr. Waggoner, I know now that your main source was . . ." he said, making a show of changing his regular glasses for his reading glasses and searching a piece of paper to get the name, ". . . a Mr. Aguilar Benicio, whom we allow on the premises to perform a service for our employees." Bigelow glared at me for a response.

I was too shocked to speak. How had he found out about Gil? "I've been talking to quite a few people," I said carefully.

He ignored me. "Is this your idea of responsible journalistic practices, Mr. Waggoner? Interviewing a shoeshine boy so you can give your readers embarrassing details about one of the most respected and successful financial firms in the world. I don't read your magazine, but I thought it was a bit higher quality than that."

"I think we might be talking about more than a few embarrassing details," I said. Now was the time to bring up St. Joe's. He was clearly flustered. But I couldn't risk pissing him off further until I found out where Gil was and that he was safe. I reasoned Bigelow wasn't a gangster. He might intimidate Gil, but he wouldn't hurt him or disappear him. Would he?

"Yes, I imagine you are. But, whatever it is you are talking about, you didn't get it from a very reliable or informed person, now did you?"

I didn't say anything.

"Clearly, you are only interested in publishing the kind of salacious gossip that one finds in the *Star* or the *Enquirer*.

"It might interest you to know," he continued, "that I have spoken to the young man in question, this Mr. . . . uh," he looked down at the paper again, "Benicio, and he has admitted to me that everything he told you was entirely invented by him. He made the whole thing up in order to impress you. He is now sorry for what he did, and he realizes that such falsehoods can hurt innocent people. I have a signed statement from him to that effect." He held something up.

"I think I would like to ask him about it myself."

"I'm afraid that will be impossible. Mr. Benicio, as I just told you, has realized the folly of his actions and the damage it could have potentially caused this firm. He will not make himself available to you any longer, and if need be, he will testify in court that everything he told you is untrue and that he warned you to that effect." Bigelow handed me Gil's statement.

Dear Mr. Waggoner,

I'm sorry for my writing. But what I want to tell you is more important then my life. When I start these whole thing I never thought about the consequences. I told you a story that was not true, and people found out about what I said to you it was a fake. I just want some one in your level to like me for who I am, like the guys at the firm, but no one would

ever going to understand me, so please everything that I said
was false. Please believe me!

Dead or life, Gil.

I had visions of Gil gagged and tied to a chair in a warehouse on the New Jersey waterfront. "Are you completely certain this letter was not written under duress and that no kind of pressure was applied?"

"What are you saying, Mr. Waggoner?"

"What does he mean by 'dead or life'?"

"I have no idea, but I can assure you that Mr. Benicio is entirely well and that he has no desire to see you or speak to you. And if you print any of the stories that he now admits he made up, we intend to pursue every legal remedy at our disposal, and I have informed my good friend Al Lieberman of that."

Bigelow stood up and smiled sourly. "Thank you very much for stopping by today, Mr. Waggoner. My wife says she doesn't see your byline much anymore. You must be getting rather desperate."

I FELT SICK as I was escorted by a security guard to the elevator. When I got to the lobby, I dialed Gil's cell phone, only to get his voice mail again: "Hi, this is Gil. Please leave it me a message and I will get back at you as soon as possible." Was Gil possibly in the building? If he was, how would I find him? Rona! I called her cell phone, but there was no answer. I remembered that Gil worked on nine and ten, so perhaps she was on one of those floors.

I went to the other elevator bank, took it up to nine, and asked the receptionist for Rona Bakalar.

"Your name?"

"Could you just say I'm an old friend, and I want to surprise her?"

The receptionist got Rona on the phone. A minute later, she came through the glass doors to the reception area. The second she saw me, she blanched and wheeled about.

"Rona," I said, running over to her. "I've got to talk to you. Please."

She hissed into my face, "Look, talking to you has already fucked up my relationship. I don't want to lose my job as well. Don't contact me again. Or Gil, either."

"I just want to know. Is Gil okay? Do you know where he is?"

"I'm sorry, you must think I'm someone else," she said in a loud voice, for the benefit of the receptionist. "Maybe you should try the personnel department. They're on four." She marched back inside.

A knot of people came out, and I managed to grab the door and slip inside without the secretary noticing. I was in a narrow, dark, paneled hallway; I followed it until it opened up onto the trading floor: a vast sea of desks and people and computer screens. I started to panic. Cold sweat was trickling from my underarms. Fortunately, nobody paid any attention to me. Keeping to the aisle running along the inside wall, I walked slowly, trying to look like I belonged, smiling and nodding at people I met. I searched each row for Gil, but there were so many, and I couldn't see below desk-level. If he was sitting on his box, shining somebody's shoes, I'd never see him.

I turned a corner to find an identical football-field's worth of desks. I had no idea money had undone so many.

Somebody, over in a far corner, was pointing at me. It was Rona, talking to two security guards. The last thing I needed was to get busted for trespassing. The guards started to maneuver their way through the maze of desks toward me. I walked away as fast as I could without actually running. I rounded another corner. I could hear jangling keys and thudding footsteps behind me.

I spotted a men's-room door, ducked inside, ran into a stall, locked it, and sat on the toilet, with my feet pulled up. A minute later, somebody burst through the door to the men's room.

"Jesus, did a guy just run in here?"

"Nobody here but me."

"Fuck. You sure? They told me he came in here."

"Nobody been coming here for a while."

"Okay." The man ran out.

"You better come out of there, mister. They going to find you if you stay."

I came out sheepishly to find a black guy wearing a blue workman's uniform with a name tag that identified him as JESUS.

"I'm a friend of Gil Benicio's," I said. "You know him?"

The guy nodded.

"I'm trying to find him. I'm worried he might be in trouble."

"Well, you ain't going to find him here."

"Do you have any idea where he is? It's very important."

"I hear things."

"Look, you have no reason to trust me, but I'm trying to save him from people who might harm him."

"Then maybe you should check out Mrs. Alice Norther's house, up in Greenwich, Connecticut."

"Oh, my God. Thank you."

"Come over here, mister."

He led me to a closet that contained a utility sink and cleaning supplies—maybe the same one Steed had made his suspicious phone call from, I wondered—and pulled out a blue work shirt, like his own, and a baseball cap. "Put these on." He indicated a large garbage can on wheels. "Just keep your head down and help me wheel this thing to the back elevators."

Outside, everyone was rubbernecking. The security guards ran around like Keystone Kops, a voice on the loudspeaker announced for everyone to remain calm and that a thief was in the building. My heart was racing, but Rona and a security guard walked right past and didn't give me a second look. I was invisible. The invisible man.

Jesus and I wheeled the garbage can to the freight elevators. Then he took me down and out a back hallway lined with the wire and pipe innards of the building, and showed me out onto the street.

FIFTY-EIGHT

Greg

I GOT A CAB back to my apartment and went online. Within two minutes, I had a street map, showing me the way to Bill and Alice Norther's house. I poured myself a thermos full of strong coffee, got my car from the garage, and drove. On the Merritt Parkway, I spilled coffee and burned my hand, which caused me almost to rear-end a Porsche. The driver glared at me as I passed him.

I had no trouble finding the house, a big Georgian brick pile with a stone wall around it. Alice and her husband were probably at work, so I pulled into the circular driveway. I didn't go up to the front door, but around to the back, where a door to the kitchen proved to be unlocked.

Inside, I found myself face-to-face with Natalia.

She was dumbfounded at seeing me. "Natalia," I said calmly, "I know Gil is here. Whatever these people are telling you guys, you can't trust them. You are not safe with them. You've got to get Gil right now and come with me."

Without saying a word or betraying an emotion, she walked out of the room. I wondered: Should I wait there? Follow her? Try to find Gil on my own?

Before I could decide, she returned.

With Alice.

Alice was acting cool, but there was fire in her eyes. "Mr. Waggoner," she said. "Nice to meet you. Gil has been telling us all about you."

I couldn't think what to say.

"I'm afraid my boss, Bill Bigelow, is quite upset with you at the moment, though," she continued. "We got a memo telling us not to talk with you under any circumstances, so I'm going to have to ask you to leave."

"I don't want to talk to you, Mrs. Norther. I want to talk to Gil."

"I'm afraid that is not possible. Gil does not want to talk to you. He realizes that you have been taking advantage of him and that he was wrong to cooperate with you. So, please leave, now, and don't make me have to call the police. You're trespassing on private property."

"Mrs. Norther," I said, playing for time, "I don't know how much you know, but I believe that a person associated with your company will be the subject of an SEC investigation sometime very soon. It's not going to look too good for you if you are seen to be trying to hide an important witness."

She looked down, weighing my words. Then she said, "Nice try."

She headed for the phone and picked up the receiver.

At that moment, Gil came through the door. "Hold on, Alice," he said. "I just wanted to talk with Greg a little."

"Gil, I think that is a terrible idea," she said. "We already discussed what could happen. He doesn't care what happens to you or anyone else. The minute he finishes his article, you're never going to see him again."

Gil looked torn.

"Gil," I said. "I've always been straight with you, haven't I? Trust me."

"Greg, it's not that I don't have that trust for you, but I worked over there for three years now. They always treat me good. I don't want them to be embarrass with stuffs that you put it in the magazine."

"Gil, there isn't going to be any article. They won. The only thing that matters right now is getting you out of here. These people are dangerous."

"Gil, that is total bullshit," Alice said. "Lies. All lies. He's just using you. Can't you see that?"

"Gil, let's just get out of here, and then I'll explain everything."

"Don't listen to him, Gil. He's just here because he needs you for the article," said Alice.

I couldn't read Gil at all. I didn't know that . . .

FIFTY-NINE

. . . MRS. ALICE and Mr. Bigelow had put it I can go to prison for talking to Greg. I went there once, man. I was drinking on the street. I was nineteen, drinking out of the paper, and this police car came, and me and my friend were in the corner of this busy street. The police car stop, and they ask me for my ID, so I hand it out to the guy. He was probably not going to give me a ticket, but then he ask me for my age, and I was like, Can't you read? That's what I answered him. That's when he came out of the car, grabbed me by my neck, took me to the little corner, and say stupid shit to me. He handcuff me.

They treat you like dogs.

First we go to this cell, and then they ask us questions there. From there they tow us to this other cell, and they ask us more questions there. From there they tow us to the big cell, where everybody stays. Until you see the judge, you got to wait there. You can't do anything. You got to sleep on this dirty floor, and every other minute there's peoples coming in. If somebody goes crazy and kicks you, you can't complain about it, because they do that. If the person comes and punch me, who the fuck I'm going to cry to?

I was there twenty-nine hours. I had to take a shit in front of like eighteen peoples. If I didn't had done that, I was going to die. It was dirty-ass metal on the toilet, you got to do standing up. You can't even sleep, because people talking, talking, talking, playing jokes. Because most of them just wants the time go fast, and they just talk, talk, talk. And then they come early morning to clean up the floors, around six-thirty. You not capable to sleep on the floors anymore. You got to stand up until the stuffs dries. It smells like motherfucking hell.

I don't want to go back to that place. And Greg is going, Don't you trust me, man? I do trust him, but I was so fucking scared. Mrs. Alice is like, He doesn't care about you, Gil. He just wanted to write this articles.

I was really confuse.

Then Mrs. Alice say, Gil, doesn't that mean anything to you, though? This times we be spending together?

I'm like, OH. MY. GOD. Because Natalia is standing right there the whole time. Everybody forgot her.

Natalia's face grow all red, because that's how it usually do when she really, really pissed. She's like, *What* time that you been spending with her?

I'm like, NO, NO. It's not like that. Me and Alice, we just friends. Right, Alice? But Alice fucking smile that little smile like she knows stuffs that we been doing it, but doesn't tell.

Natalia's like, Are you serious? I. CAN'T. BELIEVE. IT. THIS. IS. OVER.

Natalia fucking curses me. She's like, How the fuck could you do some shit like that to me? How the fuck you fuck an old womans like her? How the fuck can you be fucking this old lady and not be here—young and beautiful. You just go and fuck this trash.

Mrs. Alice goes, nicily, but you can tell she kind of pissed, Excuse me, what did you say, Natalia?

Natalia just goes to me, Why you did this to me?

I'm like, No, no, no, it's not what you thinking, Natalia.

But she look like a Tasmanian. Her eyes were popped. She's like to me, I. DON'T. WANT. YOU. TO. EXIST. She grab her hair. She pull out her hair. You could see hair in her hand, man. When I saw that, I was really fear.

Then she scream, I'M GOING TO KILL BOTHS OF YOU, and she grabs this HUGE kitchen knife. And she cut herself on the arm! There's blood on the arm! And showing to us that her pain is nothing, and she's down for whatever.

Greg is talking really nicily to her, trying to calm her down. And

I'm saying, Natalia, this is a different country than Colombia, the laws is different here, a lot of people doesn't think about that.

But I can see it she doesn't care. She doesn't care about my life. She doesn't care about her own life. When you in that position, you really don't care. You just living for the moment. I couldn't say nothing. No matter what I say, even though I will offer her money or whatever, she wouldn't listen to me. Because people like Natalia, they always want to get even first. That's the main thing in her head.

Greg look into my face, and I look in his face, and then really, really fast we grab Natalia and push her down. She drop the knife, and she scream like crazy. Alice is screaming. Now the kids is come in, and they screaming. Natalia trying to bite us, she really red in the face, she wouldn't stop fighting and fighting.

Then she pass out. She got heart problems. I seen her do that before. I thought she probably died from a heart attack.

We get some tape and wrap this girl up, her hands, her legs. We carry her to the car. I tell Greg how Alice promise me this whole new life that I was capable to live, but Alice told me I had to lie, and I didn't like it. I didn't think it was nice.

Then Natalia wakes up. She still fucking cursing me to death. I'm like, Natalia, I'm going to call the police, and you going to jail for life. I take Greg's cell and call up Natalia's mom. I get her mom to the phone and try to talk to her. I was like, Look, I did something really bad to your daughter. Cheated on her and she found out. Now, she wants to kill me, which is not right. Because if she try to kill me, I will kill her first. If your daughter don't calm down, I will have to kill her and dump her body. Her mom was crying. I put Natalia on the phone. Her hands tied so I have to hold the phone on her ear. Her mother probably talk bad about me like they do all the time. Her mom say stuffs like, This fucking kid's not worth. I don't know why you waste your time on him. He's really good-looking, but good-looking guys always give you headaches. Date an ugly guy that will give you a future.

Her mom calms her down like 73 percent. We get out of the car. Natalia's just in her own little world. Her eyes all glassy-like. She just look at me and say, I can't believe it. She say only those words.

SIXTY

Greg

I FELT TERRIBLE. I'd risked Gil's life. I'd lost him and Natalia their jobs. They were barely speaking to each other, although that, at least, was not my fault.

I dropped them at Natalia's mother's apartment. We untied Natalia and she stomped off without looking at Gil.

"I'm fucked," he said.

"Did you really fuck Alice?" I asked.

"I'm not going to lie to you."

"Oh, my God! You better deny it like hell to Natalia. And when she cools down, you better deny it all over again, and maybe she'll believe you. Sort of."

"So, Greg. You really not doing this article? Or did you said it just to get me to leave that place."

"No, I wasn't lying. You signed a paper for Bigelow saying you made up everything you said to me."

"But I had that fear. They explain me I was going to jail if I didn't sign it!"

"They can't put you in jail. I promise. And I'm not blaming you for signing. I know they scared you."

"But I will go there now and tell the truth if anyone ask me."

"It won't really help. With that statement, they'll be able to say in court that I confused you. And I'll say they confused you. And the judge won't know who to believe. But that's not the only problem. I needed to get Bigelow to crack, and he didn't."

"What you mean, crack?"

"I needed him to make some slip-up to show that I was right, that I had him. But, I failed. He was too good for me."

"I will go talk to Mr. Bigelow. He will tell me."

"Nah, that's okay. Thanks, though."

Now, I had to go tell Ed.

Before I went to his office, I sat on that same bench in the Broadway median where I'd read my first byline in the newspaper. It seemed fitting to end my career at the same place it had started. I sat there for a long time.

When I got to Ed's office, he was just getting off the phone with our publisher. "You'll never believe this," he said. "Gucci just took a $2 million, twelve-page spread in the issue. They want to photograph the shoeshine boy shining their shoes."

"Ed, we can't publish the article."

"What do you mean?" He was incredulous.

"I have to withdraw it."

"Oh, God. Don't tell me this. Why?"

"I compromised my sources, and Bigelow got to them and made them recant."

"Jesus Christ."

"I take full responsibility."

"Great. I'm happy to hear it. But what's going to fill the hole in the issue? It's more like a crater, actually."

"I apologize to you personally. I want to offer my resignation."

"Hold on a minute. Just explain to me exactly what happened."

I did, and Ed refused to let me resign. He said it probably wasn't my fault that Bigelow had found out Gil was talking to me. (He was right: Gil later told me how he had spilled the beans to Alice.) He told me to turn the story and all my notes over to my buddy Harry in exchange for an exclusive on any investigation that resulted. That way I could write the article eventually, and it would be even better. (I did give everything to Harry a few days later, and without even consulting his boss, he gave me the exclusive.)

The only problem was I still had two frightened, confused kids on my hands. I called Gil, and we arranged to meet at the bar of the Brazil Grill.

When he came through the door of the restaurant, a huge grin was plastered across his face.

SIXTY-ONE

Gil

I WAS LIKE, Greg, you never going to believe it. I'm going back to Brazil tomorrow. This the situation. Mr. Bigelow call me up and offer me $500,000 to go there, because he doesn't know that you not writing this articles. He put it, Just go back to Brazil and buy yourself a couple of properties, lay back, work out, enjoy the beach, go to college. Not go too crazy. Greg, I don't even know what to do with money like that, to tell you the truth. I never saw money like that in my life.

Greg is like, Gil, that's the best thing I ever heard, but maybe you should stay just a week more to talk to the feds, because they going to investigate Mr. Bigelow and Jeff Steed and they might need to ask you questions.

I'm like, I know this guys do some bad stuffs, but, seriously, between them, they all smart, and they all make money and went to college. And most of them always had that great fucking life. If they steal $100 millions from each other, and they best fucking friends, I don't give a fuck. I'm not lying to you. That could happen today. If someone comes in, Oh, he stole from the other person fifty millions, and he left the other motherfucker butt-naked, I'm going to look and laugh, because I think it's funny. They all went to college. They fucking smart. They make money like that. They all ambitious. They the most ambitious men on the face of the fucking earth. They don't care who you are. They tougher than anyone. They will step on you, and they will be like, Yeah, I know I did you wrong—who gives a fuck?

You can't do shit to me. I'm worth money. This traders make more money than movie stars. People never realize this. This guys are the stars of fucking America.

Greg is like, Gil, I know I lose you your job, and I lose Natalia out of her job, so it's good that you going to get all this money.

I'm like, I can't even explain it to you how important this money will mean to me. With that kind of money I can go back to my own country. I just want to get there and do things I never had done it.

Greg is like, Probably the feds don't really need you, so it's cool if you want to go back. But I'm really going to miss you, man. Who is going explain me the words to those Tupac songs?

I'm like, Don't cry. I was just joking with him, but I was really sad. I'm going to miss that guy.

SIXTY-TWO

Gil

IN THE MORNING we going to the airport, I'm thinking I'm going to end up leaving everything that I always liked—this country.

I told my mom that I'm going to take a trip down to Florida. I had done that before. I'm very spontaneous. I don't care. I don't wait, that's just what I would do. I can't tell her I'm going to Brazil. She would never let me go to Brazil, no matter what, in what situation. She would go crazy. She would go nuts. When I go to Brazil, I will call her up and just tell her the truth. If she like it, good. If she doesn't, what can I do?

Greg and Fabio's coming with us to the airport. Natalia and I both crying, even though if I'm a guy, and I don't fucking cry that easy. I'm quiet the whole driving. I don't say anything. There's not much for me to say. I'm the type that I just want to observes for the last time what I'm passing. I don't know if I'm coming back to this place, so let me just observe. Even Fabio is crying.

We get to the airport, and I'm there doing my luggages, check-in. I'm just thinking about all the life that I had it here. And how I have to give up that so easily. It's hard, man. The flight is leaving in three hours.

My heart feel so tight, and my throat feel like I have something in it. As we about to go into the gate, Natalia give Fabio a huge hug, and I'm like, Cool, man. See you when you go down in Brazil. Natalia stopped crying, but now she start again at the end. I give Greg a big hug. I'm like, I'm so grateful to you, man, for all that you had done for me. You taught me so much. He is crying, too. Man, I never thought I ever see that guy cry.

The worst is looking out the plane window. I look and then I put my head down right away. I try to think what I have to do with my life.

SIXTY-THREE

Greg

AFTER GIL GOT to Brazil, I helped him transfer the $500,000 into a new account. I didn't want Bigelow trying to take back the money once Harry's people got in touch.

About six months later, Harry asked me to meet him for dinner at Peter Luger, the famous Brooklyn steakhouse. Evidently, we had something to celebrate.

At the restaurant, Harry ordered a bottle of ridiculously expensive French Bordeaux. "Boy, government expense accounts have really improved," I said.

"They're paying for this, as a personal thank-you to both of us. Tomorrow, you're going to read on the front page of every newspaper that Bill Bigelow is stepping down."

"Holy shit! No kidding! Tell me everything."

"To make a long story short, we found that Jeff Steed—just as you figured—was giving tips to Joe Cantone, telling him which stocks were on Medved, Morningstar's restricted list, giving him advance information about mergers and takeovers."

"Did you figure out what information he was leaking when the janitor found him in the bathroom closet?"

"Ironically, at that particular moment he wasn't leaking. He was talking to a private detective he hired to tail a Russian stripper he was dating. She's actually kind of famous. Did you see *Vladimir's Cunning Stunts #16*, by any chance?"

"Missed that one." Christ, Harry watched porno? What next?

"Anyway, Steed suspected she was having affairs with other men. He told us she bilked him out of quite a bit of money, too. As if all that wasn't bad enough, she turned into a star witness for us against him. He must rue the day he ever met her."

I found it kind of ironic that the incident that set the entire chain reaction in motion was not what I assumed it to have been. Did that mean I shouldn't have been pursuing the story in the first place? Maybe my father was right. Maybe I just wasn't that good. At anything. "Are you going to prosecute Steed for blackmailing Bigelow?"

"No, we offered him immunity. It might have started out as a blackmail attempt, but Bigelow turned it into an opportunity by investing $50 million in Persimmons. That was the paperwork Gil brought back from the Bahamas. There's nothing illegal about it, but Bigelow used a web of foreign corporations to make the investment. We suspect he planned to feed Persimmons a stream of hot tips, but we felt we had to act before he could put that plan into action."

"So, the main thing you're going after Bigelow for is insider trading in the St. Joe's case?"

"Yup."

"Christ, this is huge for you, Harry."

"Thanks to you." Harry toasted me with the wine.

"How much jail time is Bigelow going to get?"

"Actually, none. He's retiring."

"I don't understand."

"I'm going to tell you now, but I want you to know that this will never be repeated or confirmed by me or anyone I work with. The boss decided Bigelow's too big to take down publicly."

"Who's the boss?"

"The really, really big boss."

"Get out of here."

"You can believe it or not."

"Harry, I've always had a great deal of respect for you. I can't believe you would agree to be part of something like this."

"I didn't make this decision. I may not even agree with it. But, I do understand the logic. They feel it would be too damaging to investor confidence if we hauled him off to prison, especially with all the corporate scandals of the last few years. Bigelow is paying, believe me. We negotiated a huge, secret settlement, and he's out of the firm, as of today."

"What about the exclusive you promised me?"

"I have to apologize about that. I was in no position to make that promise."

"This isn't right."

"Maybe not, but it's reality. I'm telling you only because without you none of this would have happened, and I think you deserve to know."

"In my opinion this makes you guys even bigger crooks than Bigelow is."

"Sorry you feel that way. Not much I can do about it."

"I don't know about that. I never agreed you were off-the-record for tonight. I'm going to run with the real story, with or without your permission."

"Be my guest. We'll deny everything. And Bigelow will take you and your magazine to court and make back all the money he gave us. And we'll even testify on his behalf."

Harry downed his glass. "Look, I'm sorry. I really am. But, what's the point of throwing out the baby with the bathwater?"

SIXTY-FOUR

Gil

IT'S LIKE YOU playing the Lotto, and you never know when you going to win. You play that Lotto, and you look at the numbers, and you see the numbers they show on TV matches with your numbers, you don't know if you cry.

It's just that chill—a great feeling. With that amount of money, an unbelievable feeling.

So the five hundred thou, it's worth a millions and a half down here.

I got into São Paulo. The feeling, getting back to São Paulo, is just chill, a different vibration that not even with words I'm capable to describe. I had people at the airport that I hadn't seen for more than ten years. I didn't want that many people there, like fifteen to twenty. My dad was there. Eddy was there. It was so good to see that kid. I was crying so much, I just cried for five minutes. Because I think everyone usually wait for that moment, and that was the moment that I just went bananas. It was stupid.

I didn't tell nobody that the money I have, because I didn't want them to be thinking, Oh, Gil has all this money, Gil has to be the center of attention. I wanted to be the center of attention just for the fact that I lived in the U.S., and they want me to tell them how it was. And that's natural of them.

Two month after I arrive, I married Natalia. That was tough, man. Because I got so many womens in Brazil that I wanted to get married.

The thing about Brazil is weddings over there they celebrate a lot more than this country. There was no less than four hundred peoples. It was out in this farm thing, where everyone goes and eat the whole day, like meat. They wake up early in the morning and they kill two cows, they clean the cows, and they do the barbecue right there. Brazilians do that. So many different foods: nice pieces of meat, rice, beans, salads, pasta, beers, wine. Greg and Annie and my mom travel the whole way from U.S. It was just this HUGE celebration. I have a microphone and talk to the people and just tell them how happy. The music was hip-hop on one side, with Brazilian music on the other side.

First thing we did we rented ourself a ranch by the beach. We stayed there and looked around the area and see if it's good for me to build a hotel around. Not a big hotel, a simple one, a ten-rooms hotel. It's near São Paulo, like you going to the Hamptons.

The peoples that I hired to work for me were most guys that I kept in touch with, a couple of family members, friends that I really trusted. I know they were peoples that never has got the lifestyle and the salary that I give it to them. It wasn't hard at all, and they were capable to do it. They needed so much, and I didn't give the money to them, but made them work for it, and just have a great life. Because they felt so miserable before. One worked as a security guy, the other used to have to carry fucking heavy boxes, to earn pennies, a couple hundred dollars a month.

I spent a good $220,000 building that place. Top-of-the-line everything. It took me two years. We got a nice pool and a little gym inside there. Flat-screen TVs in every room, with a DVD. Good liquors that I got to mark each one of them, so they don't get stole. I put cameras inside the hotel. It takes the privacy a little bit out of the peoples, but it's more secure if you have cameras around. I'm trying to do something sophisticated, but not too big. I wanted to make a familiar hotel.

Fabio came. He want to do the hooker thing. He's like, Leave it for later on at night. You tell the guys, we got this hookup. We got this VIP room. Make sure that you give your wife some of this pills that they sleep for hours, and just come along. You guys are going to enjoy the night! But I'm like, Nah. We don't need.

I don't let Natalia be the boss of the hotel, because she is really bossy. Really, really bossy. She try to get all my friends fired. The way that the guys at my hotel usually work, they go do the job and then sit down and relax. She is the type if she see someone relaxing, she's like, Hey, we paying you. You cannot sit down. She is always tacking on people and making the complaints to me. I listen to her and I'm just like, Okay, I will do some arrangements here and there. Like I'm really going to do it. I don't think no one's perfect. I don't want no one pretending to be something, and then meanwhile I'm there, and when I'm gone, they like, Oh, fuck this guy. I'm not going to have that. I let Natalia run this little boutique that sell Brazilian bikinis and stuffs like that.

I'm the boss, but I'm just like one of them. I don't put onto this peoples that I'm the owner. I want them to think I'm the manager of the hotel, not the owner. Being the manager, it's one thing. Being the owner, they going to be like, Wow!

I don't want that. I'm just like, I got this guy, Mr. Greg, this American guy that got money. You can never tell the truth down here. You can never be flashy, flashy. You just got to go with the flow and treat people nice.

I'm not greedy with money. I charge $50 a night, which is not a lot. I just charge it once, for the staying. There is a tiny restaurant. Every morning is breakfast. There is a time for lunch. The cuisine in the kitchen is different, because Brazilian food is very different from American food. I brought a lady from the States, this lady that when I first came back from Brazil, she treat me like a mother. She used to work at this Brazilian restaurant in Newark. It's Brazilian, but most people that goes there is American.

There is a bar inside and outside the hotel. The inside bar is for the guests, and the outside bar is for the peoples outside. I got a guy who is security that is taking care of the guests' stuffs.

You always got to renew the hotel, because you can't built up something and let it go with time. I work my ass if I have to. I don't want to sit around. I got to be on top of the peoples that work for me all day, the cook, the people in the kitchen, the cleaning peoples, the receptionist, but I'm cool toward everybody. I'm not nasty to them. I don't want them to be nasty to the customers of the hotel. That's how you get peoples to like you and work for you as a pleasure. I don't want to be forcing them to work for me. So I'm capable to provide my guests with peoples treating them nice, because those are peoples that I know. I talk to the guests. That is me all the time, just talking, talking, talking. Just trying to be nice. Trying to be cool. Because I think the nice you could be in life, the more guests you capable to bring.

Greg and Annie come here to stay every six month. Now they got little baby girl twins. I'm serious! Greg's writing a book about our experience. I tell him that I wanted peoples to know that I got to experience a lot of things that I wasn't able to experience if I was rich. I just want him to tell it how I change. I think the way I talk, I don't curse as much as I used to. It's not cool anymore for me. The way I try and present myself. I don't know if I'm trying to be or if it's already in me, but I think I'm a cooler person. I think I became more responsible in some certain things. The way I dress. I don't pick my ears anymore. The way I use my hands today when I talk. I used to use it like the rappers do. Like that, very aggressive. Now, I'm calm. I use my hands just like Greg. I want Greg to show this HUGE change, how can a person educate themself if they really wanted to.

At the same time I used to be in a place that I usually used to deal with peoples that was not famous, the type of peoples you usually don't see on the TV, but that make good money. Some of these guys were making fun of me, and they used to laugh in my face. There was peoples that do that because they ignorant. But some of them, they treat me as well as they treat anybody else. A lot of people that is rich think they can treat peoples like they nobody, but most of the peoples I used to work with, they used to treat me very nicily.

ACKNOWLEDGMENTS

I HAD A LOT of help with this book. Above all, it must be obvious to the reader that I had an inside track into the life of shoeshine guys. I spoke to more than one, but one was my muse. He wishes to stay in the background and be known only as Flamenguista at this point, but he wants to thank his mother, his father, and Eleontina Laurelli Martin.

Two great friends—Jonathan Burnham and Kevin McCormick—believed in this book when it was in the mere talking stage and became its godfathers.

Bryan Burrough, Sam Kashner, Kim Kessler, Anne Lee, David Margolick, Vicky Ward, and Ned Zeman all generously shared their experiences with me to help shape characters. Sam and Ned gave me entire scenes; Ned's included the best jokes in the book, which I shamelessly used.

I relentlessly pushed the manuscript, in various drafts, on anyone who expressed the slightest interest. Jim Windolf, David Margolick, and Aimee Bell did particularly brilliant and sensitive edits. For their insights and support I would also like to thank Chris Garrett, Walter Owen, Jonathan Franzen, Kathy Chetkovich, Beth Kseniak, John Fanning, Kurt Brungardt, Fred Turner, Greg Waggoner, Chris Bateman, Lynn Nesbit, Richard Morris, Francesca Stanfill, Marc Goodman, John Ortved, Chris George, Keenan Mayo, Jon Kelly, Peter Newcomb, Lisa and Claire Howorth, Will Schwalbe, Lisa Queen, and Mitch Kaplan.

Gratitude without end to my mom and dad and Graydon Carter,

for giving me the opportunities that enabled me to write the book, and to my agent and old friend, Mary Evans, for her unwavering support.

A huge bouquet to the incredible Don DeLine, Paula Weinstein, Jeff Levine, and Len Amato for their Herculean efforts.

At HarperCollins I thank Claire Wachtel, for making me go through the manuscript one time more than I thought I could; Lauretta Charlton, for always being a pleasure to work with; and Carl Lennertz and Tina Andreadis, for their early and enthusiastic support.